Tessa Dale

A Lady by Midnight

AVON

An Imprint of HarperCollinsPublishers

AVON BOOKS
An Imprint of HarperCollins*Publishers*
10 East 53rd Street
New York, New York 10022-5299

Copyright © 2012 by Eve Ortega
ISBN 978-0-06-204989-6
K.I.S.S. and Teal is a trademark of the Ovarian Cancer National Alliance
www.avonromance.com

First Avon Books mass market printing: September 2012

Avon Trademark Reg. U.S. Pat. Off. and in Other Countries, Marca Registrada, Hecho en U.S.A.
HarperCollins® is a registered trademark of HarperCollins Publishers.

Printed in the U.S.A.

10 9 8 7 6 5 4 3

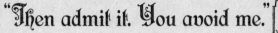

In an impulsive move, she brought his hand to her face, touching his fingertips to her birthmark. He tried to pull back, but she wouldn't let him escape.

"This is the reason. Isn't it? The reason you don't take an interest."

"Miss Taylor, I—" His jaw tensed. "No. It isn't like that."

"Then what is it?"

No reply.

Her face burned. "What is it? For God's sake, what is it about me you find so intolerable? So wretchedly unbearable, you can't even stand to be in the same room?"

He muttered an oath. "Stop provoking me. You won't like the answer."

"I want to hear it anyhow."

He plunged one hand into her hair, startling a gasp from her lips. Strong fingers curled to cup the back of her head. His eyes searched her face, and every nerve ending in her body crackled with tension. The sinking sun threw a last gasp of red-orange light between them, setting the moment ablaze.

"It's this."

With a flex of his arm, he pulled her into a kiss.

By Tessa Dare

A LADY BY MIDNIGHT
A WEEK TO BE WICKED
A NIGHT TO SURRENDER
THREE NIGHTS WITH A SCOUNDREL
TWICE TEMPTED BY A ROGUE
ONE DANCE WITH A DUKE
A LADY OF PERSUASION
SURRENDER OF A SIREN
GODDESS OF THE HUNT

Chapter One

Corporal Thorne could make a woman quiver, from all the way across the room.

An inconvenient talent, so far as Kate Taylor was concerned.

The man didn't even have to try, she noted with a rueful twinge. All he had to do was stride into the Bull and Blossom, claim a bar stool, glower into a pewter tankard and keep his broad, hulking back to the room. And without a word . . . without so much as a *glance* . . . he had poor Miss Elliott's fingers trembling as she laid them to the pianoforte keys.

"Oh, I can't," the girl whispered. "I can't sing now. Not with him here."

Yet another music lesson ruined.

Kate never had this problem until a year ago. Before then, Spindle Cove had been chiefly inhabited by ladies, and the Bull and Blossom was a quaint tea shop serving iced cakes and jam tarts. But ever since a local militia had been organized, the establishment had become both the ladies' tea shop and the gentlemen's tavern.

She wasn't opposed to sharing—but there could be no "sharing" with Corporal Thorne. His stern, brooding presence took up the whole room.

"Let's try again," she urged her pupil, striving to ignore the intimidating silhouette looming in her peripheral vision. "We almost had it that time."

Miss Elliott blushed and knotted her fingers in her lap. "I'll never get it right."

"You will. It's only a matter of practice, and you won't be alone. We'll keep working at the duet, and we'll be ready for a trial performance at this Saturday's salon."

At the mere word "performance," the girl's cheeks went crimson.

Annabel Elliott was a pretty young lady, delicate and fair—but the poor thing flushed so easily. Whenever she was flustered or nervous, her pale cheeks blazed as though they'd been slapped raw. And she was flustered or nervous far too much of the time.

Some young ladies came to Spindle Cove to recover from shyness, or scandal, or a debilitating bout with fever. Miss Elliott had been sent in hopes of a different cure: a remedy for stage fright.

Kate had been tutoring her long enough to know that Miss Elliott's difficulty had nothing to do with a lack of talent or preparation. She only needed confidence.

"Perhaps some new sheet music would help," Kate suggested. "I find a folio of crisp, new-smelling music to be even better for my spirits than a new bonnet." An idea struck. "I'll go into Hastings this week and see what I can find."

In truth, she had been planning to visit Hastings for a completely different purpose. She had a call to pay there—one she'd been putting off. Purchasing new music made an excellent excuse.

"I don't know why I'm so stupid," the blushing girl lamented. "I've had years of excellent instruction. And I love to play. Truly, I do. But when others are listening, I always freeze. I'm hopeless."

"You are *not* hopeless. No situation is ever hopeless."

"My parents . . ."

"Your parents don't believe you're hopeless, either, or they wouldn't have sent you here," Kate said.

"They want me to have a successful season. But you don't know the pressure they've put on me. Miss Taylor, you can't possibly understand what it's like."

"No," Kate admitted. "I suppose I can't."

Miss Elliott looked up, stricken. "I'm sorry. So sorry. I didn't mean it that way. How thoughtless of me."

Kate waved off the apologies. "Don't be silly. It's the truth. I'm an orphan. You're absolutely right—I can't possibly know what it's like to have parents with such high expectations and soaring hopes."

Though I'd give anything to experience it, just for one day.

She continued, "But I do know what a difference it makes to know you're among friends. This is Spindle Cove. We're all a bit unusual here. Just remember, everyone in the village is on your side."

"Everyone?"

Miss Elliott's wary gaze slid to the enormous, solitary man seated at the bar.

"He's so big," she whispered. "And so frightful. Every time I start to play, I can see him wince."

"You mustn't take it personally. He's a military man, and you know they're all addled by bomb blasts." Kate gave Miss Elliott an encouraging pat on the arm. "Never mind him. Just hold your head high, keep a smile on your face, and continue playing."

"I'll try, but he's . . . he's rather difficult to ignore."

Yes. He was. Didn't Kate know it.

Even though Corporal Thorne excelled at ignoring *her*, she couldn't deny his effect on her own composure. Her skin prickled whenever he was near, and on the rare occasion that he looked her way, his glare had a way of slicing deep. But for the sake of Miss Elliott's confidence, Kate set her personal reactions aside.

"Chin high," she quietly reminded Miss Elliott, and herself. "Keep smiling."

Kate began playing the lower half of the duet. But when the time came for Miss Elliott's entrance, the younger lady faltered after just a few bars.

"I'm sorry, I just . . ." Miss Elliott lowered her voice. "Did he wince again?"

"No, worse," she moaned. "This time he shuddered."

With a little gasp of indignation, Kate craned her neck to view the bar. "No. He didn't."

Miss Elliott nodded. "He did. It was terrible."

That sealed it. For him to ignore her pupils was one thing. Wincing was another. But there was no excuse for shuddering. Shuddering was beyond the pale.

"I'll speak with him," Kate said, rising from the pianoforte bench.

"Oh, don't. I beg you."

"It's all right," Kate assured her. "I'm not afraid of him. He might be brutish, but I don't believe he bites."

She crossed the room and came to a stop just behind Corporal Thorne's shoulder. She almost gathered the courage to tap the tasseled epaulet of his red uniform.

Almost.

Instead she cleared her throat. "Corporal Thorne?"

He turned.

In all her life she'd never known a man who could look so hard. His face was stony—composed of ruthless, chiseled angles and unyielding planes. Its stark terrain offered her no shelter, nowhere to hide. His mouth was a grim slash. His dark brows converged in disapproval. And his eyes . . . his eyes were the blue of river ice on the coldest, harshest winter night.

Chin high. Keep smiling.

"As you might have noticed," she said lightly, "I'm in the middle of a music lesson."

No response.

"You see, Miss Elliott is anxious when it comes to performing for strangers."

"You want me to leave."

"No." Kate's own reply surprised her. "No, I don't want you to leave."

That would be letting him off too easily. He was always leaving. This was their standard interaction, time after time. Kate screwed up her courage and attempted to be friendly. He always found some excuse to promptly leave the room. It was a ridiculous game, and she was weary of it.

"I'm not asking you to leave," she said. "Miss Elliott needs practice. She and I are going to play a duet. I'm *inviting* you to lend us your attention."

He stared at her.

Kate was accustomed to awkward eye contact. Whenever she made new acquaintances, she became painfully aware that people saw only the bold, portwine splash on her temple. For years she'd tried to obscure her birthmark with wide-brimmed bonnets or artfully arranged ringlets of hair—to no avail. People always stared straight past them. She'd learned to ignore the initial hurt. In time, she went from being just a birthmark in their eyes, to being a woman with a birthmark. And eventually they looked at her and just saw Kate.

Corporal Thorne's gaze was altogether different. She didn't quite know *who* she was, in his eyes. The uncertainty set her on a razor's edge, but she kept struggling to find her balance.

"Stay," she dared him. "Stay and listen while we play our best for you. Applaud when we finish. Tap your toes to the rhythm, if you like. Give Miss Elliott a bit of encouragement. And shock me to the fingernails by proving you've a smidgen of compassion."

Eons passed before he finally gave his succinct, gravelly response.

"I'll leave."

He stood, tossed a coin on the counter. And then he walked out of the tavern without looking back.

When the red-painted door swung shut on its oiled hinges, mocking her with a loud slam—Kate shook her head. The man was impossible.

At the pianoforte, Miss Elliott resumed playing a light arpeggio.

"I suppose that solves one problem," Kate said, trying, as always, to see the bright side. No situation was ever hopeless.

Mr. Fosbury, the middle-aged tavern keeper, arrived to clear Thorne's tankard. He pushed a cup of tea in Kate's direction. A wafer-thin slice of lemon floated in the center, and the aroma of brandy drifted toward her on a wave of steam. She warmed inside before she'd even taken a sip. The Fosburys were good to her.

But they still weren't a substitute for a true family. For that, she would have to keep searching. And she *would* keep searching, no matter how many doors slammed in her face.

"I hope you don't take Thorne's crude manners to heart, Miss Taylor."

"Who, me?" She forced a little laugh. "Oh, I'm more sensible than that. Why should I take to heart the words of a heartless man?" She ran a fingertip around the teacup's rim, thoughtful. "But kindly do me a favor, Mr. Fosbury."

"Whatever you ask, Miss Taylor."

"The next time I'm tempted to extend an olive branch of friendship to Corporal Thorne . . . ?" She arched one brow and gave him a playful smile. "Remind me to whack him over the head with it instead."

Chapter Two

"More tea, Miss Taylor?"

"No, thank you." Kate sipped the weak brew in her cup, masking her grimace. The leaves were on their third use, at least. They seemed to have been washed of their last vague memory of being tea.

Fitting, she supposed. Vague memories were the order of the day.

Miss Paringham put aside the teapot. "Where did you say you're residing?"

Kate smiled at the white-haired woman in the chair opposite. "Spindle Cove, Miss Paringham. It's a popular holiday village for gently bred young ladies. I make my living offering music lessons."

"I am glad to know your schooling has provided you with an honest income. That is more than an unfortunate like yourself should have hoped."

"Oh, indeed. I'm very lucky."

Setting aside her "tea," Kate cast a surreptitious glance at the mantel clock. Time was growing short. She despised wasting precious minutes on niceties when there were questions singeing the tip of her tongue. But abruptness wouldn't win her any answers.

A wrapped parcel lay in her lap, and she curled her fingers around the string. "I was so surprised to learn you'd settled here. Imagine, my old schoolmistress, pensioned just a few hours' ride away. I couldn't resist paying a call to reminisce. I have such fond recollections of my Margate years."

Miss Paringham raised an eyebrow. "Really."

"Oh, yes." She stretched her mind for examples. "I particularly miss the . . . the nourishing soup. And our regular devotionals. It's just so hard to find two solid hours for reading sermons nowadays."

As orphans went, Kate knew she'd been a great deal happier than most. The atmosphere at Margate School for Girls might have been austere, but she hadn't been beaten or starved or unclothed. She'd formed friendships and gained a useful education. Most important of all, she'd been instructed in music and encouraged in its practice.

Truly, she could not complain. Margate had provided for her every need, save one.

Love.

In all her years there, she'd never known real love. Just some pale, thrice-washed dilution of it. Another girl might have grown bitter. But Kate just wasn't formed for misery. Even if her mind could not recall it, her heart remembered a time before Margate. Some distant memory of happiness echoed in its every beat.

She'd been loved once. She just knew it. She couldn't put a name or face to the emotion, but that didn't make it any less real. Once upon a time, she'd belonged—to someone, somewhere. This woman might be her last hope of finding the connection.

"Do you remember the day I arrived at Margate, Miss Paringham? I must have been such a little thing."

The old woman's mouth pursed. "Five years at the oldest. We had no way to be certain."

"No. Of course you wouldn't."

No one knew Kate's true birthday, least of all Kate herself. As schoolmistress, Miss Paringham had decided all wards of the school would share the Lord's birthday, December 25. Supposedly they were to take comfort from this reminder of their heavenly family on the day when all the other girls had gone home to their own flesh-and-blood relations.

However, Kate always suspected there'd been a more practical motive behind the choice. If their birthdays were on Christmas, there was never any need to celebrate them. No extra gifts were warranted. Wards of the school made do with the same Christmas package every year: an orange, a ribbon, and a neatly folded length of patterned muslin. Miss Paringham did not believe in sweets.

Apparently she still didn't. Kate bit a tiny corner off the dry, tasteless biscuit she'd been offered, then set it back on the plate.

On the mantel, the clock's ticking seemed to accelerate. Only twenty minutes before the last stagecoach left for Spindle Cove. If she missed the stage, she would be stranded in Hastings all night.

She steeled her nerve. No more dithering.

"Who were they?" she asked. "Do you know?"

"Whatever do you mean?"

"My parents."

Miss Paringham sniffed. "You were a ward of the school. You have no parents."

"I do understand that." Kate smiled, trying to inject some levity. "But I wasn't hatched from an egg, was I? I didn't turn up under a cabbage leaf. I had a mother and father once. Perhaps I had them for as many as five years. I've tried so hard to remember. All my memories are so vague, so jumbled. I remember feeling safe. I have this impression of blue. A room with blue walls, perhaps, but I can't be certain." She pinched the bridge of her nose and frowned at the knotted carpet fringe. "Maybe I just want to remember so desperately, I'm imagining things."

"Miss Taylor—"

"I remember sounds, mostly." She shut her eyes, delving inward. "Sounds with no pictures. Someone saying to me, 'Be brave, my Katie.' Was it my mother? My father? The words are burned into my memory, but I can't put a face to them, no matter how I try. And then there's the music. Endless pianoforte music, and that same little song—"

"Miss *Taylor.*"

As she repeated Kate's name, the old schoolmistress's voice cracked. Not cracked like brittle china, but cracked like a whip.

In a reflexive motion, Kate snapped tall in her chair.

Sharp eyes regarded her. "Miss Taylor, I advise you to abandon this line of inquiry at once."

"How can I? You must understand. I've lived with these questions all my life, Miss Paringham. I've tried to do as you always advised and be happy for what good fortune life has given me. I have friends. I have a living. I have music. But I still don't have the truth. I want to know where I came from, even if it's difficult to hear. I know my parents are dead now, but perhaps there is some hope of contacting my relations. There has to be someone, somewhere. The smallest detail might prove useful. A name, a town, a—"

The old woman rapped her cane against the floorboards. "Miss Taylor. Even if I had some information to impart, I would never share it. I would take it to my grave."

Kate sat back in her chair. "But . . . why?"

Miss Paringham didn't answer, merely pressed her papery lips into a thin slash of disapproval.

"You never liked me," Kate whispered. "I knew it. You always made it clear, in small, unspoken ways, that any kindness you showed me was begrudged."

"Very well. You are correct. I never liked you."

They regarded one another. There, now the truth was out.

Kate struggled not to reveal any sign of disappointment or hurt. But her wrapped bundle of sheet music slipped to the floor—and as it did, a smug little smile curved Miss Paringham's lips.

"May I ask on what basis was I so reviled? I was appropriately grateful for every small thing I was given. I didn't cause mischief. I never complained. I minded my lessons and earned high marks."

"Precisely. You showed no humility. You behaved as though you had as much claim to joy as any other girl at Margate. Always singing. Always smiling."

The idea was so absurd, Kate couldn't help but laugh. "You disliked me because I smiled too much? Should I have been melancholy and brooding?"

"Ashamed!" Miss Paringham barked the word. "A child of shame ought to live ashamed."

Kate was momentarily stunned silent. *A child of*

shame? "What can you mean? I always thought I was orphaned. You never said—"

"Wicked thing. Your shame goes without saying. God Himself has marked you." Miss Paringham pointed with a bony finger.

Kate couldn't even reply. She raised her own trembling hand to her temple.

With her fingertips, she began to idly rub the mark, the same way she'd done as a young girl—as if she might erase it from her skin. Her whole life, she'd believed herself to be a loved child whose parents met an untimely demise. How horrid, to think that she'd been cast away, unwanted.

Her fingers stilled on her birthmark. Perhaps cast away because of *this*.

"You fool girl." The old woman's laugh was a caustic rasp. "Been dreaming of a fairy tale, have you? Thinking someday a messenger will knock on your door and declare you a long-lost princess?"

Kate told herself to stay calm. Clearly, Miss Paringham was a lonely, warped old woman who now lived to make others miserable. She would not give the beastly crone the satisfaction of seeing her rattled.

But she would not stay here a moment longer, either.

She reached to gather her wrapped parcel of music from the floor. "I'm sorry to have disturbed you, Miss Paringham. I will leave. You needn't say any more."

"Oh, I *will* say more. Ignorant thing that you are, you've reached the age of three-and-twenty without understanding this. I see I must take it upon myself to teach you one last lesson."

"Please, don't strain yourself." Rising from her chair, Kate curtsied. She lifted her chin and pasted a defiant smile on her face. "Thank you for the tea. I really must be going if I'm to catch the stagecoach. I'll see myself out."

"Impertinent girl!"

The old woman lashed out with her cane, striking Kate in the back of the knees.

Kate stumbled, catching herself in the drawing room entryway. "You struck me. I can't believe you just struck me."

"Should have done it years ago. I might have knocked that smile straight from your face."

Kate braced her shoulder on the doorjamb. The sting of humiliation was far greater than the physical pain. Part of her wanted to crumple into a tiny ball on the floor, but she knew she had to flee this place. More than that, she had to flee these *words*. These horrible, unthinkable notions that could leave her marked inside, as well as out.

"Good day, Miss Paringham." She placed weight on her smarting knee and drew a quick breath. The front door was just paces away.

"No one wanted you." Venom dripped from the old woman's voice. "No one wanted you then. Who on earth do you think will want you now?"

Someone, Kate's heart insisted. *Someone, somewhere.*

"No one." Malice twisted the old woman's face as she swung the cane again.

Kate heard its crisp *whack* against the doorjamb, but by then she was already wrestling open the front latch. She picked up her skirts and darted out into the cobbled street. Her low-heeled boots were worn thin on the soles, and she slipped and stumbled as she ran. The streets of Hastings were narrow and curved, lined with busy shops and inns. There was no possible way the sour-faced woman could have followed her.

Still, she ran.

She ran with hardly a care for which direction she was going, so long as it was away. Perhaps if she kept running fast enough, the truth would never catch up.

As she turned in the direction of the mews, the booming toll of a church bell struck dread in her gut.

One, two, three, four . . .

Oh no. Stop there. Please don't toll again.

Five.

Her heart flopped. Miss Paringham's clock must have been slow. She was too late. The coach would have already departed without her. There wouldn't be another until morning.

Summer had stretched daylight to its greatest length, but in a few hours, night *would* fall. She'd spent most of her funds at the music shop, leaving only enough money for her passage back to Spindle Cove—no extra coin for an inn or a meal.

Kate came to a standstill in the crowded lane. People jostled and streamed about her on all sides. But she didn't belong to any of them. None of them would help. Despair crawled its way through her veins, cold and black.

Her worst fears had been realized. She was alone. Not just tonight, but forever. Her own relations had abandoned her years ago. No one wanted her now. She would die alone. Living in some cramped pensioner's apartment like Miss Paringham's, drinking thrice-washed tea and chewing on her own bitterness.

Be brave, my Katie.

Her whole life she'd clung to the memory of those words. She'd held fast to the belief that they meant someone, somewhere cared. She wouldn't let that voice down. This sort of panic wasn't like her, and it wouldn't do a bit of good.

She closed her eyes, drew a deep breath, and took a silent inventory. She had her wits. She had her talent. She had a young, healthy body. No one could take these things from her. Not even that cruel, shriveled wench with her cane and weak tea.

There had to be some solution. Did she have anything she could sell? Her pink muslin frock was rather fine—a handed-down gift from one of her pupils, trimmed with ribbon and lace—but she couldn't sell the clothes off her back. She'd left her best summer bonnet at Miss Paringham's, and she'd rather sleep in the streets than retrieve it.

If she hadn't cut it so short last summer, she might have tried to sell her hair. But the locks barely reached below her shoulders now, and they were an unremarkable shade of brown. No wig maker would want it.

Her best chance was the music shop. Perhaps if she explained her predicament and asked very nicely, the proprietor would accept his music back and return her money. That would afford her enough for a room at a somewhat respectable inn. Staying alone was never advisable, and she didn't even have her pistol. But she could prop a chair beneath her door and stay awake all night, clutching the fireplace poker and keeping her voice primed to scream.

There. She had a plan.

As Kate started to cross the street, an elbow knocked her off balance.

"Oy," its owner said. "Watch yerself, miss."

She whirled away, apologizing. The twine on her parcel snapped. White pages flapped and fluttered into the gusty summer afternoon, like a covey of startled doves.

"Oh no. The music."

She made wild sweeps with both hands. A few pages disappeared down the street, and others fell to the cobblestones, quickly trampled by passersby. But the bulk of the parcel landed in the middle of the lane, still wrapped in brown paper.

She made a lunging grab for it, desperate to save what she could.

"Look sharp!" a man shouted.

Cartwheels creaked. Somewhere much too near, a horse bucked and whinnied. She looked up from where she'd crouched in the lane to see two windmilling, iron-shoed hooves, big as dinner plates, preparing to demolish her.

A woman screamed.

Kate threw her weight to one side. The horse's hooves landed just to her left. With a squalling hiss of the brake, a cartwheel screeched to halt—inches from crushing her leg.

The parcel of sheet music landed some yards distant. Her "plan" was now a mud-stained, wheel-rutted smear on the street.

"Devil take you," the driver cursed her from the box, brandishing his horsewhip. "A fine little witch you are. Near overset my whole cart."

"I—I'm sorry, sir. It was an accident."

He cracked his whip against the cobblestones. "Out of my way, then. You unnatural little—"

As he raised his whip for another strike, Kate flinched and ducked.

No blow came.

A man stepped between her and the cart. "Threaten

her again," she heard him warn the driver in a low, in-human growl, "and I will whip the flesh from your miserable bones."

Chilling, those words. But effective. The cart swiftly rolled away.

As strong arms pulled her to her feet, Kate's gaze climbed a veritable mountain of man. She saw black, polished boots. Buff breeches stretched over granite thighs. A distinctive red wool officer's coat.

Her heart jumped. She *knew* this coat. She'd probably sewn the brass buttons on these cuffs. This was the uniform of the Spindle Cove militia. She was in familiar arms. She was saved. And when she lifted her head, she was guaranteed to find a friendly face, unless . . .

"Miss Taylor?"

Unless.

Unless it was *him*.

"Corporal Thorne," she whispered.

On another day, Kate could have laughed at the irony. Of all the men to come to her rescue, it *would* be this one.

"Miss Taylor, what the devil are you doing here?"

At his rough tone, all her muscles pulled tight. "I . . . I came into town to purchase new sheet music for Miss Elliott, and to . . ." She couldn't bring herself to mention calling on Miss Paringham. "But I dropped my parcel, and now I've missed the stage home. Silly me."

Silly, foolish, shame-marked, unwanted me.

"And now I'm truly stuck, I'm afraid. If only I'd brought a little more money, I could afford a room for the evening, then go back to Spindle Cove tomorrow."

"You've no money?"

She turned away, unable to bear the chastisement in his gaze.

"What were you thinking, traveling all this distance alone?"

"I hadn't any choice." Her voice caught. "I am completely alone."

His grip firmed on her arms. "I'm here. You're not alone now."

Hardly poetry, those words. A simple statement of fact. They scarcely shared the same alphabet as kindness. If true comfort were a nourishing, wholemeal loaf, what he offered her were a few stale crumbs.

It didn't matter. It didn't matter. She was a starving girl, and she hadn't the dignity to refuse.

"I'm so sorry," she managed, choking back a sob. "You're not going to like this."

And with that, Kate fell into his immense, rigid, unwilling embrace—and wept.

Bloody hell.

She burst into tears. Right there in the street, for God's sake. Her lovely face screwed up. She bent forward until her forehead met his chest, and then she heaved a loud, wrenching sob.

Then a second. And a third.

His gelding danced sideways, and Thorne shared the beast's unease. Given a choice between watching Miss Kate Taylor weep and offering his own liver to carrion birds, he would have had his knife out and sharpened before the first tear rolled down her face.

He clucked his tongue softly, which did some good toward calming the horse. It had no effect on the girl. Her slender shoulders convulsed as she wept into his coat. His hands remained fixed on her arms.

In a desperate gesture, he slid them up. Then down.

No help.

What's happened? he wanted to ask. *Who's hurt you? Who can I maim or kill for distressing you this way?*

"I'm sorry," she said, pulling away after some minutes had passed.

"Why?"

"For weeping all over you. Forcing you to hold me. I know you must hate it." She fished a handkerchief from her sleeve and dabbed at her eyes. Her nose and eyes were red. "I mean, not that you don't like holding women. Everyone in Spindle Cove knows you like women. I've heard far more than I care to hear about your—"

She paled and stopped talking.

Just as well.

He took the horse's lead in one hand and laid the other hand to Miss Taylor's back, guiding her out of the street. Once they reached the side of the lane, he looped his horse's reins about a post and turned his sights toward making her comfortable. There wasn't anywhere for her to sit. No bench, no crate.

This disturbed him beyond reason.

His gaze went to a tavern across the street—the sort of establishment he'd never allow her to enter—but he was seriously considering crossing the lane, toppling the first available drunk off his seat, and dragging the vacated chair out for her. A woman shouldn't weep while standing. It didn't seem right.

"Please, can't you just loan me a few shillings?" she asked. "I'll find an inn for the night, and I won't trouble you any further."

"Miss Taylor, I can't lend you money to pass the night alone in a coaching inn. It's not safe."

"I have no choice but to stay. There won't be another stage back to Spindle Cove until morning."

Thorne looked at his gelding. "I'll hire you a horse, if you can ride."

She shook her head. "I never had any lessons."

Curse it. How was he going to remedy this situation? He easily had the money to hire another horse, but nowhere near enough coin in his pocket for a private carriage. He *could* put her up in an inn—but damned if he would let her stay alone.

A dangerous thought visited him, sinking talons into his mind.

He could stay *with* her.

Not in a tawdry way, he told himself. Just as her protector. He could find a damned place for her to sit down, as a start. He could see that she had food and drink and warm blankets. He could stand watch while she slept and make certain nothing disturbed her. He could be there when she woke.

After all these months of frustrated longing, maybe that would be enough.

Enough? Right.

"Good heavens." She took a sudden step back.

"What is it?"

Her gaze dropped and she swallowed hard. "Some part of you is *moving.*"

"No, it's not." Thorne conducted a quick, silent assessment of his personal equipment. He found all to be under regulation. On another occasion—one with fewer tears involved—this degree of closeness would have undoubtedly roused his lust. But today she was affecting him rather higher in his torso. Tying his guts in knots and poking at whatever black, smoking cinder remained of his heart.

"Your satchel." She indicated the leather pouch slung crossways over his chest. "It's . . . wriggling."

Oh. That. In all the commotion, he'd nearly forgotten the creature.

He reached beneath the leather flap and withdrew the source of the wriggling, holding it up for her to see.

"It's just this."

And suddenly everything was different. It was like the whole world took a knock and tilted at a fresh angle. In less time than it took a man's heart to skip, Miss Taylor's face transformed. The tears were gone. Her elegant, sweeping eyebrows arched in surprise. Her eyes candled to life—glowed, really, like two stars. Her lips fell apart in a delighted gasp.

"Oh." She pressed one hand to her cheek. "Oh, it's a *puppy.*"

She smiled. Lord, how she smiled. All because of this wriggling ball of snout and fur that was as likely to piss on her slippers as chew them to bits.

She reached forward. "May I?"

As if he could refuse. Thorne placed the pup in her arms.

She fawned and cooed over it like a baby. "Where did you come from, sweeting?"

"A farm nearby," Thorne answered. "Thought I'd take him back to the castle. Been needing a hound."

She cocked her head and peered at the pup. "*Is* he a hound?"

"Partly."

Her fingers traced a rust-colored patch over the pup's right eye. "I'd suppose he's partly many things, isn't he? Funny little dear."

She lifted the pup in both hands and looked it nose-to-nose, puckering her lips to make a little chirping noise. The dog licked her face.

Lucky cur.

"Was that mean Corporal Thorne keeping you in a dark, nasty satchel?" She gave the pup a playful shake. "You like it so much better out here with me, don't you? Of course you do."

The dog yipped. She laughed and drew it close to her chest, bending over its furry neck.

"You are perfect," he heard her whisper. "You are just exactly what I needed today." She stroked the pup's fur. "Thank you."

Thorne felt a sharp twist in his chest. Like something rusted and bent, shaking loose. This girl had a way of doing that—making him *feel*. She always had, even years upon years in the past. That long-ago time seemed to fall beyond the reach of her earliest memories. A true mercy for her.

But Thorne remembered. He remembered it all.

He cleared his throat. "We'd best be on the road. It'll be near dark by the time we reach Spindle Cove."

She tore her attention from the dog and gave Thorne a curious glance. "But how?"

"You'll ride with me. The both of you. I'll take you up on my saddle. You'll carry the dog."

As if consulting all the concerned parties, she turned to the horse. Then to the dog. Lastly, she lifted her gaze to Thorne's. "You're certain we'll fit?"

"Just."

She bit her lip, looking unsure.

Her instinctive resistance to the idea was plain. And understandable. Thorne wasn't overeager to put his plan into action, either. Three hours astride a horse with Miss Kate Taylor nestled between his thighs? Torture of the keenest sort. But he could see no better way to have her swiftly and safely home.

He could do this. If he'd lasted a year with her in

the same tiny village, he could withstand a few hours' closeness.

"I won't leave you here," he said. "It'll have to be done."

Her mouth quirked in a droll, self-conscious smile. It was reassuring to see, and at the same time devastating.

"When you put it that way, I find myself unable to refuse."

For God's sake, don't say that.

"Thank you," she added. She laid a gentle touch to his sleeve.

For your own sake, don't do that.

He pulled away from her touch, and she looked hurt. Which made him want to soothe her, but he didn't dare try.

"Mind the pup," he said.

Thorne helped her into the saddle, boosting her at the knee, rather than the thigh, as might have been more efficient. He mounted the gelding, taking the reins in one hand and keeping one arm about her waist. As he nudged the horse into a walk, she fell against him, soft and warm. His thighs bracketed hers.

Her hair smelled of clover and lemon. The scent rushed all through his senses before he could stop it. *Damn, damn, damn.* He could discourage her from talking to him, touching him. He could keep her distracted with a dog. But how could he prevent her from being shaped like a woman and smelling like paradise?

Never mind the beatings, the lashings, the years of prison . . .

Thorne knew, without a doubt, the next three hours would be the harshest punishment of his life.

Chapter Three

The strangest thing happened during their first hour on horseback. Before Kate's eyes, Corporal Thorne transformed into a completely different man.

A good-looking one.

The first time she stole a glance at him, letting her gaze make the slow, perilous climb from his lapel to his face—she found his appearance just as hard and intimidating as ever. The planes of his face were lit with harsh, late afternoon sun. She cringed.

But then, a few hundred yards farther down the road, she glanced up again as they passed beneath a stand of trees. This time she caught him in profile, and his features were touched with shadow. She fancied him to look . . . not so much forbidding as protective. Strong.

The wall of heated muscle at her back only reinforced this impression. So did the massive arm braced around her middle and the effortless manner with which he guided his horse. No shouting or flicking the crop— just gentle nudges of his heels and the occasional quiet word. Those words shivered through her bones like cello notes, each one settling to a low, arousing thrum at the base of her spine.

She closed her eyes. Deep voices touched her in deep places.

From that point on she kept her gaze stubbornly trained on the road ahead. Nevertheless, her mental image of Thorne continued to change. In her mind's eye he went from forbidding and stern, to protective and strong, to . . .

Handsome.

Wildly, improbably, outrageously handsome.

No, no. It just couldn't be. Her imagination was playing tricks. Kate knew many of the working-class women in Spindle Cove fancied Corporal Thorne, but she'd never understood why. His features just didn't appeal to her—probably because he was usually employing them to send a frown or a glare in her direction. On those rare occasions when he looked in her direction at all.

By the time they traveled another few miles, the puppy had fallen asleep in her arms. Kate had rummaged through her many unpleasant encounters with the man and succeeded in reminding herself that she did not find him attractive.

One more look, she told herself—just to confirm it.

But when she did glance up, the worst possible thing happened.

She found him looking down at *her.*

Their gazes locked. The piercing blue of his eyes *invaded* her being. To her distinct horror, she gasped aloud. And then she hurried to look somewhere, anywhere else.

Too late.

His features were seared on her imagination. When she closed her eyes, it was as though the back of her eyelids had been painted with that same intense, transfixing blue. Now the idea came to her that he was perhaps the most handsome man she'd ever seen—an assessment with no rational basis whatsoever. None.

Kate realized she had a grave problem.

She was infatuated. Or mildly insane. Possibly both.

Mostly, she was miserable. Her heartbeat was a frantic trill, and close as they were situated on this saddle, she knew he must feel it. For God's sake, he could likely *hear* it. That racing, prattling beat was spilling all her secrets. She might as well have piped up and said, *I am an affection-starved, addle-brained fool who has never, ever been this close to a man.*

Desperate to create some small buffer between them, she straightened her spine and leaned forward.

Just then the horse stepped into a rut, and Kate lurched perilously to one side. She knew the brief, helpless sensation of falling.

And then, just as quickly, she was caught.

Thorne corrected the horse with a flex of both thighs. He pulled on the reins with one hand, and his other arm contracted about her waist. The motions were fluid, strong, and instinctive—as if his whole body were a fist, and he'd gripped her tight with everything.

"I have you," he said.

Yes, he did. He had her so tight and so close, her corset grommets were probably leaving small round marks on his chest.

"Are we almost there?" she asked.

"No."

She stifled a plaintive sigh.

As the sun dipped toward the horizon, they stopped at a turnpike. Kate waited with the puppy while Thorne purchased a tin pail of milk and three loaves of hot, crusty bread from a cottager. She followed him as he carried this picnic out over a stile and onto a nearby slope.

They sat near one another in meadow ablaze with flowering heather. The fading sunlight touched each tiny purple blossom with orange. Kate folded her shawl into a square, and the puppy circled it several times before settling down to attack its fringe.

Thorne handed her one of the loaves. "It's not much."

"It's perfect."

The loaf warmed her hands and made her stomach growl. She broke it in two, releasing a cloud of delicious, yeasty steam.

As she ate, the bread seemed to fill some of the yawning stupidity inside her. Sensible behavior was a great deal easier to manage on a full stomach. She could almost bear to look at him again.

"I'm grateful to you," she said. "I'm not certain I said that earlier, to my shame. But I'm very thankful for your help. I was having the most miserable day of my year, and seeing your face . . ."

"Made it that much worse."

She laughed in protest. "No. I didn't mean that."

"As I recall it, you burst into tears."

She ducked her chin and gave him a sidelong glance. "Can this be a flash of humor? From the stern, intimidating Corporal Thorne?"

He said nothing. She watched him feed the puppy scraps of bread dipped in milk.

"My goodness," she said. "What will be your next trick, I wonder? A blink? A *smile*? Don't laugh, or I may faint dead away."

Her tone was one of mild teasing, but she meant every word. She was already suffering these fierce pangs of infatuation on the basis of his looks and strength alone. If he revealed a streak of sharp wit in the bargain, she might be in desperate straits.

Fortunately for her vulnerable emotions, he responded with his usual absence of charm. "I'm the lieutenant of the Spindle Cove militia in Lord Rycliff's absence. You're a resident of Spindle Cove. It was my duty to help you and see you home safe. That's all."

"Well," she said, "I'm fortunate to fall within the scope of your duty. The mishap with the cart driver truly was my fault. I'd dashed into the lane without looking."

"What happened beforehand?" he asked.

"What makes you think something happened beforehand?"

"It's not like you to be that distracted."

It's not like you.

Kate chewed her bread slowly. He was correct, perhaps, but what an odd thing for him to say. He avoided her like a sparrow avoids snow. What right had he to decide what was and wasn't like her?

But she had no one else to talk to, and no reason to hide the truth.

She swallowed her bite of bread and wrapped her arms about her knees. "I went to pay a call on my old schoolmistress. I was hoping to find some information about my origins. My relations."

He paused. "And did you?"

"No. She wouldn't help me find them, she said, even if she could. Because they don't want to be found. I'd always believed I was an orphan, but apparently I . . ." She blinked hard. "It seems I was abandoned. A child of shame, she called me. No one wanted me then, and no one will want me now."

They both stared at the horizon, where the oozing egg-yolk sun topped the chalky hills.

She risked a glance at him. "You have nothing to say?"

"Nothing fit for a lady's hearing."

She smiled. "But I'm no lady, you see. If I know nothing else of my parentage, I can be certain of that."

Kate lived in the same rooming house as all the Spindle Cove ladies, and a few were true friends, like Lady Rycliff or Minerva Highwood, lately the new Viscountess Payne. But many others forgot her when they left. In their minds, she fit the same pigeonhole as governesses and companions. She would do for company in a pinch, but only if no one better was available. Sometimes they wrote to her for a while. If their valises were too full, they gave her their cast-off frocks.

She touched the muddied skirt of her pink muslin. Ruined, beyond repair.

At her feet, the puppy had crawled halfway into the milk pail and was happily licking his way back out. Kate reached for the dog, turning him on his back for a playful rub.

"We're kindred spirits, aren't we?" she asked the pup. "No proper homes to speak of. No illustrious pedigrees. We're both a bit funny-looking."

Corporal Thorne made no attempt to contradict her statement. Kate supposed it was what she deserved, going fishing for compliments in a desert.

"What about you, Corporal Thorne? Where were you raised? Have you any family living?"

He was quiet for an oddly long time, given the straightforward nature of her question.

"Born in Southwark, near London. But I haven't seen the place in almost twenty years."

She scanned his face. Despite the gravity in his demeanor, she wouldn't put him much older than thirty. "You must have left home quite young."

"Not so young as some."

"Now that the war is over, you've no desire to go back?"

"None." His gaze caught hers for a moment. "The past is better left behind."

Point taken, Kate supposed, given the disaster that had been her day. She plucked a long blade of grass and dangled it for the puppy to nip and bat. His long, thin tail whipped back and forth with joy.

"What do you mean to call him?" she asked.

He shrugged. "I don't know. Patch, I suppose."

"But that's horrible. You can't call him Patch."

"Why not? He has a patch, doesn't he?"

"Yes, and that's exactly why you can't call him that." Kate lowered her voice, gathering the pup close and smoothing the splash of rust-colored fur around his right eye. "He'll be self-conscious. I have a patch, but I shouldn't like to be named for it. It's not as though I need a reminder it's there."

"This is different. He's a dog."

"That doesn't mean he has no feelings."

Corporal Thorne made a derisive noise. "He's a *dog*."

"You should call him Rex," she said, tilting her head. "Or Duke. Or Prince, perhaps."

His gaze slid sideways. "What about that dog says 'royalty' to you?"

"Well, nothing." Kate set the pup down and watched him scamper through the heather. "But that's the point. You'll balance his humble origins by giving him a grand-sounding name. It's called irony, Corporal Thorne. As if I were to call you 'Cuddles.' Or if you were to call me Helen of Troy."

He paused and frowned. "Who's Helen of Troy?"

Kate almost betrayed her surprise at his question. Fortunately, she caught herself just in time. She had to remind herself that "corporal" was an enlisted officer's rank, and most of the army's enlisted men had only a basic education.

She explained, "Helen of Troy was a queen in Ancient Greece. They called hers the face that could launch a thousand ships. She was so beautiful, every man wanted her. They fought whole wars."

He was quiet for several moments. "So calling you Helen of . . ."

"Helen of Troy."

"Right. Helen of Troy." A small furrow formed between his dark eyebrows. "How would that be ironic?"

She laughed. "Isn't it obvious? Just look at me."

"I am looking at you."

Good heavens. Yes, he was. He was looking at her in the same way he did everything. Intensely, and with quiet force. She could all but feel the muscle in his gaze. It unnerved her.

Out of habit, she raised her fingers to her birthmark, but at the last moment she used them to sweep locks of hair behind her ear.

"You can see for yourself, can't you? It's ironic because I'm no legendary beauty. No men are fighting battles over me." She gave a self-effacing smile. "That would require at least two men to be interested. I'm three-and-twenty years old, and so far there hasn't even been one."

"You live in a village of women."

"Spindle Cove's not entirely women. There are some men. There's the blacksmith. And the vicar."

He dismissed these examples with a gruff sound.

"Well . . . there's *you*," she said.

He went stone still.

So. Now they came to it. She probably shouldn't have put him on the spot, but then again—he was the one pressing the topic.

"There's you," she repeated. "And you can scarcely bear to share the same air I breathe. I tried to be friendly, when you first arrived in Spindle Cove. That didn't go over well."

"Miss Taylor—"

"And it's not that you're uninterested in women. I know you've had others."

He blinked, and the small motion made her uneasy in her skin. Amazing. His blink had the same effect as another man pounding his palm with his fist.

"Well, it's common knowledge," she said, quietly grinding her toe in the dirt. Digging for courage. "In the village, your . . . arrangements . . . are the subject of far too much speculation. Even if I don't want to hear about them, I do."

He rose to his feet and began walking toward the road. His massive shoulders were squared, his heavy paces measured. There he went again, walking away. She'd had enough of this. She was tired of shrugging off his rejections, dismissing the wounded feelings with a good-natured laugh.

"Don't you see?" She rose and waded through the heather, hurrying to catch the border of his long, monumental shadow. "This is exactly what I mean. If I smile in your direction, you turn the other way. If I find a seat toward your end of the room, you decide you'd rather stand. Do I make you itch, Corporal Thorne? Does the scent of my dusting powder make you sneeze? Or is there something in my demeanor that you find loathsome or terrifying?"

"Don't be absurd."

"Then admit it. You avoid me."

"Very well." He drew to a stop. "I avoid you."

"Now tell me why."

He turned to face her, and his ice-blue eyes burned into hers. But he didn't say a word.

Kate's breath left her lungs in a sigh, and her shoulders fell. "Come along," she coaxed. "Say it. It's all right. After all these years, I think it would be a mercy to hear someone speak the truth. Just be honest."

In an impulsive move, she reached for his hand and brought it to her face, touching his fingertips to her birthmark. He tried pull back, but she wouldn't let him escape. If she had to live with this mark every day, he could bear to touch it just this once.

She stepped closer, pressing her pigment-stained temple to his palm. His hand was cool.

She said, "This is the reason. Isn't it? The reason you don't take an interest. The reason no men take an interest."

"Miss Taylor, I—" His jaw tensed. "No. It isn't like that."

"Then what is it?"

No reply.

Her face burned. She wanted to beat at his chest, crack him open. "What is it? For God's sake, what is it about me you find so intolerable? So wretchedly unbearable you can't even stand to be in the same room?"

He muttered an oath. "Stop provoking me. You won't like the answer."

"I want to hear it anyhow."

He plunged one hand into her hair, startling a gasp from her lips. Strong fingers curled to cup the back of her head. His eyes searched her face, and every nerve ending in her body crackled with tension. The sinking sun threw a last flare of red-orange light between them, setting the moment ablaze.

"It's this."

With a flex of his arm, he pulled her into a kiss.

And he kissed her the way he did everything. Intensely, and with quiet force. His lips pressed firm against hers, demanding a response.

Acting out of pure instinct, Kate shoved at his chest. "Release me."

"I will. But not yet."

His grip kept her immobile. She had no escape.

Nevertheless, she didn't fear him. No, she feared whatever was rapidly filling the space between them. The raw hunger in his eyes. This heat welling between their bodies. The sudden heaviness in her limbs, her abdomen, her breasts. The mad acceleration of her pulse. The air around them seemed charged with intent. And not all of it was on his side.

He bent to kiss her again, and this time her instincts were different.

She stretched to meet him halfway.

When his strong lips touched hers, she went soft everywhere. He pulled her close, wrapping his other arm about her waist. She didn't even try to resist. The voice of her conscience went mute, and her eyelids fluttered in exquisite surrender. She sighed into the kiss. A shameless confession of longing.

His lips were so warm. And for all his cool, stony appearance, he tasted delicious and comforting. Like freshly baked bread, mixed with some faint memory of bitters by the pint. She had a vision of him earlier that day, drinking in a dimly lit tavern. Alone. The poignant solitude of that image made her want to hold him. She had to settle for clutching his coat lapels, nestling close to his chest.

She let her lips fall apart, the better to breathe him in. He caught her top lip between his, then sipped at the lower. As though he craved the taste of her, too.

He brushed firm kisses to the corner of her mouth, her jaw, the pounding pulse in her throat. Each press of his lips was swift and strong. She could feel each kiss's imprint linger like a fiery brand on her skin. He was marking her with stamps of his approval.

Her passion-swelled mouth . . . *Wanted*.

Her softly arching neck . . . *Desired*.

The sweep of her cheekbone . . . *Lovely*.

And last—the wine-splashed mark at her temple . . . *Sweet*.

His kiss lingered there for several moments. His breath moved in and out, stirring her hair. Standing like this, pressed so close to him, she could feel the barely restrained power coursing through his body. His whole being shuddered with palpable desire.

Then he pulled away.

She clung to his coat, dizzied. "I—"

"Don't be concerned. That won't happen again."

"It won't?"

"No."

"Then why did it happen in the first place?"

He put a single fingertip under her chin, tilting her face to his. "Don't ever—*ever*—think no man wants you. That's all."

That's all?

She stared up at the hardened, handsome, impossible

man. He would kiss her at sunset in a field of heather, make her feel beautiful and desired, set her whole body throbbing with sensation . . . only to set her back on her feet and say, "That's all"?

His weight shifted, as though he would retreat.

"Wait." She tightened her grip and held him in place. "What if I want more?"

Chapter Four

More.

Thorne braced himself. That word shook the ground beneath him. He could have sworn the hillside rolled and swayed.

More. What did it mean to her, that word? Certainly something different from the visions his own mind supplied. He saw the two of them, tangled in the heather and the rucked-up muslin of her skirts. This was why he sought out experienced women who shared his definition of "more"—and had no qualms about telling him exactly when and where and how often they'd like it.

But Miss Taylor was a lady, no matter how she denied it. She was innocent, young, given to foolish dreaming. He cringed to imagine what "more" meant in her mind. Sweet words? Courting? A vinegar jar had more sweetness in it than he did. His experience with courting had been limited to courting danger.

That wrongheaded kiss had been just one more example.

Stupid, stupid. His own mother had said it best. *Your head's as thick as it is ugly, boy. You never will learn.*

"You can't just walk away from me," she said. "Not after a kiss like that. We need to talk."

Brilliant. This was worse than sweetness, more fraught with danger than courting. She wanted *talking*.

Why couldn't a woman let an action speak for itself? If he'd wanted to use words, he would have used them.

"We have nothing to discuss," he said.

"Oh, I beg to differ."

Thorne stared at her, considering. He'd spent the better part of a decade on campaign with the British infantry. He knew when his best option was retreat.

He turned and whistled for the dog. The pup bounded to his side. Thorne was pleased. He'd been divided as to whether to leave him with the breeder so long, but the extra weeks of training seemed to have paid off.

He walked toward the place where he'd left the horse grazing, near a wooden stile that served as the only gap in the field's waist-high stone border.

Miss Taylor followed him. "Corporal Thorne . . ."

He vaulted the stile, putting the fence between them. "We need to get back to Spindle Cove. You've missed lessons with the Youngfield sisters this evening. They'll be wondering where you are."

"You know my schedule of lessons?" Her voice carried an interested lilt.

He cursed under his breath. "Not all of them. Just the irritating ones."

"Oh. The irritating ones."

He tossed the pup a scrap of rabbit hide from his pocket, then began checking over the horse's tack.

She placed both hands on the evenly mortared top of the stone fence and boosted herself to sit atop it. "So my lessons and your drinking sessions just happen to coincide. At the same times and on the same days, to the point that you know my schedule. By heart."

For God's sake. What heart?

He shook his head. "Don't tell yourself some sentimental story of how I've been pining for you. You're a fetching enough woman, and I'm a man with eyes. I've noticed. That's all."

She gathered her skirts in one hand, lifted her legs, and swung them to his side of the fence. "And yet you've never said a word."

With her sitting on the stone wall, they were almost equal in height. She crooked one finger and swept a curling lock of hair behind her ear—in that graceful, unthinking way women had of pushing men to the brink of desperation.

"I'm not a smoothly spoken man. If I put my wants into words, I'd have you blushing so hard your frock would turn a deeper shade of pink."

There. That ought to scare her off.

She colored slightly. But she didn't back down.

"Do you know what I think?" she said. "I think that maybe—just maybe—all your stern, forbidding behavior is some strange, male form of modesty. A way to deflect notice. I'm almost ashamed to say it worked on me for the better part of a year, but—"

"Really, Miss Taylor—"

She met his gaze. "But I'm paying close attention now."

Damn. So she was.

He'd been avoiding precisely this for a year now— the possibility that she'd someday catch sight of him in church or the tavern, hold that glance a beat longer than usual, and then . . . remember everything. He couldn't let that happen. If Miss Kate Taylor, as she existed now, were ever connected with the den of squalor and sin that had served as her cradle, it could destroy everything for her. Her reputation, her livelihood, her happiness.

So he'd stayed away. Not an easy task, when the village was so small and this girl—who wasn't a girl anymore, but an alluring woman—had her toes in every corner of it.

And then today . . .

A year's worth of avoidance and intimidation, all shot to hell in one afternoon, thank to that wrongheaded, stupid, goddamned glorious kiss.

"Look at me."

He leaned forward and braced his hands on the stone wall, confronting her face-to-face. Daring her; daring fate. If she was ever going to recognize him, it would be now.

As she took him in, he did some looking of his own. He drank in the small details he'd denied himself for long months. Her sweet pink frock, with ivory ribbons threaded through the neckline like little dollops of confectioner's icing. The tiny freckle on her chest, just below her right collarbone. The brave set of her jaw, and the way her pink lips crooked fetchingly at the corners.

Then he searched those clever, lovely hazel eyes for any hint of awareness or flash of recognition.

Nothing.

"You don't know me," he said. Both a statement and a question.

She shook her head. Then she spoke what were quite possibly the most foolish, improbable words he'd ever heard. "But I think I'd like to."

He gripped that stone wall as if it were the edge of a precipice.

She said, "Perhaps we could—"

"No. We couldn't."

"I didn't finish my thought."

"Doesn't matter. Whatever you meant to suggest, it won't happen." He pushed off the wall and gathered his gelding's lead, loosing it from the stile.

"You'll have to talk to me sometime. We do live in the same tiny village."

"Not for long."

"How do you mean?"

"I'm leaving Spindle Cove."

She paused. "What? When?"

"In a month's time." A month too late, it would seem.

"Are you being reassigned?"

"I'm leaving the army. And England. That's what I was doing in Hastings today. I've booked passage to America on a merchant ship."

"My." Her hands fell to her lap. "America."

"The war's over. Lord Rycliff's helping me arrange for an honorable discharge. I've a wish to own some land."

She moved as though she'd hop down from the wall. By reflex, he took her by the waist, slowly lowering her to the ground.

Once there, she showed no inclination to leave his embrace.

"But we're only just getting to know one another," she said.

Oh, no. This stopped right here and now. She didn't truly want him. She was overwrought from the day, clinging to the only soul in reach.

"Miss Taylor, we kissed. Once. It was a mistake. It won't happen again."

"Are you certain?" She laced her arms around his neck.

He froze, stunned by the intent he read in her eyes.

Sweet merciful God. The girl meant to kiss *him*.

He could tell the exact moment she dared herself to do it. Her gaze lingered on his lips, and he heard her sharp intake of breath. She stretched up, and as her lips neared his, he marveled over every fraction of an instant in which she didn't change her mind and turn away.

Her eyelids slipped shut. He might have closed his eyes, too, but he couldn't.

This, he needed to see to believe.

She pressed her lips to his, just as the last wash of sunlight ebbed. And the world became a place he didn't recognize.

She smelled so good. Not just pleasant, but *good*. Pure. Those light hints of clover and citrus were the essence of clean. He felt washed by that scent. He could almost imagine that he'd never lied, never stolen, never shivered in prison. Never marched into battle, never bled. That he hadn't killed four men at distances so intimate, he could still recall the colors of their eyes. Brown, blue, another blue, then green.

This is wrong.

A dark growl rumbled in his chest. He kept his hands on her waist, but he fanned his fingers wide.

His thumbs skimmed upward, skipping from rib to rib until they just grazed the soft undersides of her breasts. With the little finger of each hand, he touched the gentle flare of her hip. His hand span was stretched to its limits. This was as much of her as he could possibly hold.

He needed every bit of that leverage to push her away. When they broke apart, she gazed up at him. Waiting.

"You shouldn't have done that," he said.

"I wanted to. Does that make me loose?"

"No. It makes you soft in the head. Young ladies like you don't pass time with men like me."

"Men like you? You mean the sort of men who rescue helpless young ladies in the street and carry puppies in their satchels?" She gave a playful shiver. "Lord preserve me from men like you."

A timid smile played at the corner of her mouth. He wanted to devour it. To catch her in his arms and teach her the consequences of teasing a fiercely lusting, barely civilized beast.

But saving this girl was the one decent thing he'd done in all his life. Some nineteen years ago, he'd sold the last bits of his own innocence to purchase hers. He'd be damned if he'd ruin her now.

With firm motions, he unlaced her arms from around his neck. He held her by the wrists, making his hands tight as manacles.

She gasped.

"Have a care for yourself, Miss Taylor. I'll take blame for the kiss. It was a liberty and my mistake. I let a carnal impulse distract me from my duty. But if you're imagining tender feelings on my side, they're just that—imaginings."

She twisted in his grip. "You're frightening me."

"Good," he said evenly. "You should be scared. I've killed more men than you'll kiss in your lifetime. You don't want anything to do with me, and I don't feel a damned thing for you."

He released her wrists. "I'm finished discussing it."

* * *

He was finished discussing it.

Kate only wished she were finished *living* it.

Sadly, she had another two hours on horseback in which to recline, mortified, against his chest and savor her full humiliation. What a horrid, horrid day.

She wasn't used to riding horseback. As the miles wore on, her muscles began to knot. Her backside hurt as though it had been paddled. And her pride . . . oh, her pride smarted something fierce.

What was wrong with the man? Kissing her, telling her he wanted her, and then so callously pushing her away? After living with his standoffish treatment for an entire year, she supposed she should have known better. But today she'd fancied that maybe she'd found his hidden emotional side. Perhaps, she'd thought, the hardened beast had a tender underbelly—a soft spot, just for her. She couldn't resist giving it a poke.

He'd all but snapped her finger off.

So mortifying. How could she have misread his intentions so completely? She should have refused his offer of a ride home and spent the night singing for pennies in the Hastings streets instead. It would have been less degrading.

I don't feel a damned thing for you.

The only consolation was that he'd be leaving Spindle Cove in a matter of weeks, and she need never speak to him again.

Erasing him from her thoughts would be a more difficult trick. No matter how long she lived, this man would always be her first kiss. Or worse, her *only* kiss.

The cruel, teasing ogre.

Eventually they reached familiar bends in the road. The scattered amber lights of the village appeared on the horizon, just below the silvery stars.

Kate had a quiet laugh at her own expense. She'd left the village early this morning with a heart full of foolish hopes and dreams. Tonight, she returned with her spine wilted from six kinds of humiliation and her arms full of mongrel dog.

"If you're still taking suggestions, I'd name him Badger," she said when the silence became too much. "It suits him, I think. He's all nose and teeth and tussle."

His reply was a long time in coming. "Call the pup whatever you wish."

She bent her head and nuzzled the dog's fur. "Badger," she whispered, worrying the soft flap of his ear, "you'd never spurn my kisses, would you?"

The pup licked her fingertip. She blinked away a silly tear.

As they neared the church and the heart of the village, she looked to the Queen's Ruby. Lights burned in nearly every window. The sight kindled a warm glow in her heart. Badger's tail began to wag, as if he sensed the lift in her spirits. She did have friends, and they were waiting up for her.

Thorne helped her dismount and loosed the horse to graze on the village green.

"Do you plan to come in and eat something?" she asked.

He shrugged back into his coat. "That's a bad idea. You know there's talk about me. I'm bringing you home well after dark. Your frock's torn, and your hair's a shambles."

She cringed at the blow to what remained of her vanity. "My hair is a shambles? Since when? You might have said something."

Tucking Badger under one arm, she plucked at her hairpins with her free hand. His concern for appearances wasn't unfounded. Small villages were buzzing hives of gossip. She knew she must keep her reputation unsoiled if she wanted to continue living in the Queen's Ruby and tutoring the gently bred ladies who summered there.

"Just give the dog here, Miss Taylor, and I'll be on my way."

In an instinctive reaction, she hugged the puppy close to her chest. "No. No, I don't think I will."

"What?"

"We get along, he and I. So I'm going to keep him. I believe he'd be happier that way."

The severity of his frown seemed to slice through the darkness. "You can't keep a puppy in a rooming house. Your landlady won't allow it, and even if she would—a dog like that needs space to run."

"He also needs *love*. Affection, Corporal Thorne. Are you telling me you can provide it?" She playfully tugged at Badger's scruff. "Tell me right now that you love this dog, and I will return the pup at once."

He didn't answer her.

"Four little words," she taunted. " 'I . . . love . . . the . . . dog.' And he's yours."

"I *own* the dog," he said tersely. "He is mine. I paid coin for him."

"Then I'll pay you back. But I will not surrender this sweet, defenseless little creature to a man with no feeling, no heart. No capacity to care."

Just then the front door of the Queen's Ruby burst open.

Mrs. Nichols came running out from the inn—as much as the poor old dear *could* run. Her hands were flapping. "Miss Taylor! Miss Taylor, oh, thank goodness you're here at last."

"I'm so sorry to have worried you, Mrs. Nichols. I missed the stagecoach home, and Corporal Thorne was good enough to—"

"We've been waiting and waiting." The older woman put her arm through Kate's and pulled her toward the door. "Your visitors have been here for hours. I've run through three pots of tea, exhausted all possible topics of conversation."

"Visitors?" Kate was stunned. "I have visitors?"

Mrs. Nichols gathered her shawl about her shoulders. "Four of them."

"*Four* of them? Whatever do they want?"

"They won't say. Except that they've insisted on waiting for you. It's been hours now."

Kate paused in the threshold, scraping the mud from the soles of her boots. She couldn't imagine who these visitors might be. Perhaps a family seeking music lessons. But at *this* hour of night? "I'm so sorry I've put you to such trouble."

"Not a trouble, dear. It's an honor to have a man of such rank and stature in my parlor."

A man? Of rank and stature?

"Might I just nip upstairs and see to my appearance first? I'm all mussed from the road."

"No, no. That won't do, my dear." The inn's landlady tugged her inside. "One can only keep a marquess waiting so long."

"A *marquess*?"

While Mrs. Nichols closed the door, Kate turned to catch her reflection in the looking glass. She jumped in her skin when she found herself nose-to-button with Corporal Thorne instead.

"I thought you weren't coming in," she accused his lapel.

"I changed my mind." When she finally dared look up, she found his eyes narrowed in suspicion. He asked, "Do you know any marquess?"

She shook her head. "The highest-ranking man I know is Lord Rycliff, and he's an earl."

"I'll go in with you."

"I'm sure that's not necessary. It's a parlor, not a crime den."

"I'll go anyway."

Before they could argue it further, Kate found herself being hustled into the parlor. Thorne followed close behind. Several of the rooming-house guests lined the corridor. They gave her wide-eyed, speculative glances as she moved past.

When they reached the parlor, Mrs. Nichols pushed Kate through the door. "Here's Miss Taylor at last, my lord and ladies."

With that, the landlady shut them in. Kate could hear her on the other side of the door, chasing the residents away from the corridor.

There seemed to be a dozen guests in the parlor, though a quick count assured Kate they numbered just four. Wealth and elegance crammed the room. And here she stood in a torn, dirt-streaked frock. Her hair wasn't even pinned.

A dark-clad gentleman rose to his feet and bowed. Kate had barely managed a slight dip of a curtsy when a loud, collective gasp nearly guttered the candles.

"It *is* her. It *must* be her."

Kate swallowed hard. "Er . . . I must be who?"

A pretty young woman rose from a chair. She looked a few years younger than Kate, and she wore a frock of spotless, snowy muslin and an embroidered jade-green shawl. As she came to the center of the room, her ex-

pression was one of pure wonderment. She regarded
Kate as one might a ghost, or a rare species of orchid.

"It must be you." The girl raised her hand and
stretched two fingertips to the birthmark at Kate's
temple.

Kate flinched out of instinct. She'd already been
called a witch and a child of shame for that mark today.

Now she found herself wrapped in a warm, impulsive
hug.

Caught between the two of them, Badger yipped.

"Oh, dear." Kate pulled back, flashing an apologetic
smile. "I'd forgotten him."

The young woman in front of her laughed and smiled.
"The pup is right to object. Where *are* my manners?
Let's begin again. Introductions first." She stuck out
her hand. "I'm Lark Gramercy. How do you do?"

Kate clasped the proffered hand. "Delighted, I'm
sure."

Lark turned and indicated her companions in turn.
"Here we have my sister Harriet."

"Harry," the woman in question said. She rose from
her chair and pumped Kate's hand firmly. "Everyone
calls me Harry."

Kate tried not to stare. Harriet, or Harry, was the
most stunningly beautiful woman she'd ever seen. Without a trace of adornment in the form of rouge or jewels,
her face was a symphony of perfection: pale, luminous
skin, wide eyes, wine-red lips. A small beauty mark on
one cheekbone added a sultry punctuation to the sweep
of her dark eyelashes. She wore her jet-black hair parted
to the side and pulled back in a severe chignon that em-
phasized the swannish curve of her neck. And despite
all her classic feminine beauty, she was dressed in what
seemed to be men's attire. A chemisette with hardly

any frill at the neck, a waistcoat cut in the style most gentlemen wore, and—most shocking of all—a divided skirt of gray wool, hemmed several inches too short for modesty.

Good heavens. Kate could see the woman's *ankles*.

"My brother Bennett is off traveling the Hindu Kush, and our other sister, Calista, is married and living up North. But we have with us Aunt Marmoset." Lark patted the shoulder of a seated woman in her later years.

Kate blinked. "I've heard you wrong. I thought you said Aunt—"

"Marmoset. Yes." Lark smiled. "It's properly Millicent, but as a child, I could never pronounce it. It always came out Marmoset, and the name just stuck."

"I resemble the name more every year," Aunt Marmoset said good-naturedly.

"Yes, old dear," said Harry dryly. "I was just complaining the other day, if I have to pluck you down from one more tree—"

"Oh, hush. I meant I'm small and spry and infectiously adorable." The diminutive older woman stretched a bony hand toward Kate. Her grip was warmer and stronger than Kate would have expected. "It's remarkable to see you, child."

Before Kate could puzzle out the old woman's meaning, Lark was making her final introduction.

"And this is our brother Evan. Lord Drewe."

Kate turned to the gentleman standing near the window. The marquess, she presumed.

Lord Drewe made a deep, formal bow, which she tried to repay with her best curtsy. Here was a man, as they said, in his prime of life. Handsome, assured, worldly, and though he was doubtless responsible for hundreds, if not thousands, of tenants and dependents, he appeared to be in command of no one more than himself.

Kate found herself rather awed in his presence. She could understand Mrs. Nichols's excitement now.

"The ancestral home is in Derbyshire. But we have a property over near Kenmarsh," Lark explained. "It's called Ambervale. Just a cottage, really. We've been summering there."

"It's a pleasure to meet you all." Kate dropped into a chair so the marquess might be seated. "And you've come to Spindle Cove for . . . ?"

"For you, Miss Taylor," Lark said, taking a seat nearby. "Naturally."

"Oh. Were you wanting music lessons? I offer instruction in voice, pianoforte, harp . . ."

All the Gramercys laughed.

Behind her, Thorne cleared his throat. "Miss Taylor has had a long day. Surely your business can wait for the morning."

Lord Drewe nodded. "Your concern is duly noted, Mister . . ."

"Thorne."

"Corporal Thorne," Kate put in. "He's in charge of our local militia."

She might have embellished the introduction, she supposed. *He's good friends with the Earl of Rycliff,* or *He served honorably on the Peninsula under Wellington.* But she wasn't feeling particularly charitable toward him at the moment.

She lifted Badger. "He gave me a puppy."

"And it's a lovely puppy," Aunt Marmoset cooed.

Lark clapped her hands with impatience. "Corporal Thorne is right. It's ungodly late. Harry, just show her the painting."

Harry rose and came forward, bearing a rectangular, paper-wrapped parcel.

As her sister removed the paper covering, Lark chattered away. "I needed a summer project, you see. Ambervale is quiet, and I do go a bit mad without something to occupy my hands. So I decided to go through the attic. Just old crockery, mostly. A few moldering books. But tucked back under the rafters, I found this canvas wrapped in a tarpaulin." Her voice pitched with excitement. "Oh, do *hurry*, Harry."

Harry continued at the same pace. "Settle your feathers, pigeon."

At last she had the thing unwrapped and held it up in the lamplight.

Kate gasped. "Oh my Lord."

She clapped a hand over her mouth, horrified by her accidental blasphemy. Cursing, in front of a marquess?

The Gramercys didn't seem perturbed, however. They all sat quite calmly and quietly as Harry revealed a painting of a reclining, flagrantly nude woman tangled in white bedsheets and a red velvet counterpane. Swollen, ruby-tipped breasts rested like twin pillows atop a rotund, creamy belly. The woman in the portrait was obviously pregnant.

And she looked like Kate. She looked a great deal like Kate, save for some differences about the eyes and chin, and the absence of any birthmark. The resemblance was uncanny, disturbing, and readily apparent to everyone in the room.

"Oh my *Lord*," Kate breathed.

Lark beamed. "Isn't it gorgeous? When we found it, we just knew we had to search you out."

"Put that away." Thorne stepped forward. "It's vile."

"I beg your pardon," Harry replied, proudly propping the nude painting on the mantelpiece and standing back to admire it. "The female form is beautiful in all its natural states. This is *art*."

"Put it away," Thorne repeated in a low, threatening tone. "Or I will make it kindling."

"He's just being protective," Aunt Marmoset said. "I think it's sweet. A little savage, but sweet."

Harry yanked Lark's jade-green shawl from her shoulders and draped it over half the painting, obscuring most of the nudity. "This backward little village. Philistines, all. When we showed it to the vicar, he developed a stammer and visible hives."

"You . . ." Kate swallowed hard, staring at the painting now boldly displayed above the fire. "You showed this to the *vicar*?"

"But of course," Lark replied. "That's how we found you."

Kate crossed her arms over her chest, feeling unaccountably exposed. She leaned forward and peered at the face of the woman in the painting. "But it can't be *me*."

"No, Miss Taylor. It's not you." With a long-suffering sigh, Lord Drewe stood and addressed his siblings. "You're making a right hash of this, I hope you know. If she wants nothing to do with us after tonight, you'll have only yourselves to blame."

What on earth could he mean? Kate's brain made a lazy twirl in her skull.

The corporal addressed the room in a deep, commanding voice. "I'm giving you one more minute to start making sense. Otherwise, I don't care if you *are* lords and ladies—you'll be leaving. Miss Taylor's under my protection, and I won't have her treated ill."

Lord Drewe turned to Kate. "I'll make this brief. As

my youngest sister has attempted to explain, I am the much-beleaguered head of this traveling circus. And we've been waiting for you, Miss Taylor, because we believe you may be a part of it."

"I beg your pardon," she said. "A part of what, precisely?"

He gestured with one hand, as though it should be obvious. "A part of the family."

Chapter Five

The room swam in Kate's vision. Badger scampered to the floor, and she made no effort to stop him. All around her, the Gramercys argued.

"I told you we shouldn't have sprung it on her this way."

"It's been sprung on us all. It wasn't as though we knew, starting out this morning . . ."

"Oh, dear. She's so pale."

They were such a . . . such a *family*. Kate could scarcely believe that she might be a part of it. The temptation to hope was so great, and optimism came to her too easily. But she didn't want to make a fool of herself. She had to make some sense of this first.

While the rest of them talked, Aunt Marmoset came and sat next to her. She pulled a small, paper-wrapped candy from her pocket. "Have a spice drop, dear."

Kate accepted it numbly.

"Go on," the old woman urged. "Eat it now."

Uncertain how to refuse, Kate unwrapped the sweet and popped the hard lozenge into her mouth.

Oh . . . blazes.

Her eyes watered instantly. The disc of pure, sugared fire burned on her tongue. It took everything she had not to spit it out.

"Strong, isn't it? A bit overwhelming at first. But with patience, and a bit of work, you'll arrive at the sweetness." Aunt Marmoset patted Kate's arm. "This family's like that."

Then the old woman sharply addressed the room. "All of you, be calm."

They were all of them instantly calm. Even the one who was a marquess.

"The only way to tell this is as a story, I think." Aunt Marmoset's papery, age-spotted hand clasped Kate's. "Once, there was a man named Simon Gramercy, the young Marquess of Drewe. Like all Gramercys, he tended toward tempestuous, inappropriate passions. Simon's particular interests were art, and the charms of a highly unsuitable girl. The daughter of a tenant farmer from his Derbyshire estate, can you imagine?"

Kate shook her head, her tongue still puckered around the evil spice drop.

"Simon's mother, the dowager, was scandalized. The girl's parents disowned her. But Simon would hear no censure. He set up a love nest with his muse at Ambervale. They lived ensconced there for several months, merrily painting and posing and making passionate—"

"Aunt Marmoset."

"Really, after the portrait, I don't think it can come as a shock." The older woman continued, "Anyhow, poor Simon's health took an ill turn. The next the family heard of him, he was dead. Suddenly, tragically, dead. And no one knew what had become of the farmer's daughter. She seemed to have vanished completely. Perhaps she'd taken ill, as well . . . Perhaps she'd gone on to be another man's muse. No one could guess. The title passed to Simon's cousin, my brother-in-law. And then, on his death, to Evan." She waved in Lord Drewe's direction.

"Are you confused yet?" Lark asked.

"We'll draw you a chart later," said Harry.

Kate stared at the painting. "We do look rather alike, I'll admit, but I'm only twenty-three. And I have this." She raised her hand to her birthmark.

"Oh, but that's a family trait," Lark said. "Several of the Gramercys have something like it. Harry has only the small beauty mark, and most of mine is covered by my hair. Evan's is behind his ear. Show her, Evan."

Lord Drewe gamely turned to display the side of his neck. Yes, he did have a port-wine mark that disappeared beneath his crisp, immaculate cravat.

"Is it making sense now?" Lark asked. "When we found this painting in the attic, we knew she must be Simon's lover. But no one ever knew she was pregnant. The question was, what became of the child?"

"Dead, we assumed," Harry said. "Otherwise we surely would have heard something. But Lark couldn't resist the chance to investigate."

Lark smiled. "I do love a mystery. If the babe had been born from Ambervale, we knew some record of the birth ought to exist. So we went to the local parish, but there we learned that the church had burned in 1782 and not been rebuilt for a decade. Some sort of accident with a censer and a tapestry . . ."

Lord Drewe cleared his throat. "Keep to essentials, Lark. For Miss Taylor's sake."

Lark nodded. "So there were no records. During those years, the parish was divided between the three neighboring churches. We decided to make family outings, visiting one per week."

"Only in this family," said Harry, "would we consider it high entertainment to go searching musty parish registers for a stillborn cousin."

Lark ignored her sister. "We started at St. Francis, the closest. No luck there. This week was a choice between St. Anthony in the Glen and St. Mary of the Martyrs. I must admit, I was lobbying for St. Anthony's, because I liked the pastoral sound of it, but—"

"But our resident martyr had his way, and St. Mary's it was."

"Yes, thank goodness. The book, Evan?"

Lord Drewe withdrew a large volume that looked to be a well-thumbed parish register. Kate was surprised he would have been allowed to remove it from the church. But then, he likely paid the vicar's living. She supposed any requests from the local marquess would be difficult to deny.

He opened it to a previously marked page, found a line with his fingertip, and read aloud, "Katherine Adele, born February the twenty-second, in the year seventeen hundred and ninety-one. Father, Simon Langley Gramercy. Mother, Elinor Marie."

"Katherine?" Kate's heart began to pound. "Did you say Katherine?"

Lark bounced in her chair with excitement. "Yes. We scanned the next several years' worth of records—no death listing. No christening either, but no death. We asked the vicar if he knew of any Katherine living in the area who might be the right age now. He replied that he didn't. However, he said he'd recently received a letter."

"A letter?" Badger nosed at Kate's shins, and she lifted the pup into her lap. "*My* letter?"

For the past several years, she'd played the organ for Sunday worship at St. Ursula's. She asked no financial compensation for the service. Only a favor. Each week, Mr. Keane gave her an hour in the vicar's office. She chose a parish from his enormous Church of England directory and penned a letter, requesting a search of parish registers for any female children born between 1790 and 1792, given the Christian name Katherine, who had since fallen from the local record. She'd begun with the parishes nearest Margate and worked outward.

Slowly. Over weeks and months and years.

The vicar signed and posted the letters for her. He also did her the favor of keeping them secret. Most of the villagers would have laughed at her for spending so much time and effort on a fruitless enterprise. In their eyes, she might as well have spent her time sticking notes in bottles and heaving them into the ocean.

But Kate hadn't been able to let the idea go. She'd made hope her weekly habit. Every time the post brought another crushing "No"—or worse, when months passed with no reply at all, letting her know a perfectly good stone had gone unturned—she listened to that voice inside her heart: *Be brave, my Katie.*

And now . . .

Now Aunt Marmoset's spice drop had nearly dissolved in her mouth—and the older woman was right. A thick, delicious sweetness coated her tongue.

Kate savored it.

"Yes," Lark said. "It was your letter. And I just knew in my heart, *our* Katherine must be you. We set off at once, traveled all afternoon, and arrived here a few hours ago."

"We showed your vicar this"—Harry indicated the painting—"and once he recovered from his small apoplexy, he told us that Miss Kate Taylor did indeed bear a remarkable resemblance to the portrait."

"From the neck up, of course." Lark directed this comment—and a timid smile—at Corporal Thorne.

"So there you have it, my dear." Aunt Marmoset patted Kate's knee. "The tale has a miraculous ending. We have found you. And by all evidence, you seem to be the long-lost daughter of a marquess."

The words hit Kate like an avalanche. In the aftermath, her emotions were frozen, scattered things. It was all too much. She had parents named Simon and Elinor. She had a birthday. She had a middle name.

If . . .

If this could all be believed.

"But I never lived anywhere near Kenmarsh," she said. "I was raised as a ward of Margate School until just four years ago. That was when I came here to teach music lessons."

"And before Margate, where were you?" Lord Drewe asked.

"I haven't any clear memory, unfortunately. I asked my schoolmistress for details." Goodness, had her horrid interview with Miss Paringham only been that afternoon? "She told me I was abandoned."

Kate stared at the woman in the portrait. Her *mother*, if this could be believed. Had she died? Or given her baby up, unable to care for a child on her own? But it was plain from the way the woman's hand draped affectionately over her rotund belly, she'd loved that infant in the womb. How amazing, Kate thought, to think she could be *in* that painting, underneath the skin of it, fetal and wriggling and . . .

Loved.

"You poor thing," Lark said. "I can't imagine how you must have suffered. We can't undo those years, but we will do our best to make up for them now."

"Yes," Drewe agreed. "We must install you at Ambervale as soon as possible. When I'm home tonight, I'll send a lady's maid to help with your packing."

"I'm sure that won't be necessary."

"Did you already have your own lady's maid?"

Kate laughed, astonished. "No. I haven't that many belongings to pack. What I meant was, it's not appropriate for you to invite me to your home."

Lord Drewe blinked. "Of course it's appropriate. It's a family home."

A family home.

The words made her breath catch painfully. "But . . . wouldn't I be an embarrassment?"

"Absolutely not," Harry said. "Our brother Bennett holds the position of family embarrassment, and he jealously guards it against all would-be usurpers."

"Why would you embarrass us, dear?" asked Aunt Marmoset.

"Even if all you say is true . . . I'm your illegitimate second cousin, by a tenant farmer's daughter."

Kate waited for the import of her words to sink in. Surely people at the Gramercys' level of society didn't associate with bastard relations?

"If you're concerned about scandal, don't be," Lark said. "Scandal comes with the Gramercy name—along with enough wealth that no one much cares. If there's one lesson Aunt Marmoset instilled in us from our youth, it's—"

"Beware of spice drops," said Harry.

"Family above everything," countered Lord Drewe.

"We may be a motley assortment of aristocrats, but we stand by one another through scandal, misfortune, and the rare triumph." He pointed to the parish register. "Simon claimed his daughter and gave her the family name. So if this infant is you, Miss Taylor . . ."

A dramatic pause thickened the air in the room.

" . . . then you are not Miss Taylor at all. You are Katherine Adele Gramercy."

Katherine Adele Gramercy?

Like hell she was.

Thorne clenched his jaw. He wasn't a man of words. This situation called for eloquence, but he could only think of action. Chiefly, he wanted to fling open the door and turn all these queerly chattering aristocrats out on their arses. Then he'd lift Miss Taylor in his arms and carry her upstairs to have the restful lie-down she'd been needing for the past several hours. Her cheeks were deathly pale.

He would want to lie down next to her, but he wouldn't. Because unlike these presumptive intruders, *he* had restraint. Thorne had heard of aristocratic in-breeding being to blame for imbecility and bad teeth. This family seemed to have contracted a sort of verbal cholera. Everything they spouted was rubbish.

He couldn't believe these people proposed to take Miss Taylor away. He couldn't believe she'd consider going with them. *She* had sense.

And she promptly displayed some of it.

"You're so kind. But I'm afraid I can't leave Spindle Cove so hastily. I have obligations here. Lessons, pupils. Our midsummer fair is just a week or so away, and I'm responsible for all the music and dancing."

"Oh, I love a fair." The youngest one bounced in

her seat again. She had an irritating way of doing that, Thorne noticed.

"It isn't much, but we have a good time with it. It's a children's festival, mostly—up at the ruined castle. Corporal Thorne and his militiamen are helping, too." After throwing him a hesitant look, Miss Taylor continued, "At any rate, surely you'd wish for this . . . connection . . . to be more official before inviting me to your home? If we find that your suppositions are wrong, and I am actually *not* your relation . . ."

"But the portrait," the young lady protested. "The register. Your birthmark."

"Miss Taylor is right," Lord Drewe said. "We must prove it's not merely coincidence. I'll dispatch men to interview at the school, canvass the local area around Ambervale. I've no doubt we'll find the link between your infancy and Margate easily enough, with a bit of digging."

Thorne knew Lord Drewe's men would find no link between that parish register and Margate school. He could have cleared his throat and informed them precisely where Kate Taylor had spent her early years. She could see how eager these people were to claim her as a Gramercy then. There was high-class scandal, and then there was immoral squalor.

He said, "Miss Taylor isn't going anywhere with you. All you've presented are suspicions of her identity. And we don't even know who you are."

Miss Taylor bit her lip. "Corporal Thorne, I'm sure—"

"No, no," the mannish one interrupted. "The good corporal is absolutely right, Miss Taylor. We could be a gang of white slavers, or bloodthirsty cannibals. Or occultists looking for a virgin sacrifice."

Thorne did not believe the Gramercys to be white

slavers or cannibals or occultists—though they seemed to him the genteel version of bedlamites. And though he knew something of Kate Taylor's childhood, he had to admit—he could not say with certainty that they were *not* her cousins. It was possible, he supposed. She hadn't been born in that place. And she had the right name, the right year of birth. Those facts, plus the portrait and birthmark, made an argument that couldn't be easily dismissed.

Still, the odds remained against it, and he didn't trust these people. There was something wrong about them and their story. Perhaps they were mistaken about the connection—in which case Miss Taylor would end up dismayed and potentially the object of ridicule. Alternatively, they *were* her relations and had somehow misplaced her for the better part of twenty-three years, allowing her to languish in cruel, isolating poverty.

They were careless, at best. Criminal, at worst.

He didn't trust them with the next five minutes of Miss Taylor's future, much less the entirety of her life.

"She's not leaving with you," he repeated. "I won't allow it."

"Remind me," Drewe said coolly, "exactly who *you* are. In relation to Miss Taylor, I mean."

Thorne saw the choice before him, clear as a fork in a road. He either spoke the words hovering on the tip of his tongue—words he would never have dared to dream, let alone give voice. Or he let Miss Taylor go with the Gramercys, surrendering any claim on her safety and happiness. Forever.

There was no choice at all. He spoke the words.

"I'm her betrothed," he said. "We're engaged to be married."

Chapter Six

Kate startled in her chair. Surely she'd misheard him.

Engaged? To be married?

"Congratulations, dear." Aunt Marmoset squeezed her hand. "Have another spice drop."

"Truly," Kate said, finally finding her voice. "I've no—"

Before she could get the words of protest out, Thorne's big hand landed on her shoulder. And squeezed, hard. It was a concise, unmistakable message:

Don't.

"No one mentioned that you were betrothed," Lord Drewe said, looking suspiciously from Kate to Thorne and back. "Not the vicar, not the landlady . . ."

"We hadn't told anyone yet," Thorne replied. "It's recent."

"How recent?"

"She accepted me today, on the way home from Hastings." Thorne lifted his hand from Kate's shoulder and smoothed a stray wisp of her hair, subtly calling attention to its unbound state.

Kate's cheeks burned as his implication spread through the parlor, working as a joist to lift eyebrows in every corner of the room.

Lark beamed. "Oh, I knew there was something between you. Why else would you have come home so late, looking so . . ." Her voice trailed off as her gaze wandered to Kate's bedraggled hem and her mussed hair. " . . . so natural."

Her chair legs screeched as Kate shot to her feet. "Corporal Thorne, might I have a word?"

She excused herself with a nervous smile in the Gramercys' direction.

"What are you on about?" she whispered, once he'd followed her to a corner near the pianoforte. Kate knew from experience they could speak quietly there without being overhead. "Hours ago you told me you don't feel a . . . a dratted thing for me, and now you declare that we're engaged?"

"I'm looking out for you."

"Looking out for me? You just implied that we . . . that we've been . . ."

"They were already thinking it," he said. "Believe me. I brought you home late at night, looking like you've been tumbled."

"I—"

"And then *you* told them I gave you a puppy. What else are they going to conclude?"

Her cheeks blazed and she looked away.

"All that blushing doesn't help, either."

How could she *keep* from blushing? Her face heated further as she thought of his fingertips teasing that lock of her hair so presumptively.

"We won't go through with it," he said. "Marriage."

"We won't?" In the ensuing silence, Kate worried

that she'd sounded disappointed. "I mean, of course we won't. I've no desire to marry you. I'm going to tell the Gramercys so right now."

"That would be a mistake." His hands went to her shoulders, keeping her in place. "Hear me now. You're overwhelmed."

"I'm not over—"

Her voice broke. She couldn't even find the strength to complete the objection. Of course she was overwhelmed. Overwhelmed, exhausted, confused. And it was at least partly his fault. Perhaps mostly his fault.

To his credit, he didn't deny it.

"It's the end of a very long day," he said. "Your schoolmistress treated you ill. The cart driver treated you ill. I treated you worst of all. Then these people show up with their fairy tale, their pockets full of candy and riches. You want to see the best in them, because that's your nature. But I tell you, there's something not right about them and their story."

"What makes you say that?"

A long hesitation. "It's a feeling."

She opened her eyes and regarded him keenly. "A feeling? I thought you didn't possess those."

He ignored her baiting comment. "You can't be sure what they're after. They're not yet sure of you. This is a risky situation, and you have no guardian or relations to safeguard your interests. That leaves me. But I can't claim an interest in your well-being without making some claim on you."

A claim on you. Kate didn't know how to take those words. Her whole life, no one had ever tried to make any claim on her. Now two in one night.

The entire situation had an air of unreality about it.

The lateness of the hour, the string of coincidences, the sheer strangeness of the Gramercys. She didn't know whom or what she could trust at the moment—after the foolish way she'd thrown herself at Thorne that afternoon, her own desperate heart seemed the least reliable thing of all.

She needed an ally. But *him*?

"You're honestly suggesting we pretend to be engaged? You. And me."

He frowned. "I don't do playacting, Miss Taylor. There'd be nothing pretend about it. I'm proposing a real betrothal, so that I can offer you real protection. As soon as your situation is more certain, you can release me."

"Release you," she echoed.

"From the engagement. A lady can break an engagement at any time, and her reputation suffers no ill effects. If you're proved to be a Gramercy, no one would expect you to go through with marrying me."

"And if I'm *not* proved to be a Gramercy?"

His brow quirked. "No one would expect you to go through with it then, either."

She supposed they wouldn't. As all of Spindle Cove knew, she and Thorne were the social equivalent of oil and water. They didn't mix.

"Why are you doing this?" she asked, searching his hard expression for clues. "Why do you care?"

"Why do I—" With a gruff sigh, he released her. "It's my duty to look out for you, Miss Taylor. In the next fortnight I'll be seeing Lord Rycliff about my honorable discharge. If I've just handed his wife's closest friend to the custody of questionable strangers, he might not look so favorably on my request."

"Oh," she said. "I see. That does make sense."

Well, at least his stone-hearted, emotionless response was a touch of the familiar.

"I'm sorry," she said, turning to the Gramercys. "I should have mentioned the engagement earlier." She reached for Thorne's hand and tried to gaze affectionately into his eyes. "It's only so new. We haven't even had time to tell our friends, have we . . ." Her voice trailed off as she realized she didn't even know his Christian name.

Use a pet name, she told herself. *An endearment. Dear, darling, sweetheart, pet, love. Anything.*

" . . . have we, Cuddles?" she finished, smiling sweetly.

Ah. Now *there* was a crack in the ice sheeting those blue eyes. His grip tensed around her palm. Kate felt oddly comforted by these overt signs of his annoyance. Somehow, needling him made this all seem normal again.

Lord Drewe stood tall in the center of the room, radiating nobility and command. "Here is what will happen."

And Kate had sudden, complete confidence that whatever Lord Drewe said next would indeed happen. Even if he announced that spice drops would rain from the sky.

"Miss Taylor, I can see that we're rushing you. You have this midsummer fair in the offing, personal affairs to attend. And naturally, you're reluctant to leave when you're so newly betrothed."

She leaned into Thorne's arm. "Yes, of course."

"Obviously, we can't ask you to leave Spindle Cove at this time."

She exhaled with relief. Thank goodness. Lord Drewe was a clear-headed man, and he understood. He would return with his family to Ambervale, undertake his investigations, and notify her of the result. In writing, perhaps, rather than with a midnight visit.

"You're busy," Lord Drewe went on, "whereas we are merely on holiday. But there's no reason we can't spend our holiday here."

Kate swallowed hard. "Y-You mean to stay here in Spindle Cove? In the Queen's Ruby? All of you?"

"Is there some other inn in the village?"

She shook her head. "But this one doesn't accept male guests."

Lord Drewe shrugged. "I noticed a tavern across the green. Surely the proprietor has a room or two for let. I don't require anything special."

Oh, of course not. You're only a marquess.

This was an unforeseen complication. It was one thing to *tell* these people she was engaged to Thorne, and another thing altogether to *live* so here, in Spindle Cove.

Heavens. No one in the village would believe it.

Drewe said, "I'll speak with Mrs. Nichols about securing rooms for the ladies, and I'll send the coaches for our things straightaway."

"Surely this isn't necessary," Kate said.

"Holidays rarely are," said Aunt Marmoset. "That's the beauty of them, dear."

"I don't want to inconvenience you."

"It's no inconvenience. Spindle Cove is a seaside resort for unconventional ladies, isn't it?" Lord Drewe spread his hands, indicating his sisters and aunt. "I happen to have three highly unconventional ladies in tow, all of whom will be glad for the amusement. As for myself, I conduct all my affairs through correspondence. I can do that from anywhere."

"I'm dying to see the fair," Lark said.

"A little sea-bathing would set me up nicely," said Aunt Marmoset.

"I'm quite keen on the idea of a stay in Spinster Cove," said Harry, tugging her waistcoat straight as she rose from her chair. "It will make Ames deliciously jealous."

"So you see, Miss Taylor, it's ideal. This way, we needn't take you from your friends, but we'll have ample time to grow acquainted."

"Yes, about that . . ." Kate bit her lip. "This is a small village. Might I ask that we keep this potential kinship to ourselves? I should hope to keep speculation and gossip to a minimum, in case . . . in case it all comes to naught."

She could only hope that there weren't three girls pressing their ears to the parlor door this moment.

"Yes, of course," Lord Drewe said, pausing a moment to consider. "We have a hearty dislike of gossip, too—one bred from familiarity, sad to say. As far as people outside this room are concerned, we are engaging your services as Lark's personal music tutor. Will that suffice?"

Lark moved to her side. "In truth, I could use the lessons. I'm a disaster on the pianoforte, but perhaps I'd take to the harp."

The young lady's warm smile touched Kate's heart. So did Harry's reassuring nod, Lord Drewe's confident demeanor, and the lingering taste of Aunt Marmoset's spice drop on her tongue.

They were a family, and they wanted to spend time with her. To know her. Even if it only lasted a few days, that alone was worth anything—even suffering a bit more awkwardness with Thorne. Here was one benefit to his cruel rejection in the heather. Now she knew better than to imagine any feelings on his side.

"Well," Kate said, turning a guarded smile from one Gramercy to the next. "I suppose it's all settled."

Settled.

As she crawled into bed some time later, Kate felt anything but settled.

When last she slept between these linen sheets, she'd been an orphan and a spinster. During the course of this wild day, she'd managed to accumulate four potential cousins, a mongrel puppy, and a temporary betrothed.

"Settled" did not describe her state. Quite the opposite. Her mind was abuzz with excitement, possibility . . .

And that kiss.

Even after all that happened with the Gramercys, she still couldn't forget that kiss.

This was horrible. She was bone weary and mentally exhausted. She desperately wanted to fall asleep. But every time she closed her eyes, she felt the heat of his strong lips on hers.

Every. Time.

If only she'd kept her eyes open for the kiss, maybe she would have avoided this association. But no. The connection was drawn: eyes shut, kiss recalled. The instant her eyelashes fluttered against her cheeks, her lips plumped and her whole body throbbed with heady, unwanted sensation.

She should have taken more pains to be kissed years ago, so the feeling wouldn't be so novel now. Really, what self-respecting girl had her first kiss at the age of twenty-three?

She didn't even like him. He was a horrid, unfeeling man.

Think of family, she admonished herself, staring wide-eyed up at the ceiling beams. *Think of birthdays in February. Think of that unabashedly naked woman in the portrait, lovingly patting her swollen belly. She might have been your mother.*

If she was going to lie abed sleepless, it ought to be *these* thoughts that kept her awake. Not a kiss that had meant nothing, given by a man who didn't feel a damned thing for her, who saw engagement to her as a means of career advancement.

She would not think of him any longer. Would *not*.

She grabbed the pillow, put it over her face and growled into it. Then she clutched the same pillow to her chest and hugged it very tight.

"See the garden of blossoms so fair. Roses in bloom, orchids so rare."

She whisper-sang the familiar words into the darkness, letting the melody curl around her like a blanket. The silly nursery song was Kate's earliest childhood memory. The lilting tune always calmed her nerves.

"Lilies tall and sweet," she continued. "Rounder mums, too. All of them dancing, dancing for you."

As the last note faded, her eyelids slipped shut and stayed there.

She dreamt of a hot, stormy kiss that lasted all night long.

Chapter Seven

"Oh, Miss Taylor! I was so hoping you'd come in this morning."

Kate froze in the entryway of the All Things shop.

Sally Bright, the village shopgirl and gossip, looked up from her ledger and cast her a sly smile. "I can't wait to hear *everything.*"

Oh, please. Please, don't let word have gotten around.

Kate herself could scarcely believe last night's interview with the Gramercys, much less be pressed to explain it. "Hear everything about what?"

"Everything about you and Thorne, of course. Miss Taylor, you must tell me. I'll forgive your entire line of credit, but I want to hear every detail. I heard you're betrothed." The girl hopped for emphasis. "*Betrothed!*"

Kate closed her eyes. Oh. *That.* The girl wanted to hear about her and Thorne. She was having a hard time crediting those events, too.

"Did you say *betrothed*?" In her peripheral vision she saw a lace cap swivel.

Kate adjusted the heavy basket on her arm. Mrs. Highwood, a matron in her middle years, stood at the far corner of the shop, accompanied by the eldest of her three daughters, Diana.

"Who is betrothed?" the older woman demanded.

Mrs. Highwood was a woman of advancing age—but when it came to the subject of matrimony, her hearing was positively canine in its acuity. Between her voracious interest in all things nuptial and Sally's love of gossip . . .

Well, at least this would be over quickly.

"It's Miss Taylor and Corporal Thorne," Sally jumped to inform her. "It happened just yesterday, on their way home from Hastings."

"How do you even know all this?" Kate asked, marveling.

"Your new music pupil came in the shop. Lady Lark, is it? She popped in first thing this morning for tooth powder and told me everything."

Mrs. Highwood crossed to the counter. "Miss *Taylor*? Betrothed to Corporal *Thorne*? I cannot believe it."

"Is this true, Kate?" Diana asked. "I must admit, that's . . . rather a surprise."

Of course it would be a surprise. She and Diana were friends, and not only had she never said a thing to the eldest Miss Highwood about liking Corporal Thorne— she'd given every indication of despising the man.

Because she *did* despise him. He was horrid and cold and unfeeling and now . . .

"It's true," Kate said, inwardly cringing. "We're engaged."

It's all right, she reminded herself. *It's only temporary.*

"But how did this happen?" Diana asked.

"Very suddenly." Kate swallowed. "I'd gone into Hastings for new music, and I missed the last stage-coach home. I chanced across Corporal Thorne in the street, and he offered me a ride home."

"And then . . . ?"

"And then we stopped to rest the horse near a turn-pike. We . . . discussed the past and the future. By the time I settled in for the night at the Queen's Ruby, we were engaged." There, all of that was the truth.

Sally pouted. "That is the worst recounting I've ever heard! You owe us more than that. Did he go down on one knee, declare mad love for you? Was there a kiss?"

Kate didn't know how to answer. Yes, there had been a kiss. And her first kiss *should* have been an occasion to bubble over with excitement and regale all her friends with breathless details. Instead, she just wanted to conceal her humiliation.

"Look at your face," Sally said. "Red as sealing wax. It must have been a very good kiss indeed. The man's no kind of monk. You'll be a lucky bride, Miss Taylor. I've heard such tales . . ." She scribbled in her ledger.

Mrs. Highwood snapped open a fan and worked it vigorously. "Insupportable. My Diana's poor health has us confined to this seaside hamlet, while all England celebrates the allied victory. Here we stay, doomed to watch her chances of marriage sail by, like so many ships viewed from the shore. And now Miss *Taylor* is engaged?"

Diana gave Kate an apologetic smile. "Mama, I believe what you mean to say is that we are thrilled for Kate, and we wish her much joy."

"Much joy," the older lady muttered. "Yes, Miss Taylor may have much joy, but what of us? I ask you, Diana, where is our joy? Where?" She drew the last word into a wavering lament. "Everyone who is anyone is in Town this summer. Including your sister, who—I remind you—has recently married a viscount."

"Yes, Mama. I do recall." Diana coughed pitifully into a handkerchief. "It's so unfortunate my health has taken a sudden turn."

"You do look very pale today," Kate said.

Diana and Kate exchanged knowing looks. Minerva Highwood's recent marriage to Lord Payne was the entire reason for this subterfuge. Left to her own devices, Mrs. Highwood would have descended on the newlyweds within a day of their arrival in Town, demanding introductions be made and balls be held. Diana wanted her sister to have a quiet honeymoon—hence the mysterious and sudden "decline" in her health.

"I tell you," the older woman muttered, "in *my* youth, I should not have let consumption, malaria, and typhoid put together keep me from the celebrations of the Glorious Peace."

"But you would not have been much fun at parties," Kate couldn't help but say. "All that hacking and shivering with fever."

Mrs. Highwood sent her a sharp look.

Just then Sally Bright slammed her ledger shut. "There, that's done. Now, Miss Taylor, spill everything."

What Kate spilled were the contents of her hamper. Inside it, Badger startled at the crack of the ledger closing. The pup leapt from the wicker basket, then darted about the shop, rocketing from one corner to another.

"It's a rat!" Mrs. Highwood cried, displaying the spryness of a woman ten years her junior as she climbed a nearby stepladder.

"It's not a rat, Mrs. Highwood."

The puppy scampered under a bank of shelves.

Kate ducked and scouted under the cupboards. "Badger! Badger, do come out."

"Even worse," the matron moaned. "It's a badger. What sort of young woman carries a badger in a hand-basket? It's like a harbinger of the End of Days."

"I believe it's a puppy, Mama," Diana said. Crouching, she joined Kate in the search. "Now where's the dear thing gone?"

Down on hands and knees, Kate peered under the cupboard. Badger was there, wedged far at the back. She stuck her hand into the gap and groped for a handful of scruff. Drat. Just out of her reach.

Diana knelt beside her. "Poor dear. He must be frightened."

"Here. Try this." Sally joined them, holding out a bit of salted bacon she'd taken from a barrel in the storeroom. "Before he leaves a puddle under there."

Kate blew out a swift breath, lifting a lock of hair that had fallen over her brow. The puppy had already left two puddles in her room at the Queen's Ruby. One on the floorboards, and another in her bed. By the time she'd returned from breakfast with a slice of ham and a roll tucked in her pocket, the little beast had chewed up the handle of her good fan and one half of her most comfortable pair of slippers.

"Come now, Badger. That's a good boy." Kate pursed her lips and made encouraging noises. The pup sniffed and advanced a little, but not quite far enough.

Recalling Corporal Thorne whistling for the dog yesterday, she pressed her lips together and gave a short, chirping whistle. That did the trick. The pup came darting out—a furry bullet shooting straight into her lap.

Kate fell back on her backside with an *oof*. She

laughed as Badger devoured the bacon from her hand, then set about licking every trace of salt from her palm and fingertips.

"You will get me into so much trouble," she whispered. "And I've no strength to chide you."

Badger knew it, too. He cocked his head. Then his ear. Twitched his nose. Wagged his tail. As if to say, *Look upon my arsenal of adorable behaviors . . . and tremble.*

"This naughty little dear is Badger," she said. "He's the reason I came in today, Sally. I was hoping you'd have something I can use as a leash. Carrying him in the basket obviously won't do. And perhaps you'd have some stray bits of something for him to chew? Last night, I let him destroy a copy of *Mrs. Worthington's Wisdom.*"

Sally crossed her arms. "I might have a dog lead in back. As for things to gnaw . . ." She considered a moment, then snapped her fingers. "I know. What about Finn's old leather foot? He's been fitted with a nicer prosthetic now."

Kate shuddered at the thought of Badger gnawing away at a human limb, even a false one. How macabre. "That's a . . . creative . . . thought, but perhaps we'll just stick with *Mrs. Worthington's Wisdom.* It is a very useful book."

Mrs. Highwood came down from the stepladder and examined the dog. "Wherever did you acquire such a mongrel, anyhow?"

She gave Badger a brisk rub. "Corporal Thorne picked up the little urchin from a farmer."

Sally perked up. "That's Thorne's dog?"

"Well, he's my dog now." She covered Badger's ears, lest he hear himself being disparaged. "It's only a mongrel pup he took in on a whim."

Kate knew she couldn't offer a growing puppy the most suitable of homes. But she could give Badger love, and that was what he needed most.

Sally shook her head. "Are you certain? Rufus told me Corporal Thorne's been wanting a coursing hound. He's had one on special order from a breeder. The pups come quite dear, I understand."

Kate stared at the dog in her arms. Valuable? Badger? Such a funny-looking thing, all long, thin limbs and patched fur that was not quite straight, not quite curly. He was like an animated heap of cowlicks.

And if Thorne prized him, surely he would have told her so.

"Sally, I think you must have your puppies confused."

"For the love of St. Ursula!" Mrs. Highwood cried. She'd moved to the window. "This, I'll have you know, is why this place is called 'Spinster Cove.' While you featherbrained girls carry on about mongrel dogs, there is a gentleman walking down the lane. A tall, marvelous-looking one, carrying an expensive walking stick. I detect no hint of marriage in his demeanor."

Diana laughed. "Mama, you cannot determine a man is single just by viewing him from across the lane."

"But I can. My intuition has never failed me."

"His name is Lord Drewe," Kate said. "He's here on holiday with his two sisters and an aunt." She prolonged the suspense another moment. "And he's a marquess."

"A marq—" Mrs. Highwood swayed on her feet. "An unmarried *marquess*. Oh, my nerves. I will faint."

The men of the Spindle Cove militia were *not* particularly interested in a visiting marquess. And the addition of a few more female oddities to the Queen's Ruby coterie was simply the normal course.

But it wasn't every day they had a chance to needle their commander.

"Engaged to Miss Taylor?" Aaron Dawes exclaimed, once drill was finished for the morning.

Thorne ignored the question. He stretched his neck to one side until it cracked.

"Thought you went to Hastings for a hunting dog," Dawes said, "not a wife." The blacksmith shook his head. "I must say, never saw that coming."

"None of us saw this coming," said Fosbury. "Exactly how did you woo her, Corporal?"

"This is Thorne we're discussing," Dawes said. "He doesn't woo. He commands."

"But that wouldn't work on Miss Taylor. She's got spirit."

"And humor," said the vicar. "And good sense."

Yes, Thorne silently agreed. All that, plus distracting beauty and a mouth so lush and sweet, he'd spent the whole night dreaming about it and woken with a rod of forged steel between his legs.

"Yes, Miss Taylor's a very sweet girl," Fosbury said. He eyed Thorne with good-humored curiosity. "Makes a man wonder . . . What's she see in you?"

Nothing. Nor should she.

"Enough," he said. "We have a great deal to make ready before the ladies have their fair. My personal affairs are none of your concern."

"Don't think we're concerned for *you*," Dawes said. "We're concerned for her. Miss Taylor has a great many friends in Spindle Cove. None of us want to see her hurt. That's all."

Thorne cursed silently. If all Miss Taylor's friends knew the truth, they'd thank him. He was only trying to protect her from a far more dangerous threat.

The Gramercys.

It made no sense that the family would so eagerly take up residence in Spindle Cove, and even less sense that Lord Drewe himself would remain. Thorne could only conclude the marquess was reluctant to let Miss Taylor out of his sight. Why would he feel so protective of an illegitimate second cousin?

Higher mathematics might not be his strength, but he knew when something didn't add up.

"Corporal Thorne!" Rufus Bright called down from the turret. "Miss Taylor's climbing up the path."

Thorne dismissed the men with a curt nod. "That will be all. Go assist Sir Lewis with the trebuchet."

The men groaned. But they obeyed, crossing through an arch and wandering out to the bluffs where Sir Lewis Finch had his monstrosity erected.

Spindle Cove denizens whispered a prayer whenever the aging, eccentric Sir Lewis approached a trigger, a fuse, a powder charge—or in this case, a medieval catapult designed to lay whole cities to waste. However, instead of launching flaming balls of pitch over fortified walls, this trebuchet's sole purpose was lobbing melons out to sea. Just a bit of show for the midsummer fair.

The mechanics of the ancient weapon were apparently more sensitive and twitchy than a virgin's inner thigh. A great many test runs were needed before it would be ready.

Sir Lewis's sonorous baritone carried over the castle ruins. "Ready, men! Three . . . two . . ."

A great whomping and whooshing noise coincided with the count of one, as the men released the trebuchet's counterweight. The sling made its groaning orbit upward, then lurched to a halt and sent its missile soaring in the direction of the sea.

In the *direction* of the sea. Not all the way there.

From the loud squelch that followed, the thing couldn't have flown more than fifty feet before smashing to pulp on the rocks.

"Corporal Thorne?"

"Miss Taylor." She'd appeared out of nowhere while he was distracted, Badger nosing at her heels.

"I've a matter to discuss with you. Can we have a private word?"

He led her through the remains of a crumbled archway and around a low sandstone wall. It was a place apart, but not enclosed. The armory was no place for her, and he damned well couldn't take her into his quarters alone.

If he got her anywhere near a bed . . . this temporary engagement could all too easily become permanent.

God, just look at her this morning. The sunlight gave her hair hints of cinnamon and threw gold sparks in her eyes. The exertion of a steep climb up the bluffs showed her slight figure to its best advantage. And the heart-shaped mark at her temple . . . it was the worst and best of everything. It made him painfully aware she wasn't some unearthly apparition, but a flesh-and-blood woman who'd warm in his embrace.

None of this was for him, he reminded himself. Not the careful curl of her hair, nor the spotless new gloves that gave her hands the look of bleached starfish. She wore a pale blue frock that seemed more froth than muslin. A border of delicate ivory lace trimmed the low, squared neckline. He shouldn't be noticing that lace. Much less staring at it.

He wrenched his gaze up to her face. "What's wrong? What do you need?"

"Nothing's wrong. Except that I'm not accustomed to having a puppy for a roommate."

"Ready to give him back, then?"

"Not a chance. I adore him." She bent to give the dog a brisk rub. "But how do I keep him from chewing things?"

"You don't. It's what he's born to do—chase down small animals and rip them apart."

"My. What a little savage."

He pulled a handful of rabbit hide twists from his pocket. He tossed one to the dog, then offered the rest to her. "Give him these, one at a time. They should last a few days, at least."

"Can I buy more at the shop when these are gone?"

"I wouldn't know. I don't purchase them."

He expected her to give the knotted bits of scraped hide a faintly disgusted look, now that she knew just where they'd originated. Instead, she regarded him with the same soft, liquid eyes she used on the pup.

"You had all those prepared? She must have been right. You do value this dog."

"What? Who must be right?"

She pocketed the extra rabbit hide scraps. "Sally Bright told me—"

"Sally Bright says a lot of things."

"—that you had a puppy on order from a breeder. Bred from some kind of superior hunting stock. She said the pups come very dear. Corporal Thorne, if Badger means something to you, I'll give him back. I just need to know he'll be cared for."

Not this again. "The dog is mine. That's all I should need to say."

"What's so horrible about admitting a fondness for

the creature? I'm a music tutor, as you well know, and music is just another language. Unfamiliar phrases come easier with practice. Say it with me now, slowly: 'I care about the dog.' "

He didn't say a thing.

"That's a very intimidating scowl," she teased. "Do you practice that look in the mirror? I'll bet you do. I'll bet you glare into the looking glass until it shatters."

"Then be a clever girl and turn away."

"Unfortunately, I can't. I came up here to talk privately because we need to make our stories straight. The whole village has heard of our betrothal already. Everyone's asking me how we came to be engaged, and I don't know what to tell them. Aren't the men asking you the same? What have you said?"

He shrugged. "Nothing."

"Of course. How could I forget? No one expects you to talk. You're Corporal Taciturn. But it's different with la—"

Shouts from the other side of the wall interrupted. "Ready, men! Three, two . . ."

Thunk. Creak. Whoosh.

Then, a few seconds later, *splat.*

"More sand in the counterweight," Sir Lewis shouted to the men. "We almost have it."

"It's different with ladies," Miss Taylor said, continuing where she'd left off. "You don't understand. When a girl gets engaged, they want to know everything. Every glance, every touch, every whispered word. I can't abide lying to them, so I'd prefer we hold to the truth. We became engaged yesterday. Our first kiss was on the way home from Hastings. We've—"

He held up a hand, halting her mid-sentence. "Wait. You're telling people about the kiss?"

She blushed. "I haven't really, not yet. But I think I must. They're skeptical as it is. No one believes we've been courting. Because we haven't been." Her gaze dropped to the turf. "Oh, this is miserable. I should have never agreed to the idea."

"If it's causing you that much anguish, release me from the engagement."

Her eyes widened. "I couldn't do that so fast. I would look fickle, even mercenary. What kind of woman would engage herself to a man one evening, then throw him over the very next day just because her circumstances changed?"

"A great many women would do that."

"Well, I'm not one of them."

Thorne knew very well she wasn't.

"The Gramercys might be my relations," she went on. "I want them to like me—and to *know* me—for who I truly am. I'm not the kind of woman to marry for convenience. Unless we lie a little bit, I'll feel dishonest."

Thorne frowned. Was she asking him to behave like an interested suitor? He'd made concealing his attraction to her such a habit, he wasn't sure he knew how to do the reverse.

He opened his mouth to speak, but from beyond the wall came another shout: "Ready!"

Another count: "Three, two . . ."

Another shot from the trebuchet. This time, after several seconds of silence, he heard a distant, watery splash.

"Better," Sir Lewis called. "The force is right, but the aim is off. I need to adjust the mechanism."

"Our stories," Thorne said, once the men had gone quiet again. "Let's make them matching, as you say."

"First, what are our plans after the wedding? Supposedly you're going to America."

"I am going to America. So supposedly you're coming with me."

"Are we headed for New York? Boston?"

"Philadelphia, but only to gather supplies. I've a plan to claim some land in Indiana Territory."

"Indiana Territory?" She scrunched up her face. "*Indiana*. That sounds very . . . primitive."

Thorne shifted his weight. Through the lacy castle ruins, he could see the glistening, aquamarine cove and the expansive Channel beyond. Clearly the prospect of wide-open spaces didn't appeal to her the way it called to him. He'd been planning this for some time now—his own tract of land. He'd been clinging to the idea so long, he could feel the grit under his fingernails. There'd be rich soil to till, game to hunt and trap. Ample timber for the felling.

True freedom, and the chance to make his own life.

"Where would we live?" she asked.

"I'd build a house," he said.

"How would I continue with my music? I couldn't give it up. Not plausibly. This is me we're talking about. Everyone knows I'd never have agreed to marry you—or anyone—unless music was part of the bargain."

"I'll see that you have a pianoforte." He had no idea how one would be transported to the middle of the woodlands, but the logistics hardly signified.

"And pupils?"

He gestured impatiently with one hand. "There'd be children, eventually."

"I've tutored the daughters of dukes and lords. And now I'd be teaching frontier neighbor children?"

"No, I meant ours. Our children."

Her eyebrows soared. A rather long time passed before she said, "Oh."

He made no apology for the insinuation. "This is me we're talking about. Everyone knows I wouldn't offer marriage to you—or anyone—unless bedding were part of the bargain."

Her cheeks colored. Thorne had a vivid, sudden vision of the two of them in a rough-hewn log cabin, tucked between a straw-tick mattress and a quilted counterpane. Nothing but heat and musk between their bodies. He'd curl his strength around her softness, keeping out the cold and howling wolves. The scent of her hair would lull him to sleep.

That picture looked damn near paradise to him— which meant it was unattainable. And he could imagine she wouldn't see the charms.

"What about love?" she asked.

He jerked his head, surprised. "What about it?"

"Do you mean to love me? What about all these children you mean for us to create? Am I to believe you'll laugh and play with them, be open with them, let them into that stony thing you call a heart?"

He stared at her. If he thought he could ever give her those things, he would have offered to do so. Months ago.

He said, "No one needs to believe love's involved."

"Of course they do. Because I would need to believe it."

"Miss Taylor . . ."

"This will never work." She rubbed her brow with one hand. "No one will credit that I've agreed to leave my friends, my work, my home, and my country behind. And for what? To cross the ocean and take up residence in a remote wilderness cabin with a man who can't fathom the meaning of love? In *Indiana*?"

He took her by the shoulders, forcing her to face him. "We're ill suited. I know that. I could never make you happy. I know that, too. I'm so far beneath you, the best I could ever offer would be a paltry fraction of what you deserve. I'm aware of all of this, Miss Taylor. You don't have to remind me."

Regret softened her eyes. "I'm sorry. So sorry. I shouldn't have said—"

"Save the apologies. You spoke the truth. I was only agreeing."

"No, no. I can't stand for you to believe that I'd . . ." She reached for him.

Holy God. She reached for him, and before he could duck or step back or fall on his sword to prevent it, her gloved hand was on his cheek. Her palm flattened there, warm and satiny. Sensation jolted through his body.

When she spoke, her voice was quiet, but strong. "You're not beneath me. I'd never think that."

Yes, you are beneath her, he reminded himself, bracing against the forbidden bliss coursing through his veins. *And don't dare imagine you'll ever be atop her. Or curled behind her. Or buried deep inside her while she—*

Bloody hell. The fact that he could even think such a thing. He was crude, disgusting. So undeserving of even this slight caress. Her gesture was made out of guilt, offered in apology. If he took advantage, he would be a devil.

He knew all this.

But he flexed his arms anyway, drawing her close.

"You're worried you've hurt my feelings," he murmured.

She nodded, just a little.

"I don't have those."

"I forgot."

Amazing. He marveled at her foolishness. After all

he'd said to her, she would worry about *him*? Within this small, slight woman lived so much untapped affection, she couldn't help but squander it on music pupils and mongrel dogs and undeserving brutes. What was it like, he wondered, to live with that bright, glowing star in her chest? How did she survive it?

If he kissed her deeply enough and held her tight—would some of its warmth transfer to him?

"Wait," came a call, echoing vaguely in the distance. "Hold still! Not yet!"

Perhaps the voice belonged to his conscience. He couldn't bring himself to pay it any mind. All he knew was her touch and her caring and the raw, trembling force of his own need.

He drew her closer still. Her eyes went wide. Larger and more lovely than he'd ever seen them before. A whole world of possibility was opening in those dark pupils.

And then . . . Her gaze drifted up and a little to the side. Her lips fell apart in wonder.

A strange shadow appeared on her face.

A shadow that was round, and growing larger by the instant. As though some projectile were rapidly approaching from above.

Jesus, no.

Thorne had been here before, many times. Battle, sieges, skirmishes. Thought ceased, and instinct took over. His grip tightened on her shoulders. His already thundering heart pumped faster, powering strength to his limbs.

The word "Down!" tore from his throat.

He threw himself forward, wrapping her body in his arms and flattening her to the ground—

Just as the explosion hit.

Chapter Eight

I t took Kate several seconds to register what had happened.

One moment she'd been staring, incredulous, as an object plummeted toward her from the sky. She'd stood transfixed by the sheer absurdity of it. This strange, roundish thing silhouetted against the sun, growing larger and closer . . . and greener.

The next thing she knew, she was on the ground. Corporal Thorne was on top of her. And they were both covered in wet, sticky melon pulp. Shards of rind littered the ground nearby. A pungent sweetness filled her heightened senses. Evidently, Sir Lewis's adjustments to the trebuchet had gone awry.

Really, there was nothing else for it. She had to laugh. Softly at first, but soon her whole body shook with mirth.

Thorne didn't share her amusement. He didn't rise or roll to the side. He kept her in his arms, covering her with his body. His muscles had gone rigid, everywhere. When she sought his gaze, she found his blue eyes searching and unfocused. His nostrils were flared and his breaths were harshly won.

"Thorne? Are you all right?"

He didn't answer. She didn't think he *could* answer.

He wasn't there.

It was the only way she could think to describe it. His body lay atop her, heavy as sacks of grain. She knew he was alive, from the way his heartbeat slammed against hers. But mentally, he wasn't there. He was somewhere else. On some scorched, smoking battlefield, she imagined, where round objects falling from the sky had a great deal more destructive force than the average over-ripe melon.

She touched his face, just lightly. "Thorne? It's all right. It was only a melon. I'm not hurt. Are you?"

His arms flexed, squeezing her until she winced with pain.

He forced a strange growl through his clenched teeth. The sound was inhuman. Each hair on her arms stood tall, as if to wave a tiny flag of surrender, and her pulse drummed in her ears. She was truly afraid now. For him, and for herself. She lay small and defenseless beneath him. If he'd mistaken her for the enemy on his phantom battlefield, he could do her true harm.

She caressed his face with trembling fingers, reaching to sweep the hair back from his brow. Between the velvet of his thick, soft hair and the wetness of the melon pulp, it felt like stroking a newborn foal. Tenderness swelled in her heart.

"All's well. We're unharmed. This is Rycliff Castle. Spindle Cove." Kate tried to keep her voice low and steady, aiming to soothe them both. "You're home. And it's only me. Miss Taylor. Kate. I'm the music tutor, remember? I'm your . . . I'm a friend."

His jaw tensed. And not in a friendly way.

She'd never been more aware of the brute power contained in a man's body. If he wished, he could snap her in two. Though perhaps not very cleanly—which was all the more reason to avoid the experience, she thought. Somehow, she needed to remind him of his humanity. The gentleness these same bones and tendons and muscles could produce.

"I'm Miss Taylor," she repeated. "Yesterday, you came to my rescue in Hastings. You brought me home on your horse. We stopped to take bread, and—and you kissed me. In a field of heather, just at sunset. I've tried so hard to forget it, but I've thought of little else since. Can you recall it?"

She brushed a thumb across his lips.

His mouth softened a little and a shaky exhalation rushed over her fingertips. She thought she glimpsed a spark of awareness returning to his eyes.

"Yes," she said, encouraging him. "You're well. We're both safe. It's only me."

A shudder racked his body. He blinked hard, and his gaze began to focus on her face.

From his throat came a raspy, "Katie?"

She half sobbed with relief. "Yes. Yes, it's me."

He stared blankly at the melon pulp splattering her shoulder. "You're hurt."

"No. No, I'm fine. It's not blood. The militiamen were adjusting Sir Lewis's trebuchet, and there was a mishap. You took a melon for me." She smiled, even though her lips trembled.

He trembled, too. All over.

He wasn't so far away anymore—but he wasn't quite home yet, either.

She raked her fingers through his hair, desperate to bridge that last divide. Perhaps she could have wriggled free of his grip now. But she couldn't leave him wandering in that shadow world, with bombs and blood and whatever other unimaginable horrors it held.

"It's safe now," she whispered. "It's safe to come back. I'm here." She stretched her neck and pressed a light kiss to the corner of his mouth. "I'm here."

She kissed his mouth again. Then again.

Each time their lips met, his mouth warmed a degree. She prayed his heart was warming back to life, too.

"Please," she murmured. "Come back to me."

And he did. Oh, he did.

The change in him was swift, abrupt. And it meant a complete inversion of her world.

Once again Kate found herself breathless, scarcely understanding what had happened. Last she'd known, she'd been pressing chaste kisses to his lips.

Now his tongue was in her mouth, and hers seemed to be partly in his. Her fingers were tangled in the sticky mess of his hair.

They were fused together. One creature. And all she could think was . . .

Sweet. He's so sweet.

The sugar-musky tang of melon was everywhere. She kissed him with abandon, thirsty for more of it—and just so happy to know he was here again, and not worlds away. She still sensed all that raw, frightening power coiled in his body. Only now it wasn't marshaled to the task of survival, but another instinctive, basic drive.

Desire.

"Katie," he moaned again, pulling her closer still. Her breasts flattened beneath his broad chest. As he kissed her deeply, his muscled firmness rubbed and chafed against her nipples. The teasing sensation was unbearably exquisite. It drove her wild in her skin, made her forget everything.

His leg snaked between hers, pressing her thighs apart. When he thrust his tongue deep into her mouth, his hips rocked against hers, setting off a cascade of unprecedented pleasure. She moaned, mindlessly craving more.

Then he stopped abruptly, gasping for breath. Raised his head. Swore.

And then Kate realized what she couldn't have noticed, in her single-minded determination to bring him back from shadow and hold him skin close.

Everyone was watching them. Sir Lewis Finch. The entirety of the Spindle Cove militia. Oh, heavens . . . even the vicar. They'd all come running to track the melon's trajectory. And they'd come upon her and Thorne, tangled on the ground. Kissing like lovers.

Thorne rolled to the side, blocking her from their view. She tried her best to evaporate into the air. Meanwhile, he gruffly scolded the men for the mishap and ordered them back to work.

When they were gone, Badger came out of hiding and attacked Kate with puppyish vigor, licking the melon juice from her wrist and cheek.

Thorne stood and paced the small area. "Damn it." His hands were still faintly trembling. He balled them in fists. "Are you well? I didn't hurt you?"

"No."

"You're certain? I want to know the truth. If I hurt you in *any* way, I'd . . ." He didn't complete the statement.

"I'm unharmed. I promise. But how are you?"

He kept pacing, dismissing her question with a small flick of his hand. As if his own well-being were completely irrelevant.

"Has . . . *that* ever happened before?" she asked.

"I'm not mad," he said. "If that's what you're thinking."

"Of course not. Of course not. It was an absurd accident. I mean, what are the chances? A melon, of all things. A soldier is trained to react to bombs, grenades, cannon fire. No one's prepared for a *melon*. I understand completely."

He drew to a halt. He wouldn't look at her.

She closed her eyes, frustrated with herself. "That was a thoughtless thing for me to say. I don't understand at all. I can't possibly imagine what it is to go to war." She approached and laid a tentative touch to his sleeve. "But if you'd ever want to tell someone, Thorne, I am a good listener."

His cold blue eyes held hers for a long moment, as though he were considering. "I'd never burden you with that."

"It might as well be me. I am your betrothed, for the time being."

"Still?"

She nodded. There was no denying that something between them had changed. They'd survived a battle together—even if it had been an imaginary siege. The fearful pounding of her heart had been very real, and the same was true of the cold sweat on his brow.

She had long been accustomed to thinking of Thorne as an enemy, but after that incident . . .

They were on the same side.

The two of them, against the melons of the world.

Kate smiled. With her fingertips, she flicked a seed from his sleeve. "You have to admit, this solves one problem. They'll all believe the engagement now."

"That's one problem solved, perhaps. But several more created."

She gathered his meaning. Her pristine reputation was now spattered in melon pulp. Unless she were proved to be a Gramercy and offered a living outside Spindle Cove—it would be nearly impossible for Kate to call this betrothal off.

Kate declined Thorne's offer of an escort home and hurried back to the rooming house. By the time she arrived at the back entrance, the late morning sun had dried the moisture from her sticky frock. She took the back stairs two at a time, ducking into her room to wash and change.

Exhausted from the morning's excitement, Badger made a nest of her discarded gown and curled up to sleep.

When Kate had made herself presentable, she went downstairs and found the Gramercys assembled in the parlor. As she entered the room, she stopped dead in the doorway.

Oh, Lord.

The painting. It was still there, on the mantelpiece. Half draped, at least, to conceal all the flesh. She hoped no one else had taken notice of it. She would take it up to her room later.

"Why, Miss Taylor!" Lark looked up from a book. "What a pleasant surprise."

Lord Drewe, being a conscientious gentleman, rose to his feet and bowed. "We weren't expecting you yet. We thought you'd be occupied with music lessons, over at the Bull and Blossom."

"Not just now. I thought I'd come and . . . sit with you, if you don't mind."

"Don't be silly." Aunt Marmoset patted an empty

section of divan. "We're in this village for you, dear. We don't mind."

"But please don't let me interrupt," Kate said. "Just be as you are, and go on as you were."

From her seat at the escritoire, Harry laughed. She set her quill aside and sprinkled a letter with blotting powder. "We're hardly busy. Lark's reading quietly. Aunt Marmoset's aging quietly. I've just finished venting my spleen with a scathing letter to Ames. As for Evan—" She swept a hand toward her brother, who'd taken a seat by the fire. "Evan's sitting with his precious agricultural newspapers and trying to pretend he's not a tightly wound ball of seething passions."

"What?" Evan lowered his newspaper and regarded his sister over it. "I do not seethe."

"Of course you seethe. You seethe the way other men drink brandy. A little bit daily as a matter of habit, and more than's good for you when you think no one's looking."

With a bored sigh, Lord Drewe turned his gaze to Kate. "Do I have the appearance of a man who seethes?"

"Not at all," Kate answered, studying his calm expression and unperturbed green eyes. "You look the picture of equanimity."

"There, Harriet. Satisfied?" He raised his newspaper again.

"Don't let appearances fool you, Miss Taylor," Lark whispered. "My brother only looks even-tempered. He has fought no fewer than five duels in his life."

"Five duels?"

"Oh, yes." Lark's eyes brightened. She counted them down her fingers. "Let's see. There was the one for Calista. Before that, three for Harry—"

Kate looked to Harry, who was dressed today in the same divided skirt and tailored waistcoat. The outfit was something like a riding habit, only . . . there were no horses about.

"My goodness, Lady Harriet. Three?"

Harry shrugged as she folded and sealed her letter. "My season was eventful."

"And one for Claire," Lark finished, reaching her little finger.

"Claire?" Kate asked. "Who is Claire?"

Aunt Marmoset lifted her brows. "We don't talk about Claire."

"To the contrary," Lord Drewe said from behind his paper. "You all talk about Claire a great deal. I refuse to join the discussion."

"Because you prefer seething," said Harry.

"Because it's not kind to speak ill of the dead." The tone of his voice told everyone the conversation was finished. A snap of newspaper served as punctuation.

The ensuing silence was awkward.

"Oh, dear," said Lark. "I was hoping to avoid it. But Harry, I think you had better acquaint Miss Taylor with the truth."

The truth?

"What is the truth?" Kate asked. Her heart pounded in her chest. Perhaps Thorne was right, and they'd been hiding something from her.

Harry put away all her ink and paper. "The truth is . . . as aristocratic families go, we Gramercys aren't what you might call—"

"Civilized," Aunt Marmoset suggested.

"Typical," Harry finished. "It goes back to our childhood, I think. We spent the entirety of it up North, at

Rook's Fell. Enormous old place, more cobweb than mortar in its walls. Our father suffered with a very prolonged, debilitating illness, and our mother was devoted to his care. The servants couldn't make us mind, and no thought was ever given to school. No one expected Evan would inherit the title, of course. It was to stay in your father's line. So we simply ran wild, like vines in a neglected garden. Until Aunt Marmoset came to mind us, and even then it was too late for us older ones. Except for dear, sweet Lark there, we've all of us grown up twisted in some way."

"Twisted?" Lark echoed. "Harry, you do make it sound so perverse."

"If Kate is to associate with us, she should know. The plain fact of it is, we are not really 'good society.' But we are obscenely rich, highly ranked, and so utterly fascinating the *ton* cannot look away."

"That's going to change," Lord Drewe said. "The 'good society' part. I am determined that Lark will have the debut she deserves. I have failed twice to bring out my sisters with any success. Harriet's season was an unmitigated debacle."

"Only if you judge by Society's standards."

"That is the entire point of a season. To be judged by Society's standards. And by the end of your season, we were not only judged by Society, but convicted, sentenced, pilloried, and exiled for the better part of a decade." Lord Drewe folded his papers, set them aside and massaged the bridge of his nose. "Calista never even made it to London."

"She didn't want to," Lark said. To Kate, she explained, "She fell in love with Mr. Parker, the stable master. Now they live together at Rook's Fell, and we cleared out this summer to give them run of the place. Calista always did love horses, and she and Parker have turned their efforts to breeding."

Aunt Marmoset tittered with laughter. Kate tried not to join her.

"What?" Lark looked around, bemused. "What have I said now?"

"Nothing," Harry assured her. "Do not think on it, chicken. You are everything good and pure, that's all."

Lark turned to Kate and gave her an uncertain smile. "There you have it. To be a Gramercy is to be embroiled in one scandal after another, it seems. Do you despise us already? Do you want us to leave?"

"Not at all." She looked around the room. "I'm so happy, I can't tell you. I'm delighted that you're not fusty and proper, or I don't know how I'd ever fit in. I'm in heaven just sitting here, listening to you talk and tease and turn the pages of your newspapers. You can't know what a pleasure it is for me, to be in the presence of a family. Any family."

"We are not just *any* family," Lark said. "We may be *your* family."

"If you'll have us," Harry said. "I shouldn't blame you if you won't."

Kate looked around at their earnestly hopeful faces. "In all my life, there's never been anything I wanted more."

But as she spoke the words, they had the faintly acid taste of a lie. Earlier that day, she'd craved a man's touch with a fierce, primal intensity. She'd wanted it more than comfort, more than family. More than breath. Beneath her skin, her muscles still yearned and ached.

She closed her eyes and willed the forbidden feelings away. "I only wish there was some way we could be certain."

"I've begun inquiries," Lord Drewe said. "I've already sent letters directing my man of business to Margate, to see what he can stir up there. We're also exploring other avenues."

"I don't suppose it's too much to hope that you might . . . remember something?" Lark asked. "I don't want to pressure you, but we thought that perhaps after seeing the portrait and being around our family, some forgotten detail might shake loose."

"Perhaps it will in time. But truly, I have so few memories." Kate let her eyes go unfocused. "I've tried, so many times, to recall. It's as though I'm traveling down a dark, endless corridor, and my past is at the end of it. And I know . . . I just know . . . if I could open the door at the end of that corridor, I'd remember everything. But I never quite get there. I only hear pianoforte music, and I have some memory of the color blue."

"Perhaps it's the pendant," Lark said. She fetched the portrait from the mantelpiece. "The one about her neck, see?"

Kate looked closely. She'd noticed the pendant before—but in the dark last night, it had appeared to be black. Now she could see that it was actually a deep, almost indigo blue. Too dark to be a sapphire. Perhaps lapis?

She lifted her head, excited. "I suppose that could be the blue I recall. Especially if my mother wore it always."

"She must have done," said Harry. "She even wore it when she wore nothing at all."

Kate startled. "Oh. And there's a little song. A song about flowers."

She sang it all the way through for them, beginning with, "See the garden of blossoms so fair . . ."

"It's been lodged in my memory all my life, but in all my years of teaching music, I've never met anyone else who knew that song. I always fancied my mother sang it to me. Is it familiar to any of you?"

The Gramercys shook their heads.

"But the fact that we don't know the song doesn't mean anything," Lark said. "We never would have met your mother at all."

Kate's shoulders relaxed. "It would be nice if that could have been the link. The proof. But I suppose it was too much too hope."

"Nothing is too much to hope." Aunt Marmoset patted her hand. "And dear, we really must decide what to call you. If you're family, 'Miss Taylor' just doesn't seem right."

"It's not even my name at all," Kate admitted. "The surname Taylor was assigned to me at Margate. Really, I'd love it if you'd call me Kate. All my friends do."

Even though her full name had been listed as Katherine, she'd always gone by Kate. It simply fit. "Katherine" sounded too refined and regal. "Kitty" brought to mind a flighty young girl. But "Kate" sounded like a sensible, clever young woman with lots of friends.

She was a "Kate."

Except to someone, somewhere, she'd once been "Katie."

Be brave, my Katie.

And today, when Thorne had pinned her to the ground, acting with courage to guard her life with his own—even if the threat was a wayward fruit, rather than a mortar shell—he'd called her "Katie," too. So strange.

"Will you show us the local sights?" Lark asked. "I'm dying to explore that old castle on the bluffs."

Kate bit her lip. "Perhaps we should save that for tomorrow. The militia are undertaking some drills. But I'd be delighted to give you a tour of the church."

"Hold that thought." Lord Drewe held back the curtain. "I believe our things have arrived."

Kate watched, amazed, as a caravan of one, two . . . *three* carriages pulled up before the Queen's Ruby, all of them bursting with valises and trunks. They must have contained enough belongings and supplies to launch a small colony.

"Thank the Lord," said Aunt Marmoset. "I'm down to my last three spice drops."

Chapter Nine

T horne was a man of habit.

That evening, after all the men had left, he re-turned to his solitary quarters—one of the four turrets that comprised the Rycliff Castle keep. He brushed the dust from his officer's coat and polished his boots to a fresh shine, so they'd be ready the next day.

Then he sat down at the small, simple table to review the day's events.

This, too, was routine. In the infantry, he'd served under then-Lieutenant Colonel Bramwell, now Lord General Rycliff. After every battle, Rycliff would sit down with his maps and journals to painstakingly re-create the order of events. Thorne would help him to recall the details. Together, they laid it all out before them. What had happened, exactly? Where had key decisions been taken? Where had ground been gained, lives been lost?

Most importantly, they asked themselves this: Could anything have been done differently, to achieve a more favorable outcome?

In most cases, they arrived honestly at the same

answer: no. Given a chance, they would do the same again. The ritual dampened any whispers of guilt or regret. Left unchecked, such whispers could become echoes—bouncing off the walls of a man's skull. Growing louder, faster, more dangerous over weeks and months and years.

Thorne knew the echoes. He had enough of them rattling around his brain already. He didn't need any more. So tonight he poured himself a tumbler of whiskey and reviewed the events of his most recent conflict.

The Melon Siege.

Could he have reasonably predicted the danger to Miss Taylor?

He didn't think so. The trebuchet had been firing reliably seaward, if with varying degrees of strength. Sir Lewis had said afterward he could not have replicated that trajectory if he tried. A freak accident, nothing more.

Had he acted rightly to tackle her?

Again he could not regret his actions. Even if he'd been aware that the missile was a melon, he likely would have done the same. Had the fruit been any less ripe, it might not have exploded on contact. She could have been seriously injured. Thorne's head was still pounding from the impact.

No, it was everything that came afterward. That was where he'd gone wrong. The shock had rocketed him to some other place. A place filled with smoke and the stench of blood. He'd found himself crawling on his belly toward the sound of her voice. For miles, it seemed, collecting scrapes on his knees and hands. Until he found the source—a clear, calm pool of water amidst the ugliness, with her face reflecting up at him instead of his own. He'd lowered his face to drink from it, lapping up that cool, refreshing peace. But it wasn't enough. He'd wanted to bathe in her, drown in her.

That kiss . . .

Even when he came to his senses, he hadn't pulled back. Not immediately, as he should have done. He'd never forgive himself for that. He could have truly hurt her.

But Lord. She'd been so sweet.

He lifted—and swiftly gulped—the tumbler of whiskey. Didn't help. Even a second dose of liquid fire couldn't burn her taste from his lips. He let his pounding head fall back until it met with the uneven stone wall.

So sweet. So soft in his arms. Christ, she'd been *under* him, every bit as warm and alive as he'd known she would be. Stroking his face and his hair, murmuring gentle words. The recollection made his chest ache and his groin tighten.

Good God. Good God.

He sipped the liquor again. As he forced the swallow down, a groan of raw pain and longing rose in his chest. All the whiskey in the bottle couldn't numb this ache.

But he knew one thing.

This lusting stopped here. With these queer, mysterious Gramercys in the picture, she needed his protection. He needed to keep his wits sharp. If he came too close, he risked compromising her and losing his own focus. So there could be no more closeness. Only the bare minimum of contact. Handing her down from carriages and the like. Perhaps he'd be pressed to offer his arm on occasion.

But on this, he was resolved—

There would be no more kisses. Ever.

Someone pounded on the door.

"Corporal Thorne! Corporal Thorne, come out."

Thorne's heart kicked into a gallop. He thrust his feet into his boots and punched to a standing position. As he made for the door, he snagged his coat from its hook.

"What is it?" He flung open the door to view a red-faced, out-of-breath Rufus Bright.

The young man's eyes were serious. "Sir, you're needed down in the village at once."

"Where? What's happened?"

"The Bull and Blossom. And I can't describe it, sir. You'll see when you get there."

That was all Thorne needed to hear. He broke into a run. From there it was a footrace with trouble—which particular kind of trouble, he hated to imagine. Was she sick? In danger? Had the Gramercys heard about the melon incident and departed in disgust, leaving her heartbroken and alone?

Damn, damn, damn.

Walking from the castle to the village normally took about twenty minutes. Going this direction, he had the advantage of the downslope—but with the light fading, a man had to watch his step.

Nevertheless, Thorne would venture no more than five minutes had passed by the time he reached the bottom of the path and plunged into the village lanes. A few moments later he was tearing across the green and throwing open the tavern door.

Bloody hell. It seemed that every soul in Spindle Cove was packed into the place. He saw villagers, militia-men, ladies from the Queen's Ruby. Like fish in a net they were, just a mass of wriggling bodies with gaping mouths.

To a one, they turned and hushed as he burst through the doorway. Thorne could imagine why. He was panting, sweating, growling, and furious with the need to know just what the hell was going on.

But he was so winded, he hadn't the breath for extensive questioning. Only three words mattered, in his mind. He used the last of his air to bark them out.

"Where is she?"

The crowd rustled and sorted itself, pushing Miss Taylor forward as if she were the wheat amid the chaff.

He swept his gaze up her body, then studied her face. She was whole, and not bleeding. Her eyes were clear, not red with tears. That alone was enough to make her the most beautiful thing he'd ever beheld. As far as he was concerned, her low-cut, fitted yellow gown was merely in the way. She had better not be bruised or broken under all that shimmering silk.

"Surprise," she said. "It's a party."

"A . . ." He worked for breath. " . . . A *party*."

"Yes. An engagement party. For us."

He swept a look around the crowded tavern. This might have started as a party. It was going to end as someone's funeral.

"Wasn't it a nice idea?" She forced a smile. "Your militiamen planned it."

"Oh, did they?"

Thorne turned to the bar, where his militiamen stood in a lazy, substandard line. Pursing their lips like buglers, to keep from laughing aloud.

He wanted to murder them all. One by one by one. Unluckily for them, he'd left his pistol at the castle. But there had to be knives in this place.

She took a few steps closer. With every labored breath he drew, he now got a dizzying lungful of her lemon-clover scent. It calmed him in some ways and inflamed him in others.

"It wasn't my idea," she murmured at the floorboards. "I can see you were frightened. I'm so sorry."

"Not frightened," he replied curtly.

Just ready to fight. And she needed to stop looking so pained, or he'd be seriously tempted to put his fist through the wall.

Fosbury, the tavern keeper and confectioner, came out from the kitchen wearing an embroidered apron and bearing a large tray. "Come along, Corporal Thorne. Even you have to celebrate sometime. Look, I made you a cake."

Thorne looked at the cake.

It was baked in the shape of a melon, iced with green. There were letters swimming on it—they spelled out congratulatory wishes, he supposed—but he was too angry and exhausted to push them together into words. Heaped atop all his other frustrations, that last insult to his pride was enough to turn his vision red.

"There's a fly on it," he said.

Fosbury bristled. "No, there's not."

"There is. Look close. In the center."

The tavern keeper bent his head and peered closely at the center of the cake.

Thorne grabbed him by the hair and pushed downward, mashing his face straight into the icing. The man came up blinking and sputtering through a mask of green, sugary scum.

"Do you see it now?" Thorne asked.

A thick glob of piped icing fell from Fosbury's brow. It landed with an audible plop. The entire room had gone silent.

They were all staring at him, aghast. *What's the matter with you?* their horrified looks said. *We're your neighbors and friends. Don't you know how to enjoy a party?*

No. He didn't.

No one had given him a party before. Never in his life. And the way everyone was staring at him, it was clear that no one would ever dare to give him one again.

Then it started. Just a light ripple of musical sound, coming from Miss Taylor's direction. It grew louder, gained strength, until it was a full-force cascade.

She was laughing. Laughing at him, laughing at the stupid cake, laughing at Fosbury's green-covered face. Her peals of melodious, good-natured laughter rang from the exposed ceiling timbers and shivered through his ribs.

Before Thorne's heart could remember its rhythm, everyone else was laughing, too. Even Fosbury. The mood went from black to some iridescent color only found in rainbows and seashells. The party was a party again.

Damn. If only he had it in him to love, to give her what she needed—he would claim her for his own and keep her so very close. To tease him, to kiss him back from the shadows, to laugh merrily when he terrorized his friends. To make him feel almost human, every once in while.

If only.

"For goodness' sake," she said, still laughing behind her cupped hand. "Someone fetch the poor man a cloth."

A giggling serving girl handed a rag over the counter, and Miss Taylor took the cake from Fosbury's hands so he could wipe his face clean.

She stuck her finger in the mussed icing, then held Thorne's gaze while she sucked it clean. "Delicious." She held the cake out. "Care to try?"

God above. No man could resist that. He had to take at least this much.

He reached—not for the cake, but for her wrist. While she stared at him, wide-eyed, he dipped her finger in the icing and brought it to his own mouth.

He sucked the creamy, sugary confection from her finger, and then he sucked the sweeter treat that was her bare fingertip, working his tongue up, down, and around it. The same way he would savor her nipple, or that hidden nub between her legs.

She gave a little gasp, and he fancied he heard pleasure in it. If she were his, he'd have her making that sound every night.

He released her hand and pronounced, "Delicious indeed."

A raucous whoop went up from the assembled crowd.

She gave him a chastening look. Her cheeks were as red as his coat.

He shrugged, unapologetic. "It's our engagement party. Just giving them what they came to see."

Sometime later, Kate was seated at a corner table with Thorne and the Gramercys. Slices of half-eaten cake sat before each place.

She was having a difficult time attending conversation—not only because the tavern had only grown louder after two rounds of drinks, but because her thoughts were entirely absorbed by a tongue.

His tongue.

She'd gained a great deal of familiarity with that tongue today. It was nimble, impertinent, and had a way of ending in places she wasn't expecting. It also gave her an inordinate amount of pleasure, when he wasn't employing it to send her harsh words.

But right now, perhaps his tongue was fatigued from the day's exertions, because he wasn't using it. At all.

He'd been sitting at this table for a half hour, at least, and hadn't spoken a word.

"Why don't you tell us how you and Corporal Thorne met," Aunt Marmoset said.

Kate sent a nervous glance in Thorne's direction. "Oh, no. It's a boring story."

Harry lifted her wine. "It can't be a more boring topic than estate management and agriculture, and that's all we ever hear from Evan."

Beneath the table, Kate twisted her fingers in her lap. There was no way she could spin a plausible tale of courtship. She didn't want to lie to the Gramercys at all, and Thorne's taciturn presence across the table would only undermine any tales of romance she might concoct.

"It's been a year," she said. "So long ago. Truthfully, I'm not even sure I could remember the time and place of our first—"

"It was here."

The reply came from Thorne. The silent oracle had spoken. The collective surprise was such that the glassware rattled on the table.

Even more astonishing—he appeared to have yet more to say.

"I arrived with Lord Rycliff last summer, to help assemble the local militia. Our first day in the village, we entered this tea shop."

Lord Drewe looked around. "I thought this was a tavern."

"It was a tea shop then," Kate explained. "Called the Blushing Pansy. But since last summer, it's been the Bull and Blossom. Part tea shop, part tavern."

"So go on," urged Aunt Marmoset. "You came in to the tea shop, and . . ."

"And it was a Saturday," Thorne said. "All the ladies were here for their weekly salon."

"Oh," said Lark with excitement. "I see where this is going. Miss Taylor was playing the pianoforte. Or the harp."

"Singing. She was singing."

"She sings?" Drewe looked to Kate. "We must have you perform."

"It's a rare thing to hear her," Thorne said. "Too often, she's accompanying one of her pupils instead. But that first day, she was singing."

Dreamy-eyed, Lark propped her chin with one hand. "And right there, that first moment, you were struck by her celestial voice and rare, ethereal beauty."

Kate cringed. *Celestial?* Lark was taking it much too far. Surely he'd balk at confirming that.

Thorne cleared his throat. "Something like it."

Lark sighed. "So romantic."

Of all the words Kate had never expected to hear applied to Thorne, "so romantic" had to rank near the very top. Right beneath "talkative," "dainty," and "choirboy." She had to admit, he was doing an admirable job of making this sound believable, without resorting to lies. He must have worried she'd give away the truth, with all her hesitant stammering on the subject.

"What was she wearing?" This question came from Lord Drewe. It had the sound of a quiz, not friendly curiosity. As if he didn't believe Thorne was telling the truth.

"Lord Drewe, it was a year ago," Kate interjected lightly, trying to divert this line of questioning. She was lucky they'd progressed this far without a misstep. "Even I don't remember what I was wearing."

"White." Thorne regarded Lord Drewe across the

table. "She was wearing white muslin. And an India shawl embroidered with peacocks. Her hair was dressed with blue ribbons."

"Is that true?" Lark asked Kate.

"I . . . If Corporal Thorne says so, I suppose it must be."

Kate struggled to conceal her shock. She remembered that shawl. It had been on loan from Mrs. Lange. Since she was angry with the husband who'd given it to her, she'd let Kate have use of the shawl all last summer. But Kate never imagined that Thorne would recall it. Much less the matching peacock ribbons in her hair.

She stole a glance at him as the serving girl removed the empty glasses. Had he truly been "struck by her" that day, the way Lark said?

"So he clapped eyes on you right here in the Spindle Cove tea shop," Lark said dramatically, "and he knew at once—he must make you his own."

Kate's cheeks burned with embarrassment. "It wasn't like that."

"You know nothing of men, goose," Harry said. "It's been a whole year. Corporal Thorne is a man of action. Just look at him. If he'd made up his mind to have her, he would have done so long before now."

"See, he didn't like me," Kate said. "Not at first. Perhaps there was some superficial attraction, but no emotions were involved." She looked at him over her wineglass. "He didn't feel a thing for me."

"Oh, I won't believe that." Aunt Marmoset unwrapped another spice drop. "I think he liked you too well, dear. And he made up his mind to stay away."

Kate looked to Thorne. She found him staring back at her with unnerving intensity.

"Well?" Lark asked him. "Does my aunt have it right?"

Does she? Kate asked him silently.

She didn't know what answer to read in those ice-blue eyes, but she discerned there was a great deal going on behind them. For a man who claimed to feel nothing . . . the "nothing" went very deep.

"Miss Taylor, are you going to keep our new friends all to yourself?"

Kate shook herself back to the present. Mrs. Highwood stood behind her, Diana and Charlotte in tow.

"Introduce us, dear," the matron said through a clenched smile.

"Yes, of course." She rose, and so did the men at the table. "Lord Drewe, Lady Harriet, Lady Lark, and Aunt Marmoset, may I introduce Mrs. Highwood and her daughters, Diana and Charlotte."

"I have a third daughter," Mrs. Highwood said loftily, "but she is lately married. To the Viscount Payne of Northumberland." The older woman turned and made a strange, awkward motion with her fan.

"Congratulations," Lark said, smiling at the matron and her daughters. "We've seen you in the rooming house, but it's a pleasure to be properly introduced."

"Yes, of course," said Mrs. Highwood. "What a boon it is to have a family of your caliber in Spindle Cove. We are quite starved for society this summer." Once again she turned and made the same swoop of her fan.

"Are you swatting a wasp?" asked Aunt Marmoset.

"Oh, no." Mrs. Highwood flicked an agitated gaze toward the same corner of the room. "It's nothing. Will you excuse me for just a moment?"

As Kate—and all the Gramercys—looked on, the matron turned away, walked two steps, and hurled her closed fan with such force that it smacked an unsuspecting man on the back of the head.

"Music," she half growled. "Now."

The man rubbed his head, offended, but he drew out a fiddle and began to saw a few creaky strains of a dance. Around the tavern, guests came to their feet to clear tables and chairs.

"Oh, look," said Mrs. Highwood, turning back to the Gramercys with an innocent smile. "There's going to be dancing. What a happy surprise."

Kate shook her head, dismayed. Of course the woman would do anything in her power to engineer a dance between her eldest daughter and Lord Drewe. But dancing wasn't a good idea for Diana. The last time she'd danced with a lord in this tavern, Diana had suffered a serious breathing crisis.

"Lord Drewe, I do hope you will honor us with a dance," said Mrs. Highwood. "Spindle Cove offers no shortage of lovely partners." She nudged Diana a step forward. "Ahem."

Kate began to grow truly panicked. She didn't know how to stop this. Even if he had no interest, Lord Drewe would not embarrass Diana with a refusal. And Diana was too shy and sweet to countermand her mother in company.

She cast a frantic, pleading glance at Thorne. He must understand what was going on. But unlike the others involved, he wasn't the sort to let etiquette stop him from doing something about it.

Standing tall, he lifted his voice and called to the fiddler. "No dancing. Not tonight."

The music died a quick, plaintive death. Around the room, guests muttered with discontent. Once again Thorne had single-handedly destroyed the celebratory spirit.

Only Kate knew the true reason, and it wasn't surliness. Neither was it a lack of empathy.

Quite the opposite. There was good in him. Raw, molten goodness, bubbling deep in his core. But he didn't possess the charm or manners to control it. It just erupted periodically in volcano fashion, startling anyone who happened to be nearby. Whether they were neighbors he prevented from dancing or teary-eyed spinsters he kissed in fields of heather.

He recalled the color of her hair ribbons on the first day they met. And she'd been blind to his essential nature all this time.

"Of course we can't have any dancing," Diana said, restoring peace with a smile. "How could we think of it, when we haven't yet raised a glass to the happy couple?"

"That's right," someone called. "There must be a toast."

"I'll say something. I'm the host." Fosbury raised a glass from behind the bar. "I don't think I'll be speaking out of turn to say this betrothal came as quite the surprise to everyone in Spindle Cove."

Kate glanced at Lord Drewe, worried he'd suspect something was amiss.

Fosbury continued, "For a year, we've all been watching these two square off on opposites of every argument. I had it on good authority that Miss Taylor had diagnosed Corporal Thorne as possessing a stone for a heart and having rocks in his head."

A wave of laughter rippled through the crowd.

"And considering these infirmities"—the tavern keeper stretched his glass in Thorne's direction—"who would have thought the corporal could make so wise a choice?" He smiled at Kate. "We're all terrible fond of you, m'dear. I think I speak for the entire militia when I say—we wouldn't let you go to anyone less worthy. Or less capable of calling us up on court-martial."

"Hear hear!"

Everyone laughed and drank, and the collective affection in the room created a knot in Kate's throat. But it was another emotion that made her chest ache.

Fosbury was right. Over the past year, she'd abused Thorne thoroughly, to his face *and* behind his back, when he'd done nothing more egregious than ignore her. After tonight, she suspected all that neglect had been his clumsy attempt at chivalry.

Here she was, surrounded by friends—and possibly family—who believed her to be in love with the man. Engaged to marry him. But in reality, she knew she'd treated him ill.

He told her he had no feelings to hurt, but no one could be completely without emotion. And if all Thorne's brusqueness had goodness beneath . . .

What sort of heart was hidden under all those staunch denials?

She regarded him now: arms crossed, face hard, eyes glazed with ice. He was a living suit of armor. If she listened hard enough, she might even hear him creak as he walked.

He wouldn't surrender any secrets willingly. If she wanted to know what was truly inside the man, she would have to crack him open to find out. It seemed a dangerous proposition, and a sensible, clever young woman—a "Kate"—would turn and run the other way.

But she wasn't a "Kate" to him. He'd called her Katie. And Katie was a courageous girl, even in the face of her fears.

Be brave, my Katie.

Yes. She would need to be.

Chapter Ten

I must say, that's a true disappointment. He hasn't
any phallus."

"What?" Kate asked, laughing.

When they'd reached their picnic spot, Harry placed
her hands on her hips, clenched her teeth around a cheroot, and regarded the immense green slope a few pastures distant.

"No phallus at all." She exhaled a puff of smoke.
"And here I had such high hopes, considering he's
known as 'the Long Man'."

Kate exchanged amused glances with Lark. They both
turned to regard the giant outline of a man carved into
the chalk hillside. The ancient figure ranged over the
entire slope, standing out in white lines against green.

"Ames and I went to see the Cerne Abbas carving in
Dorset," Harry went on. "The giant depicted on their
hillside is magnificently pagan. He has a horrific grimace on his face, and he's waving a big, knobby club
in his hand. Not to mention, sporting a monumental
erection."

Lord Drewe frowned. "Really, Harriet. That's enough

discussion of phalluses. I don't see why you and Ames should even care."

Harry sent her brother a look. "It's an artistic appreciation." She gestured at the ancient carving on the slope. "This one's just an outline. No facial expression whatsoever. Rather rigid and staid-looking, isn't he? And confined, locked up between those two lines."

"I think they're staffs," Kate suggested. "So perhaps that's some consolation. He's missing the monumental erection, but he does have *two* impressive staffs."

Harry took the cheroot from her mouth and gave her a shocked look. "Why, Miss Kate *Taylor.*"

Kate knew a moment of pure distress. What had she been thinking, to overstep and speak so crudely? The Gramercys were the aristocracy. She was their poor relation at best, and a complete stranger at worst. Just because Harry could make scandalous jokes, that didn't mean she should do the same.

Harry turned to her brother. "I like her. She can stay."

"She stays, whether you like her or not."

"I suppose that's right," Harry said. "If amiability were a requirement for inclusion in this family, Bennett should have been handed his permanent exile years ago."

Kate breathed a sigh of relief. She couldn't cease marveling at the notion that she might be a part of this. This wild, impolitic, eccentric, creative assortment of individuals. They *liked* her.

Now, if only Thorne would join in. The pagan figure carved on the distant hillside was a more active participant in the conversation.

He'd separated himself from the group, on the excuse of letting Badger tumble through the heather. As she looked closely, Kate thought he had the dog engaged in a training exercise. However, she couldn't follow quite what he was training Badger to do, because she kept getting distracted by the flexing of his thighs whenever he crouched to praise or correct the pup.

It wasn't only his physical firmness that drew her attention. His character was solid, too. She'd long known him to be stern and immutable, but since their engagement party, Kate was beginning to glimpse the good qualities his silence masked. Patience, confidence, steadfastness. Such traits didn't clamor for attention. They just quietly . . . existed, waiting to be noticed.

She'd made it her hobby these past few days—noticing. And the more she noticed, the more she yearned to know more.

"Well, that's a lovely view for a picnic," Aunt Marmoset said, joining them. "I do enjoy gazing upon a well-carved man."

"He's called 'the Long Man of Wilmington,' Aunt Marmoset." Lark scribbled in her journal.

"How odd. I'd been under the impression his name was Corporal Thorne." Aunt Marmoset came and put her hand in Kate's pocket. "My dear, hold onto that one. Tightly, and with all four limbs."

Kate blushed. "I don't know what you mean."

"Yes, you do. We have similar tastes."

The old lady withdrew her hand, leaving Kate's pocket oddly heavier—full of spice drops, she assumed.

"Remember what I told you," Aunt Marmoset whispered. "Strong. Overwhelming at first. But with a bit of work, you arrive at the sweetness."

Kate had to laugh. "I am coming to adore you, Aunt Marmoset. Even if you're not truly my aunt."

Over the past few days, she had begun to sort out the web of Gramercy family relationships. She knew Harry

had meant it as a joke the first night, but she secretly
had made herself a chart. Aunt Marmoset was Evan's
mother's sister, come to live with the family when
their father took ill. Therefore, the old lady was not a
Gramercy and no potential blood relationship to Kate
whatsoever. But that fact didn't seem to diminish Aunt
Marmoset's efforts to welcome her with warmth and
good humor and a great many spice drops.

All the Gramercys had blended in with Spindle Cove
life. Drewe had rightly pointed out that the village was
a haven for unconventional ladies—and Harry, Lark,
and Aunt Marmoset certainly met the standard. They'd
been enjoying regular activities with the other ladies:
country walks, sea-bathing, making decorations for the
fair.

But today the family had decided on an outing—not
only to satisfy Harry's curiosity about the Long Man,
but to give them time alone. In the village, they'd still
kept the possibility of kinship a secret. Here, they could
speak freely.

Kate haltingly approached Lord Drewe. As always,
his aristocratic presence and sheer male splendor hum-
bled her. His gloves alone . . . they held her rapt. They
were things of seamless, caramel-colored perfection,
encasing deft, elegant hands.

"Any news from your men of business?" She hated
to pry, but she knew from Sally that he'd had several
expresses since arriving in Spindle Cove.

"No information of value at Margate," he said re-
gretfully. "No information at all."

Kate only wished she could claim surprise.

"But now they're canvassing the area around Ambervale, looking for any servants from Simon's time. Perhaps one of them would remember Elinor and the babe."

"That sounds like a possibility." If a slim one.

His gloved fingertips touched her elbow, drawing her gaze up to his face. "I know the uncertainty is difficult to bear. For us all. Lark, in particular, is growing very attached to you. But today we should simply enjoy the outing."

"Yes, of course."

On the flat green, two liveried servants had been working hard to erect a canvas pagoda, topped with red banners gaily striping the blue sky.

The Gramercys did nothing without a certain degree of pageantry, Kate was coming to understand. From the carriages, the footmen unloaded two large hampers stocked with a variety of savory dishes and freshly baked sweets provided by the Bull and Blossom. This might be a picnic, but it wasn't a rustic affair.

As she and Lark helped unpack and arrange a tray of jewel-bright jam tarts, Kate realized there was one question her charts hadn't helped her settle. "Who is this Ames that Harry's always talking of? Another cousin? A family friend?"

"No," Harriet called back, overhearing them. "Not a cousin and certainly no kind of friend."

"Now, Harry," Lark said. "Just because the two of you had a little argument . . ."

"A little argument?" Aunt Marmoset scoffed. "More like a waterless reenactment of the Battle of Trafalgar, with saucers and teacups launched in place of cannonballs."

"Ames must have been playing Lord Nelson, then," Harry replied. "Because she has been dead to me ever since."

"'She'?" Kate had been picturing someone male.

Lark sighed and drew her into confidence. "When my

sisters and I were younger, Miss Ames was our paid companion. And now . . . now she is simply Harriet's companion. Her life companion."

"Oh," Kate said. And then, more slowly, as the import sank in—"*Oh.*"

"I know it's not very usual. But nothing is in this family. Are you terribly scandalized?"

"No, not . . . terribly." Though the revelation certainly put a few things in perspective. "But what of all those engagements? The duels Lord Drewe fought?"

"Harry tried her best during her season, and she loved the drama of suitors battling for her attention. But she could never go through with the weddings," Lark explained. "Her heart was with Miss Ames all along. Don't let her ranting mislead you. They're devoted to one another. They've had a falling out, but they always mend it in time."

"I heard that," Harry said. "And you're wrong, Lark. This time, we're through. If we were true companions, as you say, she would have allowed me to accompany her to Herefordshire."

Lark tilted her head. "Oh, Harry. You know Miss Ames's family isn't nearly so understanding as ours."

Very few families were, Kate imagined.

"I know it well. They're horrid to her." Harry kicked at a tent pole with the squared toe of her boot. "Always have been, or else she wouldn't have needed to be a paid companion in the first place. If she'd let me go along, I could have protected her."

"I'm certain she misses you sorely," Lark said.

Harry looked off at the horizon and released a sigh. "I'm off for a ramble. Perhaps the Long Man's phallus is embarrassingly small and only visible on closer inspection."

As Harry started off across the pastures, legs striding free in her divided skirt, Kate watched her with a twinge of sadness. Obviously, it pained her to be parted from someone she loved.

And what pained Harry, pained Kate. She was truly coming to care for these people. To lose them now would devastate her.

As if he knew her spirits needed a lift, Badger came shooting up from the meadow, attacking Kate's skirts with muddy paws, sniffing around all the refreshments and smothering her in delightfully cold, tickling kisses.

Thorne approached soon after, but offered no pawing or kisses. A keen disappointment.

Aunt Marmoset tapped Kate's shoulder and pointed. "There's a picturesque church in that direction. I noticed it as we drove by, but I couldn't make out the name. Be a dear, Kate, and satisfy my curiosity. Corporal Thorne," she added, "kindly escort her."

Kate smiled and rose to her feet, glad of the excuse to walk. She pocketed a few meat pies for Badger, and the three of them set off across the field, walking in the direction of the church.

Once they were safely out of earshot, Kate said gently, "You could try to be a little more sociable, you know."

He made a gruff noise. "I'm never sociable."

True enough, she supposed. "Why do you dislike the Gramercys so much?"

"I'm looking out for you." He looked over his shoulder at the picnicking group. "There's something not right about those people."

"They're unusual, I'll grant you. But it's only eccentricity. It's what makes them so amusing and interesting and lovable. It's what gives me hope that they might accept and love me. They value family bonds above scandal, disagreements, convention. Just because they're a bit odd, I don't see any reason for suspicion."

"I do. I don't trust them or their story."

"Why not?" she said, hurt. The more agitated she became, the faster she walked. By now they were hurrying toward the church, and Badger ran to keep up. "Because you don't think I could possibly be related to lords and ladies?"

He pulled to a halt, turned and fixed her with an intense look. "If I hadn't spent the last year thinking of you as a lady, I promise you—things would be different between us."

Her face heated. Other parts of her heated, too. She hadn't regarded him this closely or directly in days, and now . . .

He was so stunning it hurt.

For a man with few manners and little grace, she now saw he was always immaculate in his attire, be it full uniform or what he wore today—crisply fitted breeches and a simple, dark coat that stretched capably across his broad shoulders. Nothing was fussy, just precise. It was as though fabric didn't dare rumple in his presence. No button would be so bold as to fall out of line. His boots were polished to a blinding gloss.

And his face . . . Almost a week now since he'd seen her home from Hastings, and every time she looked at him, she still found his face to be that inexplicable, unbearable degree of handsome.

"Must you make this so difficult?" she asked. "You must know I'm all nerves, purely on the Gramercys' account. They've been so kind. I want to be open and honest, and yet I'm afraid of letting my hopes soar too high. I don't know my place with them, and that's difficult enough without feeling confused about you, too. I'm pulled in too many directions."

"I'm not pulling you anywhere. I'm staying close enough to look out for you, without interfering."

"Of course you're interfering. You interfere with my breathing, you teasing man. I can't just ignore you, Thorne. I've never been able to ignore you, even when I disliked you. Now I'm a toy on your string, dangling on your every move and word. One minute, you're paying me no mind at all, and the next . . . you're staring at me the way you're doing now. As though you're a voracious, starving beast and I'm . . ."

His jaw tightened.

She gulped and finished in a whisper, "Edible."

His exhalation was prolonged, measured. An impressive display of restraint.

"Well?" she prompted. "You can't deny it. There's something between us."

"There isn't nearly enough between us, and that's the danger. Don't you have a modest frock in your wardrobe? For God's sake, just look at that gown."

She cast a glance downward. She'd dressed for the outing in her best traveling frock—a handed down dove-gray silk. The hues were modest enough, and the sleeves rather long for summer. But from the direction of his gaze, she supposed he'd taken an interest in the row of ribbon bows that marched down the front of the bodice, holding two edges of gray silk together across a thin slice of white lace. It was all part of the gown's design, of course, but the garment was cleverly stitched to create the illusion that just a few ribbon ties stood between demure modesty and a state of undress.

"You're like a gift," he said, his voice rough. "All

wrapped up for someone else. A man can't look at you, but think of loosing those bows, one by one."

"They're false bows," she stammered. "They're sewn together."

His gaze never left her bodice, surveying. Strategizing. "I could rip them with my teeth."

And then what? a foolish part of her longed to ask.

They stood like that, facing one another. Saying nothing, breathing hard, and imagining far too much.

Eventually Badger nosed at her boots, impatient to be on with things. They couldn't stand here and look at each other all day. No matter how exhilarating it was.

"It's only physical," he said, walking on. "It will pass. You'll be able to release me soon enough."

It would have been comforting to believe so, but Kate wasn't convinced.

"I need to know something of you," she said as they neared the church. "Lark is always asking me questions about you. About us. And I don't know how to answer. What's your birthday, to begin?"

"Don't know it."

Kate felt a twinge of sadness for him, but then—she'd survived without a proper birthday for twenty-three years.

"How about your favorite color?"

He threw a careless, sidelong glance at her frock. "Gray."

"Be serious, please. I'm engaged to you, temporarily, and I know nothing of you. Nothing of your family, your history, your childhood." And after their engagement party, Kate knew he'd been paying a great deal of attention to her.

"There's nothing to tell."

"That can't be true. I was raised at a miserable girls'

school, but even I have amusing stories from when I was a child. There was the time it was my turn to help in the kitchens, and I decided to be creative with the seasonings for our evening soup. I accidentally dumped the entire contents of the pepper pot into the broth, and I was too afraid to own up to it. And then it was supper, and I still couldn't say a word. I'll never forget watching all my friends and teachers take that first mouthful of soup—"

She broke off, laughing. "Oh, I caught so much trouble. Everyone went to bed hungry, of course. They had me copying out Proverbs for days."

She waited for him to dredge up some similar story of youthful foolishness. Everyone must have at least one. *Everyone*. But she waited in vain.

Before she could ask him another question, Badger suddenly perked to attention. His funny little ears stood straight up, pointing skyward like twin church steeples. Then they flattened and he was off like a flash of lightning, streaking toward the church.

"Badger, wait," she called, rushing after the pup.

Thorne paced her in easy strides. "Don't call him back. He's got his sights on a hare or a rat, most likely. Chasing is what he's bred to do."

The dog darted toward the small churchyard tucked behind the main buildings. Evidently, the pup's quarry had escaped through a small hole in the bottom of the stone wall. Badger wriggled through the crack, disappearing from their view.

"Drat," Kate said, breathless. "We'll have to go around."

"This way."

They quickly skirted the circumference of the small cemetery until they came to the wrought-iron gate.

Thorne opened it, and she rushed past him, into the crowded jumble of the high-walled churchyard. Mossy, timeworn monuments tilted at various angles, like rows of rotten teeth.

"Badger! Badger, where have you gone?" Kate started down a row of monuments, ducking and peering at the uneven ground. Remembering the meat pie in her pocket, she fished it out and held it as a lure. "Here, darling. I have a lovely treat for you."

Thorne skirted the slab of an aboveground sepulcher and came to a halt in the center of the churchyard. He whistled.

After a brief pause, Badger came bounding out from behind a bit of crumbled stone.

"Thank goodness. Did he catch something?" Kate was almost afraid to look.

"No. But that's good. He'll run faster next time."

There was real pride in his voice. And genuine affection in the way he rubbed the dog's scruff and ears. He *must* care about that dog, despite all his disavowals.

There was so much more to him than he was allowing anyone to see. Right now they were secluded from the Gramercys, the Spindle Cove gossips . . . from the rest of the living world. This might be her only chance to get at it.

"Give me *something*," she pleaded. "Your father's trade, or the names of your siblings. The house where you were raised. A friend, your favorite plaything. Anything."

His face hardened as he rose to his feet.

"For goodness' sake, Thorne. Do you realize, I don't even know your Christian name? I've been stretching my brain to recall it. Surely someone in the village would have used it, at least once. It would be in Sally's ledger of accounts in the shop, maybe. Or Lord Rycliff would have mentioned it sometime. Perhaps in church. But the more I think on it, the more I'm certain . . . no one else in Spindle Cove knows it, either."

"It's not important."

"Of course it is." She grabbed him by the sleeve. "*You* are important. And you need to let someone know you."

His eyes bore into hers, nailing her in place. His voice sank to a low growl. "Stop pushing me."

When a powerful, unpredictable man loomed over a girl and glared at her that way, her every instinct was to back down. He knew that, and he was using it against her.

"I won't give up," she said. "Not until you give me something."

"Fine." He spoke in a remote voice, utterly devoid of emotion, as if rattling off a list of drill commands or ordering up a list of dry goods. "I never knew my father. Never wanted to. He got my mother with child too young, out of wedlock, and then abandoned us both. She turned whore, found a place in a bawdy house. I could sleep in the attic, so long as I worked for my keep and stayed out of the customers' sight. I never went to school. Never learned a trade. My mother came to like her gin, and she came to hate my face, the more I grew to resemble my father. Never missed a chance to tell me I was useless, stupid, ugly, or all three. If she had anything solid to hand, she'd beat the message in for good measure. I left when I had the chance, and I never once looked back."

Kate couldn't respond. Words failed her.

"There," he said, taking the forgotten meat pie from her hand and tossing it to the waiting dog. "Charming story for the breakfast table."

Her own silence mocked her. She'd asked for the truth. She'd pushed him for information, and now she was allowing him to push her away.

Kate willed her tongue to work. *Say something nice. Anything.*

"I . . ." She swallowed hard. "I find you unbearably handsome."

He stared at her. "Miss Taylor . . ."

"I do. I find you unbearably, painfully handsome. I didn't always." The words spilled from her lips, unconsidered. "But ever since Hastings . . . it's hard for me to even look at you sometimes. It can't come as much surprise. You must be aware how many women are attracted to you."

He made a derisive sound. "It's not for my fine looks."

Kate went silent, suddenly keenly aware of all his other attractions. His strong body, that air of command, the fiercely protective instincts. The talents that must fuel those "tales" Sally Bright mentioned in the All Things shop.

"I'm certain women are attracted to you for a host of reasons," she said. "But I can only speak for myself. And I find you unbearably handsome."

He frowned. "Why are you saying this? I don't need this from you."

"Perhaps you don't."

But I think you do.

She might not be able to comprehend the horrors he'd faced on a battlefield, but she knew how it felt to be an unwanted child. She understood how it felt to be deemed worthless and ugly by the very person charged with her care. She knew how each and every unkind remark worked on a child's confidence for weeks, months, years. Bruises faded from the skin, but insults worked like weevils, burrowing into a person's soul.

She knew it took dozens of kindnesses to counteract just one slight, and even then—she knew how she'd come to dodge compliments, even well into adulthood, dismissing them as mere pity or insincerity. Because how could they be true? The ugly words were still there, deep inside, and they outlasted everything. They were the bones in this churchyard. No matter how much soil was heaped atop them, no matter how many cheerful flowers were planted over the grave—they would always be there.

Those hateful words could outlive dirt.

She *knew*. And she couldn't watch him hurting and not do something to counteract it.

"I find you unbearably handsome," she said. "I know you're modest and guarded and you don't need to hear it. But I need to say it. So there it is."

She touched her fingertips to his cheek. He flinched, and his Adam's apple bobbed in his throat.

"Stop that."

Make me.

Reveling in the thrill of disobedience, she framed his face in her hands, letting the tips of her longest fingers graze the dark fringe of his hair. The icy chips of his eyes sent a shiver down her spine.

So she let her gaze fall to his lips, wondering—not for the first time—how that grim slash of a mouth could transform into something so passionate and warm when they kissed. She touched the pad of her thumb to the hollow of his cheek. Where a dimple might appear, if he could ever be coaxed to smile.

She very much wanted to see him smile. She wanted to make him laugh, long and loud.

"You're handsome," she said.

"You're absurd."

"If I am speaking absurdities, it must be your fault. This hard angle of your jaw"—she traced it with a fingertip—"quite scrambles my thoughts, and your eyes . . . There's some puzzle in them I want to solve."

"Don't try. You don't know me." His voice was harsh, but his gaze was stark with hunger. Open, naked hunger.

Yes. Triumph surged through her veins. She was getting somewhere now.

"I know you took a melon for me." She smiled. "That's a start. And when you look at me the way you're doing right now, I scarcely know myself. I feel womanly, to a degree I've never felt before. But then I feel girlish, too. I have to remind myself not to do something silly, like twirl my hair or bounce on my toes. I think that's quite definite proof that you're handsome, Thorne. At least, to one woman."

And if she was right—and that small spark in his eyes was a deeply buried yearning . . .

Kate thought she could live with being beautiful to just one man.

He took her by the waist, pulling her close. She gasped at the suddenness and strength in the motion. She suspected her shock was his purpose.

"I don't fear you," she said.

"You should fear me." He tightened his hold on her waist. In a matter of three paces he had her backed against the nearest wall. A lush green curtain of ferns and ivy framed her hair and face. "You should fear *this*. Every minute we're in this churchyard together, you're risking ruin. You could lose everything you've wanted most."

She knew he spoke the truth. Just a few hundred yards away were four people who offered the human connection and family love she'd grown up dreaming of and hoping to find. The Gramercys represented her heart's desire.

And yet she was here, with him. Sharing a highly improper embrace on sacred ground, with only the dead to chaperone. Had she lost her mind?

Perhaps.

Or perhaps she'd found another heart's desire.

Was there some limit on them? Couldn't a girl have more than one?

The Gramercys made her feel accepted. But Thorne made her feel *desired*. Needed. In her youth, she never could have known to wish for this.

She murmured, "What have you done to me?"

"Not a fraction of what I'd like to do."

She smiled. There it was again—a flash of that dry, disarming wit. Oh, she was in so much trouble. Wringing affection from this man would be like squeezing honey from a stone. But he'd brought her this close, and she couldn't resist reaching for something more.

Don't hide from me, she willed. *Don't pull away.*

"Handsome," she whispered, taking a chisel and hammer to the stone. Chipping away as best she knew how. "Fine-looking. Attractive. Striking. Noble. Body-thrilling. Swoon-inducing. Beauti—"

His kiss made a liar of her.

She'd blithely told him she didn't fear him—but that was before his lips came crushing down on hers. Before his tongue invaded her mouth. Plunging deep, and then deeper still. Exploring, stroking, demanding. Stirring up emotions she didn't know how to control.

A low growl rose from his chest. He moved forward,

pressing his hard, masculine body to hers, and together they burrowed into the ivy covering the wall. The air was a dark, glossy green in her senses. Tiny, grasping tendrils pulled at her, scratched like small fingernails along her skin. They made her feel wild and part of something larger than herself, something elemental and natural and old as time.

As they kissed, his strong hands began to roam her body, shaping and claiming her in ways that must be wrong, but felt so necessary.

She wondered—if she were a woman with more experience, where would she be touching him? Stretching her arms about his waist, perhaps? Might she work her hand inside his coat, to feel the sculpted contours of his chest?

She wasn't that daring. Instead, she touched her hand to his jaw, robustly formed and rough with new whiskers when the hour was barely noon. She slid her hand around the strong column of his neck, letting her fingertips graze the shorn hair at his nape. She stroked him there, softly. Tenderly. Because everyone deserved a bit of tenderness, and she was so very hungry for it herself.

What he gave her was something far more primal.

He clutched her tight, moaning into the kiss and holding her fast against him. The thrill of power was immediate. It shot through her, forking into every limb and electrifying her senses as he ravaged her mouth.

He muttered a curse as his lips slid to her neck, as though he kissed her unwillingly, against all morals and reason. She thrilled to that bit of blasphemy. It excited her to know that here, in this tiny, walled churchyard, she'd torn down his barriers. He'd lost all sense of duty or restraint, and she'd done this to him.

And then . . .

Then there was what he was doing to *her*.

His kisses worked lower along the left side of her throat, and his right hand worked higher from her waist, and the two seemed destined to meet at a specific point. That reddish, round, helpful point that now puckered and jutted against her garments, presenting itself as an eager target.

I should put a stop to this.

She watched the idea pass through her mind. It came, and it went, and she did nothing about it.

When his hand stroked over her fabric-cloaked breast, she nearly fainted with pleasure and relief. His palm ironed the modest globe flat, and then his thumb found the taut, straining peak of her nipple, chafing back and forth in a delicious manner. Her body throbbed with a deep, sweet ache. He kissed the sensitive skin over her pounding heart, then pushed her breast higher, nuzzling the overflowing scoop of warm feminine flesh in his palm.

Nuzzling. Who could have known this cold, ruthless man had it in him to nuzzle? At all?

"Katie." He groaned. "I burn for you."

Just a few husky words, but coming from a man so taciturn, she thought they must equal reams of poetry.

I burn for you.

So hot, those words. So dangerous. Their effect was incendiary.

The potent heat of his desire changed her everywhere. Her stockings itched. She wanted them off. Between her legs, she swelled and ached. Her breasts challenged the corset's limits with her every fevered, panting breath. They rose impatient and quivering, begging for more of his skillful attention.

He hooked his finger beneath the fabric of her bodice

and ran it up toward her shoulder, loosening her gown just enough to slide it over one shoulder and down. With his thumb, he eased her neckline lower, all the while kissing and sucking lightly at her neck.

He was going to touch her bare breast.

She was going to let him.

It would happen. Soon.

Please. Now.

He kissed her lips, just as his fingers curled inside her bodice, cupping the slight handful of her breast. She tasted his dark, sensual moan. The pleasure was so intense, she arced off the ivy-covered wall, mindlessly thrusting her hips against him. Her belly met with the hard, pulsing ridge of his arousal.

My goodness.

Someone notify Lady Harriet. There was a monumental erection to be found in Wilmington, after all.

He growled against her lips as he kneaded and fondled her flesh, teasing her nipple with the pad of one finger. Rolling it under his touch, chasing round and round. Kate thought she would go out of her skin with pleasure.

"I must—" He broke the kiss, gasping. "Katie, I want to taste you. I have to taste you."

"Yes," she urged. "Yes."

She worked a hand between them, reaching for the ribbon bow just at the top of her bodice. She hadn't lied to him earlier—the bows on the gown were ornamental, sewn together.

All except this one.

She watched his eyes widen as she grasped the edge of the ribbon and teased the bow loose. It was like she'd given him a lifetime of Christmas and birthday gifts, all at once. And any self-consciousness she'd ever felt about her smallish breasts and dark nipples . . . it all disappeared in an instant when he pulled the fabric down, exposing her to the cool air and his hot, hungry gaze.

She might not be perfect, but he liked what he saw.

At least, she supposed that was what it meant when a man whispered, *"Sweet God above."*

He shook his head, still staring rapt at her naked breast. "This can't happen."

"Oh, yes. It's happening." She hoped more would be happening rather soon.

"I don't use women. Ever."

"You're not using me."

"And I don't take advantage of innocent girls. Ever."

For goodness' sake. He wasn't taking advantage of her, and she wasn't a girl. Would it help if she begged?

The longer he delayed, the tighter her nipple puckered. It looked like a raspberry now, jutting out from a scoop of blancmange. Ready to be devoured.

"Thorne." She wriggled, pressing her breast into his hand. "I need . . . something."

He looked up, pinning her gaze with his. "I know precisely what you need." The deep richness of his voice melted and spread over her skin.

"Then please." She tugged at his coat, trying to pull him closer. "Please."

After a long hesitation he pulled her sleeve back up over her shoulder, then covered her breast.

"You need more than a moment's stolen pleasure," he said. "You need care and affection. Tenderness and love."

With jerky motions, he retied the ribbon bow, then stepped away. "You need a different man. A better man than me."

Chapter Eleven

No sooner had Thorne stepped away, loins throbbing with unspent lust, than Lady Lark Gramercy came dashing into the churchyard.

He quickly moved behind a stone cross, which was conveniently waist high. There was no concealing his labored breathing, however. Nor Katie's.

"Oh, there you two are," Lark said, smiling. "For a moment, I worried you were having some sort of tryst. I should hate for anything to tempt Evan to a sixth duel." The young woman laughed. "Five is impressive, but six . . . ? Six would just look predictable."

Katie—*Miss Taylor,* he scolded himself—plucked a bit of ivy from her hair as she stepped away from the wall. Her cheeks and throat were washed with pink.

"We've had a time of it," she said. "Badger dashed into the churchyard through a hole in the wall and we've been searching."

Bloody hell. Thorne scanned the rows of graves. The pup was missing again.

What a blackguard he was. Not only had he been moments away from desecrating Miss Taylor's virtue in a churchyard and ruining her future of wealth and comfort—he'd neglected the damn dog. He scrubbed a hand through his hair, furious with himself.

"Go on with Lady Lark," he told Miss Taylor. "I'll find him."

He needed a few minutes to bring his lust into submission anyway.

Once the ladies had left, he whistled. The dog came running straightaway.

And then Thorne spent a quarter hour or so reading the inscription on every last monument in the churchyard, at his usual painfully slow rate. Might as well get acquainted with the people he'd given such a salacious show.

Four rows of dead Wilmingtonians later, his loins had calmed and he believed he might be able to think clearly again. As he left the churchyard, Badger at his heel, he ran both hands through his hair.

What the devil was he doing? Hadn't he resolved there would be no more kisses? He knew how to withstand purely physical temptation, but her sweetness . . . this was a force unlike any he'd faced before.

If he hadn't chosen that moment to stop . . . If Lady Lark had arrived just a few seconds earlier . . . Katie— *Miss Taylor*—would have been caught with her bosom hanging out of her dress. With him hulking and slavering over her like a randy youth getting his first flash of tit.

Thorne had meant what he'd told her. He didn't use women. Growing up in a whorehouse had left him with contempt for any man who paid for pleasure. And an exchange of coin wasn't the only way a woman could be used. He'd seen men wield power, privilege, circumstance, and physical violence to have their way.

Sometimes—many times—it all made him disgusted to be a man.

But he *was* a man. One like all the others, rank with dark cravings and base needs. So he took lovers—but only when he knew the relationship would be mutually satisfying, uncomplicated, and brief.

Nothing with Miss Taylor could be uncomplicated. As for brief . . . ? They had a connection spanning decades.

Today he'd been tempted to use her anyway. Oh, she would have argued that she was willing enough. But he knew what she truly wanted from life. And it sure as hell didn't involve reclining against a churchyard wall and offering her breast to a crude, uneducated convict. If he'd given in to her pleadings and his own lust, he would have only been using her. To make himself feel stronger, more powerful.

More human.

You are important, she'd said. *You need to let someone know you.*

When it came to his emotions, no one could get past the stalwart defenses he had erected. No one, that was, until her. She'd been close to him long before all those fortifications were completed. And though she didn't remember his face or his name, she seemed to recall her way through the network of tunnels. She was gaily skipping past all his Keep the Hell Out barricades, working her way to the center of his soul.

Where all the demons lurked.

He had to find some way to fence her out, before she got hurt. He'd said too much about the past already, and he could never let her know more.

It would ruin her life.

As the Gramercys' ridiculous picnic pagoda came into view, he drew to a halt in the middle of the meadow and stared at the thing. It seemed that wherever these people went, they built a queer little kingdom of their own—and he was always outside its borders.

Badger sat at his heel, waiting on further direction.

Thorne tossed the pup a bit of dried beef from his pocket, rewarding his patience.

He'd been waiting a long time for a hound like this. While noblemen kept purebred greyhounds and such for their fancy fox hunts, the lurcher was a common man's hunting dog—a coursing hound specially bred for speed, sight, and intelligence. A good lurcher could chase down rabbits, fowl. Even foxes and deer.

A dog like Badger would make a fine companion in the American wilderness. He was perfectly bred to be obedient, swift, and ruthless in pursuit of the kill.

Miss Taylor couldn't care less about any of that. She wrung her hands at the idea of Badger catching a vole.

Yet she claimed to love the creature. And for what? The too-long nose, or unevenly patched fur? The pup's propensity to chew her belongings to bits?

The longer he stared at the dog, the less sense it made.

"What the hell does she see in you?"

"Oh, Badger. What do we see in that man?"

As Kate curled up with the puppy that night, she found and plucked a hidden burr from his undercoat.

"You like him, too," she said to the pup. "Don't try to deny it. I can tell you do. Your eyes go all melty when he tosses you the smallest scrap of affection, and when he's near, you have a tendency to pant."

She sighed, cupping the puppy's cone-shaped muzzle

in her palm. "Do you want to know a secret? I'm afraid I have the same reaction, and it's every bit as obvious."

Badger pawed at a bit of loosened leather binding from a copy of *Mrs. Worthington's Wisdom for Young Ladies.*

"Go on, destroy it," she urged. "There are several hundred more where it came from."

Copies of the insipid, damaging etiquette book littered the village in scores—and very few of them remained anywhere else in England. As the original patroness of Spindle Cove, Susanna Finch—now Lady Rycliff—had made it her personal mission to remove every possible copy of *Mrs. Worthington's Wisdom* from circulation.

Badger was welcome to chew his way through them, one by one. Because right now, Kate had no use for proper, ladylike behavior. She flopped back on the mattress and stared up at the ceiling, giving in to the temptation to remember.

Her nipples peaked beneath her nightrail. With each rise and fall of her breath, the thin linen teased them harder still. She wanted his hands on them. His *mouth* on them. His body atop hers, heavy and strong.

She wanted that yearning look in his pale blue eyes, and the sweet, sweet taste of his kiss.

Oh, Thorne.

She lifted one hand to the valley between her breasts and lightly stroked up and down her sternum, dragging the muslin with her touch.

If only he hadn't suffered that attack of conscience in the churchyard.

Well . . . she had to be honest. Considering the timing of Lark's appearance, she was rather glad Thorne had stopped when he did.

But if he were here with her right now, he wouldn't need to stop at all.

Kate slipped loose one button of her nightrail. Then two. She closed her eyes and summoned the green, earthy scent of moss and ferns, blended with a more masculine smell of leather and musk. She recalled the scrape of his whiskers against her palm.

She slipped her hand inside her nightrail, trying to relive the experience through his senses. How did she feel, to him?

Soft, she decided.

So soft. Like warm satin—or the well-worn palms of her oldest, dearest kid gloves. A little springy, like bread dough, in a way that tempted fingers to knead and squeeze. At the areola . . . amusingly wrinkled. A rosette of tightly ruched silk.

She rolled that pursed bud of her nipple beneath her fingertip, trying to recapture the excitement and pleasure of his touch. Imagining his mouth and his wicked, skillful tongue.

It felt good. Very good.

But nowhere near the same. If there was one thing she'd learned over the course of her life, it was that no amount of imagining could make her forget she was alone. If she wanted to recapture that intense, forbidden thrill, Thorne would have to be involved.

She sighed and brought her hand out from the nightrail, flinging her arm above her head.

In the next moment, she was seized by a paroxysm of torment. Badger had found something interesting to nose and lick on the underside of her arm.

"Stop." Kate convulsed with helpless, ticklish laughter. "Stop, you little imp."

His cold nose burrowed into the crook of her elbow,

rooting and sniffing. She had to clap a hand over her mouth to keep from yelping aloud. It was torture of the sweetest, furriest kind.

Once she'd managed to turn on her side and restore order, the dog leaped down from the bed and began circling and sniffing at the carpet.

Kate sat bolt upright.

Oh, no. Oh, no you don't.

Kate jumped out of bed and jammed her feet into a pair of slippers. She grabbed her dressing gown and pulled it on over her nightrail, hastily knotting the belt at her waist.

"Just wait, Badger darling. Just hold it one minute more . . ."

Scooping up the dog in one arm and taking a candlestick with the other, Kate shouldered open the door of her bedchamber and padded softly down the corridor. The hour was well past midnight, and she didn't want to wake anyone.

After descending the stairs, she opened the front door of the rooming house a crack. Cool night air rushed over her exposed throat. She set Badger on the ground and pulled her dressing gown closed at the neck.

"Go on." She shooed him with a hand. "Do your business and come back. I'll just wait here."

As Badger scampered across the front garden to have his choice of the hitching posts, a light caught Kate's eye.

There was a lamp burning in the Bull and Blossom.

Odd.

To be sure, the Bull and Blossom was a tavern, but this was the country—Fosbury always closed up shop by nine or ten at the latest. Village life began with the crack of dawn. What man would be up drinking at this hour?

Perhaps a man occupied by the same thoughts that kept her awake, when all the other ladies were asleep.

It had to be Thorne.

And she simply had to see him.

Kate rewrapped her dressing gown, tying it as modestly as possible. Anyway, it was dark. No one could see much. She blew out her candle, leaving it on the small entry table. Then she shut the door behind her and moved into the garden, summoning Badger to her side with a little chirping noise.

"Come along," she told him. "We're going to have an adventure."

A chill crawled down her spine as she crossed the dark, shadowy village green, but having the dog at her heel was some comfort. Badger might not be fully grown, but he could tickle an attacker into submission, if nothing else.

When she reached the red-painted front door of the Bull and Blossom, she put a hand to the door latch and tested it. It was unlocked.

And vibrating.

She held her breath and opened her ears. From inside the tavern, she detected soft strains of pianoforte music. But they sounded as if they were coming from a long distance away.

The faint chords threw her back to those first hazy memories. She was in that long dark corridor again. Pianoforte music played from somewhere. From below? In her memory, she felt the distant strains of music shivering up through her heels. The arches of her feet tingled.

"See the garden of blossoms so fair . . ."

The corridor was cramped and dark. Endless. But in the darkness, there was something blue.

Be brave, my Katie.

Kate awoke from her trance with a gasp, sucking breath into air-deprived lungs. Her white-knuckled hand remained clasped on the door latch.

She gathered Badger with her other arm, then opened the door and entered.

What she found inside surprised her.

Lord Drewe.

He was seated at the pianoforte, and he had not noticed her entrance.

Light from a small lamp revealed him to be dressed in an open shirt with rolled cuffs and a dark pair of trousers. His feet were hard to see through the shadows, but Kate thought they were bare—just long, pale wedges against the dark floorboards.

He was playing the pianoforte, but with the top closed and the damper pedal pressed to the floor. The result was that no matter how vigorously he attacked the keys—and he was going at them with true fervor—only a faint, music-box sound escaped the instrument.

She could have laughed, if she weren't so afraid of being caught. Watching a powerful marquess play the pianoforte in this fashion . . . Well, it was a little like watching a side of beef being butchered with a penknife.

Badger wriggled free of her grip.

Kate held her breath, mortified, as he hit the floor with a clatter of tiny claws.

Lord Drewe's hands froze on the keys and he looked up sharply. He peered hard toward the shadows that concealed her.

"Who's there?" His voice had a rough, end-of-day quality to it, and his jaw had a dark sprinkling of whiskers. For the first time, he seemed less of an elegant marquess and more of a . . . man.

"It's only me," she managed to whisper. "Kate."

"Oh." In an instant he'd mastered his shock. He rose from the bench and waved her forward. "Please come in. What a surprise."

She hated for him to see her in her dressing gown, but it seemed a greater sin to remain hidden. "I'm so sorry. I just took Badger out for a minute, and then I saw the light burning. I was curious. I didn't mean to interrupt your . . ." She bit her lip. "Your seething."

He smiled and laughed a little.

Kate released her breath, relieved. "I'm so glad you laughed."

"Were you thinking I wouldn't?"

"I wasn't sure. To tease you felt like a risk, but I couldn't resist." She approached the pianoforte. "I didn't know you played."

"Oh, yes. My brother Bennett does as well—or at least, he used to. Oddly enough, none of my sisters show much inclination for it. It seems to be a trait confined to the Gramercy men." A half smile tugged at his mouth. "That is, on *our* side of the family."

"Do you know if my—if Simon Gramercy played?"

"I believe he did." Lord Drewe slid down the bench and gestured for her to sit. "Shall we try a duet?"

"I'd like nothing more."

She choose a simple piece—one of those easy duets that all novice pianists learn with their tutors. Kate had played the lower part of it countless times with her students. Today, she took the upper part, and Lord Drewe quickly entered with the bass.

He was good. Very good. Within a few measures, she could discern his skill. He had long, deft fingers and a reach that she envied. But his talent went deeper than mere skill—he possessed a natural musicality that even a gifted teacher could not impart. Seldom did she have a pupil who could match her for training, but occasionally one came close.

This was the first time in years she'd felt herself truly *bested*.

But it was marvelous. As they played, she felt him making her better. She soon left the proscribed boundaries of the exercise, taking the melody down different paths. He followed her lead, occasionally made his own suggestions with a new, surprising chord. It would have been difficult to explain to anyone who didn't play— but the duet was a conversation. They responded to one another, adjusting tempo and dynamics. They finished one another's phrases. They even told each other jokes.

His technique was flawless; his style, restrained. But she sensed true passion beneath it all.

When they ended the duet with a playful flourish and one final, muted secret of a chord, they looked to each other.

"Well, then," he said. "That seals it. You must be part of the family."

Her heart missed a beat. "What are you saying? Did you have some news, some result from the inquiries . . . ?"

He shook his head. "Not yet. But there's so much indirect evidence. We've spent the whole week with you, and we're all agreed. You simply fit in, Kate. This"—he indicated the pianoforte—"is just one more reason. In my mind, the investigation is concluded. Don't you feel it, too?"

Kate didn't feel certain of anything—except that she was most certainly going to cry. She tried to hold the tears back, but a few spilled over. She swiped at them with the side of her wrist.

A few moments passed before she could speak. "Lord Drewe, I don't know how to thank you."

"To begin with, you must call me Evan now. And no thanks are necessary."

Kate drew up her legs beneath her dressing gown and angled to face him on the piano bench. If he was truly her cousin, she now had the right to fuss over him. "Why are you up so late, Evan?"

"I might ask you the same thing." One dark eyebrow arched. "I won't believe it was only the dog."

When she stammered a bit in response, he waved off her explanations.

"It's all right. You needn't manufacture excuses. We're all a bit haunted, we Gramercys. Each of us has a passion. My sister Calista—you'll meet her soon—has always been wild for nature. Harriet lives for drama, and Lark loves a puzzle. Our brother Bennett would tell you his passion is vice, but he once had nobler pursuits."

"So your passion is music?"

He shook his head. "I enjoy music, and I often take refuge in it. But music is not what makes me . . ."

"Seethe," she finished.

He smiled. "Precisely."

"Then what is it? Or whom?" The moment the words left her mouth, she regretted them. "I'm sorry. It's not my place to ask."

"No, it is your place. Because you're part of it now. My passion is the family, Kate. This title I've inherited, the responsibilities of managing several estates. Being a good steward of the land. Taking care of those in my protection. Guarding my siblings from themselves."

He stared into the corner, and Kate took the opportunity to study him. She noted the small creases at the corners of his eyes. Here and there she could glimpse a thread of silver in his dark hair. But these subtle signs of age looked well on him. They harmonized with his worldly demeanor, as though his body were learning to reflect the maturity of the soul inside. He was a fine-looking man by any standard, but she suspected his most handsome years were yet to come.

He pushed a hand through his hair. "Corporal Thorne does not like me."

She startled at the abrupt change of topic. "Oh, please don't believe that. If you go by appearances, Corporal Thorne doesn't like anyone. He's very . . . reserved."

"Perhaps. But he resents me in particular, and for good reason. He believes that I should have known of your existence, and that I should have tried harder to find you. I know he's right."

"You couldn't possibly have known. You were only a youth when you inherited."

"But you were just a girl, living penniless and alone." He rubbed his temple. "As you might have gathered . . . a violent temper is one of my worst faults. I have no patience for those who cross my family."

A rather grave understatement, Kate thought, given the five duels. His having walked away unscathed from one or two such confrontations would be impressive enough, but . . .

Five.

Evan sighed heavily. "This is what Corporal Thorne does not appreciate. No one can be angrier with me than I am with myself. You've been wronged, Kate, and I have no one to call out. No malfeasance to blame but my own inattention. Someday, I will ask you to forgive me. But not tonight."

Kate leaned forward, boldly placing her hand on his arm. "There is no need. Please believe me when I tell you I have no room for bitterness or rancor in my heart. It's too full of joy and gratitude. I'm so happy to have a family at long last."

"I am soothed to hear it." He took her hand in his and regarded it carefully. Thoughtfully. "Do you care for him?"

"Thorne? I . . ." She hesitated, but only to choose her phrasing. The answer was instinctive. "I do care. I care very much."

"Do you love him?"

Now here was something she'd been avoiding asking herself. But she couldn't let pass the opportunity to unburden her heart. Evan was family.

"I think I could come to love him," she said. "If he would let me."

Evan's thumb rubbed a lazy circle on the back of her hand. "It's plain you have a brave and generous heart. I imagine you could love just about anyone, if you made up your mind to do it. But you deserve a man who can love you in return."

Kate smiled a little, nervously.

His grasp on her hand was warm and firm. "I mean to take care of you. I want you to know this. If there's no legacy allotted in the terms of Simon's estate, I will ensure that you have one. You will be an independent woman of significant wealth. A woman with choices." He leaned meaningfully on that last word.

She swallowed. "Evan, you needn't do that for me. I've never had any expectation of—"

"I have expectations of myself, Kate." His eyes glittered in the dark. "I have a passion for protecting this family. And that passion now extends to you."

A silence opened between them. As they regarded one another, Kate's curiosity grew.

He had a "passion" for her. The insides of her elbows tingled. What did that mean, exactly?

"Corporal Thorne is a good man," she said.

"Perhaps. But is he the best man for *you*?" He looked down at where their hands remained linked. "Kate, it's possible we won't accumulate enough evidence to satisfy the courts of your identity. But that's not the only way I can give you the family name."

She stared at him through the flickering shadows. Surely he didn't mean that the way it sounded. He couldn't possibly be hinting at—

A floorboard creaked, and Kate startled.

Evan released her hand. "Just the dog. Don't be alarmed."

Relief washed over her. Nothing improper had passed between the two of them. At least, she didn't think it had. But she cringed to imagine how the scene could have looked to a gossip-minded villager. That would be a juicy rumor for Sally Bright to stock in the All Things shop—Miss Taylor holding hands with Lord Drewe, when she was engaged to Corporal Thorne?

But no one would believe that rumor, Kate assured herself. A girl like her, courted by two virile, powerful men—and one of them a lord? She felt silly for even entertaining the idea herself.

Wrapping her dressing gown tight around her chest, she rose from the chair and gathered Badger.

"I'd best go back to the rooming house," she said. "Please don't stay up too late seething on my account."

He gave her an intent look and a cryptic smile. "I make no promises."

Chapter Twelve

By Spindle Cove custom, the midsummer fair was a children's festival. But readying the crumbling Norman castle for its annual day of merriment required all the foresight and strategy of a military campaign.

There were so many preparations to complete. Music, dancing, food, displays, general amusement. Kate was responsible for the first two items on that list, and she'd worked hard toward the success of the latter three as well.

By mid-morning, however, she seemed doomed to fail at them all.

First Miss Lorrish brought distressing news about the decorations. "Miss Taylor, we've tried three times now. The swags simply won't stay put on the southeastern turret."

Kate shaded her brow with one hand and gazed up at the limp purple bunting dangling sadly from the crenellated parapet. "I'll ask the militiamen to climb up and secure it."

Next, it was Miss Apperton's turn for a crisis. "Oh, Miss Taylor. I've broken the last good string for my lute."

"You may borrow mine," she offered.

Another hour smoothed most of the wrinkles, as children and families began to stream in from the countryside and village.

But then there was Miss Elliott. Poor, petrified Miss Elliott. The hapless young lady came skittering to Kate's side moments before the ladies were to sing the madrigal.

"I can't." Beneath her bonnet's wide brim, her cheeks blazed scarlet. "I just can't do it."

"You won't be alone," Kate assured her. "We're all singing together."

"But there are so many people. I didn't realize—" Her voice broke. "Please don't force me."

"Don't weep." Kate drew her into a tight hug. "Of course I won't force you. Just as long as you understand, I'm not giving up on you, either. We'll hear you sing another day." She pulled back and tilted her head to view under Miss Elliott's bonnet. "Now, then. Chin high, keep smiling. Right?"

Miss Elliott sniffed and tried to smile. "Yes, of course."

Poor girl.

When Kate considered that she might have been reunited with exacting relations like Miss Elliott's, she felt the magnitude of her good fortune.

Her gaze slid to the Gramercys, seated under the canopy reserved for guests of honor. In the center were two flower-bedecked thrones. Kate had asked Evan to sit as ceremonial king of the fair, with Diana Highwood playing the part of his regal, placid queen.

After the dancing, Kate had a short break while the children's hoop race went off. She made her way toward the canopy, meaning to check on Aunt Marmoset's comfort.

Mrs. Highwood intercepted her, however, and drew her quickly aside. "Don't they make a handsome couple?" she said. "I always knew Diana would do better than Minerva. Minerva might have caught herself a viscount, but now Diana will be a marchioness."

"Mrs. Highwood," Kate whispered through her teeth. "Please. They're sitting just a few feet away."

But the matron went on, undeterred. "Lord Drewe must fancy her. Why else would he have stayed in the village so long?"

"I've been giving Lady Lark music lessons."

Mrs. Highwood erupted in laughter. "Oh, Miss Taylor. Do you expect me to believe a man of Lord Drewe's fine looks, intelligence, manners, and stature would remain in this tiny village just for you?"

Kate sighed. No, she didn't expect Mrs. Highwood to believe it.

She didn't expect anyone to believe it.

Two days had passed since the night she came upon Evan playing the pianoforte in the Bull and Blossom, but those days were wholly consumed with preparations for today's festivities. There hadn't been any quiet opportunity to talk.

She kept thinking back to his cryptic comments that night. "That isn't the only way I can give you the family name."

Never in her life would she have dreamed that a marquess would hint at marrying her. And Mrs. Highwood was right—no one else would believe it, either.

It didn't matter, anyhow. Kate was otherwise engaged. Her public intentions, private attention, and, increasingly, tender emotions were all engaged by the man now taking the green.

The hoop race finished, and the militiamen claimed the center of attention for a short rifle drill. As they marched forward in formation, Kate delighted in the opportunity to stare. Pride swelled in her heart.

Thorne was a sight to behold. He wore his best officer's coat, of course. The uniform was designed to make any man look tall and fit, and when the man in question was already tall and fit, it made him look positively godlike.

"Of course," said Mrs. Highwood, "you should not feel bad, Miss Taylor. You have snagged yourself a corporal, and that is nothing to sniff at. For a young woman in your circumstances, a corporal is a fine catch indeed. Though I do think you could have managed a lieutenant. That would have been better."

"Would it?"

Kate couldn't imagine any man looking fitter, stronger, or more attractive than Thorne appeared to her eyes right now. She would not have traded him for a prince.

Lately, everyone—Mrs. Highwood, Evan, even Thorne himself—kept telling Kate she belonged with a different man. Perhaps common sense would argue the same.

But her heart was saying otherwise, and she couldn't ignore it any longer. There was a connection between them. Some bond she simply couldn't give up.

As the militia review concluded and Sir Lewis prepared for the grand finale—his demonstration with the trebuchet—Kate couldn't stay away.

She left the canopy and plucked the shiny brass helmet

from a displayed suit of medieval armor. Jogging across the green, she presented it to Thorne. She just had to be near him.

"Here," she said, breathless but smiling. "In case of melons."

He took the helmet and gave it a stern glare.

"Still no laugh?" She ducked and tilted her head, trying to catch his attention. "I was hoping you'd smile, at least. Well, I suppose I'll just have to keep trying."

His icy eyes met hers. "Don't."

She winced at the curt rejection. It seemed that whatever progress they'd made in Wilmington had vanished. He was shutting the door again.

She would find a window. "I mean to stay after the fair, to help put things to rights. We need some time to talk. Alone."

"I don't think—"

"We need to talk. It's important."

She took his silence as reluctant agreement.

"Miss Taylor!"

Kate turned to see Lark careening at her like a lawn bowl. Laughing, she grabbed Kate by the hand. "I'm stealing her, Corporal. Don't try to stop me."

Little did Lark know, she wasn't likely to encounter much resistance from Thorne's quarter. He looked only too pleased to see her go.

"What is it?" Kate asked as Lark tugged her away to a quiet corner of the ruins.

"Oh, Kate." The young lady flung her arms wide and captured her in an effusive hug. "I've been dying to talk to you alone. This is the perfect time, while everyone's paying attention to the demonstration."

"What's the matter?"

"Nothing's the matter. Everything's *perfect*. Evan

tells me we're going to consider it official. He has solicitors coming down to meet you and make everything right. We're going to claim you as a Gramercy." Lark gave a little squeal. "We're cousins. Isn't it wonderful?"

"Yes," Kate agreed, grinning. "It is."

Lark clasped Kate's hands, swinging them back and forth a bit. "Our holiday will be ending soon. We'll be leaving Spindle Cove."

"Oh. Oh, I'll miss you all very much."

"Goose." Lark squeezed her hands. "You'll come with us to Town, of course. I need you. I have ever so much shopping to do for my season, and it will be so much more fun if you're there. Harry couldn't care less about plumes and bonnets. I suppose I should have some actual music practice, too."

Kate turned her head and blinked hard.

"What's wrong, dear?"

"I . . ." She tried to smile. "It's too much to believe. I only wish I knew why you want me."

Lark put her hands on Kate's shoulders. "Because you're you. And because you're family. Family above everything." She cast a glance toward the bailey. "Honestly, I'm not sure why you'd want us, either. We've little to recommend ourselves, save pots of money."

"No," Kate said, earnestly shaking her head. "*No*. I would want to be a Gramercy even if you were poor pig farmers on the Isles of Scilly."

Lark laughed. "Well, Evan does pay a great deal of mind to agriculture. It's rather a bore sometimes. Don't worry about anything. There may be a touch of gossip, but this family has weathered many a scandal. Once the *ton* has a chance to meet you, you will only improve our overall standing, I suspect."

Kate couldn't quite believe that, but living with the Gramercys was social acceptance enough. When it came to the *ton,* she would simply do her best to stay out of the way.

"Oh!" Lark exclaimed. "I'm so stupid, I forgot. That's the entire reason I wanted to speak with you today. Evan says we must keep it all quiet a few days longer. But you'll be wanting to tell Corporal Thorne, of course. Now that you're part of the family, he'll be marrying into the Gramercys, too."

Kate's breath left her. "I hadn't even thought of that."

Goodness. If ever a man needed the acceptance of a family, it was Thorne. And despite his rocky start with Evan, if the Gramercys would so happily bring her into the fold, they would surely accept Thorne, too. Why would he want a cold, lonely cabin in the American wilderness when he could be a part of this?

But that would mean marrying him. And staying married to him, so long as they both should live. No simple prospect.

"Should you like to have the wedding at Ambervale?" Lark asked. "I thought it might be nice, since your parents were so happy there. It's your birthplace, you know. Your true home. I know you have your own plans, but promise me you'll discuss it with Corporal Thorne."

"I promise you," Kate said. "We'll discuss it."

"Have you been letting the dog chew books?"

"What?" Miss Taylor smiled. "Thorne, when I asked to speak to you alone, it wasn't about Badger's discipline. I told the Gramercys I'd be down to join them for dinner. We don't have much time."

Thorne glanced around the rapidly emptying castle

grounds. The fair was over, and daylight was fading. Everyone had gone down to the village for drinks and refreshments at the Bull and Blossom.

He pulled a small green volume from his pocket and waved it at her. "I had to pull this away from the dog yesterday. It's Lord Drewe's, you know." He displayed the chewed binding. "Now it's ruined. I don't know what to do about it."

"Well, don't concern yourself overmuch. Lord Drewe has other books to read, I'm sure."

Thorne snorted. Didn't he know it. Fosbury had told him the marquess had two full crates of books delivered to the village, along with all his other belongings.

Two *crates* of books. What possible use could a man have for them all? The sheer puzzle of it irritated him.

And the books themselves weren't even useful. He glared at the shredded volume. "Who the devil is . . ." He blinked and frowned at the letters again. "Ar . . ."

She took the book from him and peered at the chewed spine. "Aristotle. It's a Greek name."

"More Greeks? I don't suppose he was one of the men fighting over that Helen of Troy."

"He was a philosopher." She sighed. "It's not important right now."

"It is important. You shouldn't be letting Badger chew on these."

"I know, I know. He must have gotten that one when I wasn't looking." She shrugged. "We can get a replacement. Evan won't be angry."

"Evan?" Thorne jerked his head in surprise. A bright red burst of irrational jealousy pulsed through him. "So he's 'Evan' now?"

"Yes. That's what I needed to tell you. It's the most wonderful news. Lord Drewe has—"

She broke off abruptly and clapped a palm over her mouth.

A quick glance down told him why. A freshly killed rat had just been dropped at her feet, its hairless, worm-like tail still twitching.

As for the puppy who'd proudly delivered the kill— his furry tail was wagging like mad. A pink tongue dangled loose from a canine grin.

"Don't scream," Thorne warned her in a low, calm voice. As he spoke, he crouched beside the puppy and gave him a firm, affectionate rub. "Don't scold him, either. You'll only confuse him. This is a good thing."

"*This?*" she squeaked through her cupped palm, gesturing toward the lifeless rat with her free hand. "This is a good thing? I think I'm the one who's confused."

"After the fair, people will have left refuse everywhere around the castle. Apple cores, little morsels of cake. Draws the vermin. Badger chased down a rat, caught it, and denied himself the pleasure of eating it. That's precisely what he's been bred and trained to do, and now he deserves praise."

"What do I do?" she asked, still staring wide-eyed at the lifeless rat. "Don't ask me to touch it. I can't possibly touch it. It's only just stopped moving."

"You don't need to touch it. Just act like it's the best, most charming thing Badger's done in all his furry little life. And distract him, so I can toss the bleeding thing over the cliff."

She nodded. "All right."

While she fawned and cooed over the pup, Thorne found a shovel and disposed of the rat. Once he'd finished the work and rinsed his hands, he returned to find her cupping the pup's funny face in both her hands.

She made kissing noises. "You are the most clever puppy in all Sussex, Badger. Did you know that? So very brave. I just adore you."

Thorne watched her, quietly amazed. It just came so easily to her—loving encouragement. He supposed this quality was what made her a successful tutor.

She'd handled the shock of the rat quite well. Better than most ladies would, he imagined. She deserved some encouraging praise of her own—someone to frame her lovely face in his hands and tell her she was clever, beautiful, brave, adored.

But Thorne just didn't have that talent. It wasn't born in him, and he'd never had lessons, either. If love were music, he would be tone deaf.

"So what was your wonderful news?" he asked. "From 'Evan.'"

"Oh, yes." With one final loving pat, she released the dog and stood. "Lord Drewe says the family will claim me as their cousin."

Thorne's insides clenched. Wonderful news, indeed.

"Have they found some proof?" he asked.

She shook her head. "But Evan says there's proof enough for him. The birthmark, the parish register, the painting. And . . . I simply seem to fit. So they're making me part of the family. They want me to come with them to Town, to Ambervale . . . everywhere."

As she spoke of it, her face lit up. There she went again, glowing with happiness. Like a star, only further out of his reach.

He told himself not to be churlish. Perhaps this was the best possible outcome. The Gramercys . . . maybe they truly were just odd, not sinister. If they would accept her, with no further inquiries into her past . . .

Katie could have a glittering new life. She would never be forced to face the horrid truth.

This was good for her. And for him. He could go to America and not worry for her. He would think of her, always. But he wouldn't have to worry.

"Thorne," she whispered, "you should come. They're expecting it."

He shook his head. "Time's growing too short. My ship leaves from Hastings in just a few weeks. I suppose I could escort you as far as—"

Her hand clasped his. "I'm not asking you escort me," she said gently. "I'm asking you to come with me. And stay with me. With the family."

Stay? With the family?

He gazed at her in disbelief. "If you don't feel safe with them on your own, you needn't go."

"I feel perfectly safe. That's not my meaning." She paused. "I want you there, too. I know your own childhood was . . . less than idyllic."

He harrumphed. "Something less than it. Yes."

"Well, perhaps this can be your chance to feel a part of something larger than yourself. Part of a strange, delightful, loving family. Don't you want that, deep inside? Just a little?"

"I could never be a part of that."

"Why not?"

He blew out a breath. "You don't know me."

She bit her lip. "But I do. I *do* know you. Because I know myself. And I've been a lonely person, too." She took another step toward him, speaking softly. "I know how it wears on a soul. How it eats little pieces of your heart at unexpected times. How you can go whole weeks happily occupied, feeling no melancholy or deprivation, and then the smallest thing . . . Someone opens a letter, perhaps. Or stitches up a ripped garment that belongs to someone else. And it makes you realize how . . . adrift you are. Not tied to anyone."

"I don't—"

"And don't try to tell me that you have no emotions. That you're incapable of feeling anything at all. I know there's a heart in there."

It would seem there was. The cursed thing was pounding like a damned drum.

"Think this through," he said sternly. "You're not making sense. If the Gramercys make you part of their family, you will move in new circles of society. You could have a gentleman for a husband."

"A gentleman who wants me for connections and money? Perhaps. I'd rather have the man who wants me." She slid her arms around his neck. "You said you wanted me once."

Her nearness tormented him. Like all the ladies, she'd taken a great deal of care with her appearance today. Embroidered flowers covered the overskirt of her lavender gown. The high waistline of her bodice plumped her breasts like twin pillows—pillows edged with gold lace. She wore ribbons and flowers carefully braided into her hair.

It was far too quiet. They were much too alone.

"Of course I want you," he said roughly. "Every thought in my head is of you. Tasting you, touching you, taking you in ways your innocent mind can't even fathom. I don't know a cursed thing about art or music or Aristotle. My every thought is crude and base and so far beneath you, it might as well be on the opposite side of the earth."

Her cheeks colored. "I've told you, you're not beneath me."

Damn it. How could he make her understand?

"I own four books. Four."

She laughed a little. "What on earth does that signify?"

"It signifies everything. Your life is about to change, forever. I won't let you cling to me just because you're scared. It's not right. It's not what's best."

She moved closer. "We could marry, Thorne. I'm not asking for much. You can just . . . be yourself, and I'll amuse myself trying to make you happy. I know it'll be a challenge, but I'm strangely keen to try."

"For God's sake, Katie. Why?"

"I don't know how to explain it." Her gaze searched his face. "Have you ever known true hunger, Thorne? Not just a missed meal or two, but prolonged deprivation. No proper food for days on end."

He let a few seconds pass before affirming it. "Weeks."

Years.

"Then you must understand. Even now, surrounded by plenty, food looks different to you than it does to others, doesn't it? It tastes richer, means more. Years later, and you can't bring yourself to let the smallest scrap go to waste."

He nodded tightly.

"Let's not waste this," she whispered, reaching for him. "I don't know what it is between us, but I know I've hungered for it all my life. Maybe other women could walk away, but not me. Never me." She touched his cheek. "I think you're hungry for it, too."

She could have no notion. None. His heart was starved to a wasted shadow, with nothing left to offer now.

A smile spread across her face, broad with mischief. "Just think of all we could have. Two unwanted orphans, taking on London society. We'd wring more pleasure from every moment than people like the Gramercys can find in a year. Can you tell me honestly that you want no part of that life?"

Staying here in England and living on Lord Drewe's charity? Enduring endless balls and dinners and hunting parties? Always feeling like the outsider; forever knowing he was so much less than she deserved? He wouldn't even be able to support her like a real man.

He looked her in the eye. "I want no part of that life. It's time for you to release me."

Her lovely hazel eyes softened and her gaze fell to his lips.

"I just can't," she said. "I'm not letting you go."

Chapter Thirteen

Kiss me, Kate willed silently.

Please. I've just laid my heart at your feet. Kiss me now, or I'll die of disappointment.

She knew he was tempted. He stared at her mouth so intently, she could taste the softness and strength and heat of his lips. Her own jaw softened in response. She could see it so clearly, in her mind's eye. Just how that kiss would go. She would be yielding and open, inviting him in. The boldness of his possession would shock and excite her. She would cling to him, and his big hands would roam every bit of her body. Their kiss would be frenzied at first, and then slow, sweet.

"Thorne."

She caught his gaze. His pupils were so dilated, his eyes were almost entirely black. Even so, that thin orbit of blue was so intense, so piercing—she felt it *inside* her.

A sudden realization gave her a thrill. In *her* imagination, they were kissing. In *his* mind, they were doing something much more intimate. More animal, with far fewer clothes.

The thought enflamed her. Inexperienced as she was, she knew enough to sense her feminine power in the situation. He might say no to family and comfort and connection. But could he truly refuse this?

She leaned forward until her cheek met his. Just a simple press of skin to skin, and it was like nothing she'd ever felt.

"Is it . . ." She forced herself to ask, "Is it always like this? With your other women?"

He shook his head slowly. The scrape of his whiskers against her jaw—oh, it made her wild. But it wasn't enough.

"No?" she prompted. She had to hear him say it. She had to hear him say *something*. His voice could stroke her, so very deep.

At last he gave her what she craved. "No."

That dark, thrilling syllable whispered hot against her ear and sank into her very bones.

"Well?" she asked, breathily. "Shouldn't we do something about it?

He groaned and shuddered, and she suspected he was mentally thumbing through a whole catalog of things he would *like* to do about it. Some sort of lovemaking drill book with all possible positions and maneuvers clearly defined. The precise contents would be a mystery to her—but she was ready and willing to learn.

Shameless, she tugged on his neck and pulled him forward until she could kiss his ear.

He sighed. "I can't give you what you need."

"Oh, I think you can." She caught his earlobe in her teeth and worried it.

With a husky groan, he gave in. He dipped his head, and his strong lips brushed her pulse.

"You don't see yourself," he said. "When you're

around the Gramercys, it's like a flame comes to life inside you." He marched a column of kisses down her neck. "You don't light up for me."

She pressed her body to his. "I *burn* for you, Thorne. I've never felt this way. I never knew I *wanted* to feel this way."

She pulled at his neckcloth, unknotting the fabric and tugging it free. She pressed a kiss to the dark notch at the base of his throat, then nuzzled there, inhaling the arousing musk of his skin. His raspy breathing gave her hope.

She was getting to him. Delving through the layers, uncovering the man beneath.

All those buttons of his coat must come next. She worked the top one loose with trembling fingers.

"You called me scared," she said, "and I am frightened. But not the way you think. I'm terrified that I'll part ways with you, and I'll live my whole life without feeling this again."

She chanced a look at him then, pleading with her eyes. Begging him to give in to her, to take control of this . . . just do *something,* before she was forced to rip open her bodice and say something truly embarrassing like, *Make me a woman.*

"It's only desire you're feeling." His brow was heavy, disapproving. "Curiosity. If I give in to it, you'll despise me afterward."

"I could never despise you."

"Yes, you could. You spent a full year doing just that."

She cursed under her breath. He *would* have to point that out. "I was a fool. I didn't know you. I didn't know my own heart."

His gaze sharpened. "What makes you think you know it now?"

"I don't know," she said honestly. "I don't know. But this afternoon, Lark Gramercy came to me and offered everything I ever thought I wanted. A family. A home. Security, friendship, society. More wealth than I'd ever dreamed. And at that moment, I knew in my heart it still wouldn't be enough. Either I'm the most greedy, ungrateful woman in England, or I'm . . ."

God, could it be true?

Her heart told her it must be. Nothing else made sense.

"Thorne, I think I'm falling in love with you."

"Katie." He took her face in his hands. Roughly, and with a possessive power that thrilled her. A brooding divot formed between his eyebrows. "Katie, you're so—"

She wondered what delightfully misanthropic word he would choose this time. Wrongheaded? Foolish? Stubborn?

Kissable, apparently.

He gave up on words and claimed her mouth instead, kissing her with more passion and fire than she would have ever dared to hope. One of his hands slid down her back, coasting over silk and sweeping hot sensation all the way to the base of her spine. But he didn't stop there. His touch dipped farther. He spread his fingers to cup her backside, then lifted and squeezed, pulling her pelvis flush against his. Pleasure sparkled through her veins. She moaned into his kiss and clutched his neck so hard, her fingernails would surely leave marks. He didn't seem to mind.

He kissed her deeply, pushing her jaw wide and swallowing her desperate gasps of pleasure. She writhed against him, pressing close to feel the abundant evidence of his lust for her. The solid ridge of his arousal pulsed against her belly. She wanted to feel that heat where it belonged—against her sex. As they kissed, she twined one leg around his booted calf, grasping his shoulders to work herself higher . . . closer . . .

Drat.

Badger pulled them back from the brink of paradise. Some yards away, the puppy started barking like a creature possessed.

"Ignore the dog," she murmured, tugging Thorne back to the kiss. Catching and sipping at his bottom lip. "He's perfectly fine."

"He's fine," he echoed. "It's just another rat."

"Yes."

Yes.

His hand swept over her curves, lingering for a brief, delicious squeeze of her backside before dipping to caress her thigh. He gathered a large fistful of her skirt and tugged, drawing her body just as tight and close as she craved and exposing her ankles to the cooling afternoon air.

With one hand, he delved under her skirts and petticoats, encircling her thigh in his grip. The feel of his work-roughed palm against her stockinged leg inflamed her. And her desire only mounted as he swept his touch higher still. Over her ribbon garter, up the sensitive slope of her bare inner thigh, and . . .

There.

It amazed her, how easily he claimed her most intimate, untouched places, and how little timidity she felt. His fingertips traced the cleft of her sex, slipping easily over her aroused flesh.

"So wet," he murmured.

The words shocked her. She wanted to hear more.

He stilled, resting his temple against hers. His breath

stirred her hair as he traced her intimate flesh in slow, tantalizing strokes.

"For me?" he whispered. The vulnerable rasp in his voice undid her.

She kissed his jaw. "For you. Only you."

He rewarded her boldness. Deftly parting her folds, he slipped one broad, callused fingertip inside.

A startled cry of joy escaped her.

"Hush," he soothed. "Hush. I won't take too much. Only let me ease you this once." He nibbled lightly at her ear and neck, stroking deeper. "You'll feel better afterward, see matters clearer. It will be enough."

Enough? What foolishness. She'd never known such an exquisite blend of sensual relief and desperate hunger for more. He claimed her lips in a kiss, and their moans mingled as he cupped her sex in his clever, wicked hand. His tongue and his finger thrust in unison, moving deeper by gentle yet steady degrees. She gripped his shoulders, rocked by wave after wave of devious pleasure.

Yes. Oh, yes. She wanted this. Him inside her. The two of them, joined in every way. And it would never be enough. She would always crave more.

More.

His hand stilled.

Kate panted for breath. Was something wrong?

Apparently so. He withdrew his touch completely, letting her skirts fall loose to the ground, and Kate's muddled senses finally gathered why.

It was Badger again. More barking. More dashing about. More ruining everything.

Drat, drat, *drat.*

With a muttered curse, Thorne turned to follow the dog with his eyes. "He's got his sights on something."

"Only a rat, surely."

"Perhaps."

The dog disappeared around a corner of the castle ruins, growling and snarling as he went.

"But perhaps not." Thorne released her with a sigh of obvious regret. "It's not like him to behave that way."

That was it, then. The moment was gone.

Thorne strode off in pursuit. Resigned to it, Kate picked up her skirts and followed after both dog and man.

They rounded the corner of a crumbling sandstone wall.

Badger had his quarry cornered in a shadowy niche. The puppy stood at attention, growling at whatever it was he'd captured.

"I don't see any rat," Kate said, drawing nearer. "Perhaps it's only a tiny vole?" She moved closer to investigate.

Thorne caught her by the arm, holding her back. "Don't."

Kate froze. When uttered in that tone, it wasn't a command she could refuse.

Then she saw the reason for his sudden change in demeanor. It wasn't a rat or a vole Badger had cornered, but a snake. A long, thick adder curling in on itself and weaving figure eights in the matted grass—less than a yard from her slippers. A thin tendril of tongue flickered out, and the snake's hiss crawled down her spine.

The puppy—brave, foolish thing—stood his ground at her feet, still snarling and preparing to pounce.

She could see very easily what would happen. The snake was backed into a corner, and the creature no doubt knew—in whatever way snakes knew these things—its only chance of escape was to strike.

"Oh. He'll be bitten." Kate struggled against Thorne's grip. "Badger, no. Come away from that horrid thing."

She attempted to reach for him, but Thorne held her back.

"Shush," he said firmly. "I'll see to him. Just don't move."

He released her arm. Kate clenched her fists at her sides to keep still. Her fingernails bit into her palms.

Thorne planted his boots in the grassy turf. Then, moving with excruciating slowness, he stretched his right arm as he leaned forward, spreading his fingers wide. As he leaned, the full length of his hard thigh pressed against the back of her leg. She could feel the leashed power in his every small motion.

Just a little farther. A few inches more and he'd be able to snatch the puppy by the scruff, deliver him up and away.

Oh, hurry, she pleaded inwardly, even though she knew sudden movements would be disaster.

Thorne ceased moving altogether. His outstretched right arm went ramrod straight, and she could feel the energy tensing in his muscles. It made the hairs on her arm lift. Like quiet thunder rumbling through a cloud.

Then came the lightning strike.

With a powerful lunge forward, he reached out—

And grabbed the snake.

Five seconds and it was over. Once Thorne had the adder in hand, he doubled the length and snapped its spine. The writhing coil of green-sheathed muscle fell lifeless to the ground.

Badger kept right on barking.

Kate fell to her knees, scooping up the dog, clutching him to her chest and peppering his fur with kisses.

"Why did you do that?" she asked Thorne. "You might have just reached for Badger and pulled him out of harm's way."

Thorne shook his head. "That snake was going to strike when I did," he said. "If I'd reached for the dog, those fangs would have found your ankle instead."

Good Lord. He'd never had any intention of reaching for Badger. He just grabbed for the snake with his bare hand, rather than risk it biting her. How exceedingly reckless and stupidly brave.

"You shouldn't have done that."

Leaning against the stone wall, he turned his hand this way and that. "I reckoned I could weather it."

Kate's heart stalled. "What do you mean? Were you bitten?"

When he didn't answer, she released Badger and scrambled to her feet.

"Let me look." She reached for his wrist, and he did not fight her as she raised his big, roughened hand to the light for examination. "Oh, no."

There they were. Two neat, round punctures just where the heel of his hand met his wrist. The area around the bite was already puffing with blood.

"We must go to your quarters. Do you have a medical kit? This needs to be treated, and quickly."

"It's only an adder bite."

"*Only? Only* an adder bite?"

He shrugged. "Just a scratch."

"A scratch infected with venom." She pulled on his sleeve, tugging him back toward the castle keep.

"There's a lot of me. It would take more than a few drops of poison to bring me down."

Nevertheless, he walked with her to the corner of the

keep that served as his personal quarters. As he nudged the door open with his left shoulder, she saw him misjudge his step and stumble against the door.

"Are you dizzy?"

"Just . . . a misstep." But he stayed there, leaning against the door, his eyes unfocused. "Give me a minute."

Absolutely not. At the rate his hand was swelling, she wouldn't give him another second.

She found a stool beside the lone, small table and braced it against the turret's interior stone wall.

"Sit down," she ordered. He might be a big, intimidating infantry officer, accustomed to having men march, load, and fire at his command—but she would not be countermanded on this score. She grabbed his good arm and pulled with all her might.

Oof. He barely budged. Goodness, he was just an enormous lump of masculinity, all muscle and heavy boots. There was a lot of him, as he'd said.

"I'm well," he protested.

"I'm worried. Humor me."

Kate coaxed him to the stool and made sure he sat with his back well braced against the wall. Badger came to his heels, sniffing about his boots and making small whining noises.

Once Thorne was seated, she began tugging at his sleeve. "I'm sorry. We have to remove your coat."

She began with the sleeve of his injured right arm, carefully drawing the red wool sheath down until he could pull his entire arm free. She eased a hand behind his shoulder to help him out of the sleeve. An involuntary tremor passed through his sculpted shoulder muscles—a whispered confession of the danger he faced, despite his impressive size and strength. Kate shivered in response.

While she propped his wounded wrist on the table for examination, he twisted his torso and shook the garment down his left arm. The red coat slid to the floor.

He gave the discarded coat a regretful look. She knew it must pain him to see the uniform crumpled on the ground. But he didn't bend to retrieve it.

"Perhaps I'm not so well," he said.

Her pounding pulse accelerated. If he admitted it, he must be very bad off indeed.

A serrated knife lay on the table. She reached for it.

"Be still," she warned.

With clumsy swipes of the blade, she laid open the linen sleeve of his shirt, rending it all the way up to the elbow. Angry streaks of red blazed from the adder bite. She could follow those streaks halfway up his thick, muscled forearm, even through the covering of dark hair. She needed a tourniquet.

When she raised her head to ask Thorne where one might be, she saw that his face had gone pale. A thin sheen of perspiration covered his brow, and his breathing was uneven. She reached for his unknotted cravat and worked it loose with trembling fingers. He tilted his head back to assist her. As her fingers brushed the freshly shaven skin of his throat, she could see the pulse beating beneath his jaw, as though a butterfly were trapped under his skin.

His Adam's apple bobbed. "You're undressing me," he said thickly.

"It can't be helped."

"Wasn't complaining."

Once she had the cravat free, she doubled the arm's-length strip of fabric and wound it around his arm, just below the elbow. She took one end of the fabric and clenched it in her teeth, then pulled the other end with both hands. Her efforts wrenched a groan of pain from his throat. By the time the thing was in place, she was huffing for breath and sweating just as much as he was.

"Where is your medical kit?" she asked, already scanning the room for likely places.

He slid his gaze toward a battered wooden chest on a high shelf.

Kate hastened to the shelf and stretched up on her toes to retrieve the box.

When she turned back, she nearly dropped it. Thorne had the knife in his left hand. His sweat-covered brow was furrowed with concentration and he was pressing the serrated blade against the angry, swollen skin at his wrist.

"Oh, don't—"

He grimaced and twisted the knife. A growl of pain forced through his clenched teeth, but his hand didn't falter. Before she could reach his side, he'd turned the blade a quarter turn and slashed through the distended flesh again. Blood flowed freely from the crossed incisions.

He let the knife fall to the table and slumped back against the wall, breathing hard.

"Why'd you do that?" she asked, carrying the kit to the table.

"So you wouldn't have to."

Kate was thankful. She knew he'd done the right thing. Releasing the blood—and venom—from the swollen area was necessary, lest it travel to other parts of his body. But the sight of so much blood stunned her motionless for a moment. She had helped Susanna a time or two when she'd treated the villagers' illnesses and injuries. But that was offering a bit of assistance to a skilled, competent healer. This was the two of them, alone with desperate measures.

He could die.

A wave of nausea passed through her. She rode the crest of it, then put a hand to her belly and willed herself to be calm.

Kate opened the chest and found a clean-looking length of gauze in the medical kit. She used it to dab blood from the seeping wound.

"Don't bind it," he said. "Not yet."

She nodded. "I know. What do we do next?"

"You go back to the village. I either live or I don't."

The words were so absurd, she choked on a wild laugh. "Are you mad, Thorne? I'm not leaving you."

She rifled through the bottles and jars in the medical kit, straining to read the faded labels. None of the contents looked familiar. "You said you own four books. I don't suppose any are books of physic?"

He nodded toward a shelf. Kate dashed to it and found a well-thumbed military drill book, a Bible coated in dust, a bound collection of geographical magazines . . .

"Aha." She seized on a large black volume and peered at the title. *"Treatment of Ailments and Injuries in . . ."* Her hope dwindled as she read the remainder aloud. " *. . . in Horses and Cattle?* Thorne, this is a veterinary book."

"I've been called a beast." He closed his eyes.

Kate decided she didn't have the time to be particular. She quickly paged through the book until she found the section on bites and stings. "Here we are. Adder bites. 'The sting of the adder is rarely fatal.' Well, that's reassuring."

Although she would have felt a great deal better had it read "the sting of the adder is never fatal." To say adder bites were "rarely fatal" seemed to her the same as saying "adder bites are *occasionally* fatal," and Thorne did pride himself on being an exception to ordinary conduct.

But there was a lot of him, she reminded herself. And all of it was young, healthy, and strong. Very strong.

There were several possible remedies suggested in the text.

She read aloud, " 'First, squeeze out the blood.' We've done that, haven't we? Good." She made an impatient swipe at a lock of hair dangling in her face and continued. " 'Take a handful of the herb crosswort, some gentian and rue, boil together in a thin broth with Spanish pepper and some ends of broom, and when that is done, strain and boil with some white wine for about an . . .' " She growled. "About an *hour*?"

Drat. She didn't have time to go scouting for a dozen different herbs, much less boil them for an hour. She didn't even dare leave Thorne for the time it would take to run to the village for help.

She glanced at his face again. God, he was so pale. And his arm was entirely swollen now. Despite the tourniquet, those streaks of red had reached his elbow and beyond. His fingers were purple in some places.

"Do be calm," she said, even as anxiety pitched her voice. "I've several more remedies to go through."

She went back to the book. The next suggested remedy was to wash the affected area with salt and . . .

Urine.

Oh, good Lord. At least *that* substance was obtainable, but still. She couldn't. She couldn't possibly. Or perhaps she could, to preserve a man's life. But she'd never be able to look at the preserved man again.

She sent up a fervent prayer that the third remedy would prove suitable to save both his life and their combined dignity. She read aloud with rapidity. "'Lay a plaster to the area, with a salve made of calamint pounded with turpentine and yellow wax. And give the animal some infusion of calamint to drink, as a tea or mixed in milk.'"

Calamint. Calamint sounded perfect. If only she had some.

Kate went back to the medical kit and peered at all the contents of the bottles. She uncorked a vial stuffed with a dried herb that looked promising. When she held it to her nose and sniffed, she supposed it smelled as much like calamint as anything.

She looked around the room. There was a great deal to be done. Light a fire, boil water, melt wax, pound the salve, make a tea. And Thorne was tilting dangerously on that stool she'd given him. At any moment he'd topple the small pedestal table and crash to the floor.

She decided his wound had bled long enough. The extreme swelling had slowed the blood flow to an ooze, anyhow. She wrapped a bit of linen about his wrist as a loose bandage, then made her way to his good side.

"Up," she directed, sliding her shoulder beneath his unbitten arm. "We're going to take you to the bed."

As she helped him to his feet, she could feel his eyes on her. His stare was heavy and intent.

"Am I causing you pain?" she asked.

"Always. Every time you're near."

She turned her face away to hide her wounded reaction. "I'm sorry."

"Not what I meant." He sounded drunk. With his healthy hand, he nudged her jaw until she faced him. "You're too beautiful. It hurts."

Wonderful. Now he was hallucinating.

Together, they shuffled toward his narrow bed. It was

only a distance of a half-dozen feet, but it felt like miles. Her spine hunched under his formidable weight.

At last they reached the edge of the mattress. She managed to turn them so that when she removed her support, he sat down on the edge of the bed. Without much urging from her, he reclined onto his back.

There. That took care of head, shoulders, and torso. Now, to get his legs on the mattress, too.

"I feel strange," he said dreamily. "Heavy."

"You *are* heavy," she muttered, straining to lift one of his massive boots from the floor and heave his leg onto the bed. Goodness, lifting him felt like lifting a statue carved of granite. Once she had the first leg in place, the second came easier. Badger leapt onto the bed and curled between his boots.

She leaned over him to place the pillow under his head.

"I can see down your bodice," he remarked.

A thrill shot down her spine, leaving her body through the soles of her feet.

Really, Kate. This isn't the time.

She laid the back of her hand to his forehead. Hot to the touch.

"You're feverish. I need to strip the rest of your shirt, to cool your body and ease your breathing."

She reached for the knife, wiped it clean of blood, and used it to make a notch in the neckline of his shirt. Then she grabbed both sides and ripped it straight down the front, pushing the halves to either side and working the remaining sleeve down his good arm.

When she'd bared his chest, she startled. He didn't seem to notice her shock, and she wasn't sure whether his insensibility was a fortunate thing or a very bad sign.

But since he didn't notice . . . she openly stared. His

chest was hard, sculpted muscle covered with tanned skin. She saw a liberal sprinkling of dark hair, a few healed scars . . .

And tattoos. Several tattoos.

Kate had heard of such things. She knew many sailors had patterns or pictures inked into their skin, but she'd never seen an example in person, to her recollection. Definitely not this close.

Not all of Thorne's tattoos were patterns or pictures. There was an abstract design of some kind on his upper right chest, encircled by a medallion just smaller than her palm. On his shoulder was a tiny, crudely drawn flower—rather like a Tudor rose. A row of numbers marched up the underside of his left arm. And on the side of his rib cage, she found a pair of letters: B and C.

So primitive. So *fascinating*. She couldn't help but lay her fingers to those letters and wonder what they meant. The initials of some former sweetheart, perhaps? She knew he'd had lovers, but the notion of Thorne with a sweetheart seemed absurd. Almost as absurd as the spike of jealousy twisting in her chest.

But when she touched his skin, the scalding heat reminded her of the larger task at hand. Keeping this immense, stubborn, tattooed man alive.

She tried to rise from the bed, but his good arm shot out to catch her. He still had some strength in him, apparently, and he used it to pull her close.

"What is it?" she asked.

"You smell so good." His eyes were closed, and his voice was a low, rummy drawl. "Like clover."

She swallowed. "I don't even know what clover smells like."

"Then you need a good roll in it."

She laughed a little. If he was making jokes, he couldn't be beyond hope.

Then his muscles seized and his eyes rolled back as he thrashed on the mattress. She put her hands to his chest and leaned all her weight on them, holding him to the bed.

He fell limp, panting. His hand found and tangled in her loosened hair. "Katie. I'm dying."

"You're not dying. Adder bites are rarely fatal. That's what the book said. But I need to make you some salve, and a tea."

He held her fast, forbidding her to move. "I'm dying. Stay with me."

Desperation pressed on her, but Kate forcibly held it at bay. She reminded herself of what Susanna had once told her—big, strong men always made the worst, most infantile patients when forced to a sickbed. If they took sick with a cold, they moaned and complained as though they were at death's door. Thorne was simply overreacting. She hoped.

She stroked a touch over his perspiring brow. "You'll be fine. I'll just go make you some—"

"You don't know me."

"I do. I know you far better than you give me credit for. I know you're brave and good and—"

"No, you don't know. You don't recall me. But it's best. When I first arrived, I worried. Feared you might place me. At times, I almost hoped you would. But it's . . ." He drew a raspy breath. "It's best this way."

"What do you mean?" Kate's every nerve jumped to attention. "It's best what way?"

"You've done so well for yourself, Katie. If she could see you, she'd be . . . so proud . . ." His voice trailed off and he closed his eyes.

What did he just say?

She shook his arm. "Who? Who'd be proud?"

"Sing for me," he whispered. "Your sweet voice will be the last thing I hear. I'll carry a little echo of heaven with me, even when they drag me down to hell."

She didn't know what to make of any of his rambling. Perhaps he was simply delirious. That had to be the explanation.

"I have to pound the herbs," she choked out. "There's a salve you need, and then some tea."

"Sing." His grip on her hair went slack, and he pulled his fingers through her loosened curls. "Only not . . . not the garden. Not the blossoms so fair. Don't sing that verse for me."

She froze, stunned. "How do you know that song? When did you hear me sing it?"

"Always hated . . . hearing it from your lips."

She searched her memory, trying to recall if she'd ever sung that verse in his presence. She didn't think so. Even if she had, why would he hate it? "Have you been following me? Spying on me?"

He made no answer.

Well, Kate needed answers, and she was going to have them. She extricated herself from his grasp. "Lie still in that bed and let me make you some salve. We will talk about all this when you've recovered."

"Katie, just sing to me. I'm dy—"

She grabbed him by the jaw and gave his head a brisk shake, forcing him to open his eyes. His pupils were so wide, there was almost no blue in them.

"You are not dying," she told him. "Do you hear me, Thorne?"

"Aye." His eyes slowly focused on her face. "But just in case . . ."

He pulled her mouth down to his, catching her in a kiss.

A wild, feverish, dangling-on-the-brink-of-death kiss.

He'd caught her unawares, lips parted. The result was a passionate, open-mouthed tangle of tongues and teeth. There was nothing tender in this kiss, nor even seductive. It was hot, possessive, fierce, and it held nothing back for tomorrow. As his tongue swept deep into her mouth, again and again, she could taste his hunger and desperation. His need resonated as a deep ache in her bones.

And she found herself answering. Out of pure instinct, she was kissing him back. Letting her tongue rub against his. With each slide of that sweet friction, desire spiraled through her. He moaned against her mouth and gripped her so tightly it hurt.

When the kiss broke apart, Kate was left reeling.

Which put her better off than Thorne, who slumped back onto the bed, unconscious.

"No. *No.*"

Frantic, she put a hand to his throat and felt for his pulse. It was there. Steady, if rather fast.

She had to act quickly. She rose from the bedside. From the table, she gathered up the vial of calamint.

Salve first. Tea, second. Prayers, third.

Extensive questioning later on.

As she took the tinderbox to the hearth, she spoke to him. "You are not going to die, do you understand me? I will not allow it. I am going to save your life if I have to barter with the devil for it."

Whatever information Thorne was hiding, she'd be damned if she let him take it to his grave. She needed answers.

And she needed *him.*

Chapter Fourteen

He dreamt of a giant serpent. A thick rope of ominous power, sliding down the narrow alleys of London. Twining through gardens and thickets in Kent. Last, snaking over the low, rolling hills of Sussex . . . tracing the scent of salt all the way to the ocean. It had followed him here, to this ancient castle, where it slithered in through the turret's smoke vent and dropped to the bed. It wound its length again and again about his arm.

It squeezed.

Devil take me.

The pressure was so intense, Thorne sensed his very bones pulverizing. Then, as if inflicting that flesh-grinding pain wasn't enough, the dream snake settled on his chest. Each breath felt like a struggle to lift a hundredweight with his ribs.

Thorne wrestled the scaly beast for untold hours, thrashing and grappling with the pain. Finally, mercifully, it faded into blackness.

Sometime later he woke with a start.

All was dark, save for firelight. He couldn't move.

Repeated efforts to draw up his legs or rise to a sitting position came to naught. His limbs wouldn't obey his commands.

He stared up at the ceiling, panting for breath. A bead of sweat trickled from his brow to his ear. The room was thick with the scents of herbs and tallow.

How much time had passed? Hours? Days?

He heard someone rustling over by the hearth.

"Katie?" he croaked.

She didn't hear him. As she went about stirring the fire, she hummed a little tune.

He closed his eyes and went back to that very first day. He'd entered the Bull and Blossom and there she'd been. Singing.

He hadn't recognized her, not at first. How could he? She was a woman now, near twenty years older than when he'd seen her last. And her profile was to him— the unmarked side. To his battle-weary eyes, she was just a fresh-faced girl in white.

To his ears, she was some sort of angel.

She hit this note—a soft, plaintive trill—and that was it. He was done for.

That note found the vulnerable slot between his plates of armor, wriggled in deep and sank in teeth. Her voice was the sweetest venom. It was in his blood, his heart, pumping all through his body before he could muster any defense. All sorts of impulses swelled in response: affinity, desire, protectiveness. An intense, sudden hunger for her approval.

Naturally, a well-bred lady of accomplishment would not look at a man like him. Nor should she. He'd formed no plans or expectations. But simply to know he *could* feel such things was a source of true wonder. He'd been numb for so long.

She'd struck the last chord, and the music eased into a full, vibrating silence. He would not have noticed a powder blast in the lane.

Then she'd risen from the pianoforte to take her seat. He saw the mark at her temple, and the truth detonated.

Good Lord. It was her. *Katie*.

Waifish, sweet-faced Katie, all grown up. Now it all made sense. There was a reason he felt a strong sense of recognition—because he did know her. He felt protective toward her because she'd once been in his keeping. And that hunger for her approval . . . it too had its roots in a time long past, when she'd looked up to him with something akin to worship in her eyes.

All these impulses inside him . . . they were echoes of something he'd lost long ago. Some memory of the humanity that had long since been beaten, starved, and flogged out of him.

She didn't know him, of course. She couldn't have remembered—she'd been too young, and now they were too different. They'd started in the same low trough of their youth but climbed opposites sides of the valley. Now there was a chasm between them, and even if she shaded her brow and peered hard, she'd probably never recognize him across it. But what mattered was that she had survived. She'd forged a new life well apart from that squalid misery they once shared. And he'd vowed to himself then and there—no matter how alluring he found her, he would never do anything to jeopardize her happiness.

A year of mostly successful avoidance. And then he made the idiot mistake of letting her hold his dog. A lurcher pup bred too well for his own good, cornering the first snake he happened to meet.

Badger lay curled at the foot of the bed. Thorne glowered at the sleeping ball of fur. *This is all your fault, I hope you know.*

"You're awake." Soft footfalls crossed to the bedside. A cool hand pressed to his brow. "I'm here."

"How long have I been insensible?"

"Since yesterday afternoon. It's a few hours yet before dawn, I think." She stroked the hair back from his brow. "Thank God your fever's broken. And the swelling's much improved."

He let his head fall to one side and surveyed his condition. Most of his body was draped with a clean white linen sheet, save for his injured right arm, which lay atop the bedclothes. The tourniquet was gone. A fragrant plaster covered his wound, held in place with strips of flannel. His entire arm had been washed clean, and the swelling had abated. The discoloration remained, however—red streaks and purple-black bruises covered his skin. It looked as though his arm had been caught in a clothespress.

He'd lived through worse. His arm scarcely hurt anymore. Instead, it felt numb. He flexed his muscles, attempting to make a fist. His fingers gave a feeble twitch.

Then he tried once more to draw up his legs. Nothing. That worried him.

"Drink this."

She brought a cup of tea to his lips. He bent his head and sipped. The infusion had an herbal, faintly familiar taste. He thought he recalled her spooning it through his cracked lips sometime during the night.

"You stayed by me," he said. "All night."

She nodded. "I could not have done otherwise."

"I'm in your debt."

"I'll think of ways you can repay me." She gave him a wry, cryptic smile.

He glanced down at his uncooperative limbs and hesitated. "I . . . I can't move. I can't move my body below the neck."

She didn't show quite the concern or dismay he might have expected. "Oh, I know you can't."

He frowned with confusion.

She reached for the edge of the linen and lifted it, so he might peer beneath. Several lengths of bedsheet and neckcloth were tied about his torso and left arm, lashing him to the bed.

Bindings. Now that he understood they were there, he could feel similar restraints on his legs. All the knots were well out of reach.

"Why would you do that?"

"At first, because you were thrashing so much."

Damn it. If he'd lashed out at her while he was insensible, he'd never forgive himself.

"Did I—" The words stuck. He cleared his throat with a harsh, desperate cough. "Did I hurt you?"

"No."

Thank God.

"But you were delirious, and I worried you'd do yourself more harm. So I bound you. And then I left the bindings on because"—she replaced the linen sheet, brought a chair to the bedside and fixed him with a challenging look—"you have some explaining to do."

His heart began to pound. "I don't know what you mean."

"Don't you? When you fell ill yesterday, you did a great deal of talking. About you and me."

"Must have been delirious." He eyed the cup in her hand. "I'll take some more of that tea, if you will."

"Not just yet." She balanced the pewter mug between

her hands and twisted it back and forth. "You seemed to think we knew each other."

"We *do* know each other."

"In the past," she said. "As children."

A knot formed in his throat. He struggled harder against his bindings. "You must be confused. I don't recall saying any such thing."

"I thought that might be the case." She set the mug aside and reached for a sheet of paper. "Fortunately, I wrote it all down."

Damn it.

She smoothed flat the creases in the paper.

He strove to look bored.

She made her voice comically deep and gruff. In an imitation of him, he supposed. "'You've done so well for yourself, Katie. If she could see you, she'd be so proud.'" She lowered the paper. "Who were you speaking of? Who would be proud?"

He shook his head. "You need to release me from these bindings so I can see you home. You're overtired. You're imagining things."

She waved the paper at him. "I'm not imagining this!"

At her loud protest, the pup came awake.

"There was something about how you'd worried I might place you, remember you," she went on. "You also mentioned that you could see down my bodice, and you told me I smelled like paradise."

"Miss Taylor—"

"So now we're back to 'Miss Taylor.' What happened to 'Katie'?" She peered at him. "That's another odd thing, you know. My name is Katherine. My friends call me Kate. No one calls me Katie. At least, no one has since I was a very small child."

"Release me." He mustered his voice of command.

"I'll see you home. It's not proper for you to be here with me. Most certainly not alone, at this hour."

"I'm not going anywhere until you give me some answers."

"Then you'll be here a very long time."

She could keep him here a month, and his resolve wouldn't crumble. He'd endured much harsher prisons, with much less comely captors. He could hold out for years.

"How does your arm feel?" she asked, changing the subject.

"How does it feel? It feels like wood."

"I did some more reading while you were asleep. You can expect it to be numb for a few days, at least." Her skirts rustled as she swept to the other side of the bed. She produced a vial of oil and pulled out the stopper. Tilting the bottle, she poured a shilling-sized pool of liquid into her palm. "This will help with the stiffness, the book said. It's only plain oil from your cooking stores. I'll fetch something aromatic from Summerfield later."

She set aside the vial and rubbed her hands together, spreading the oil over both palms. Then she laid her hands to his bare skin and began to massage his deadened flesh. Her deft fingers kneaded him, chasing away the stiffness in his forearm.

Unfortunately, the stiffness wasn't leaving his body altogether. No, it was merely relocating—to his groin. Beneath the bedsheet a familiar heaviness gathered and swelled.

He groaned. "Stop that."

"Is it too painful?"

No. It feels too good.

"Will it help if I sing to you?" she asked coyly. "The

way you begged me to sing to you last night?" She hummed a lilting melody, then sang the words that he already knew. " 'See the garden of blossoms so fair . . .' "

He sighed and closed his eyes. God, he hated that song.

" 'Roses in bloom,' " she sweetly sang on, " 'orchids so rare.' "

"Stop," he growled at her. "Enough."

Her massaging hands swept down the length of his arm, all the way to the bandage at his wrist. She turned his arm palm side up and simply laid her fingers across his hand.

"I've been staring at you all night. Searching what few memories I have from my earliest years. The more I look at you, the more I feel like there's a puzzle I should be solving. But the pieces just won't come together in my mind. And if you won't volunteer any information . . ."

He sucked in his breath.

" . . . then I have no choice but to bring out my most ruthless means of extorting it."

"You're threatening *me* with ruthlessness," he scoffed.

"Don't you think I have it in me?"

She caught the hemmed edge of the bedsheet and whisked it all the way down to his waist. His bare chest was exposed to the firelight. Every mark, every tattoo, every ridge of scar tissue. He burned with the sensation of exposure. She didn't appear shocked, however. Only curious, in a markedly sensual way. No doubt she'd had a good view of him earlier. He hated that tending his physical infirmity had robbed her of yet more innocence.

But the way she unconsciously wet her lips as she regarded him . . .

He didn't have it in him to hate that.

She uncorked the vial again and held it over his chest, tilting it by slow degrees until a trickle of oil poured forth. She drizzled the slick liquid in a lazy line down the center of his chest. Bisecting his chest and abdominal muscles, skipping over the linen binding him to the bed, tracing the furrow of dark hair that arrowed straight for his groin.

Holy God. The image was perversely sensual. Just what mischief did she intend? If she dragged her soft hands down his bared, oiled chest, he would not have to worry about forced confessions. He'd combust on the spot, leaving behind nothing more blameworthy than ash.

"I have a way of getting you to talk." Her mouth quirked in a cold smile. "Prepare yourself for my secret weapon."

Thorne steeled his loins.

"Here he is."

Christ.

She caught the pup in both hands, lifting him to a position directly above Thorne's glistening abdomen. That twitching dog nose hovered just an inch above his oil-filled navel.

Thorne's abdominal muscles flinched. So this was her grand, malevolent plan. She was going to tickle the truth from him. With the dog.

"Little Badger has been here all night with us. With nothing to eat save an old rind of cheese he sniffed out in your cupboard." She screwed up her face and spoke to the dog. "You're very, very hungry, aren't you, dear?"

"You wouldn't," said Thorne.

"Oh, just watch me."

"Katie, don't you dare."

Her eyebrows soared. "Ah. Now we're back to Katie? My tactic is working already."

He firmed his jaw and glared at her. "If you had any idea the torments I've endured in my life, you would know—I will not be done in by a puppy."

"Let's just try it and see."

Thorne inwardly cursed. He could not be done in by a puppy, but this woman . . . she was a true danger.

She made eye contact with him, direct and honest. "My whole life, I've searched for answers about my past. My whole life, Thorne. I will not rest until you tell me the truth."

"I can't."

She lowered the pup another half inch.

A quiver pulsed through Thorne's belly.

"Badger, no," he commanded, even though he knew the futility of warning a dog off such behavior.

The dog was a dog. He barked. He chewed. He chased.

God have mercy.

He licked.

Kate kept her first bout of torture brief. She lowered Badger for just a few seconds of enthusiastic tickling.

Thorne growled like an animal. An enraged animal. His nostrils flared. The muscles of his abdomen tensed in staggered rows, hard as cobblestones beneath his skin. Tendons stood out on his neck, and his good arm was solid flexed muscle, embossed with thickly pulsing veins.

Heavens.

Kate's own breathing quickened. He was massive and strong and furious and utterly at her mercy. A beast, but a beautiful one.

Near giddy with power, she momentarily restrained the pup. "Had enough?"

His breathing was heavy, his voice a hoarse rasp. "Stop this. Stop this now."

"Beg me for mercy."

"The devil I will."

She lowered the pup again. This time he strained and arched beneath the ropes so hard, he had the bed frame rocking to and fro. The entire bed scooted several inches across the floor. Beads of sweat dotted his forehead.

She gave him another brief reprieve. "How about now?"

"Devious woman. You're going to regret this."

"I doubt that." She lowered the dog once again, letting him lick Thorne's side now, just beneath his lowest rib. He seized and gasped.

"Very well," he finally growled. "Very well. You win. Just get him off me."

"You'll tell me everything?"

"Yes."

Victory surged in Kate's breast. "I knew you'd surrender."

"I'm not asking mercy for me," he panted, staring up at the ceiling. "Just for the dog. With all that oil, you'll make him sick."

She smiled to herself, knowing she'd found his Achilles' heel. "I knew you cared about him."

She brought Badger close to her chest and praised him extravagantly before setting him on the floor. Then she gave Thorne her full attention. Oh, the look on his face was murderous.

She said, "I'm listening."

"Release me from these bindings first."

"When you're fuming at me so darkly? I may be

brave, but I'm not stupid." She reached for the tea. "But I will offer you some of this."

She moved close to the head of the bed and raised the mug to his lips, putting one hand behind his head to help him drink. As he lowered his head to the pillow, she swept her fingers through his bed-mussed hair, taming it. "Go on."

He sighed. "Yes, I knew you as a child. You were just a little thing when we saw each other last. Four years old, perhaps. I was older. Ten or eleven. Our mothers—"

At the word "mothers," a lump rose in her throat.

"Our mothers?" She clasped his good hand. "You must tell me everything. Everything, Thorne."

He sighed reluctantly. "I'll tell you more. I swear it. But release me first. The tale warrants a bit of dignity."

She considered. "All right."

From the table, she retrieved the knife. With careful sawing motions, she cut loose each of the bands of linen holding him to the bed. Some of the bindings she'd wrapped over his breeches-clad legs. Others cinched against the bare skin of his chest and abdomen. To lift and cut them, she had to run her hands along his warm, oiled skin. She tried to maintain a businesslike demeanor, but it was difficult.

When she had the last binding cut, he propped his good elbow under him and slowly curled to a sitting position. A sleeping giant coming awake.

His boots hit the floor with twin thuds. She'd never bothered to try removing them.

He rubbed his squared, unshaven jaw, then pushed a hand through his hair. His gaze dropped to his bare, oil-coated chest. "Have you a sponge or damp cloth?"

She handed him a moistened towel from the bedside table.

He accepted it with his left hand and dragged the square of fabric over his throat and then around to his nape. As he tilted his head to either side, Kate stared at his sculpted shoulders, transfixed by the limber stretch of his tendons and the defined contours between each muscle. There was nothing soft on him, anywhere.

And then there were those intriguing tattoos.

When he dropped his hand and began to swab his chest, Kate's mouth went dry. She looked away, suddenly conscious that she'd been staring.

A shirt. She really ought to find him a shirt. A narrow cupboard near the turret's entry seemed to serve as his closet. It was where she'd hung his red officer's coat last night, once the danger had passed. She went to it now and found him a freshly laundered shirt of soft linen.

He discarded the damp towel, and she averted her eyes as she handed him the shirt. After a few moments she looked back. He'd managed to get his head through the wide, open collar and his good arm into the left sleeve. But she could tell he was struggling with his wounded side.

She went to him. "Let me help."

He flinched away. "I'll manage."

Chastened, she let him be. "Well. I'm glad to see you survived the ordeal with your stubborn pride intact. I'll take Badger out for a few minutes."

The morning was chill and wet with dew, and she hurried Badger about his business, not wanting to risk an encounter with another snake.

When she returned, she found Thorne seated at the table with an open flask. His hair was damp and combed. He'd put on a coat.

"Would've shaved and donned a neckcloth, but . . ."

He nodded at his right arm, dangling limp and useless at his side.

"Don't be silly." She sat with him and propped an elbow on the table. "There's no need. I can't imagine how I look at the moment."

"Lovely." He spoke the word without equivocation. His intense gaze caught hers. "You are lovely, always." He reached out to catch a stray lock of her hair. "Her hair curled like this, but it wasn't so dark."

"Where was this?" She swallowed the lump in her throat. "Where did we live?"

"Southwark, as I've told you. Near the prison. The neighborhood was rough and very dangerous."

"And you called me Katie then."

He nodded. "Everyone did."

"What did I call you?"

His chest rose and fell slowly. "You called me Samuel."

Samuel.

The name struck a chime inside her. Memories heeded the summons, crowding the periphery of her mind. If she tried to look straight at them, they vanished. But she could sense that they were there, waiting—misty and dark.

"Our mothers took rooms in the same house," he said.

"But you told me your mother turned whore."

His mouth set in a hard line. "She did."

Oh no. Kate's breath caught painfully. The implications were too horrible to contemplate. "Is my . . . Could she still be living?"

Solemnly, he shook his head. "No. She died. That's when you went to the school."

Kate blinked, staring unfocused at a groove on the tabletop. Rage built within her, swift and sudden. She wanted to scold, scream, cry, pound something with her fists. She had never known this sort of raw, helpless anger, and she didn't know just what it might cause her to do.

"I'm sorry, Katie. The truth isn't pleasant."

"No, it's not. It's not pleasant. But it's *my* truth." She pushed back from the table and punched to her feet. "My *life*. I can't believe you kept this from me."

He rubbed his face with one hand.

"Let me be certain I understand this," she went on. "When you arrived in Spindle Cove last summer, are you telling me that you recognized me at once?"

"Yes."

"By this." She touched her birthmark.

"Yes."

"So you immediately knew me as an acquaintance from your childhood. And in the present, you found me . . ." She churned the air with her hand. " 'Fetching enough' was how you once phrased it."

"More than fetching."

"How much more?" She stood and flung her arms wide, taunting him. "Pretty? Beautiful? Rapturously stunning beyond all words and comprehension?"

"The third," he shot back. "Something like that third. When you're not flapping like an outraged chicken, I sometimes think you're the most beautiful woman in the world."

She let her arms drop.

After an awkward pause, she said, "I'm not, you realize. I'm not even the most beautiful woman in Spindle Cove."

He held up a hand. "Let's just go back to desirable. I found you very desirable."

"Fine. So you recognized me and found me desirable."

"Very."

"Yet rather than speak to me about any of this, you

decided to intimidate and avoid me for an entire year. When you knew I thought myself to be an abandoned orphan. When you *must* have understood how desperate I was for any connection to my past. How could you do that to me?"

"Because it was best. Your dim memories are a blessing. We lived in a place most would wish to forget. I didn't want to inflict that unpleasantness on you now."

"That was not your choice to make!" She gestured angrily toward the unseen ocean beyond the castle walls. "I can't believe this. You would have left for America, having never said a word. Leaving me to wonder forever."

As he looked on, she paced back and forth. Badger chased the flounce of her skirt from one end of the room to the other.

"If the Gramercys hadn't found that painting and come looking for—" A horrid thought struck her. "Oh, God. *Were* they looking for me? Did my mother look like the portrait? Did she wear a pendant of deep blue stone?"

"I can't say. My memories of her aren't a great deal more reliable than yours. When I saw her, she was usually made up with rouge and kohl. Later on, pale with illness. Ellie Rose was—"

"Ellie Rose." Kate took a pouncing step in his direction. "My mother's name was Ellie Rose?"

"That's what she went by. I don't think it was her real name."

Ellie Rose. Could she have been the same woman as Elinor Marie, or was she some other unfortunate soul?

Oh, Lord.

Who was Kate? The daughter of a marquess? The child of a whore?

Both?

She crumpled to the floor, numb everywhere. Badger pounced in her lap, as though he'd won whatever game they were playing. She ignored him. Not even puppy kisses could make this moment better.

Out of habit, her fingers went to the mark at her temple. A child of shame, Miss Paringham had called her. A child of shame who ought to live ashamed.

Be brave, my Katie.

At her loneliest, most despairing moments, that voice had given her hope. She couldn't abandon that hope now. Someone, somewhere had loved her. Even if that someone had been a fallen woman, and that somewhere had been a seedy brothel—it didn't change the essence of love.

Thorne said, "Do you see? This is why I tried to protect you from the truth. Leave the past forgotten, Katie. Look at your life now. All you've accomplished, all the friendships you've made. You've found a family to accept you."

The Gramercys.

"Oh God," she breathed. "I have to tell them."

"No." Thorne tapped the table with his good fist. "You can't tell them anything of this."

"But I must! Can't you see? This could be the link. If Ellie Rose was Elinor . . . then they would know for certain I'm Simon's daughter."

"Aye, and they'd know for certain that you spent your first four years in a bawdy house. They'd cast you out. They'd want nothing to do with you then."

Kate shook her head. "The Gramercys would never do that. Family above everything. That's what they always say. They've weathered many a scandal."

"There's high-class scandal, and then there's this. It's not the same."

She knew he was right. It wasn't the same. If her mother had been an elite courtesan, then *maybe* the scandal wouldn't be too much. But coming from a low-class Southwark brothel?

Nevertheless . . .

"I owe the Gramercys the truth. I can't let them accept me into their family if there's a chance it's all a mistake."

A new thought struck her. She caught and seized it.

She rose to her feet. "Maybe *you're* mistaken, Thorne. Have you thought of that? So you knew a little girl with a birthmark once. But that was twenty years ago. You can't be sure it was me."

"What about the song, Katie?"

She crossed her arms and lifted her chin. "The song is just a silly little song. What of it?"

Never mind that in all her years at Margate, all her years of music instruction, she'd never met another soul who knew it.

For a moment he looked as though he'd argue the same point. But then he seemed to reconsider.

"Fine," he said, lifting his good shoulder in resignation. "You're right. I must be mistaken. I never knew you as a child. You were never the daughter of a whore. All the more reason why you shouldn't tell the Gramercys anything about this."

"But I have to," she whispered. "I must. They deserve to know. They've been so kind to me, offered me so much faith. I have to tell them. Today."

He struggled to his feet. "Then I'll go with you."

"No." She sniffed. "I don't want you there. I don't want you anywhere near me." She jabbed a finger to her breastbone. "I tried to see the best in you, despite all your surliness. I defended you in my heart, even in the face of your callous rejections, and yesterday . . . I was ready to *marry* you, you heartless man. I foolishly thought I was coming to love you."

Her voice broke. "And you were lying to me. All along, from the very moment you walked into this village and saw me singing in that borrowed India shawl. You lied to me. You forced me into this joke of a betrothal. You made me a fool in front of all my friends, as well as the people I hoped to call family. All this, when you knew—you *knew* how much it meant to me. I can't keep letting you hurt me, Thorne. You were right, that day in the churchyard. I need someone capable of sympathy and caring. I need a better man."

"Katie—"

"Don't call me that. Don't ever call me that again."

He caught her by the arm. "Katie, I can't let you walk away. Not like this."

"Why not?"

"Because I—"

Her racing pulse stumbled. If he told her he loved her, right here and now, she wouldn't be able to leave. Even after all he'd done, she wouldn't have it in her to walk away. He had to know that.

Go on, she silently urged. *Just say three words and I'm yours.*

"Because you've spent the night here," he said.

She narrowed her eyes. *Coward.*

"You spent the night alone in my quarters," he said. "If anyone notices that, you'll be ruined. Completely."

"I'll take my chances. I'd rather be ruined than be with you." She wrested out of his grip and went to the door. "Our engagement is over."

"You're right, it is over," he said. "We'll be married today."

Chapter Fifteen

Thorne had known all along that this would happen. He'd warned her, again and again, that if she knew him, she'd want to get as far away as possible.

He watched her now, inching toward the door, wearing an expression of pure disgust.

"Marry you? Today?" She shook her head. "You've gone mad. Perhaps it was the adder venom."

"I'd never claim to be a learned man, but I have my wits about me." He crossed the room slowly, learning his new balance with a leaden right arm. "You've spent the night with me. Alone. In my personal quarters."

"But you were ill. I couldn't leave you. I had no choice. And besides, nothing happened." A blush touched her cheeks. "Well, almost nothing."

A shudder went through him as he recalled the sweet flicker of her shy, velvet tongue and the soft heat of her sex. And all those naive, starry-eyed promises—offers to keep him and love him and give him a home, as if he were another stray pup she'd adopted.

Evidently, those offers were rescinded now.

He said, "You know as well as I, it doesn't matter what did or didn't happen. It's what people will assume." He hadn't removed her from a whorehouse all those years ago just to make her look the slattern now. "We must marry. You've no choice."

"Of course I have a choice. Watch me make it." She wrenched open the door and dashed through it. He watched her disappear in the direction of the village— running with all the haste of a bat fleeing dawn.

With a wistful thought that he'd have preferred to do this with some bread and ale in his stomach, Thorne set off in pursuit. Badger happily joined the parade, ears flattened against his head.

As she hurried down the path that led from the castle bluffs to the village, she threw him a look over her shoulder. "Stop following me. I'm not marrying you, Thorne. You're going to America. I mean to stay here in England. With my family."

The path straightened onto a gentle downslope. Thorne forced his weary limbs into a sprint, gaining ground until he could stretch out his left hand and catch her by the arm.

Ignoring her cry of outrage, he wheeled her to face him. Her hair escaped its pins, tumbling about her shoulders in heavy waves. She stared at him, breathing hard.

He found himself equally starved for air. What was it she'd said earlier?

Rapturously stunning beyond all words and comprehension.

Yes, that about summed it up.

He said, "You need to ask yourself one important question. If that family is truly *your* family and they're so very understanding . . . why did your mother never go to them? Before Simon died, why didn't he tell anyone about his child?"

"Perhaps there wasn't time. And like Aunt Marmoset explained, their parents never approved of their love. But Evan was only a boy then. Times are different now. These Gramercys are different. They will not abandon me."

"What if they do? If you're turned out of the Queen's Ruby—and after spending the night with me, you likely will be—you'll have no living whatsoever. How will you support yourself?"

She shrugged. "I do have friends. That may be a foreign concept to you, but there are people who will help me. Susanna and Lord Rycliff would take me in."

"I'm certain they would. But Rycliff's my superior officer. If I acquaint him with the circumstances, he'll agree we must wed."

She turned and stared out over the green-blue sea, looking desperate and forlorn. His chest ached.

"Katie," he said, "I am trying to do the honorable thing."

She swung a fierce glare on him. "Well, you're a year too late!"

He knew he deserved that. "It's unfair. I know it. You were too softhearted to leave me last night, and now you have to pay for it with your future. It's the way of things. Acts of kindness come with costs attached."

This was one lesson life had taught him well.

But he'd do it all again. He'd swallow an entire nest of live adders if it meant sparing her a moment's pain.

He tried to put something soothing in his voice, rather than the usual blend of sawmill grist and impersonal authority. "Come. Let me take you home. You're tired."

"I *am* tired. Tired of secrets, tired of lies. But most of

all, I'm weary of living with uncertainty, feeling pulled between two pasts, two futures. I'm going to speak with Evan and tell him everything. Exactly what happened and didn't happen last night. I'll tell him all about Ellie Rose and the Southwark brothel. We're going to have this all out in the open, and then I'll hear what he has to say."

"Why should you trust Drewe to make the decisions? You've only known him a few weeks. He hasn't—"

"I said, I'll hear what he has to say," she replied. "I will make my own decisions. I've allowed you to decide far too much ever since the Gramercys arrived in my life. I'm paying the price for it now, but I will not make the same mistake again."

"I've only been—"

"Looking out for me? Oh, yes." She spread her arms and indicated her rumpled gown. "And a fine job you've done of it, too."

"My intentions were decent."

"Please." She jabbed a finger in the center of his chest. "You betrayed me, Thorne. You lied to me. You can't fathom how to love me. I am not marrying you. Not today. Not ever."

He exhaled slowly.

Not ever.

Once a woman made her wishes that clear, a man would be a villain to keep pursuing her. She understood the risks. She did have friends, if she needed help. If she wanted him out of her life, Thorne would leave it. Today.

"I'm going home to the rooming house now." She backed away. "Don't follow me."

"I've arrangements to make in London," he said. "I'll leave this morning."

"Good." She crossed her arms over her chest, turned and strode off down the pathway. The wind gusting in from the open sea whipped her hair and gown in all directions, but her own path never swerved.

Thorne watched her go—until a high-pitched canine whimper drew his attention.

Badger stood waiting at his heel, tail thumping. The dog whined anxiously as he looked to Miss Taylor's retreating form, then back to Thorne.

"Go on," Thorne said, releasing Badger to chase. "Watch over her for me."

As Kate walked back to the village, she reached a fork in pathway. The left-hand path continued into the village, and the right led out to the main road.

She turned right and stared into the distance. Perhaps she should just keep walking—make her way to some other village and start over. She could look for music pupils again, or become a governess. She could board a ship and go anywhere in the world. Surely braving Australia would be easier than sitting down with Lord Drewe and explaining the events of last night.

No, no. She muzzled the irrational voice urging her to flee. Starting over in a strange place wasn't a prudent idea for a single, unprotected woman.

Ellie Rose, whoever the poor soul was, had probably fostered high hopes of taking her baby and doing just that. And look where she'd ended.

Kate took the left-hand path, trudging toward the Queen's Ruby in the early light of dawn. She couldn't stomach any further evasion, deception, or half-truths. It was time to make a clean breast of it with everyone and hope for the best.

As she neared the center of the village, a hiss from an alleyway startled her.

"*Kate.*"

"Who's there?"

A figure darted out from the shadows, blanketing her with an immense, dark cloak. The heavy fabric suffocated Kate and she flailed instinctively. She felt attacked.

Oh, what an irony it would be if not twenty minutes after refusing Thorne's protection, she were kidnapped and held for ransom. He might finally laugh at that.

"Stop struggling," a voice told her. "Almost have it . . ."

Kate's head finally emerged through the top of the cloak. She could breathe again. And see.

"Harry?" Stunned, she blinked at the beautiful, unconventional woman she'd come to think of as a cousin.

Harry put her arm around Kate, steering her back onto the street.

"Oh, Miss Taylor!" she proclaimed loudly. "What a lovely walk we've had this morning. So invigorating, marching all over the Downlands. The dog enjoyed it, too."

"What on earth are you talking of?" Kate whispered.

"Just play along," Harry murmured back, draping the cloak about Kate's shoulders. "Don't worry. Unless they see you're wearing yesterday's gown, no one will even suspect."

"No one will suspect *what*?"

Harry lifted her voice as they neared the Queen's Ruby entrance. "Really, what a lovely ramble. The weather's glorious. If I were the sort to gather flowers, I should have plucked dozens."

As they entered the rooming house, Mrs. Nichols came to greet them. The older woman wore an expression of true concern.

"Oh, Miss Taylor. How good to see you this morning. Are you feeling better, dear?"

Kate stammered. "I—I . . ."

"Of course she's feeling better." Harry plucked Badger into her arms. "Just look at those roses on her cheeks. I've always said, there's nothing that a good brisk walk through open country can't cure."

Before Kate could even begin to object, a smiling Harry nudged her toward the staircase.

"We'll just go freshen up for breakfast, Mrs. Nichols. I do hope we'll be treated to some of your delicious currant bread this morning."

When they reached the top of the stairs, Harry steered them both to Kate's bedchamber. She followed Kate inside, set the puppy loose, and flopped dramatically against the closed door.

"There now." She gave Kate a conspiratorial grin. "That was satisfying. And just as I told you, no one suspects a thing."

"I don't understand." Kate sank onto the edge of her narrow bed. Hers was a small bedchamber, tucked under a far corner of the eaves. The bigger rooms were reserved for the visiting ladies with larger wardrobes and more accommodating purses.

"I lied for you, of course," Harry said. "I used to do it for Calista all the time. It was obvious enough why neither you nor Thorne showed up at the tavern last night. So when someone remarked on your absence, I volunteered to go check. I told everyone you were wretchedly ill and resting in your room. I even went to the trouble of waking Mrs. Nichols for a headache powder." Her lips curved in a smug smile. "I'm very good at these things."

"Evidently," Kate said. Her head was spinning.

"I must say, it almost makes me jealous. When two women want to be alone, the sneaking around is far too easy." She came to sit near Kate on the bed. "I do hope you enjoyed your night. But next time, be a dear and give me some advance warning?"

"Oh, Harry." Kate let her head drop into her hands. She knew her cousin's interference was well-meant. But it was poorly timed. Just when she'd vowed to make a clean breast of things. "It's not at all how you think."

"You don't have to make excuses to me, Kate. Of all people, I'm not going to judge."

"I know. But I'm being truthful. I swear, nothing like that happened. In fact—" She broke off, overwhelmed.

Harry clucked her tongue and patted Kate's shoulder. "Did you and Corporal Thorne have a row? Tell me what the scoundrel did. Don't worry, you can abuse him to me thoroughly. When you two make things right again, I'll never let on. I say the most horrid things about Ames when I'm vexed."

"I don't think this will ever be made right." Kate raised her head. "I ended the engagement."

"Oh." Harry moved closer and put her arm around Kate's shoulders. "Oh, no. I'm so sorry."

"Are you? I didn't think any of you liked him."

"Well, no. But *you* liked him, so we were trying our best."

Kate smiled, even as tears welled in her eyes.

Harry handed her a handkerchief from her waistcoat pocket. In her typical style, the linen square was gentlemanly—unadorned with lace or fancy monograms.

Kate's heart twisted as she traced the neatly hemmed border of the handkerchief. She hated to think their family bond might all be a lie, a misunderstanding.

Harry asked, "You didn't break off with Thorne for our sakes, did you?"

"No. No, it was something else altogether." Kate sniffed and dabbed at her cheeks. "I must speak with Evan right away. This morning, if possible. I need to explain to him about last night."

"Oh, no." Harry's eyes flew wide. "Kate, you can't. You can't tell Evan anything about last night. He'll go into one of his . . . episodes."

"His episodes?"

"You've seen the man seethe. But you haven't seen him explode. And nothing sets him off like knowing one of his female relations has been compromised. It wasn't only for your sake that I lied last night. I've grown fond of this little village, and I should hate to see it laid waste."

Laid waste? Surely Harry had to be exaggerating.

"You'd believe me if you'd been there when Calista was discovered with Parker," Harry said. "Good Lord, it was like something from a didactic medieval tapestry. One duel, two outbuildings burnt to the ground, at least a half-dozen valuable horses running wild on the moors. Took the grooms days to retrieve them all." She shook her head. "It made Evan's efforts on behalf of *my* honor look like a few friendly bouts at the club."

"And what about Claire?" Kate couldn't help but ask.

"The less said about Claire, the better. Let's just say there's a gentleman somewhere who's missing parts. *Vital* parts."

Goodness. Kate tried to reconcile these accounts with the Evan Gramercy she knew and had come to admire.

He seemed so collected and elegant. When they'd played together that night, she had sensed the depth and intensity of emotion beneath the surface. But violence?

"I must risk it anyway," she said. "In truth, my virtue has not been compromised. My conscience is clean."

"Kate," Harry said sternly. "I am not one for social convention. But even I know, if you spent the night with Thorne, you are compromised. It doesn't matter what happened or didn't happen."

That was exactly what Thorne had said. If two human beings as completely opposite as Thorne and Harry agreed on something, Kate could only conclude it must be true.

Harry squeezed her hand. "I beg of you. Unburden your heart to me, if you wish—or find a way to tell Evan part of the truth. But unless you wish true harm upon Corporal Thorne, do not let Evan know about last night. And for the love of everything, change your frock before you speak with him."

There was a knock at the door.

Kate sucked in a deep breath and hastily dabbed at her eyes. "Who is it?"

"It's me." The door opened a crack, revealing Lark's sweet countenance. When she laid eyes on Kate, she flung the door open wide. "Kate, what is it? Are you still ill?"

Kate shook her head. "No. I'm fine."

"I've just been telling her a very sad, tragic story," Harry said, rising to her feet. "And she was deeply moved by the moral of the tale."

"Harriet. Don't provoke her so. At least not until she's stuck with us for good." Lark turned to Kate and smiled. "Evan has visitors at the tavern. The solicitors, I think. He's asking to see you."

Chapter Sixteen

As many times as she'd been in the public room below, Kate had never visited the rooms *above* the Bull and Blossom.

At Fosbury's direction, she made her way up a narrow staircase and emerged into a long, windowless corridor. She froze, struck again by that same familiar image.

She was in an endless, shadowy tunnel, and her future lay at the other end. Pianoforte music came up through the floor, tingling in the soles of her feet. She closed her eyes, and blue flashed behind her eyelids.

"Kate, is that you?" Evan's voice carried out from the first room on the left.

"Yes." She shook herself and smoothed a hand over the skirt of her fresh sprigged muslin before entering the room.

"Come in, come in." Evan waved her forward. "I trust you're feeling better this morning."

She stepped into a small yet comfortably furnished sitting room. She knew at once it had to be the Fosburys' private parlor. They must have vacated it to offer Evan a full suite of rooms, worthy of a marquess.

"Miss Kate Taylor, I'd like you to meet two of the family solicitors, Mr. Bartwhistle and Mr. Smythe."

"How do you do." Kate curtsied to the two men, who were dressed in brown coats so similar as to be nearly identical.

"And this"—Evan turned her attention to an older woman in a faded indigo day dress several years past its peak of fashion—"is Mrs. Fellows."

Kate smiled and nodded, but was dismayed when Mrs. Fellows made no acknowledgment in return. Instead, the older woman remained seated in the tufted armchair, facing the window and staring straight ahead.

"Cataracts," Evan whispered in her ear. "Poor old dear's nearly blind."

"Oh." Understanding the remoteness of her demeanor now, Kate moved forward to take the woman's hand. "Mrs. Fellows, it's a pleasure to make your acquaintance."

Evan closed the parlor door. "Mrs. Fellows was just telling us about her tenure as housekeeper at Ambervale, twenty years ago."

"Ambervale?" Kate's heart skipped an alarming number of beats. Evan had told her in Wilmington that they meant to canvass for former Ambervale servants, but he'd never mentioned it again.

He pulled up a chair for Kate, and she accepted it gratefully.

He took a seat as well. "Tell me, Mrs. Fellows. Did you keep a large house staff in my cousin's time?"

"No, my lord. Just me and my man. Mr. Fellows is gone now, some eight years. We had a cook in those days, and a girl came in daily for scullery. We sent the laundry out. Most of the house was closed up, you see.

There were never any guests. His lordship and Miss Elinor liked their privacy."

"Yes, I would imagine." Evan smiled at Kate. "And then Miss Haverford became pregnant, is that right?"

The frankness of the question obviously pained Mrs. Fellows. But she answered. "Yes, my lord."

"And she gave birth to a child. Was it a son or a daughter, do you recall?"

"A baby girl." Mrs. Fellows still faced the window, and she smiled at the dust motes whirling in the sunlight. "They named her Katherine."

From the other side of the room, Mr. Bartwhistle cleared his throat. His keen gaze fell on Kate—or more particularly, on the birthmark at her temple. "Mrs. Fellows," he asked, "do you recall whether the infant had any . . . distinguishing marks?"

"Oh, yes. Unfortunate little dear had a birthmark. Right on her face."

Unfortunate little dear? For the first time in her life, Kate blessed that mark on her temple. If she could have stretched her lips like India rubber, she would have *kissed* it.

She leaned forward in her chair, training her ears so hard, she felt her eardrums bending under the strain.

"If you ask me," said Mrs. Fellows, "it was the wine. If I told Miss Elinor once, I told her a hundred times—a woman shouldn't be drinking aught of claret while she's breeding. It's unseemly. But she had a taste for a sip from time to time, and sure enough, when the babe came, there was a great splash of it on her temple."

"Can you describe the mark in any further detail?" Evan asked. "I know it's been many years."

Mrs. Fellows shifted in her chair. "But I remember it, clear as day. It was just here." She lifted an age-spotted hand to her own temple. "Had almost the shape of a heart. I'll never forget that, because they laughed about it, you know."

"They laughed about it?" Kate asked, forgetting that she wasn't the one conducting the interview.

"Laughed with each other, yes. They were like that, always laughing with each other about everything. I heard the lady tell his lordship, 'We know she's yours, don't we?' That was on account of his having a birthmark, too. But the late Lord Drewe insisted the mark was from Miss Elinor's side. Because she wore her heart on her face, and so the child must as well."

On the other side of the room, Bartwhistle and Smythe were furiously scribbling, taking down every word.

Evan reached for Kate's hand and squeezed it. "I knew it. I knew you were ours."

"It sounds as though Simon and Elinor were very much in love," Kate said, choked with emotion.

"Oh, yes." The old housekeeper smiled. "Never seen a couple so madly devoted to one another." Her smile faded. "And after his lordship died, so sudden and so soon . . . oh, she took it so hard."

"What happened?" Evan asked.

"We never knew," Mrs. Fellows replied. "The doctor said mayhap the midwife brought in a contagion. I always suspected the painting, myself. Can't be healthy, staying shut up all day with those horrid vapors." She shook her head. "However it happened, he was gone. We were all desolate, and Miss Elinor was beside herself. Alone in the world, with a newborn babe? And there was no money. None. His lordship had never kept much in the house, and we hadn't any way to keep purchasing goods on credit."

"What did you do?" Kate asked.

"We closed up the house. Miss Elinor took the babe and left. Said she'd go back home to Derbyshire."

Evan leaned toward Kate and murmured, "I suppose she never made it that far, or certainly someone would have heard. If only we could know what happened between the closing of Ambervale and your arrival at Margate."

A sense of desperate bewilderment settled on Kate. She was heartily sick of lies and deceit. She wanted to do—and say—the right thing. But she didn't know what the right thing was.

How could she explain to Evan about "Ellie Rose" and the Southwark bawdy house—in front of two solicitors and the housekeeper who'd held her mother in such obvious regard? Did it even matter? Perhaps Thorne's story was irrelevant. The little girl he'd known might have been someone else.

The most maddening thing of all was knowing that her own brain was holding the truth hostage. The memories were in there. She knew they were. But she could never quite reach the end of that corridor.

"I wish I could tell you," Kate said. "I wish, more than anything, that I had some clear memory of that time."

"The good Lord must have taken her to heaven," Mrs. Fellows said. "I can't imagine Miss Elinor would part with her child for anything less. I've six of my own at home, and I'd go to war with the devil for each of them."

"Of course you would, Mrs. Fellows," Evan said.

Impulsively, Kate reached forward and squeezed the aging housekeeper's wrist. "Thank you," she said. "For taking such care of her. And of me."

Mrs. Fellows fumbled for Kate's hand. "Is it you, then? Are you Katherine? You're his lordship's daughter?"

Kate looked to Evan, and then to the solicitors. "I . . . I think so?"

Mrs. Bartwhistle and Mr. Smythe conferred. In the end, Mr. Bartwhistle answered for them both.

"Between the parish register," he said, "the striking physical resemblance, and the statement of Mrs. Fellows with regards to the birthmark—we feel it safe to conclude in the affirmative."

"Yes?" Kate asked.

"Yes," said Mr. Smythe.

Kate sank into the depths of her armchair, overwhelmed. The Gramercys had burst into her life less than a fortnight ago. Evan, Lark, Harry, Aunt Marmoset—each of them had accepted her into the family, individually. But there was something about the dry, actuarial "Yes" from the solicitors that made the brimming cup of emotion overflow. She buried her face in her hands, overcome.

She was a lost child, found. She was a Gramercy. She had been loved.

She couldn't *wait* to pay another call on Miss Paringham.

Mr. Bartwhistle went on, "We will draw up a statement for your signature, Mrs. Fellows. If you will be so kind as to offer a few more details. Were you present at the birth?"

"Oh, yes," the housekeeper said. "I was present at the birth. And at the wedding."

The wedding?

Kate's head whipped up. She sought Evan's face, but his expression was unreadable. "Did she just say 'the wedding'?"

* * *

After Mrs. Fellows and the solicitors had gone, Kate sat with Evan in the small upstairs parlor. The musty parish register lay open before her on the table, flipped to a page just two leaves prior to her birth record.

"Simon Langley Gramercy," she read aloud in a quiet voice, "the fifth Marquess of Drewe, married to Elinor Marie Haverford, the thirtieth day of January, 1791."

No matter how many times she read the lines, she still found them hard to believe.

Evan rubbed his jaw. "Cutting it a bit close, weren't they? Whatever scandal they began in, it seems Simon wanted to make things proper when it counted."

Kate looked up at her cousin. "Have you known this all along?"

He regarded her steadily. "Can you forgive me? We always meant to tell you, of course, once we'd—"

"We? So Lark and Harry and Aunt Marmoset . . . they all know, too?"

"We all saw it together, that day at St. Mary of the Martyrs." He reached for her hand. "Kate, please try to understand. We needed to be sure of your identity first, to avoid disappointing you, or . . ."

"Or tempting me to stretch the truth."

He nodded. "We didn't know you at all. We had no idea what kind of person you might be."

"I understand," Kate said. "Caution was necessary, and not only on your side."

"That's why you pretended an engagement to Corporal Thorne?"

She warmed with a guilty flush. How had he guessed? "It wasn't a pretense. Not exactly."

"But it was a convenience. Invented on the spot, right

there in the parlor of the Queen's Ruby. He wanted to protect you."

She nodded, unable to deny it.

"I've long suspected as much. Don't feel badly, Kate. When I think of how we surprised you that night . . . It was the strangest, most unpredictable situation. For us all. Both of us held information back. But we were only guarding ourselves and our loved ones as best we could."

His words made her think of her argument with Thorne. She'd been so furious with him for withholding what he knew—or *thought* he knew—about her past. Hadn't Evan committed the same exact transgression?

But she wasn't leaping from her chair and shouting at Evan. She wasn't heaping insults on Evan's character. Nor was she flouncing from the room in an airy huff of indignation, vowing to never see Evan again.

Why the distinction? she asked herself. Were the two men's actions so fundamentally different? Perhaps smoothly spoken Evan just explained his reasons more deftly than Thorne.

Or maybe it was merely this: Evan had concealed happy news, while Thorne's story represented a painful "truth" she'd prefer to reject. If so, she had dealt with him most unfairly.

But it was too late for regrets now.

With one long, elegant finger, Evan tapped the parish register. "You do realize what this means, don't you?"

She swallowed hard. "It means they married before my birth. It means I'm legitimate."

"Yes. You're the legitimate daughter of a marquess. Which means that you are a lady. Lady Katherine Adele Gramercy."

Lady Katherine Adele Gramercy. It was too much to be believed. The title felt like a too-large gown, borrowed from someone else.

"Your life is about to change, Kate. You will move in the highest circles of Society. You must be presented at court. And then there is an inheritance. A significant inheritance."

She shook her head, faintly horrified. "But I don't need all that. Being your illegitimate cousin already felt like a fairy tale come true. As for an inheritance . . . I don't want to take anything away from you."

He smiled. "You will not be *taking* anything. You will have what was rightfully yours all along. We've merely had it on loan, these three-and-twenty years. I still keep the title, naturally. The marquessate cannot pass to a female child."

He patted her hand. "The solicitors will sort it all out. Of course, you'll have a great deal to discuss with Corporal Thorne."

"No," she blurted out. "I can't tell him. He's gone to London on business. And before he left, we . . . *I* broke the engagement."

Evan exhaled in a slow, controlled fashion. "I am sorry, Kate—gravely sorry—for any hurt this has caused you. But for myself and for our family, I cannot pretend to be disappointed. I'm glad it ended before today's interview, rather than after."

"You needn't have worried," she said. "He's not mercenary. He wanted no part of marriage to me, even once he knew you were planning to claim me as a Gramercy. If he hears I'm a true *lady*, it will only drive him further away."

Thorne's words echoed back to her:

If I hadn't spent the past year thinking of you as a

lady, I promise you—things would be different between us.

"Evan, you must be relieved on all counts," she said. "Now that the solicitors have accepted me, there'll be no need for you to . . . devise another way of giving me the family name."

"By marrying you, you mean?"

She nodded. It was the first time either of them had admitted the idea aloud.

"The relief should be on your side, I think." A smile warmed his eyes. "For my part, I would not have viewed it as a hardship."

She cringed, hoping she hadn't caused any offense. Evan didn't seem to love her romantically, but then . . . After yesterday, what did she know of reading men's emotions?

"I'm sorry," she said. "I didn't mean to suggest that I . . . that we . . ."

He took her bumbling apology and waved it smoothly away. "Kate, you will have so many options now. Every door will be open to you. Corporal Thorne may be a fine enough fellow. He troubled himself to protect you, and that speaks well of his character."

You've no idea, she thought.

He'd taken a melon for her. And a snakebite. He'd given her his dog.

"But," Evan continued, "you can do better in your choice of a husband. You deserve better."

She sighed. "I'm not so sure that's true."

"Corporal Thorne! Here you are, at last."

Thorne made a bow. "My lady."

Lady Rycliff herself welcomed him at the door of a new, lavish Mayfair town house.

"You know you can dispense with all that." Stray wisps of copper floated about her smiling face as she hurried him inside. "It's good to see you. Bram's been so looking forward to your visit. Now that the baby's arrived, he's outnumbered by females again."

The piercing wail of an infant drifted down from the upper floor.

Lady Rycliff bowed her head and pinched the bridge of her nose. When she lifted her face, her mouth twisted in a wry smile. "Evidently, little Victoria is eager to meet you, too."

"Did I wake her?" he asked, worried.

"No, no. She scarcely sleeps." Lady Rycliff showed him into a parlor. "Will you mind waiting here for Bram? I'm so sorry to abandon you when you've just arrived. We're between nursemaids."

She disappeared, and Thorne stood awkwardly in the center of the room, surveying the evidence of genteel disorder. A few pillows lay scattered on the floor. The room smelled . . . odd.

He could scarcely believe that this was Lord and Lady Rycliff's home. Rycliff had been born and raised in the military. Order came as naturally to him as breathing. And as for his wife . . . she'd been quite the managing sort, in Spindle Cove.

Shouldn't they at least have servants?

As if reading his mind, someone said from the doorway, "Good God. This house is in upheaval. How is it that no one's offered you a drink?"

Thorne turned to see that Rycliff had joined him.

He bowed. "My lord."

Rycliff brushed off the honorific. "It's just Bram in this house."

He offered Thorne a tumbler of brandy with one

hand and a firm handshake with the other. "It's good to see you."

Thorne accepted the brandy and made excuses for the handshake. His right arm was still numb from the elbow down, though he was slowly regaining sensation.

As he drank, he sized Bram up, noting the changes a few months' time and new fatherhood had made on the man. One thing was clear—he ought to dismiss his valet. Only late afternoon, and Bram was dressed in a waistcoat and a rumpled, uncuffed shirt. To Thorne's eyes, he looked exhausted—but he'd venture to deem it a contented exhaustion, quite different from the grim fatigue of campaign.

Lady Rycliff reappeared, her arms full of wailing infant. "I'm so sorry," she called over the din. "She's a very fretful baby, I'm afraid. She cries with everyone. Our first nursemaid's already left us. No one under this roof is getting much sleep."

"She sleeps for me," Rycliff said. "Give her here."

His wife did so, with obvious relief. "Two months old, and she's already Papa's darling. I fear we're in for a time of it." She looked to Thorne. "I do hope you weren't planning on a quiet, restful stay in Town."

"No, my lady," Thorne said. "Just business."

And when he wasn't occupied with business, he imagined he'd be spending long hours engaged in self-castigation and regret. Distraction of any kind would be welcome—even if it came in the form of a wailing infant.

"Go on ahead," Bram told his wife. "I have her. I know you've dinner to oversee."

"Are you certain you don't mind? I'll just check on the corporal's rooms upstairs."

"She always sleeps for me," Bram said. "You know

that. Come along, Thorne. We can discuss our business in my library."

Squalling daughter in one arm and brandy in the other, Bram backed out of the parlor. Thorne followed him across the corridor to a richly paneled library.

Bram kicked the door shut behind them, placed his brandy on the desk blotter, and readjusted baby Victoria's weight in his arms. He paced the floor back and forth, jouncing the wailing baby as he went. His persistent limp from a war injury gave his steps an uneven rhythm.

When he caught Thorne's inquisitive look, he said, "Sometimes the walking helps."

Not every time, apparently.

When the babe's crying still didn't abate, Bram swore quietly and pushed his rolled sleeve to mid forearm. He fixed Thorne with an authoritative look. "I'm still your commanding officer. You are never to tell Susanna I did this. That's an order."

He dipped the tip of his little finger in the brandy, then popped it into the babe's mouth. Little Victoria went quiet instantly, contentedly suckling.

"God help me," Bram muttered down at her. "You're going to be a handful when you're sixteen."

He released a heavy breath and looked to Thorne. "So. Are you certain you want this?"

"Want what?" Thorne asked, wary.

"An honorable discharge from the army. Not the infant. Loud as she might be, I'm not willing to part with her."

"Of course not." He cleared his throat. "To answer your question . . . Yes, my lord. I'm certain."

"Enough with the 'my lord,' Thorne. I'm not asking you lord to servant, or even commander to soldier. I'm asking you friend to friend." The baby released his finger, falling into a shallow sleep. He lowered his voice and resumed pacing the room, slowly this time. "I want to make sure this is really your desire. You could make a good career for yourself in the army. I'm well enough placed now, I could easily grant you a commission, if you wished."

The words gave Thorne a moment's pause. What Rycliff offered was no small favor. If he accepted a commission, he could be assured higher standing in Society and a steady income for the rest of his life. Enough to support a family.

"That's very generous of you to—"

"It's not generous at all. It's piss-poor compensation. You saved my life and my leg, and you served under me faithfully for years."

"It was my duty and an honor. But I don't belong in England anymore, if I ever did. I need someplace bigger. Less civilized."

"So you're going to America. To be a farmer?"

Thorne shrugged. "Thought I'd start with trapping. I hear there's good money in it."

"No doubt. And I can't deny it would suit your talents." Bram bounced his daughter. "I'll never forget that time in the Pyrenees, when you used nothing but a bayonet to skin and gut that . . . What was it, again?"

"A marmot."

"Yes, marmot. A tough, greasy bastard. Can't say I'll be requesting marmot stew on the menu anytime soon, but it tasted fine when it was the first fresh meat in a fortnight." Rycliff nodded at his ledgers. "Can't I lend you some funds? Let me do that much. We can call it a loan."

Thorne shook his head. "I have money set aside."

"I see you're determined to be stubborn and self-sufficient. I can respect that. But I insist you accept a gift, friend to friend." He tilted his head at a long, gleaming rifle from the mantel. "Take that. It's Sir Lewis Finch's latest design."

When Thorne's eyebrows knitted in skepticism, Rycliff hastily added, "Professionally manufactured, of course. And thoroughly tested."

Thorne lifted the weapon with his good left hand, testing its balance. It was a fine rifle. He could see himself out tramping the woods with this gun in his hand. Of course, to make the picture complete, he'd need Badger at his heel.

Damn it. He would miss that dog.

Thorne watched with curiosity as his friend gently rocked the sleeping baby in his arms. "You love her," he said. "The baby."

Bram looked at him like he'd gone mad. "Of course I do. Yes."

"How do you know?"

"She's my child."

"Not every father loves his child. How do you know you love yours?"

Thorne knew this strayed beyond the normal boundaries of their conversation, but if Bram wanted to do him a favor . . . this was a favor he could use.

Bram shrugged and looked down at his sleeping daughter. "I suppose it's a fair enough question. I mean, as of yet she doesn't do much, does she? Except deprive me and her mother of sleep, food, peace of mind, and sexual congress."

Bram lowered his weight into the desk chair. Slowly, so as not to wake the babe. "When she's freshly washed, she smells better than opium. There's that. And even though

I know it's not statistically likely, no one could convince me she's not the most beautiful infant in Britain."

"So she's pretty. And she smells good. That's all you have?" If that was all there was to love, Thorne thought, he would have been chest-deep in it for ages.

"What can I say? She's not much of a conversationalist yet." Bram shook his head. "I'm no philosopher, Thorne. I just know how I feel. If you require a definition, read a book."

Sliding his daughter to his left arm, he reached for his brandy and drew a healthy swallow. "Does this line of questioning mean there's truth to the rumor? You've taken up with Miss Taylor?"

"Taken up?"

"Susanna's had some very strange letters from Spindle Cove. There's some talk of an engagement."

"It's only talk," Thorne said. "No truth to it." *Not anymore.*

"If there's no truth to it, then how would the rumor be started?"

Thorne set his jaw. "I'm not certain what you mean."

Bram shrugged. "Miss Taylor is Susanna's good friend. I just want to be certain she's been treated well."

A white flare of rage rose in Thorne's chest. He worked hard to conceal it. "My lord, when will this discharge go into effect?"

"You've permission to speak freely now, if that's what you mean."

He nodded. "Then I'll thank you to mind your own affairs. If you make any further insinuations that disparage Miss Taylor's virtue, we'll have more than words about it."

Bram stared at him, surprised. "Did you just threaten me?"

"I believe I did."

He broke into low laughter. "Good God. And here Susanna and I were placing wagers on whether you even liked her. Now I see she has you utterly tied in knots."

Thorne shook his head. She did *not* have him tied in knots. She hadn't held him tied in knots for at least . . . fifteen hours.

Bram raised a brow. "Don't take offense. Stronger men than you have been brought to their knees by Spindle Cove women."

Thorne harrumphed. "What stronger men would those be?"

A knock sounded at the study door.

"How do you do it?" Lady Rycliff asked, marveling at the sleeping babe in Bram's arms. "For a gruff old soldier, you charm lambs and babies with remarkable ease. Corporal Thorne, what is his secret?"

Bram gave him a stern look. *Don't tell. It's an order.*

Thorne wouldn't disobey an order. But neither could he let that "stronger men" remark go unanswered. "It must have been the . . . the lullabies, my lady."

"Lullabies?" Lady Rycliff laughed and turned to her husband. "I've never heard him sing a note. Not even in church."

"Yes, well," Thorne said. "His lordship sang them very softly. And then he made little kissing faces. There might have been a story about fairies and ponies."

Bram rolled his eyes. "Thanks for nothing."

Chapter Seventeen

After the midsummer fair, activities in Spindle Cove returned to the usual routine. Still nursing an adder-bitten heart, Kate embraced the familiarity as some comfort.

The ladies of the rooming house followed a predictable schedule during the summer. On Mondays they had country walks. Tuesdays were sea bathing. On Wednesdays they turned their hands to gardening.

And Thursdays were their day to shoot.

On this particular Thursday—a rather overcast, gloomy sort of morning—Kate had invited the Gramercys to join the ladies' target practice at Summerfield, Sir Lewis Finch's estate.

"I've always wanted to learn this," Aunt Marmoset said. "It's so exciting."

"Watch first, shoot later." Kate demonstrated the proper loading of a single-barrel pistol. "You must measure out the charge carefully with the powder horn," she said. "Then the ball and a patch. Like this, see?"

As she tamped down the bullet, Kate could sense Aunt Marmoset's impatience.

"That's all very interesting, dear, but when do I make it go bang?"

Kate smiled. "Let's shoot together this first time, shall we?"

She moved behind the older woman and helped her raise the pistol in both hands, bracing her arms straight as they aimed at the target.

"You'll want to close one eye," she said. "For precision. Then cock the hammer like so. And once you have it aimed and steady, gently squeeze the—"

"Oh," cried one of the other ladies, "here comes Lord Drewe!"

"Evan's here? Where?" Aunt Marmoset swung around, turning Kate with her. Together they pivoted with the loaded pistol braced in their outstretched hands—like a compass needle veering toward north.

All the ladies gasped and ducked.

"Get down!" Kate cried, struggling to regain control.

"Evan, look!" the Aunt Marmoset called. "I'm learning to shoot!"

Realizing he stood in the line of fire, Evan froze in place. "Brilliant."

With a flick of her thumb, Kate uncocked the hammer.

"Aunt Marmoset, please." She gripped the old woman's frail wrists and pulled downward, until the pistol was safely pointed at the ground. Despite her racing heartbeat, she made her voice calm. "Why don't we set this aside for now? Lord Drewe looks as though he has something to say."

Evan recovered himself. "Indeed I do." He clapped his hands together and rubbed them briskly. "I have exciting news for everyone."

"What is it?" Charlotte Highwood asked.

"Sir Lewis has agreed to loan me Summerfield's great

hall for an evening next week. My sisters and I . . ." He paused for effect. " . . . will be hosting a ball."

All the ladies went dead quiet. Nervous glances were exchanged. Kate thought she heard someone mutter a prayer.

"Did you . . ." She cleared her throat. "You did say a ball, Lord Drewe? Here at Summerfield?"

"Yes, a ball. It will be our way of thanking Spindle Cove for all the warm hospitality we've been shown during our holiday. We'll invite the militia, all the rooming house residents. We'll have a grand time."

The ladies' silence clearly wasn't the reaction Evan had been expecting. He looked around at the somber young women, nonplussed. "I don't understand. Do you not like balls?"

"We do," Kate assured him. "It's just that Summerfield balls . . . well, the last two both ended in violence and mayhem. Last summer, the ball was over before it even started, due to a tragic explosion. And then at Christmas, a French smuggler crashed into the ballroom and held poor Miss Winterbottom hostage all night. So we've developed a bit of a superstition, you see. About Summerfield balls. Some people say they're cursed."

"Well, this one will be different." Evan pulled up to his most lordly, commanding stature.

"Of course it will be," Lark said, "if the Gramercys are hosting it."

"Oh, yes," Harry added. "We are known for always showing our guests an unforgettable time."

Kate might have argued that the first two Summerfield balls had been unforgettable in their own ways.

Diana Highwood smiled, saving them all with her ever-affable nature. "Mama will be very pleased. And

I can scarcely wait myself. A ball is a lovely idea. Lord Drewe, you and your sisters are very good to us."

Evan bowed. "Thank you, Miss Highwood. It is our pleasure." To Kate, he added, "Miss Taylor, will you take a turn with me and my sisters in the garden? We'd like to solicit your advice with regards to the music."

"Very well," Kate said. She disarmed and disassembled the pistol and stored it safely away. To Diana, she whispered, "Please don't let their aunt anywhere near another weapon."

Diana laughed a little. "Don't worry. I won't."

Before heading for the garden, Kate collected Badger from the Summerfield groundskeeper. While she supposed a top hunting dog should theoretically be inured to gunfire, she hadn't thought it wise to have him underfoot during target practice.

Once they'd rounded a hedge and disappeared from the other ladies' view, Kate addressed the whole family. "I'm so sorry for that incident just now with the pistol. So very sorry. It was unforgivable of me to even put the weapon in her hand. I'd no idea the old dear would prove so strong. Or enthusiastic."

"Never mind that," said Evan. "Sir Lewis just finished showing me his medieval hall. Believe me, no humble pistol could chill my blood after viewing his collection of ancient torture devices. That's not what we called you aside to discuss."

"It's not?" She arched a brow. "Are you sure?"

"The ball," Lark whispered excitedly. "We need to talk about the ball. You do realize, it's for you. It's all for you."

"The ball is for me?"

Lark vibrated with excitement. "Yes, of course."

Harry cut in. "What Evan said about showing our

appreciation . . . that was true, too. But we want to bring you out, Kate. Give the debut you never had."

"But I'm twenty-three. That's much too old for a debut."

Evan said, "A debut, a come-out . . . they're just words that mean 'introduction to Society.' That's precisely what's in order here. We need to tell all England about you, Kate. But it only seems right to begin here. In Spindle Cove. All your friends will be so happy for you."

"I suggest a dramatic announcement at midnight," Harry said. "Make them all tingle with anticipation."

Kate tingled with some other feeling. She thought it might be dread.

She couldn't understand why this idea made her uneasy. Being announced as a long-lost lady, at a ball held in her honor—it ought to sound like a dream. A moment of fairy-tale triumph for a girl who'd grown up feeling outcast and alone. Her friends *would* be thrilled for her, to be sure. Except for perhaps Mrs. Highwood, who would likely go apoplectic with envy.

Still, she couldn't imagine the moment without feeling a flutter of anxiety. If she was going to stand before all her friends and neighbors and be announced as Lady Katherine Gramercy . . .

Kate wished she could be certain she believed it herself. Remembered it, in some undeniable fashion. Any small detail would do. With each passing day, she felt more certain that the memories were there, closer to the surface than ever before. She just needed to find the courage to unlock them.

As they turned into another section of the garden, Badger lunged at a wandering peafowl, scampering across a bed of herbs. Kate broke away from the group.

She leaned down to touch a teacup-sized pink rose blossom, sliding her finger along the velvety petal. The delicate texture held her transfixed, and a melody rose in her, instinctive as breath.

See the garden of blossoms so fair . . .

There was something in that song. Something important. She wouldn't have remembered it all her life otherwise.

She ground her slipper heel into the manicured white gravel. "Will you excuse me? Please go ahead back to the village. I—I've forgotten something. And Badger needs to have his run for the day."

Without even waiting for an answer, she turned and began walking in the other direction. The puppy followed at her heel.

She had no particular destination. But she *had* forgotten something.

She would walk and walk, and keep walking until she recalled it. Until she finally reached the end of that long dark corridor.

And when she arrived there—this time, she would open that door.

"Don't be long, Kate!" Lark called after her. "The sky looks like rain."

Thorne could not have picked a worse day for overland travel. He hadn't made it very far south before the sky darkened with ominous clouds. A few hours later he met with the rain.

It hadn't let up since.

These damned Sussex roads took no more than a sprinkle of rain to go from "passable packed dirt" to "muddy pig wallow." His progress was slow, and wet. This all would have been easier if he could have skipped returning to Spindle Cove at all and proceeded straight to America after gaining his discharge papers. But he needed to collect his personal belongings and arrange for transfer of the militia command.

And he needed to see Katie. Just one more time, even if from a distance. Conversation wouldn't be necessary. He just wanted to lay eyes on her and assure himself she was happy and safe and loved.

She deserved to be loved, by people who'd read enough books to understand what the hell "love" meant.

At last he turned off the main road and took the spur toward Spindle Cove. At that point the moors and meadows were more passable than the rutted roads, so he turned his horse off the lane and continued overland.

Through a cloud of swirling fog, the ancient specter of Rycliff Castle appeared on the distant bluffs, seeming to shift and change with every gust of wind. Beyond that the sea was obscured by a wall of gray mist. All the usual sounds of country life—sheep bleating, birds singing—were muted by the steady rain. The entire scene was unearthly. Beneath the many sodden layers of his coat, waistcoat, cravat, and shirt, his skin crawled.

Watch sharp.

At the meadow's lowest point—just before the rocky bluffs began to rise on the other side—Thorne slowed his horse to a walk. He scouted carefully for the appropriate crossing place. Centuries ago there'd been a deep moat carved here. An extra layer of protection for the castle above.

Over hundreds of years the moat had mostly filled in—but there were still pockets here and there where the meadow dropped out from beneath a man's feet, and boulders waited to catch him a few yards below.

A strange sound came to him, piercing through the thick felt blanket of rain noise. He recognized it at once.

"Badger?"

Thorne left his horse. The gelding was on familiar ground now; he'd spent a year grazing these meadows every day.

Whistling in this downpour would be futile. He cupped his hands around his mouth and shouted for the dog. "Badger! Here, boy."

The pup's barking came from one of the deep hollows in the meadow. What was he doing down there?

"This had better not be another snake," Thorne muttered, advancing to investigate.

It wasn't a snake. It was a woman.

His Katie, tucked beneath a bit of overhanging turf, soaked to her skin and shivering in a muddy hole in the ground.

"Jesus Christ."

He stepped down into the pit, bracing his boot on a ledge of stone and stretching his free hand toward her. "Katie, it's me. Take my hand."

"You're here." Her face was so pale, and her voice was frayed. "I knew you'd find me. You always find me."

Her arm looked positively ghostly as she reached up to him. He worried he'd make a grab for her hand and discover she'd dissolved to mist. Lost to him forever.

But no. When he tightened his fingers, they seized on real flesh and blood. Treacherously *chilled* flesh and blood, but he would take her any way he could have her, so long as she was alive.

With a few tugs and a bit of cooperation on her end, he had her out of the hole. She fell against him, and he caught her in his arms.

"Katie." He stared down at her, horrified. Her thin

muslin frock was soaked through, clinging to her skin in mud-streaked tatters. "Are you injured? Are you broken anywhere?"

"No. Just c-cold."

He released her—steadying her on her feet so he could strip out of his coat. The damn sleeves were fitted too well, and the fabric was damp. He had to struggle, and every moment he wasted was a moment she shivered with cold. By the time he finally had the thing off, he'd rattled through every blasphemy in his vocabulary.

"What the devil are you doing out in this?"

"I . . . I didn't mean to be. I took Badger out for a run, and we were caught in the rain. I didn't realize how much he'd hate it. I thought dogs loved the rain."

"Not sight hounds."

"S-So I've learned. At the first sprinkle of rain, he darted down into the hole. I couldn't make him leave, and I wouldn't leave him. I decided we'd just take shelter and wait the downpour out. But then it went on and on. By the time it eased a little, I was so very c-cold."

He threw his coat around her shoulders and drew it closed. For a summer rain, this one was cold, and God only knew how long she'd been out in it. Her lips were a distressing shade of blue, and now she wasn't making a damn bit of sense.

"I had to go walking, you see. I had to keep walking until I found the answer. Even if it t-t-took all day and all night. I had to know. But now I do." Her teeth chattered and she stared blankly into the distance.

"I need to get you inside. We have to get you warm."

Her eyes met his, suddenly lucid and piercing. "I remembered, Samuel."

God. When she said his name, his heart made a mad, frantic attempt to escape his chest.

She collapsed against his body, curling her fingers into the fabric of his shirt. Her breath was a puff of warmth against his skin.

"I remembered you," she whispered. "You, the music, the song. That night. I remembered everything."

Chapter Eighteen

I remembered everything.

Thorne refused to think about the implications of her words. He needed to get her to dry shelter as soon as possible. Everything else could wait.

The castle was barely a quarter mile off. He could have put her up on his horse, but the beast was exhausted from slogging through mud all afternoon. Thorne would have needed to walk alongside, which meant there'd be no speed advantage over simply carrying her himself.

So that was what he decided to do. At least she'd be able to borrow his heat.

Thorne wrapped one arm around the small of her back and slid the other beneath her thighs. With a flex of his muscles and a grunt of effort, he plucked her off her feet and settled her weight against his chest. She was a good bit heavier than when he'd done this last. But then, he was bigger and stronger, too.

He ducked his head, using his sleeve to wipe the raindrops from his face, and started walking. His boots squelched through the muddy flat, slowing his progress.

When he finally reached the bluffs, he had firmer rock beneath his feet.

Of course, he also had to trudge uphill.

He paused to rebalance her weight. "Can you put your arms around me?"

She obeyed, sliding her chilled arms free and reaching to lace them around his neck. It helped. If nothing else, the secret thrill of her touch against his skin made his heart beat faster, powering a new surge of strength to his limbs.

He made the final climb in determined strides, carrying her straight to the heart of the castle—the keep, where his personal quarters were.

Once he had her inside, he lit a lamp and assessed her state more carefully. Her damp, chilled condition appalled him, but it also gave him something to do. He made a mental list. First, dry clothing and blankets. Second, a fire. Third, nourishment. Then he'd see about restoring her gown to rights.

Badger shook himself, spraying muddy droplets everywhere. Thorne threw him an old quilt, and the dog nosed and rolled in it.

"That'll have to do for you," he said to the dog. "She comes first."

He rolled up his sleeves and went to work. There was nothing sensual in the way he helped her out of the sodden, mud-spattered frock. He moved briskly, willing himself not to notice anything of her bare body save the pale, bluish tinge of her skin and the way her muscles quivered. To take any pleasure from this would be disgusting and base.

As she sat on the hearth rug and hugged her knees to her chest, he toweled dry her hair and helped her into one of his own clean, dry shirts. For modesty's sake, he draped it over her head and shoulders before reaching beneath to unbutton and remove her chemise. He tried his best to keep his cold, coarse fingers from scraping against her bare flesh. He averted his eyes from the flash of her red, turgid nipple as he switched one garment for the other. As he pulled the folds of crisp, soap-scented lawn down her midriff, he tried to ignore the way lamp-light cast her slight, nubile form in silhouette.

He couldn't, not entirely. What a beast he was.

He would rather let her tend to such things herself, but she seemed incapable at the moment.

Once he laid a fire, she stared dully into it, mute and shivering. He wondered if it was the shock of remembering the Hothouse, and the squalid conditions there. Perhaps her mother's loss had suddenly become real to her, and she was suffering the pangs of grief.

In any event, he didn't want to rush her or press her to talk. He just relished the chance to take care of her, here and now—where this was *his* right, *his* responsibility, and no one else's. He was happy for her to stare into the fire. When she came back to herself, those hazel eyes would no doubt turn on him and fill with loathing. It might be the last time she looked at him, ever again.

"Here," he said, crouching beside her and offering her a steaming mug of tea, well-doctored with sugar and brandy. "Drink this. It will help you get warm."

He put it in her hands, wrapping her fingers around it. She held it, but only stared blankly at the contents.

"I c-can't seem to stop shivering."

He reached for another blanket.

"No." Her head turned, and her eyes focused on his face. "I want you, Samuel. I want you to hold me. Pl-Please."

Those words—just the words alone—found some

aching chasm in his soul and filled it. But damn it, he was trying to be honorable. If he took her in his arms, he wasn't sure he could keep his thoughts protective.

"I should tend to your frock," he said. "It's almost dry, but it needs—"

"The frock can wait." With trembling hands, she set the mug of tea on the floor. "I can't." Another chill racked her body. "I need you."

Reluctantly, he sat beside her on the small, threadbare rug. He stretched one of his legs behind her, propping her up with his bent knee. His other leg sprawled toward the fire. And then he put both arms around her, and she sank into his embrace, nestling close to his chest. Her cool cheek rested against his pounding heart.

"Tight," she whispered. "Hold me tight."

He obeyed, flexing the muscles in his arms.

Her discomfort was his enemy. Any chills that dared rack her frame would have to rattle him, too. He had heat and strength enough for them both.

He bent his head, burying his face in her curling hair and letting his breath warm her ear and the back of her neck.

Her fingers gathered a fistful of his shirt and clung tight. They remained like that several minutes. He kept a close watch on her bottom lip. When it pinked and ceased quivering, a stupid surge of triumph rushed to his head. He had the brief, idiot notion he'd done something good for her.

Then he remembered who she was, and who he was, and precisely why they were here. And he reminded himself that this would be the end.

He pressed his face into the curve of her neck and inhaled deeply of her lemony clover scent. He'd hold her while he could.

"Thank you," she whispered. "That's better."

When he lifted his head, she relaxed her grip on his shirt.

"I've remembered it for you," she murmured. "The amusing story from your childhood. It's like I told you, everyone has one. You see, there was this girl who shared your attic. A pestering little thing who tugged at your sleeves when you would have rather been running loose with the neighborhood boys. But late at night, sometimes, when she couldn't sleep, you took it on yourself to make her laugh and laugh—with games and shadow puppets and sweets nicked from the kitchens downstairs. One night, you bundled her up in every cloak and cape and muffler she had, and told her it was time to play gypsies. We were going to have a grand adventure, you said."

She looked up at him, eyes wide in the dim firelight. "Why didn't you tell me everything? You told me the truth of my mother, but you neglected to tell me the truth about you." She touched his cheek. "Why didn't you tell me that you saved my life?"

He swallowed hard. "I didn't save your life."

"I think you did. Or something close to it. I told you, I finally remembered."

She gazed into the fire, contemplative. "All my life, I've kept this shadowy recollection in my thoughts. I'm in a long, dark hallway, and I can feel pianoforte music coming up through the floor. I hear the song, that same little verse about the garden. There's something blue flashing in the darkness, and someone says, 'Be brave, my Katie.'"

A knot stuck in his throat. He couldn't speak.

"It was you, wasn't it? We were up in the attic, and we were escaping that place."

He forced out a reply. "Yes."

"You took my hand and opened the door. We hurried down the stairs, and we never went back. You delivered me to Margate."

"It was what your mother wanted. Before she died, she made her wishes clear. You were clever, and everyone could see it. She'd read about Margate in some subscription magazine and knew they took in foundlings. She wanted you sent to that school."

"But I wasn't?"

He shook his head. "After Ellie Rose died—"

"Why can't I remember her?" she interrupted, distressed. "I remember you now, in little bits and pieces. But no matter how I search my brain, I still have nothing of her."

"Perhaps you'll recall more, in time. It's not your fault. We had to stay out of our mothers' way, for the most part. Else we would have been branded as troublesome, and landed ourselves on the streets. Anyhow, after your mother died, weeks passed. Then months. I knew they never meant to send you to that school. They never meant to let you go at all. They would have kept you there, made you one of them far too soon. For God's sake, they were already teaching you the song." His stomach turned, just thinking of it.

"*They* taught me the song?"

"The place . . ." He blew out his breath. He hated telling her these sordid details, but they'd come this far. She needed to know everything. "It was an opera house, mainly, with music and dancing girls cavorting on stage. But all manner of other things went on abovestairs. They named it the Hothouse, and all the dancers were called 'blossoms.' "

"Like Ellie Rose," she said, understanding. "Instead of Elinor Haverford."

"Lily Belle. Pansy Shaw. Molly Thorne." He winced. "That verse you remember . . . it's what they sang for the gentlemen at the start of every performance."

"So they were teaching me . . ."

"To be part of it, yes. They'd dress you up like a doll, push you out on the stage. At first, just as a poppet to sing and smile for the crowd. But the devil only knew how long it would take, before they wanted something more of you."

"Oh." As his meaning sank in, her face twisted. "Oh, God. That's horrible."

"I know it's horrible. I know. That's why I had to take you out of that place. That's why I never wanted you to hear this." He ran a hand through his hair in agitation. "Katie, don't ask me about it anymore."

"All right. We'll speak of other things." She reached for his right wrist. "How is your arm healing?"

"It's better. Still clumsy, but improved. If I ever did save your life, I think you returned the favor that afternoon. We're even now."

"I doubt that." Her fingers found their way to the border of his open collar. She pulled the gaping shirt-front to the side, exposing the hardened surface of his chest.

She stroked her fingertips over the most prominent of his tattoos. He sucked in his breath, trying not to let her touch affect him. Too late. His groin was already rock hard. So disgusting. So *wrong*, that he should be aroused by her, so soon after relating that tale.

"These make me so curious," she whispered. "Where did you get them?"

"Different places," he answered dismissively. "None of them worth your notice."

"But I want to know."

She pulled away from his embrace. A fresh gleam of determination lit her eyes. She ran her hand down his shirtfront, then gathered the linen hem and began hiking it, exposing his belly.

His abdominal muscles flinched and went rigid. "What are you doing?"

"Won't you call me Katie? I like it when you do. Something about your voice when you say it, in that low, dangerous growl." She gathered the folds of his shirt in both hands now and raised it.

"Katie . . ." he groaned.

She smiled. "Yes. Like that. It makes me warm and tingly all over. Now raise your arms."

He could deny her nothing, and she knew it. She meant to make use of it.

She drew the gathered shirt over his head and down his arms, then cast it gently aside. Swiveling her body, she angled to face him. Her gaze roamed over his bared chest, and the look in her eyes was a mix of fascination and fear. He felt the urge to hide the truth, the unpleasantness. But it was better that she see this and understand.

She said, "Tell me."

"What do you want to know?"

"Which was the first?"

"This one." He turned his shoulder to her, to point out the small rose inked there.

"How did you get it?"

"After I left London—"

"With me. After you left London with me, and delivered me to Margate."

"Yes." He swallowed. "I couldn't go back to the Hot-house, of course. Even if I'd wished to return, and I didn't. I roamed the countryside, doing odd work here and there, but mostly sleeping in haystacks and living off what small game I could snare. I found I had a knack for it, the coursing. It was as if I lived so wild, I devel-oped an animal way of thinking. I sensed where the hare would be before it appeared, knew which direction it would flee. And the open land and fresh air . . . I think it did me good, after all those years of London soot. I was a dirty, scraggly thing, but I think those months were the closest to happiness I ever came.

"I fell in with a poaching gang, once winter arrived. I brought them game to sell, they made sure I had a barn to sleep in and a warm coat and boots. This mark"—he rubbed the crudely drawn flower—"was how the mem-bers knew one another. No names."

"No friendships," she said. "No real human connec-tions."

"I did have a dog."

"Really?" She smiled. "What was his name?"

He hesitated. "Patch."

"Oh, Samuel." She pressed a hand to her cheek and shook her head. "I was so thoughtless. I'm so sorry."

He shrugged. "Don't be. Badger suits him."

She found the row of numbers inside his left forearm. "And this?"

"Ah. Those mark the next stop in a poacher's career. Prison."

"Prison? Oh, no. How old were you then?"

"Fifteen. I think."

She rubbed the tattoo. "Was this some sort of identi-fication number they gave to all the prisoners?"

He shook his head. "I did it myself, the first month.

It's the date I was due to be released. Didn't want to risk it being forgotten."

"Forgotten by the gaolers?"

"Forgotten by me."

Neither had he been willing to prolong his sentence by accepting any comforts in prison. Bedding, meat rations, the keys to the irons—all of it came at a price, and the gaolers tallied it in ledgers. Sixpence a week for this, a shilling for that. By the time a man's sentence was served, he might have accrued debt in the tens of pounds—and he wouldn't be released until he came up with the funds to pay it. Rather than face that madness, he had refused any extra food or blankets.

"How long were you imprisoned?" she asked.

"I was sentenced to seven years. But in the end, I only served four."

The word "only" contained all sorts of lies. Only four years of sleeping on straw so old it had turned to dust, and so thick with vermin that the dust seemed alive. Only four years of surviving on a penny's worth of bread a day. Only four years of shivering in irons that never were adjusted, even though he grew bigger and taller every month.

Yes, "only" four years of violence, hunger, ugliness, and animal treatment that haunted him to this day.

"The courts took mercy on you?" she asked.

"Mercy? Hardly. England needed soldiers more than she needed prisoners. They released me on the condition that I enlist."

"So this . . ." She touched the medallion on the right side of his chest. "Is this the symbol of your regiment?"

"Partly." His chest lifted in a humorless chuckle. "Don't go fishing for deep meaning in that one. Just too much rum in a Portuguese tavern one night, soon after we shipped to the Peninsula."

Her hand slipped down his rib cage and to the left, passing right over his heart. He winced at the ripples of pure pleasure.

"And this . . . ?" she asked. "B.C. Who was she? Did you meet her in the same tavern? Was she exotic and big-breasted and terribly beautiful? Did you . . . care for her?"

He stared at her, struggling like the devil not to laugh.

"I hope she was a good person, for your sake. But however well she treated you, I must admit that I've formed an irrational, intense dislike of her already. In my mind, I've named her Bathsheba Cabbagewort."

Now he lost the struggle. He bent his head and laughed, long and low.

"Well, there's something good come out of it," she said, eyes misty. "I've been growing quite desperate to hear you laugh. And it's just as I suspected." She touched his cheek. "You do have a dimple, just here. Tell me Bathsheba never saw that."

He put his hand over hers and drew it downward. He traced the letters on his side with her fingertip.

"B.C.," he said. "Not a woman. It stands for 'Bad Character.' It's what they mark on soldiers who are drummed out of their corps for criminal offenses."

"Criminal offenses? What did you do?"

"What didn't I do would be the better question. Looting, thieving, fighting, shirking duty, insubordination. Everything short of rape, murder, and desertion— and I was primed to attempt the last. So far as I was concerned, His Majesty's government had beaten and starved everything human from me already. Then they'd sent me to die on the battlefield. Nothing mattered to me anymore, Katie. I had no loyalty, no honor, no morality. I was truly more beast than man."

"But you changed, obviously. And you did stay in the army, or you never would have come to Spindle Cove."

He nodded. "After my drumming out, I was sent to Lord Rycliff. He was Lieutenant Colonel Bramwell then. It was his to say what to do with me—prison, death, worse. But he took one look at me and said he'd be a fool to send away any man with my fitness and strength. So he kept me on, made me his personal batman. His valet, in essence."

"That was very good of him."

"You can't know. It was the first time in years that someone had entrusted me with anything. Rycliff wasn't much older than me, but he was comfortable with command. And he was nothing like my sergeants. He cared about the men in his regiment. He took pride in our mission. I worked so close to him, I guess some of that rubbed off on me. I started to see that there was honor to be found in doing a task well, no matter how small. Starching collars, mending seams, replacing buttons. But mostly the boots."

"The boots?"

He nodded. "Worth more than my life's wages, his boots were. Worth more than my life itself, I'd guess. This was the infantry. Every day, all day—we marched, dug, fought. Come nightfall his boots would be covered in dust, muck, blood, worse. I slaved for hours to make them shine again. So he'd look at them in the morning and know there was something worth saving beneath it all. And when I'd finished with his boots, I still didn't sleep—not until I'd done the same with mine.

"I wasn't loyal to the army or England so much as I

was loyal to him—or maybe even just to those boots. When he took a bullet to the knee—I couldn't let him lose that leg, you know. No leg, no boot. Would have been giving up half my purpose in life." He rubbed his face and stared into the fire. "He's offered to grant me a commission now."

"Lord Rycliff has?"

He nodded.

"What an honor, Samuel. Don't you want it?"

He shook his head. "I'm not made for that. I don't have Rycliff's ease with military politics. The open country is where I was best suited, even as a youth. It's where I belong now. Out in the wilderness, with the creatures that howl and claw and snarl. No social graces necessary."

There. He'd laid it all out before her. His checkered past, his history of crime and violence. All the reasons he needed to leave England and stay far away from her.

And in response she said the most horrible thing he could imagine.

"Would you take me with you?"

Chapter Nineteen

"Take you with me?" he echoed. "To America?"

Kate nodded. It seemed more than reasonable to her. He'd suffered twenty years of violence and misery to pay the cost of her dreams. She could handle living in a cabin.

His brow furrowed. "No. No."

As she watched, he rose from the carpet and went to the opposite side of the small room, pulling her gown from the screen where he'd hung it to dry and filling a pressing iron with hot coals.

Well. That wasn't quite the response she'd been hoping for.

"You can't leave me," she said. "The world will only push us back together. Haven't we learned that much? We're meant to be with each other."

"We're meant to be no such thing. You are the daughter of a marquess. You always were, even then. And I was always a lowborn cur. There's nothing we have in common. Nothing."

"Don't you want me to be happy?"

"Of course I do."

He spread her frock over the table, carefully layering it between pressing cloths. The muscles of his left arm bunched and flexed as he skimmed the hot iron over fabric, working with care and confidence. She never could have dreamed how arousing this would be—the sight of a massive, shirtless man pressing a gown. All she could think of was those hands roving over her body, warming and smoothing her own frayed edges.

"Katie, I want you to have everything you're entitled to—wealth, connections, Society. The family you always dreamed of finding. It's all yours now, and I'll be damned if I'll ruin that for you." He put the iron aside. "You can't be with someone like me. Look at me. That cousin of yours wouldn't hire me on as a footman."

If Thorne was this reluctant already, she wasn't about to tell him the truth of her inheritance. Not yet. He wouldn't see it as a convenience, only as one more factor widening the gulf he perceived between them.

Which wasn't a gulf at all. All that separated them was an imaginary line. But someone must take the first step across it, and Kate knew it would have to be her.

"This is about us, Samuel. No one else." She drew the blanket about her shoulders and rose to her feet. His stubbornness was a thing to be conquered, and she felt her courage rising. "I'm just me. Just Katie. *Your* Katie, as you called me once. I know you have feelings for me."

He set the iron down, agitated. "I've told you, time and again, it's only—"

"Only desire. Yes, I know you've told me that. And I know you're lying to me. Your feelings go much deeper than lust."

"I feel *nothing*." His nostrils flared. He beat his fist against his chest. "Nothing. Do you understand me?"

"I know that's not tr—"

"Look. These letters." He pointed to the B.C. marked on the left side of his torso. "Do you know how they make these marks?"

She shook her head no.

"They take a board, about so big." He measured with his hands. "And on it are protruding nails, forming the shapes of the letters. They press the points of those nails to your skin, and then they give the board a smart whack. With a fist, perhaps. Or maybe a mallet."

Kate winced. She stepped forward, but he held her off with an open hand.

"And then, when they've made all those tiny punctures, they take black powder—you know enough about weaponry to know that it's corrosive stuff—and rub it in the wounds to make the mark."

"That must have been torture."

"I didn't feel a thing. Just like I didn't feel these."

He turned, showing her his back. Kate's stomach turned as she viewed the lattice of twisted, branching scars that covered his skin.

"Floggings," he said. "A hundred lashes, for my countless offenses. They laid open my flesh to the muscle, and I swear to you, I didn't feel a stroke. Because I'd learned how to deaden myself. To pain, to sorrow, to sentiment. To everything."

Tears stung at the corners of her eyes. She couldn't decide whether he deliberately told her falsehoods or had convinced himself of these untruths, but she hated hearing him speak this way.

This man felt, and he felt deeply.

"Samuel . . ."

"No. I know what you're thinking. Today, you've remembered some boy you once knew. He was fond of you and kind to you, and he did you a good turn, once. That boy doesn't exist anymore. The man I am . . . well, you can read for yourself." He pointed out the marks on his skin, one by one. "Thief. Prisoner. Drunken soldier. Bad character, through and through. I went dead inside long ago. And I feel nothing now."

She approached him slowly, in small increments, just as she would approach a cornered wild animal she didn't want to frighten away.

"Do you feel this?" She tilted her head and leaned in to kiss his neck. The scent of him made her pulse with longing.

"Katie . . ."

"What of this?" She stretched to kiss his cheek, allowing her lips to linger on the hard edge of his jaw. "Or—"

He seized her by the arms, pushing her back. "Stop."

She dropped her gaze to his chest, surveying all the marks and scars he'd collected since they parted in her childhood—all of them incurred, in part, for her. The enormity of what those marks represented eclipsed any fear or sorrow she'd ever known. She could scarcely comprehend the magnitude of his suffering, but she forced her mind to stretch, to try. He'd sacrificed everything, including the only home he ever had. He'd bought her a bright, shiny future at the cost of his own freedom.

How could she not love him? How could he deny loving her?

"My whole life," she began, her voice faltering, "I clung to just a few scraps of memory. No matter how bleak my surroundings, those vague recollections gave me hope that someone, somewhere, had cared for me, once. And I always believed, to the very center of my being, that one day someone would love me again."

"Well now you've found the Gramercys. They will—"

"You. I found *you*." She put her hands on his chest. "The Gramercys are wonderful people. I'm so fond of them now, and they're fond of me. But they never knew I existed. My poor mother . . . she seems to have been too preoccupied, and then too sick to give me much love. None of them were that force I carried all along, that hope that sustained me for years. That was you. All you."

A tear spilled down her cheek. " 'Be brave, my Katie.' I remembered you saying that. You can never know what those words meant to me, and it was your voice, all along. And if—"

He closed his eyes and pressed his brow to hers. "Katie, I beg you. For your own good, stop this."

"And if you deny it now . . ." She worked her hands high enough to frame his face. "If you deny that you care for me, you'll make my whole life a lie."

He shook his head. "You're dreaming. Or confused. Overwrought by the day, perhaps. You can't mean to suggest you'd give up everything here. The Gramercys, the wealth, all your friendships."

"To be with the man I love? Absolutely."

"Don't." His arm whipped around her and he turned, pressing her against the wall. "Don't say it. You can't love me."

"Are you doubting my sincerity? Or are you forbidding me to love you?"

"Both."

He pinned her with a glare that was stern and fierce and ice-cold blue. So blue it made her heart sing. At last she knew why she'd carried that memory of blue in her heart.

It was him. It had always been him.

His jaw tightened. "I have nothing to offer you. Nothing."

"If that's true, it's only because you've already given me everything a man could give. You saved me, Samuel. Not just the once, but so many times. You stepped in front of a horse whip. You took a melon to the head. You caught an adder in your bare hand, you dear, foolish man."

"I did that for the dog."

"*My* dog. Which you let me keep, even though you prized him yourself." She stroked his cheek, trying to soften his expression. "I know you care. And I know you want me."

He didn't try to deny that part. The desire in his eyes was knee-melting.

"When you look at me that way, I feel so beautiful."

"You *are* beautiful." He sighed deep in his chest. His hands slid up and down her arms, caressing her roughly. "So damned beautiful."

"So are you." She put a hand to his bare chest, tracing the defined ridges of his musculature. "Like a diamond. Hard and gleaming, and cut with all these exquisite facets. Inside . . . pure, brilliant fire."

She slid her hands to the back of his neck, plunging her fingers through the velvety nap of his short hair. The clipped ends teased the webs between her fingers, setting off sparks of sensation throughout her body. She drew his head down to hers until his lips—so strong, so sensual—filled her vision. And then she closed her eyes and explored those lips with her own. Pressing slight, tender kisses to each corner of his mouth. Capturing his top lip between both of hers, and then giving the lower its due.

Nothing separated her breasts from his chest but a single layer of linen, which quickly heated and softened between them. A heavy ache settled in her breasts, and her nipples came to tight, desperate points. She rubbed them against his chest, hoping to soothe the ache, but only inflaming her desire.

And his, apparently.

His good left arm rested around her waist. He flexed his arm muscles, lifting her off her feet and drawing her pelvis flush with his. The hard ridge of his arousal pressed against her sex. The pleasure was blinding. Deafening. Numbing. It was as though all her senses sank inward, downward, the better to concentrate on that source of solid, delicious pressure between her legs.

She ground her hips against it. She could not have done otherwise. And when she'd done so once, all she wanted was to do it again.

He groaned and nipped her earlobe. "Katie, I want you. I can't make it poetry. I can't make it sound anything other than crude, because it is. I want you in my bed. I want you under me, holding me. I want to bury my cock so deep inside you."

The carnal words made her blush and stammer. "I—I want those things, too."

She wished she could have managed a more sophisticated reply. But the words worked well enough to earn her a kiss—a wild, passionate storm of a kiss—and then she was lost in the tempest of heat and longing.

His tongue thrust deep into her mouth, possessive and hot, coaxing her instinctive response. Her heartbeat quickened, and a matching pulse beat at the juncture of her thighs.

When he broke the kiss, he was breathing hard. "You should go. Leave me."

"Never."

"If you stay, I'm taking you to my bed. And once I bed you, you're mine. Always. You must know that."

"Yes." A thrill shot through her. "I want nothing more."

She gasped as he plucked her from the floor and carried her to the mattress. One-armed, as though she weighed nothing.

While she lay there, he stood back and began wrestling with the closures of his breeches. He worked left-handed, and clumsily. After a few moments she couldn't bear the suspense.

"Won't you let me help?" She sat on her knees and reached for the buttons. The buckskin was butter-soft and stretched taut as a drum. Her mouth dried as she worked one row of buttons loose, freeing one side of the falls. Then she reached for the small row of closures in the center. She slid one fingertip beneath the waistband to aid her efforts. When her touch grazed his belly, he flinched, ticklish.

Kate smiled. She loosed one button, then another, exposing the dark line of hair that widened and thickened as she moved lower. It seemed she couldn't look her fill—until the moment when she grasped the final button, and then she couldn't bear to look at all.

She tilted her face upward and found him staring down at her. His face was grim with restraint and his eyes dark with hunger. She slipped the last button free and watched his face as she slid her hand inside his breeches, exploring the hot, hard flesh within.

She marveled. He was so solid, so sleek, so intriguingly textured.

And so big.

Goodness. She was meant to take *all* this inside her?

As Kate watched him, his eyes fluttered closed and his head fell back. He pushed into her grasp with a strangled moan. She loved the sensual abandon in his expression, but she worried about the physical dimensions of his ardor. With every inch her sliding fingertips explored, he seemed to grow longer still—and she grew increasingly doubtful about the logistics involved in this enterprise.

Perhaps her sense of touch was misleading her. Maybe if she looked the organ head-on, it wouldn't seem so intimidating.

She dropped her gaze and pushed his breeches down over his hips. Up it sprang from a thatch of dark hair. A thick, dusky curve of pure impossibility.

Were all men like this?

She put her hand on him again, since he seemed to enjoy it. He filled her grip, and then some. Kate suddenly had the urge to call a temporary halt to this entire interlude and pay a hasty call on a few of her married friends. Then she'd return wiser, worldlier, and prepared with some kind of soothing poultice for afterward.

He gripped her hand, squeezing tight. "Enough."

"Did I do something wrong?"

"No. No. It's too right. Too good. I won't last."

Since she didn't suppose she could implement her first plan to dash out for education and herbal remedies, having this over with quickly didn't seem like a bad alternative.

"I don't mind if it's fast," she said shyly.

For the second time in an hour she heard him laugh.

It was such a lovely, gruff sound, she didn't even mind that he was laughing at her.

"You should mind." He stepped out of his breeches and set them aside.

She felt so stupid. He'd been with many women, and no doubt all of them had been accomplished in a way that actually mattered. Proficient in bed sport, rather than arpeggios.

"I'm sorry. I haven't any useful experience to draw on. I just hope you'll tell me what pleases you."

"You please me." He sat next to her on the mattress and drew the fabric of the borrowed shirt aside to bare her shoulder. His lips traced the slope of her neck.

"I mean, I should hate to suffer by comparison."

His lifted his head. His eyes flashed. "There is no comparison. None."

He slid his hand beneath the shirt to cup her breast. His strong fingers molded and shaped her.

She moaned as he teased her nipple, rolling it under his thumb. "Samuel."

"Yes." His voice was husky as he drew the shirt up and over her head. "Give me my name."

"Samuel," she whispered, glad that he'd given her this one way to please him. "Samuel, I missed you every day that you were gone. I've missed you so much."

He stretched his body over hers, covering her with his weight. She loved the feel of his body—hard and heavy and covered in dark hair. So very different from her own. As he kissed her, he slid one thigh between hers. It excited her to feel his bare skin against her most intimate flesh.

His tongue swirled lazy patterns over her breast, painting her with delicious, silky heat. He fastened his mouth over her nipple and suckled hard, drawing the whole peak into his mouth. She cried out with the sharp joy of it, shamelessly rubbing and bucking against the firm slope of his thigh.

As he transferred his attentions to her other breast, he adjusted his weight to the side. She whimpered at the loss of friction against her sex, but his fingers skimmed down her belly and found her cleft. He sifted through the soft curls, stroking over her swollen folds before parting her gently and sliding a finger inside. Just an inch at first, then working deeper in smooth, blissful plunges. The sense of fullness was exquisite. His thumb found that sensitive bud at the crest of her sex and worked it in devilish circles. Soon she was rolling her hips to meet each deep slide of his finger, loving the way his palm slapped lightly against her flesh.

"Samuel, it's too . . . I can't—"

The climax took her, fast and hard. She arched off of the bed, grinding down on his hand and crying out with pleasure. Her intimate muscles grasped at his invading finger, shamelessly begging for more.

As the last waves of joy rippled through her, he withdrew his touch. He settled his hips in the cradle of her thighs. His erection wedged hard and hot against her still-pulsing core.

"Do you want me?" he asked.

"More than anything."

He positioned himself at her entrance. "You want *this*? You're sure of it?"

"Yes." She tilted her hips, eager to welcome him in. "Now. *Please*. Just take me."

He took.

His first thrust was shallow—she burned a bit as her inner walls stretched, but nothing too terrible.

This might not be so bad, she thought.

"Katie," he moaned. "You feel like heaven."

Not so bad at all.

But then the second plunge—it was pure, stabbing misery. She buried her face in his shoulder to conceal her sob. As he rooted deeper in rhythmic, gentle thrusts, the pain eased a bit. But not so much that she could manage a convincing reply when he asked if she was well.

He swore.

"What is it?" she asked. "Have I done something—"

"You're perfect. I just hate that I've hurt you. I hate that it's done and I can't take it back."

"Well, I don't hate any of it. The pain's better already. I love the feel of you inside me. I love knowing I can hold you like this, so close." She smoothed the hair from his brow and stared deep into his eyes. "Samuel, I love you."

"Don't say that." But even as he resisted, he began to move again. Slowly, deeply. In ways she found tantalizing, rather than tormenting.

"Why not?" She gave him a teasing smile. "Are you afraid you might say it back?"

He flexed his thighs and slid deep, deep inside.

"I love you," she whispered.

He pulled back, frowning. Hesitating. As though he were weighing the pleasure another thrust would bring him against the pain of facing words he didn't wish to hear.

She wouldn't let him intimidate her with those stormy looks. This was the bargain. If he wanted her body, he would have to accept her heart, too.

He grit his teeth and pushed into her, hard.

"I love you," she gasped, clutching his arms.

He increased his tempo, battering her with desperate motions. As though he would force her to break, to recant.

Not a chance.

She wrapped her legs around his hips and clung stubbornly to his neck. The words became a chant in time with his thrusts. She would chip away at the stone all night, if that's what it took to break down his walls.

"Love you," she moaned. "Love you. Love . . . you."

His face twisted into a tortured mask—of agonized pleasure, or perhaps pleasurable agony. His eyebrows rose in anticipation, then crashed down into a fierce, determined line.

And then he broke away.

He pulled free of her body, turned aside, and gave those last, beautiful moments of abandon to the linen sheets instead. She tried not to feel hurt. For a whole host of reasons, a pregnancy would be ill-timed. It was good of him to think of her health and reputation, even in that wild, passionate moment.

But she couldn't hold back a whisper of disappointment. She wanted him *all*.

Spent and weakened, he slumped on the mattress. She turned and gathered him in her arms. She stroked his scarred, beautiful back, waiting to hear whatever he could bring himself to say.

After long moments he rose up on one elbow. He stared at her, still breathing hard. His eyes were dark and fathomless as he stroked the hair from her brow and trailed a gentle touch down her cheek.

Finally, he repaid all her nervous waiting with just one deep, resonant word.

"Katie."

And it was enough. Enough to make her heart soar and her eyes burn with blissful tears. Enough to make her desperate for his kiss. She tugged him close, dragging his mouth to hers and reveling in the sweet possession.

With this man, there would never be poetry. Very few parties, and even less dancing. They'd never sit down to the pianoforte and play clever duets.

She could wait her whole life, and he might never find the words to say he loved her.

But the truth of it was written all over his skin. And that was enough.

Chapter Twenty

fterward, she slept.

Thorne didn't.

He couldn't have slept, even if he'd wished to. Too many thoughts rioted in his skull. He lay awake, keeping one arm curled protectively around her shoulders and watching the smoke from the fireplace draw upward and disappear into the darkness overhead.

It was done now. There could be no undoing it. Now he was resolved to give her everything she deserved. As close to it as he could manage, anyway.

Beside him, she stirred, rousing halfway from sleep. She rolled toward him, nestling close and throwing her arm over his chest. Her fingers toyed idly with the hair there, sifting through the springy tufts and lifting them playfully.

Then her touch swept downward. If he hadn't been already hard before she started petting him, he was rock solid now.

She whispered, "Make love to me again?"

He stared at her, amazed, and stroked a wayward lock of hair from her face.

Was that what they'd done, just an hour or so ago? Make *love*? She'd certainly uttered the word enough times, like some kind of incantation. The idea was in him now, and he didn't know what to make of it.

He rather liked her phrase for bedding, though: "make love." It made the emotion sound concrete. Comprehensible. Like a product that could be manufactured from whole cloth. Take two lusting, yearning bodies and rub them briskly together, and this substance called love would simply result—simple as striking two flints to make a spark.

Unfortunately, Thorne didn't think it worked quite that way.

"It's too soon," he said. "You'll be tender. I don't want to hurt you."

"I am tender, I'll admit. But aren't there other ways?"

He lifted a brow, skeptical. "What could you know of other ways?"

She laughed. "Really, Samuel. Women do talk among themselves. And more than one risqué novel has made the rounds of the Queen's Ruby."

Thorne choked back a derisive noise. There were heroes of novels, and then there were men like him. Whatever those bawdy stories had taught her, no doubt it was some genteel, delicate imagining of lust—as evidenced by the way she trailed light, sweet caresses up and down his stiffened cock right now.

He fought the urge to take her hand, take control. He could show her how to grip him tight. He could guide her into stroking him hard and fast, relentlessly, until he snarled and bucked like a wild beast. He could put her on all fours and take her like an animal, savagely pumping her from behind.

He doubted any of *those* scenes were in her risqué

novels. They certainly had nothing to do with "making love."

His own crudeness concerned him, as it never had in the past. Unlike any other woman he'd bedded, Katie had a way of demolishing his self-control. When he'd been inside her, pushing closer and closer to release— he'd felt himself slipping closer and closer to some precipice, too. That was the reason he'd withdrawn. He'd come too close to that divide, and he didn't know what waited on the other side. It might be a dark, shadowy place. If he fell into it, he worried he could lose himself.

He could hurt her.

He folded his arms behind his head and laced his fingers together, just to forbid them from wandering. Her light, teasing touch was already more than he should hope for. He'd content himself with this.

"Go back to sleep," he said.

"I can't. I'm a newly engaged woman, and I'm too busy making plans. Do you think we can be married in St. Ursula's? It's such a beautiful church. I always dreamed of being married there."

He chuckled. "I don't suppose I was the man standing at the altar with you."

"I'm not certain. Maybe you were. His face was always rather shadowy. But exceedingly handsome." She propped herself up on one elbow and faced him, eyes bright and inquisitive. "Did you ever dream about me?"

"Sometimes," he admitted reluctantly, only because it was obvious she hoped to hear him say yes. "I tried not to."

"Why would you try not to?"

He stared into the darkness overhead. "Because my dreams didn't have anything to do with marriage or church."

"Oh," she said, drawing a coy touch down the center of his chest.

"It didn't seem right, to use you that way."

"That's absurd."

She flipped atop him, belly-to-belly, stacking her arms on his chest and replacing his view of the looming shadows with her own radiant, smiling face. Her hair tumbled about them both, making a draped, hidden room to house their kiss.

God. He couldn't believe this was real. That she was here, and his. He was almost afraid to touch her for fear she'd vanish, so he kept his hands tucked beneath his head and allowed her to kiss him, just as long and as deeply as she wished.

"Samuel," she said at length, "you have my express permission to dream about me however and whenever you like." She sat tall, straddling his torso, and jabbed one fingertip into his breastbone. "With one condition—you must tell me all about it when you wake up, so I can make the fantasies real."

"Don't say that. You've no idea the depravities a man's imagination can supply."

"Then enlighten me."

She braced her hands on either side of his body and leaned on them. Her slight breasts swung forward, taunting him, and the downy curls between her thighs brushed against his belly. His cock arched and strained upward, seeking her softness and heat. With one brisk tug on her hips, he could have her sex cradling his. Then sinking down to sheathe him, so very tight.

He groaned a little. But he kept his hands firmly pinned beneath his head.

"Tell me." Her voice was a smoky whisper. "Tell me your every last depraved, wicked, carnal desire."

"We'd be here a week."

A coy smile tipped her mouth. "I wouldn't mind."

He shook his head. No matter how smugly pleased she looked with herself, he knew she was just a few hours past the first blush of innocence.

She sat up straight, tossing her hair back over her shoulders and looking down at him. "I'm serious, Samuel. I won't have you treating me like some untouchable, delicate lady. Saving your truest, deepest cravings for dreams that feature someone else. I'm jealous. I don't want to merely appear in your dreams. I want to be the *only* woman in them, from this day forward."

He stared up at her, fingers woven behind his head. He'd never considered the matter that way.

If she was truly that determined to learn something of his darkest desires . . . he supposed he could oblige her. But he would keep to the fantasies that didn't put her in any sort of risk.

Ones that placed her in control.

He unhooked his hands from behind his head. Beginning at her shoulders, he skimmed a touch down her arms until he clasped her hands in his. He took and lifted them to the level of her torso, then fitted her palms over her own pale, smooth breasts.

"Hold these for me," he said.

Then he reclined to the pillow, once again lacing his hands beneath his head.

She gave him a quizzical look. Then she turned that quizzical expression on her own breasts, plumping them lightly in her hands. "What am I to do with them?"

"Whatever feels good."

"And you're just going to lie there and watch?"

He nodded.

Her brow wrinkled. "Truly. This is something men fantasize about?"

"With regularity."

She laughed and blushed a little, as women did when they were embarrassed. He simply lay there, waiting, and offered no excuse.

Eventually, she shrugged. "As you wish, then."

With her palms, she gently lifted and shaped the modest swells of creamy flesh. She ran her fingertips around the circumference of each breast. And then she balanced them carefully, like two weights on either side of a scale, and pressed her thumbs to her hardened nipples.

"Like this?" she asked. "Am I doing it right?"

He nodded, unable to answer aloud. His tongue had plastered itself to the roof of his mouth.

As she rolled her own nipples beneath her thumbs, a wash of pink spread across her chest and worked its way up her throat. Her lips fell apart, swollen and red, and she moistened them with her tongue.

"Pinch them," he scraped out.

She gasped faintly as she obeyed, catching the puckered, berry-red nubs between her thumbs and forefingers. As she pinched and plucked, she closed her eyes and arched her back, thrusting those luscious breasts forward for his view. Her pelvis rocked against his tensed abdomen.

She was already so wet. He was painfully hard.

"I did this once," she whispered, opening her eyes. Her gaze was dark and glittering, and a shy smile played about her lips. "That night after the outing to Wilmington. I touched myself just like this and tried to imagine your mouth on me."

Holy God. He'd never heard anything so arousing in

his life. His fingers curled like talons, biting into his scalp, but he didn't move. He didn't dare reach for her—or before she could whisper a word of caution, he'd be ballocks-deep in her tender flesh, rutting like a beast.

Still, he couldn't resist wanting more.

"Bring them here," he said. "Bring them to me. Let me taste."

She smiled. "Yes, Corporal."

Her pert response made him wild. Normally, Thorne didn't care for those power games in the bedchamber. He hated any implication that he would trade on his rank for pleasure.

But she wasn't ceding to his will. She was poking fun at him for resorting to a stern, military tone. She knew he was desperate. She knew she'd made him that way, and she was already learning to relish her sensual power.

Damn, but she was a quick study. A clever, clever girl.

And he was a lucky, lucky man.

With one hand, she gripped the headboard for balance and support. She cupped her breast with the other, leaning forward until her taut nipple hovered an inch above his lips. The scent and warmth of her skin were palpable, intoxicating. She was teasing again, waiting for him to stretch and bridge that last distance.

Minx. He could tease, as well.

He pursed his lips and blew, sending a current of air rushing over her nipple. Her skin erupted in gooseflesh, and a delicious shudder traveled through her body and straight into his.

He stretched his tongue—just the very tip of his tongue—and flicked over just the very tip of her nipple.

Then he pursed his lips and blew again.

"*Samuel.*"

He ached for contact and physical release, but the needy edge in her voice was satisfying in a different way. A deeper way.

She lowered her breast, rubbing its silky weight against his unshaven cheek. He closed his eyes as the sweet, tender berry of her nipple traced his bottom lip. He smiled—a rarity for him—just to stretch his lips and give her more distance to cover.

They spent several minutes like this—teasing, lightly tasting. Each baiting the other in turn. As if acknowledging they had a lifetime to enjoy this, so there was no reason to rush just now.

He lazily mouthed her breasts—first one, then the other. She braced both hands on the headboard and leaned close, so he might alternate at will. Her breathing went ragged and a heady musk filled the air. As he licked at her nipples, she began to rock in a slow, steady rhythm, grinding against his belly. He drew one peak into his mouth and suckled hard, until she gave a low moan.

She responded to him so naturally. He might have been able to make her come this way. But that couldn't be enough for him now. That moan pushed him past some breaking point, and he craved more.

He let his head fall back against the pillow, releasing her glistening breast to the dark, cool air. He unlaced his hands from beneath his head and grasped her by the waist.

And then he pulled forward, drawing her toward his mouth.

She tensed. "Samuel."

"You claimed to know there are other ways."

"Yes, but—"

"You wanted to know my every dark, depraved fantasy."

She sighed. "I know. It's just—"

Her words broke off as he lifted her by the waist, resettling her so her knees rested on either side of his broad shoulders. The pose spread her wide. She was pink and dewy and beautiful. Perhaps he shouldn't push her this far, this soon. But he was out of his mind with lust, couldn't rest now until he tasted her. All of her.

"Hold the headboard," he commanded.

"Are you *certain* this is right?"

"It's perfect." Then, more hoarsely, "You're perfect."

He parted her with his thumbs, opening her to his kiss. He needed to get his mouth on her, and then she'd warm to the idea.

He began slowly, just as he had with her breasts. First teasing her with his breath, then sweeping light, flickering passes of his tongue all along her crease. He explored her every ridge and fold. When he focused his attentions on the swollen pearl at the crest, he heard a little sob of pleasure catch in her throat.

Yes.

Triumph pulsed through his veins. He gripped her hip, holding her still and close for his attentions. With his other hand, he reached for his own throbbing staff.

Easier this way, he thought. If he tended to matters himself, he wouldn't be tempted to paw at her afterward. By taking himself in hand, he'd keep his baser needs under control.

It wouldn't take long, for either of them. As he stroked his eager cock, he kept up a brisk, relentless rhythm with his tongue. With a bit of trial, he found the angle

and rhythm that pleased her—one that had her gasping
and arching against his open-mouthed kiss.

Yes. Move with me. Come for me.

Her mewling sighs of pleasure drove his own excitement to a dizzying peak. He'd never known anything so
arousing in his life. She was so trusting, so completely
spread open and vulnerable. So damned delicious
against his tongue, positively molten with desire for
him. For *him*. Perhaps he would never make her light
up from within, but he could make her burn.

He could make her pant. And sigh. And moan.

This was a fantasy indeed. Lifting his eyes, he could
watch her breasts sway and bounce. Her thigh muscle
gave a sweet quiver against his jaw, and he knew whatever thin cord of restraint was left to him would surely
snap. Soon. Raw, animal need chased beneath the surface of his skin, seeking release.

He gripped his cock tighter, pumped faster. So close.

"Samuel," she gasped. "Samuel, I can't—"

She cried out and bucked against his mouth, shaking
the headboard with the force of her crisis.

Hearing his name on her lips, in that lusty voice . . .
it sent him over the edge. His own climax erupted,
wrenching his hips off the mattress. He came growling
and shuddering, spilling his seed in forceful jets.

In the aftermath, the only sounds were the crackle of
the fire, the muted patter of rain, and the hoarse, open-
mouthed rasps of their breathing.

Well. She'd wanted carnality.

As soon as he could regain some strength in his limbs,
he guided her aside and helped her settle onto the mattress. She curled next to him with her eyes closed, still
working for breath.

She was so quiet for so long, he began to worry.

Damn it. He must have shocked her too greatly. She was having regrets, wondering just what sort of beast she'd tethered herself to.

He stroked her hair, teasing out the rain-induced tangles with his fingers. "Are you well?"

"Yes," she replied. "I'm well indeed. I'm just not sure how to look at you after that."

After a moment's thought, he suggested, "With pride?"

She laughed into her pillow.

"I'm serious. You were perfect."

"You have such a wicked sense of humor. You always make me laugh at the most unlikely moments."

"Is that a good thing?"

"It's a wonderful thing." She propped her chin on his chest. "It's one of the things I love most about you. And it's what assures me we'll be happy together. We're neither of us perfect people, but we can laugh together and admit our mistakes. And there's this." She eyed the mussed bed linens, blushing.

There was "this" indeed.

"After what we just did," she said, "I don't suppose I could have a single secret from you."

"I pressed you too far just now. It's your first time. I should have been more tender, more—"

"Please. Don't apologize for giving me unfathomable pleasure. It's just . . . for a fantasy girl, I didn't even do much of anything." Smiling, she touched his flagging erection. "I'd like to help with this part next time."

A hoarse chuckle lifted his chest. "That can be arranged. Shortly."

"Do we have a little time to talk first?"

He sat up in bed, pushing a hand through his hair before reaching for his flask. "A few minutes, at least. I'm not a youth anymore."

At her chirping call, Badger abandoned his quilt and leaped onto the bed. The pup circled a good five times before finally wedging into a space between them. His tail whipped furiously.

"There we are," she said. "Just like a little family. We'll be very cozy in America."

Thorne took a casual draught off his flask. Best not tell her that with those simple words she'd gone and made his wildest, most depraved and outrageous fantasy come true. He'd keep that information to himself. Until after a few more rounds of pleasure, at least.

She dropped her gaze and picked at an edge of the bedsheet. "I'm legitimate."

He choked on his mouthful of whiskey. "What?"

"Evan and the solicitors found a marriage record. It seems Simon and Elinor—my parents—were married in secret. And the housekeeper from Ambervale identified me by my birthmark. So it seems I'm not just a Gramercy, I'm . . ."

Oh, Jesus. Don't say it.

She lifted her head and looked at him. "I'm a lady."

The room tilted. Then the walls began to spin around him.

A lady.

"Please don't look so overset," she begged. "It won't change a thing between us."

A cloud of frustration blurred his vision. She was the legitimate daughter of a marquess. A *lady*. How could that not change everything?

God damn it. It was as though every time he dared to reach for her, some cruel, vengeful deity pulled her just a little further out of his grasp. If he found a way around this hurdle, what would be next? She'd be revealed to be a princess? A mermaid?

"We're still going to marry and go to America," she said. "That's all I want, is to be with you. To be your wife."

A marquess's legitimate daughter, living as a trapper's wife in a humble, rough-hewn cabin. In *Indiana*.

Lady Katherine of the Prairie. Right.

"You're not angry with me, are you?"

"Angry with *you*? Why would I be angry with you?" Even as he spoke the words, he was aware that they sounded . . . well, angry.

He forced himself to take a deep breath and then exhale slowly.

She was right; it didn't matter. Not after what they'd just shared. They *must* marry, whether she was a charwoman or a fairy queen. He couldn't waste time feeling worthless or counting all the ways he wasn't good enough for her.

Whatever sort of woman she was . . . he had to be the man she needed.

Thorne scrubbed a hand through his hair, trying to fit his brain around the notion.

"Of course you're a lady," he said finally. He reached for her hand. "You always were, to me."

"They haven't told anyone yet," she said. "Only the family and the solicitors know. Evan's made arrangements with Sir Lewis to host a ball at Summerfield next week. It's supposed to be the Gramercys' parting gift to Spindle Cove, but they secretly plan to introduce me as their cousin that night. From there, we were meant to go to London." She reached for his hand. "But I'll explain to them that we've reconciled and plan to marry, as soon as possible."

He held up a hand for silence and listened. "The rain has slowed. The hour isn't even that late. We can dress, and I'll take you down to the rooming house. Then I'll explain matters to Drewe."

She paled. "Oh, no. We can't go to him like this. Not tonight. He has a famous temper. There's no telling how he'll react if he knows we've—"

"If he's any sort of man, he's out searching for you already. They could be pounding at the door any moment."

"Then I must go." She scrambled from the bed, wrapping one of the sheets about her torso for modesty.

He rose from the bed as well—making no such modesty attempts. "Katie, I won't let you walk home alone."

"You must. Otherwise, it will be obvious what's happened between us, and Evan would . . ." She pulled her shift over her head. "Samuel, there's a very real chance he would try to kill you."

Kill him? Thorne couldn't help but chuckle at that. His lordship was welcome to try.

"Just let me break the news gently," she said. Her fingers worked desperately to do up her buttons. "Please."

He swore, despising himself for causing her such obvious distress. Of course she wanted to break the news gently, because there was no way in hell a family of aristocrats—no matter how eccentric and unconventional—would rejoice to see their legitimate cousin marry a man like him.

Even he couldn't rejoice at the idea. The two halves of his being were at war—the half that wanted the best for her, against the half that simply *wanted* her.

He gathered a pair of loose trousers and pulled them on.

"I think I'll have a little money," she said, rolling a woolen stocking up her leg and tying it off with a simple garter. "That's the good news. We can buy ourselves a fair slice of America."

Smiling, she reached past him to take her frock from the screen. He took the garment from her hands.

"Turn away," he said. "Arms up."

He helped her into the frock, taking time with all the buttons and laces. His right hand was still clumsy, so several moments passed.

When he'd finished, he put his hands on her slender waist. "Katie, how can you truly want that life? How can you want me?"

She swiveled to face him. "How could I want anyone else?"

To be sure, she said such sweet things *now*. But in time, he worried she'd come to resent him. A solitary life on the American frontier would give her far too many quiet hours to ponder all she'd left behind. A comfortable, lavish home and every convenience money could purchase. Her pupils, her friends. The family she'd waited her whole life to find.

"You will miss them."

She nodded. "I will miss them. And I'll be happy with you. The two conditions can coexist."

Not knowing what to say without contradicting her, he instead bent his head and took her mouth in a kiss.

What started out tender quickly became passionate, feverish. He clutched her tight against his body and swept his tongue between her lips. She opened to him readily, no hint of shyness or restraint, and he kissed her as deeply as he could. Probing, searching. Desperately seeking the reassurance that would give his guilt-stricken soul some peace.

Convince me. Make me believe I can make you happy.

Light up for me.

When they broke apart, her cheeks were flushed and

her eyes were glassy. But he couldn't exactly say that she glowed. Damn.

"Samuel, I won't claim loving you is easy. But it's scarcely the hardship you're making it out to be, either." She stretched to touch his face, rubbing the spot between his eyebrows with a single fingertip. "I want to iron this flat. Stop fretting so."

"I'm not fretting. Men don't fret."

Men acted. If he saw a problem, a real man addressed it. He took bold risks, made life-altering changes.

"I'll let you go home to the Gramercys tonight," he said, "on one condition. Don't tell them anything just yet."

"But I'll have to—"

He shushed her by placing two fingertips to her soft pink lips.

"Not a word of this. Not yet." He caressed her cheek. "I want to ask for you properly. I must speak to Drewe myself, Katie. Man-to-man. You cannot deny me that."

She swallowed and nodded. "I understand. Will you come down to the village tomorrow?"

He shook his head. "I need to return to London. I need some time to make arrangements first."

"Will you be long?"

"A few days, that's all."

Her eyes shimmered. "Promise you'll return?"

"You have my word."

She had his word, his heart, his soul, his life. Always.

And he had a few days. A few days' time—to change his life and place a wild, reckless wager on the future.

Chapter Twenty-one

Kate stood before a mirror in the Queen's Ruby. Fretting.

It was all very well and good for Samuel to say men didn't fret. But he was cruel to give her so much reason to fret herself. Nearly a week had passed since their night at the castle, and she hadn't heard a word. While she had no reason to doubt his intentions, the longer she went without breaking the news to the Gramercys, the more of a liar she felt.

All week long the Gramercys had gone about making plans for Ambervale and Town. Parties they would host, places they would take her to see, people to whom she would be introduced. Kate tried to limit her responses to noncommittal nods and polite smiles, but she knew she was giving them the impression that she meant to come live with them forever.

Now it was the night of the ball. In a matter of hours she would be introduced as Lady Katherine Gramercy to all of Spindle Cove. To be sure, this was not exactly English high society—but word *would* spread to

London, and soon. When she eloped to America with an enlisted man just weeks thereafter—wouldn't that be a public embarrassment for the Gramercys?

And if her connection to the Hothouse ever became public . . . if the gossips of London ever learned that a onetime Marchioness of Drewe had lived as a Southwark opera dancer . . .

That would be a scandal of the worst order. It could affect the entire family's standing and destroy Lark's prospects.

Kate knew she could spare them pain by leaving quietly with Thorne. The inheritance didn't matter to her. But it must be done before they made her identity public.

She couldn't wait for Samuel any longer. She needed to speak with Evan, tonight.

She twisted and turned before the small mirror, judging her reflection. The color had been Lark's suggestion—a lush cobalt-blue silk with a lace overlay in a darker, midnight shade of indigo. The hue seemed rather daring for an unmarried lady, but they wanted her to stand out. And she always felt her best in blue.

"Oh, Kate. Aren't you lovely."

Aunt Marmoset entered the room. The older woman was dressed in a long, draped violet gown and matching gloves. An ostrich plume adorned her wispy, upswept hair.

Kate fidgeted with a curl at her temple, trying to arrange it just over her birthmark. "I can't make this curl cooperate."

"Let me try." Aunt Marmoset plucked a hairpin from the dressing table, beckoning Kate to duck her head. "There now."

Kate stood and looked in the mirror again. Aunt Marmoset had pinned the curl back, smoothing it away from her face entirely.

"Don't hide the mark, dear. It's what makes you one of us."

"I know. I'm sorry. It's an old habit, and I can't help being nervous tonight," she confessed.

The older woman came to stand beside her in the mirror, sliding an arm about her waist. The ostrich feather barely grazed Kate's shoulder. "Lark always likes it when I stand beside her," Aunt Marmoset said. "She says I make her look tall."

"I don't know about tall, but I do feel stronger when you're near." In the mirror, Kate watched a tentative smile spread across her own face.

"Ah," said Aunt Marmoset. "I knew your appearance wasn't quite complete, but I couldn't place the deficiency. That smile was missing."

"Thank you for helping me find it."

"You might wish I hadn't. I *was* on the verge of giving you this instead."

Aunt Marmoset unclenched one frail, knobby hand. From it unfurled a slender gold chain. And at the end of the chain dangled a pendant.

The pendant.

"Oh my goodness," Kate gasped.

A quick glance toward her mother's portrait confirmed it. It was the same teardrop of dark blue stone, veined with amber and white. So distinctive, that stone, with its lacy, scalloped layers of light and dark. It reminded her of when Sir Lewis showed the ladies a bit of butterfly wing under a magnifier.

"Where did this come from?" Kate asked, amazed.

"I asked the servants to pack my jewelry from Ambervale and send it down for the ball. Evidently, the maid found this hidden away in the dressing table and assumed it was mine. But it isn't mine at all, is it? It's yours."

"How wonderful."

"Let's have it on." Aunt Marmoset fixed the chain about Kate's neck.

Kate turned to view it in the mirror. The indigo-blue pendant dangled just at her breastbone.

"It's lovely," Aunt Marmoset said.

"It's a miracle." Kate turned to the older woman and, bending low, kissed her on the cheek. "Your kindness is worth more to me than any jewelry, Aunt Marmoset. I don't think I've thanked you properly for helping me feel at home in this family, but—"

"Bosh." Aunt Marmoset waved off the remark. "You *are* at home in the Gramercy family. When will you accept that?"

I don't know, Kate thought. I don't know.

In her heart, she did believe that she was Katherine Adele Gramercy. She also knew herself to be the daughter of an unfortunate Southwark prostitute, as well as an impoverished orphan who'd been raised as the ward of a school. Perhaps all these things *could* eventually be reconciled into one existence, but . . .

But mostly, she was just a girl named Kate, in love for the first time in her life.

She loved Samuel. She missed him, terribly.

From the corridor, a call went up. "The carriages, ladies! They're here."

As they emerged into the corridor, Kate was startled by the sight of a ravishing woman in red emerging from a side room. She was quite sure she'd never seen this lady before. Her dark hair was piled high in a profusion of sensual curls. A thick rope of gold and rubies encircled her elegant neck.

The woman turned.

Kate gasped with recognition. "Harry? Harry, is that truly you?"

Her cousin smiled. "Of course, dear. Did you think I'd wear trousers to your grand introduction ball?"

"I wouldn't ask you to be anyone but yourself," Kate said, hoping her cousin would feel the same toward her.

Harry shrugged. Her ruby-red lips curved in a seductive smile. "I do enjoy a lavish gown on occasion. Sometimes I like to remind them all just what it is they're missing."

Lark appeared at her sister's side, looking fresh and pretty in diaphanous white.

"Oh, Lark. I didn't know if you'd be joining us, since you're not yet out."

The young lady smiled and blushed. "Evan's making an exception tonight. So long as I don't dance."

Their loyalty was so touching. Look at all they'd done for her, Kate thought, tonight alone. Harry had put on a gown, and Lark was willing to undercut the excitement of her own debut. All this, at the end of a summer holiday they'd completely rearranged for the sake of spending time with her.

Little did they suspect that she was planning to bid them farewell in a matter of days. Forever. Would the Gramercys be able to understand her reasons for leaving, or would they feel betrayed?

She'd miss them, no question. But she had to be with Samuel, and he couldn't stay here in England. He needed open land and the sort of opportunities England couldn't—or wouldn't—afford a man of low birth and criminal background. After the way he'd suffered, it was her turn to make the sacrifices, and she would do so gladly.

She owed that man everything. *Everything.* If not for him . . .

She couldn't bear to contemplate her life if not for him.

Samuel, where are you?

Instead, it was Evan who stood in the Queen's Ruby entryway, watching them come down the stairs. He pressed a hand to his chest and pretended to stumble. "What a stunning collection of ladies."

Evan was rather stunning himself. Dressed in a black tailcoat and a waistcoat of embroidered gold silk, he looked every inch the marquess. And his black gloves . . . My, but the man always had *the* most elegant, exquisitely fitted gloves. They made his hands look ready for all manner of deeds—charitable, sensual, ruthless.

As Kate reached the bottom of the stairs, he offered her an arm. "All the other ladies have gone ahead in Sir Lewis's carriages. There's just the two family coaches left."

They walked out into the front garden. Indeed, the two coaches emblazoned with the Drewe crest stood waiting at attention, drawn by perfectly matched teams of warmbloods.

Evan handed Aunt Marmoset, Harry, and Lark into the first of the coaches, then signaled the driver to be on his way.

"Will it be just the two of us, then?" she asked, surprised.

"Do you mind?" He handed her into the second coach, then followed and sat opposite on the rear-facing bench, out of deference to her skirts. "I was hoping we could talk alone. Before the ball."

"Oh," Kate said as the carriage rolled into motion. "Oh, good. I was hoping the same."

He smiled. "I'm glad we're in accord."

"I've been thinking—"

They both uttered the words at once, speaking over each other. And then they both laughed.

He motioned with his gloved hand. "Please. You first."

"Evan, I'm not sure you should announce me as your cousin tonight."

He was silent for several moments, and Kate was sure she'd ruined everything.

"I agree," he finally said.

"You do?"

"I'd prefer to introduce you as my future wife."

Pure astonishment stole Kate's breath. "What?"

"That's the reason I wanted this time alone. I meant to ask you to marry me."

"But why? You can't be—" She tried again. "Evan, you don't seem to have those kind of feelings for me."

"I'm very fond of you, Kate. We have interests in common, and we get on well. If I didn't think we could make a happy life together, I would never suggest it."

"But there's something else," she intuited. "Some other reason you're proposing now."

"I won't insult you with a denial." He leaned toward her. "Kate, I've told you there would be an inheritance."

She nodded.

"But I haven't told you the precise size of that inheritance."

"Well, what size is it?" She scanned his worried expression. "Precisely?"

He looked her in the eye. "You'll have everything, Kate. Everything. I'll keep Rook's Fell—the one entailed property that comes with the marquessate. Aside from that, the entire Gramercy family fortune is yours. Eight properties. Several hundred thousand pounds."

Kate gripped the edge of the seat. "But . . . I don't want all that. What would I even do with such wealth? A fortune like that is a full-time occupation, and you're the one who has always managed everything." She blinked hard. "What of Harry's income? Lark's dowry? Aunt Marmoset's living?"

"All yours as well. I set the money aside in trusts, but they'll no longer be valid. Legally, the money was never mine to give away."

"Oh dear. Oh, Evan."

He rubbed the bridge of his nose. "So now you understand, this is the quandary that's kept me up nights."

"Seething," she whispered.

"Yes, seething." He lowered his hand and gave her a bittersweet smile. "I will no longer make pretensions otherwise. I have been exceedingly worried over the future of the family. Not for myself, but for my siblings. The Gramercys have always been a queer lot, but we've been wealthy enough that we're forgiven our eccentricities."

"And that won't be the case anymore."

Kate was no solicitor, but she understood Evan's dilemma. If she married Thorne, the entire fortune would be out of Gramercy hands. Evan would have no means to protect and support his family. They would all be her dependents—or if she married him, Thorne's.

That would be an awkward situation.

"If I'd only known about you," he said, staring out the window. "We had other properties from my mother's side. Foreign land holdings, mostly. In India, the West Indies. But then Bennett went to view them, and he came back . . . changed. I sold all the land at a loss years ago, wanting nothing more to do with plantations or slaving. The land here in England was more than enough, I thought."

"You thought right," Kate said. "You did right. And you needn't fear. I won't abandon you. We'll find some way. Can't I just refuse the inheritance, or give it all back?"

He smiled. "It's not that easy, I'm afraid."

"What if I went away?" This might be the answer to both their problems. She could go to America with Thorne, and Evan would remain the head of the family. "I could leave the country. Or stay here in Spindle Cove. No one needs to know I exist."

"*I* will know you exist. We all know, and it wouldn't be right. Kate, I want to secure my siblings' future, but I refuse to destroy our souls in the process. We can't simply deny your existence. To do so would be to deny your parents' love for each other, to deny their love for you. You can't want that."

No. She supposed she didn't.

"We wouldn't want that, either," Evan went on. "And what's more, Kate, the solicitors know about you. Legal proceedings have been set in motion. If you were to disappear now . . . we'd have to wait seven years with everything tied up in court, and then petition to have you declared dead." He made a grimace. "So please don't think of it."

"But it's just so unfair," she said. "You've been so generous and welcoming to me, and now you must pay this terrible price."

"You are the one who has suffered unjustly," he argued. "Never think otherwise."

"Did you know all along? Even when you first came

to find me, did you know that I could be taking the entire fortune?"

He nodded. "I suspected."

"But you came to find me anyway. With no hesitation."

"Yes, of course." His intelligent brow lifted. "Family above everything. That's the Gramercy way."

He was so very decent and good, and under different circumstances, she should have been overjoyed to marry a man like him. But she was in love with Samuel. She was committed to Samuel. She'd been intimate with Samuel. There was no way she could marry Evan now.

He took her hand. "Kate, if you'll marry me, I swear—I will devote everything to giving you the life you deserve. The life you always deserved. And together, we will help our family." He gave her a half-joking smile. "If you won't have me, I'll be forced to pursue some obnoxious heiress with social-climbing parents."

But would he be able to find social-climbing parents who'd eagerly support unconventional Harry, or decrepit Aunt Marmoset, or Bennett, off wandering the Hindu Kush? And poor Lark, losing her dowry just months from her debut.

Kate cast a desperate glance out the carriage window as they pulled up in the Summerfield drive. This was intolerable. To have found her family after all this time, to feel so loved and accepted by them . . . only to destroy their lives and happiness?

"So," he said, preparing to exit the carriage, "which will it be? At midnight, will I be introducing you as Lady Kate? Or may I introduce you as the future Lady Gramercy?"

"Evan, I—"

"You need some time," he finished for her. "Of course, I understand. I'll come find you before the midnight set."

And then he was out of the carriage and extending his hand to help her alight, and there was no privacy to discuss it any longer. Before them, the golden candlelit splendor of the Summerfield great hall beckoned. They were being watched by many sets of curious eyes.

"Smile," he whispered, offering his arm. "And be happy. This is your night."

As she entered the Summerfield ballroom, Kate scanned every corner and alcove of the hall. Her heart skipped every time she caught a flash of red. There was one militiaman she was particularly hoping, against all odds, to see.

She didn't find him, but she found the next best thing.

"Kate!"

"It's us. Over here."

She whirled on the heel of her slipper, heartened by the familiar voices.

"Susanna. Minerva. Oh, it's so good to see you." She embraced her friends warmly. Until Susanna's arms went around her, Kate couldn't have realized how desperately she needed a hug.

She could use some friendly advice, as well.

"I'd no idea you'd be here." She looked from one friend to the other—Susanna, now Lady Rycliff, with her flame-red hair and freckles, and Minerva, the darker, bespectacled middle Highwood sister, recently married to Lord Payne.

"We all came down from London together," Susanna said. "Papa was growing desperate to see his first grandchild."

Minerva added, "And I knew I couldn't deprive Mama of her new son-in-law much longer, either. But in truth, it was our husbands who suggested we make the trip."

"Truly?" Kate asked, incredulous. "Lord Rycliff and Lord Payne *wanted* to come? To Spindle Cove?"

"I think they secretly miss this place, though they'd never let on," Minerva said.

Susanna winced a little.

"What's wrong?" Kate asked.

"Oh, nothing. I'm just a bit achy, that's all. When the baby hasn't nursed for a few hours, it's uncomfortable." She looked to the ceiling. "Perhaps I'll just slip upstairs to the nursery."

"Can we come with you?" Kate asked. "I'm dying to meet little Victoria myself, and . . . and I'd very much appreciate the chance to talk."

"She's so beautiful," Kate whispered. "Her hair is just like yours."

"This is the only time she's quiet," Susanna said, gazing down at her suckling babe. "Unless her father is holding her. Bram has some secret method of calming her that he refuses to share, the impossible man."

"I'm so glad Colin's happy to wait on the childbearing score," Minerva said. "He's recently taken control of his estate. I've so many scholarly works in progress. We're not at all ready for parenthood."

"But, Min, how . . ." Kate lowered her voice. "How can you be sure you won't conceive?"

"Well, one can never be completely sure. But we take precautions. Colin's had some experience on the male side of things. You see, when a man spends his seed—"

Susanna gave her friend a look. "Min," she whispered, "perhaps we could save the specifics for another occasion."

"Right," Minerva said apologetically. "You know me, I speak of natural topics at all manner of inappropriate times. Anyhow, Kate—there are ways. Susanna's given me some herbs. Those help, too."

"How clever of you both," Kate said.

She was glad for Samuel's caution the other night. It wasn't as though she disliked the idea of bearing his child. Nothing would make her happier, someday. Thinking of him as a father, cradling a tiny babe in the crook of his arm . . . it made her heart float. But with so much uncertainty now with the Gramercys, a pregnancy would be ill-timed.

Especially since the father of the child had disappeared.

"Kate, what's wrong?" Susanna asked. "You look so troubled."

Kate paused, biting her lip. And then she took a deep breath and told them everything. All about the Gramercys. All about Thorne. The portrait, the melon, the snakebite, the inheritance, her night with Samuel, and Evan's proposal just now in the coach. Everything.

"My goodness, Kate," said Minerva, adjusting her spectacles. "You've been busy."

Kate laughed at the absurdity of the statement, and it felt so good. This was what she'd been needing—her best, closest friends to listen and help her see everything clear. Susanna and Minerva would not be on Thorne's side, or the Gramercys' side.

They were on her side, unequivocally.

"I always knew that someday you'd have your fairy tale," Susanna said. She called in the nursemaid and handed her the now-sleeping babe. "I didn't predict *this,* of course. But we all adored you so. I knew you couldn't go unnoticed for long."

"I never did go unnoticed," she said. "Not really."

Samuel had noticed her, even that very first day in the Bull and Blossom, when she pulled her India shawl tight around her shoulders and turned the other way. He'd always been looking out for her, asking nothing in return.

She cast a wistful glance at the darkened windowpane. Where was he now?

"I don't know what to do," she said. "Samuel has vanished. The Gramercys are depending on me to save them all. Evan wants to know whether he can introduce me as Lady Kate or his soon-to-be Lady Gramercy. Meanwhile, I feel like a maid who pilfered her mistress's gown and stole into the ball. I don't know how I'll manage as a lady of any sort."

"The same way we do," Minerva said. "Look at Susanna and me. A year ago we were confirmed spinsters, never the belle of any ball. Now she is Lady Rycliff and I am Lady Payne. And we may be a bit awkward in the roles, but society will just have to struggle on despite it."

"We'll form our own club, Kate. The League of Unlikely Ladies." Susanna came to sit beside her. "As for what you should do . . . I'm certain you already know, in your heart."

Of course she did. She loved Samuel and wanted nothing more than to be his wife. But if at all possible, she must find some way to help the Gramercys, too. They were her family, and she couldn't abandon them.

Minerva bent over and stared Kate in the bosom. "I'm admiring your pendant."

"Do you know what sort of stone it is?" Kate asked

eagerly. "I've been wondering, but I'd never seen its like."

"This is an easy identification." After peering for a moment through her spectacles, Minerva released the teardrop-shaped stone. "It's called blue john. A form of fluorite. Quite a rare formation, only found in one small area of Derbyshire."

Kate clutched the pendant. "It was my mother's. She was from Derbyshire. She must have worn it always to remind herself of home."

How strange, then, that Elinor would have left it behind at Ambervale. Perhaps she'd worried it would be lost during travel.

Minerva patted her arm. "Kate, I don't think you should worry overmuch. I have a strong suspicion your problems will work themselves out, and in hasty fashion."

"I hope you're right," Kate said. But despite her natural bent for optimism, this was one situation where she had a difficult time seeing an easy solution.

"Well," Susanna said, standing. "I suppose we've hidden ourselves up here as long as we dare. We had better go find our men before they create some mischief."

"This is a Summerfield ball," Kate agreed. "There seems to be something in the ratafia that makes male passions . . . explosive."

Chapter Twenty-two

Thorne's patience was nearing the end of its fuse.

Tucked away in the Egyptian-themed library of Sir Lewis Finch, he paced a small square of carpet, patrolling back and forth. His new boots pinched his feet. His starched cuffs chafed his wrists. Sheer agony was his companion.

And the agony had a name: Colin Sandhurst, Viscount Payne.

"Let me give you a bit of advice," Payne said.

"I don't want any more of your advice. Not on this."

"You don't want to admit you want it," Payne replied smoothly. "But I shall talk to myself, and you can merely be nearby, not listening."

Thorne rolled his eyes. He'd spent the better part of the past several days "nearby, *not* listening" to Payne. Through shopping trips, appointments with solicitors, lessons on . . . an activity Thorne hated to acknowledge in thought, let alone speak aloud.

Payne tossed back a swallow of his drink and propped one boot on an inscribed sarcophagus. "Before I found

Minerva, I'd passed nights with more than my share of women."

Thorne groaned. *Don't. Just don't.*

"I've passed time with duchesses and farm girls, and it doesn't matter whether their skirts are silk or homespun. Once you get them bare—"

Thorne drew up short. "If you start in on rivers of silk and alabaster orbs, I *will* have to hit you."

"Easy, Cinderella," Payne said, holding up his hands. "All I meant to say is this. Beneath the trappings, all women crave the same thing."

Thorne made a fist and clenched it until his knuckles cracked.

"What? I'm speaking of tenderness."

From his chair behind the desk, Bram rubbed his temple. "I think what my cousin is trying to say is, just because she's Lady Katherine Gramercy now and not Miss Taylor, that doesn't mean that she's changed inside."

Thorne resumed pacing. Perhaps he shouldn't have told them everything. He'd needed their help, but he hated that they *knew* he needed it. Feeling weak wasn't something he was accustomed to, and he didn't like it. His impulse was to crash through the doors, find his Katie, pick her up in his arms, and carry her away someplace warm and small and safe.

But he couldn't take her away. That was the whole point of tonight. She had a family now. Not only a family, but a place among the English peerage.

This new life of hers . . . it meant she could never be entirely his. No matter the promises she made about leaving everything behind and sailing with him for America, he knew it couldn't work that way. As a Gramercy, she was part of a family. As the daughter of a marquess, she would have obligations and duties here. As a lady, she would always be above him—the reminder of it would sit before her name on every letter she received or penned.

He didn't *want* to share her. But he must, if he wanted to be a part of her new life. Most of all, he was utterly resolved: He would not bring shame to her, ever.

So tonight he was pacing the library carpet, waiting for his chance. He was hardly Cinderella, but at least he'd wedged his scarred body and ashen soul into a smart new outfit.

From behind the desk, Bram regarded Thorne. "I can't believe you went to my cousin."

I can't believe it, either.

"If you needed anything, Thorne, I would have helped. You need only have asked."

"You're busy."

Payne smiled wryly. "Yes, and I was only on my honeymoon. I had nothing better to do than scrub up a noble savage, take him shopping, and teach him to dance."

"What?" Bram looked at Thorne in astonishment. "No."

Thorne turned away.

Bram's smug inquiries pursued him. "You *danced?* And Colin gave you lessons?"

"You act as though the pleasure should be mine," Payne said. "It was rather a trial on my part, I'll have you know. But thanks to my darling wife's influence, I'm learning to embrace my academic duty. I've long been a scholar of the female sex. Since I'm now happily married and devoted to one particular woman, it would be miserly of me to hoard such accumulated knowledge for myself."

"No doubt." Bram laughed. To Thorne, he said, "Good God. If you put up with this for a week, you must really love that girl."

Payne resumed his suave, professorial demeanor. "It's like this, Thorne. If you mean to ask for a woman's heart, you have to be willing to take risks of your own. Real ones. Not just dancing lessons."

Thorne set his jaw. He'd given up his home for Katie. He'd spent years hungry in the countryside, then hungry in prison, then hungry and marching in the army. "I've sacrificed for her. I've given her as much as a man like me can give."

Payne chuckled. "You may think so. But they want everything, man. You can empty your pockets and lay down your body, and they still won't be satisfied. Not until you serve up your heart, still beating."

Bram sighed. "Once again, I will translate for my cousin. Just tell Miss Taylor you love her. That's all they really want to hear."

Love. It all kept coming back to that word. It would be easy enough to tell Katie he loved her. Speaking the words wasn't any great task. But to tell her so in a way that made them both believe it . . . that was the challenge.

"Did you want to practice again?" Payne asked.

"No."

"I don't mind taking the lady's part. I'm secure enough in my masculinity."

"I said *no*."

Payne straightened his cravat. "Really, Thorne. I'm only trying to help. 'No, thank you' might be more polite."

"Etiquette isn't my strong point."

"Yes, but that's why I'm here, isn't it? It's why you

came to me for help. If you mean to win that woman—that *lady*—and make her your wife, you'll have to make it your strong point. And quickly."

Thorne shushed him. The small orchestra had struck up a new tune, and he strained to hear.

"That's the waltz," Payne confirmed. "You're on."

Bram clapped Thorne on the shoulder. "Go to it, then."

"No pressure," Payne said. "It's only your one chance at happiness, you know. It's only the rest of your life."

Thorne cut him a glare as he shouldered open the door. "Not helping."

As he made his way through the connecting door and down the short stretch of corridor to the ballroom, nerves danced in his gut. But once he spied her at the opposite end, all his anxiety disappeared—replaced by awe.

He hadn't laid eyes on her in nearly a week.

And he'd never seen her looking like this.

Good God, she was beautiful. She stood in profile to him, deep in conversation with Minerva Highwood, the new Lady Payne. He stopped in his paces a moment, just to drink in the sight of her. And to remember how to breathe.

She wore deep blue silk, the color of fathomless oceans and dark night skies. Set off by the lush fabric, her shoulders were smooth, pale perfection. Tiny brilliants spangled her dark, upswept hair, and satin gloves sheathed her arms to the elbow. He heard the sparkling melody of her laughter float high above the music.

She was too elegant for him, too beautiful for words.

But he'd come this far. He would dare to ask for her anyway.

He started to move. The crowd shifted around him.

Across the hall, Katie shifted her weight and swept the room with an unfocused gaze. She looked right through him, with no hint of recognition—then went back to her conversation.

He strode toward her, moving with purpose now.

When he'd covered half the distance, her eyes darted to him again. Once, fleetingly. Then a second time, narrowing. As though she were trying to place him. The wrinkle of her brow was one of mild concern. He could almost hear her thoughts. Who was that hulking, overdressed brute across the ballroom, staring her down?

God. She didn't know him.

It's me, Katie. You know me.

Their gazes connected. He felt it in his bones, the moment recognition struck. That sweet jolt of affinity shot down his spine.

Then a waltzing couple twirled between them, blocking his view.

Damn it.

Damn, damn, damn. He had to see her reaction. That was his entire purpose in coming here and making an entrance. How would she greet him? Would it happen this time, at long last?

By the time the waltzers passed, the whole crowd had shifted. He pushed his way through the throng, scanning for her. His heart pounded so fiercely, he thought it would burst.

"Samuel!"

He turned on his boot heel.

There she was, poised on tiptoe, her neck elongated like a swan's, the better to call over the crowd.

He changed course, veering for her. And stopped, two paces away.

Waiting, with his heart in his throat, to see if she'd light up for him.

She didn't glow. Her eyes didn't twinkle. No small flame of joy flickered to life behind her expression.

No, this was so much better than that. It made everything worthwhile—not just the past week, but the lifetime before it.

She went incandescent with the brilliance of a thousand fiery stars.

"Samuel. It's you."

Kate struggled to compose herself. He had a lot of nerve, keeping her waiting all this time and then showing up looking like *this*. He was still his unbearably handsome self, only . . . he was more.

More, in every way.

She could have sworn his new, fashionable Hessians made him a full inch taller. The tight fit of his black tailcoat made his shoulders look a touch more broad. She couldn't begin to articulate what the clinging buff breeches did for his thighs, or she might suffer an attack of light-headedness.

His hair was clipped with precision, glossed with a touch of pomade. Even from an arm's length he smelled wonderful—like leather and cologne and clean linen, blended with the essence of raw, manly strength.

Most of all, there was an air about him. It wasn't quite elegance or refinement, but perhaps . . . self-possession. Purpose. Oh, his face was still hard, and his eyes remained chips of ice. But beneath it all, there was fire.

"Might I have this dance?" he asked. So suavely. The velvet darkness of his voice sent a thrill coursing all the way to her toes.

"I suppose you may."

What was this game they were playing? Were they supposed to pretend they didn't know one another? All she wanted to do was fly into his arms.

But she put her hand in his. As he led her to the dance floor, her heart fluttered.

They faced one another, and he fit his hand between her shoulder blades. The expression on his face was so stern.

"You look magnificent," she whispered. "So handsome."

She waited for him to compliment her gown or her hair, but she waited in vain. The expression on his face was both intent and somehow uncertain. What did it mean?

"I've missed you so much."

He swung her into the waltz. They moved through several bars of the dance, haltingly. He never said a word.

"Samuel, are you . . . Have you changed your mind?"

He blinked. "About what?"

"About me."

He frowned at her, as if chiding her for the question. "No."

She waited for further assurances. He didn't give them. Her heart began to pound. She didn't know what it was, but something was wrong.

"If you don't want to be here," she said, "I don't want to force you."

He made no reply. Except to curtly sigh with impatience and stare at the orchestra.

"Won't you speak to me? I've been waiting for you all week. Hoping all night. I couldn't believe you would leave me feeling so abandoned, and now you're finally here—"

"I've been here for hours."

"Then why did you take so long to come find me? Were you ashamed? Uncertain?" Her voice broke. "At least look at me."

He came to a halt. "Blast. I can't do this." He looked about the room, his eyes searching out every possible exit. "We need to talk somewhere, alone."

Kate struggled to keep her worst fears tightly leashed, but they had tenacity. And sharp teeth.

Perhaps her new identity as a lady was too much for him. Maybe he'd decided he couldn't be part of her life.

"This way," he said.

She followed him out the nearest set of doors and down a long paneled corridor, until they passed into Sir Lewis's famed medieval hall, where the aging antiquarian's collection of arms and armor was most impressively displayed.

"It's quiet here," he said. "And safe."

Kate supposed it was. On either side of the long, narrow hall a half-dozen suits of ancient armor stood sentry. Like an escort of Arthurian knights, solemnly standing guard on either side of a plush, rose-red carpet.

A pair of wall sconces at either end provided the hall's only illumination. Candlelight quietly gleamed off the polished suits of centuries-old armor, limning the edges of their swords and the points of their staves.

The setting was either wildly romantic or vaguely threatening.

Samuel motioned for her to sit on a bench nestled into an alcove. The cool stone beneath her thighs made her shiver.

He sat next to her. "Katie, you have to let me explain."

"Please do. If you've been here at Summerfield for

hours, why didn't you come to me at once? Why did you make me wait all night?"

"You want the truth?"

"Always."

"Because I can't dance. I only had time to learn the waltz. I couldn't come claim you for the gavotte or the sarabande. I had to stand in the library like a damned fool and wait for the orchestra to play the one dance I knew."

Her heart twisted in her chest. "Oh."

"And I couldn't even manage it. For Christ's sake, it shouldn't be more difficult than marching, should it? Payne told me not to stare at my feet, but . . ."

"Oh, Samuel."

"But you looked so lovely. Every thought went right out of my head."

Now everything made sense. This explained his stern, uncertain expression and his refusal to speak or look at her. He'd been trying so hard to keep step with the dance, he hadn't been able to spare concentration for niceties.

And did he say Lord Payne had advised him? Samuel despised Lord Payne. But he'd sought the man's help. He'd asked for *dancing* lessons.

Heavens. He could have spelled out his love for her in fifty-foot letters, right on the hillside beside the Long Man of Wilmington, and it wouldn't have been any more obvious.

Those clear blue eyes sought hers, shining true through the dark. "Look at me. This is who you'll be stuck with, Katie. A clumsy oaf who can't count to three in his head and tell you you're beautiful at the same time. What the hell are you doing with me?"

"I'm in love with you, you foolish man. Falling deeper

every moment." She let her brow fall to his chest and listened sharp for the deep, steady beat of his heart. "I know you love me. You don't have to say it. I can feel it. I know."

He drew a ragged breath. "Katie, you know the life I've led. It's been brutish and bloody and cruel, and I don't know that I can ever give you the kind of tenderness you deserve. You tell me I love you . . . but I couldn't be sure. I didn't understand what the word even meant, or how a man like me could ever feel such a thing."

"It's all right," she said. "I don't need the words."

"I brought some words anyhow." He stared into her eyes. His gaze was a breathtaking, penetrating blue. "'Love is composed of a single soul, inhabiting two bodies.'"

"Samuel, that's . . ." Her voice broke. "That's absolutely beautiful."

"It's Aristotle. I did some reading."

Oh. He'd done some reading. Kate's heart was doing some wrenching and aching.

"I never thought Greek philosophy could make a damn bit of sense to me. And most of it didn't, but those words just seemed right. 'Love is composed of a single soul, inhabiting two bodies.'" He took her by the shoulders, drawing her close. "It rang true for me, in a way nothing else did. Whatever soul I had, Katie, I think I placed it in your keeping twenty years ago. And now, it's as if . . . every time we kiss, you give a little piece of it back."

She nuzzled his smoothly shaven cheek, inhaling the rich fragrance of his skin. Shaving soap and his natural musk and just the slightest hint of cologne.

He raised his head. "But I don't want you giving anything up for me. I want you to have this life. This family. Your birthright. You are a lady, and I'm no gentleman."

"It doesn't matter," she protested, feeling a sudden stab of panic. "It will never matter. You're a good man. The best man I know."

"You need a husband who is a gentleman. One who understands your new life, and all its demands. A man who can be your partner in society and help manage your inheritance."

"But I don't want any—"

"I mean to be that man, Katie. Or I mean to become him, as best I can."

Her heart swelled in her chest. "What do you mean?"

"The waltzing was only a part of it. I've spent the past several days in London, with Lord Payne. He's arranged for me to have some instruction from his land stewards at Riverchase. I understand game and horses and the run of the earth, but I need to learn how to manage crops, handle tenants. I thought you might have some property come to you, and I—"

"Eight," she said. "Evan told me just today. I have eight properties, scattered all over England. I'm terrified."

He swallowed hard. "I suppose I'd better learn fast."

"I think we both had better." She tried to smile.

He pulled away, putting distance between them, and withdrew something from his pocket, wrapped in a bit of black velvet. As he unfolded the small square of fabric, his fingers were unsteady. Finally, his thumb and forefinger closed on a slender edge of metal and he shook his treasure loose from one last fold of velvet.

He held it out to her. "I didn't know what to choose for you, but I didn't want another man choosing for you, either. So I just looked through the trays until I saw one that looked fine enough for your finger."

She looked down at the gold band in his hand, embedded with small round diamonds. In the center was mounted a square-cut, faceted stone in the palest shade of pink.

"Will it do?" he asked.

"Oh, Samuel. It's too much. This must have cost a fortune."

"Not a fortune." His mouth pulled to the side in a self-effacing way. "Just most of what I had left to my name, after the commission and this." He indicated his new coat and boots.

"The commission?"

"A captaincy. Rycliff's arranged for me to purchase one. He offered to pay for it himself, but I couldn't accept that. Katie, I'll give you everything I can—all that I am, and all I possess—but you must take me at my own worth."

Kate found herself without words. His own worth? This man was priceless.

If she'd tried, she could not have written a more perfect ending to this evening. They would be married and stay in England. She would be able to live with Samuel *and* help her new family.

He went down on one knee before her. The ring glittered on his palm. His face was grim with uncertainty. "Will you wear it? Will you marry me?"

"Yes. Yes, of course." She tugged off her gloves. "Put it on for me, please. My fingers will tremble."

His hands were none too steady, either. But he took her hand and slid the gold band over her finger.

"It fits perfectly," she said.

"And it looks almost deserving of you." He took her hand in both of his and stroked it gently. "I've only ever seen one proper wedding. What's that word, in the vows . . . to cherish? I will cherish you, Katie. Every day of my life. You're the most precious thing I've ever held."

He brought her hand to his lips and kissed it. "I will cherish every inch of you."

With tender, careful brushes of his lips, he kissed each of her fingers. He turned her hand palm up and placed a warm, open-mouthed kiss to the center. His lips brushed the pulse at her wrist, then worked slowly higher. By the time he progressed halfway up her forearm, she was trembling with pleasure and a lifetime of need.

"Samuel? If you wanted to stop cherishing and start ravishing . . . I'd be most amenable."

He froze, lips pressed to her skin. "After the wedding," he told the inside of her elbow.

She reached for him, putting her fingers under his smooth-shaven jaw and pulling his gaze to hers. "I'd prefer now."

She bent at the waist, catching his stunned, parted lips in a kiss. But she couldn't get close enough this way. So she slid from the bench and joined him on the carpet, twining her fingers into his freshly clipped hair as she kissed him deep.

He moaned with pleasure, and she slid her hands beneath the lapels of his coat, running her palms over the cool silk of his waistcoat. She found the closures in front. Such tiny buttons for such a large, powerful man. How did he ever manage them?

But they were no trouble for her fingers. She dispatched them with all the ease of a nursery rhyme. One, two, three . . . four.

Then she divided the sides of his waistcoat and placed her hands flat on his shirtfront, rubbing the crisp linen between her palms and his hardened, muscled chest. His heartbeat thudded against her palm, and she pressed her hand there, holding it close.

When they'd been together the first time, there was something he'd held back. Tonight, she needed to know he could give her everything. That here, in this hall lined with suits of armor, he'd lain down all his own shields. She wanted . . . she wanted something that sounded pagan and savage. To hold his heart—his warm, beating, pure and good heart—in her hands.

He dropped his head, nuzzling her throat and slipping his tongue into the valley between her breasts.

"Don't stop," she begged.

It was the wrong thing to say. He stopped and lifted his head.

"We should go back."

"No," she insisted, pressing her body to his. "Not yet. Please."

Kate's own brazenness shocked even her. He'd given her such lovely words, but she needed to feel the strength and purpose behind them. "I want you so badly, Samuel. I want you to make love to me."

After a thoughtful moment, he placed a hand to her cheek. He tilted her face to receive his kiss. "That I can do."

He kissed her sweetly, once.

That was all the sweetness he had left. The second kiss was deep, demanding, thorough, and wild. Their tongues clashed and dueled as they fought to get closer.

While Thorne explored her mouth, he laid her back on the plush velvet carpeting and worked his hand under her skirts. They were on the floor, in the middle of Sir Lewis Finch's medieval hall, while a ball went on mere steps away.

The wise man would have hurried, or put a stop to this entirely. But he meant to take his time. This wasn't a hasty, scandalous tryst.

This was making love.

As he lifted her blue silk skirts, he took care to arrange the folds carefully so they wouldn't wrinkle any more than necessary. He bunched the petticoats strategically, baring her legs.

Thank God. She wore no drawers.

He needn't have removed her stockings, but he couldn't resist. The garters taunted him with neat ribbon bows.

He undid them with his teeth. After easing one silk stocking down her smooth, taut thigh and shapely calf, he was filled with sorrow to reach her neatly turned toes. Then his spirits were buoyed when he realized he could immediately repeat the experience with her other leg.

Once he had the second bared, he placed a kiss to the tender arch of her foot. He worked his way upward, ignoring her little twitches and protestations when he licked the inside of her knee or the slope of her inner thigh. He had some tickling to repay.

By the time he reached the cleft of her sex, she was writhing, eager for his kiss. Her folds glistened in the dim light. He loved knowing anticipation worked just as well as application. He rewarded her patience with a single, lazy, savoring pass of his tongue. She whimpered, arching in a plea for more.

He sat back on his haunches, hurriedly unbuttoning his trouser falls while he drank in the view of her pale, sprawled legs and the dark triangle of curls guarding her sex. There was something unspeakably arousing about this perspective. From her waist up she was poised, elegant, perfect. A lady. From the waist down she was nothing but pure, natural woman.

And she belonged to him. All of her.

He freed his erection, already rock-hard and pulsing.

She bent one leg at the knee, opening herself in invitation.

He couldn't refuse.

With care not to crush her skirts, he settled into the cradle of her thighs and positioned himself at her warm, wet entrance. He told himself to go slow, to not hurt her. But she tilted her hips, and he slid straight in.

Sweet mercy.

She was tight, yes. But not guarded or clenching in pain. She was perfect, and he fitted himself deep, sinking in all the way to the root. The soft welcome he found made him want to never leave.

"Yes," she sighed.

He began to thrust slowly, steadily—knowing that this was a race more easily won at a walk than a gallop. Drawing on all the self-control he possessed, he kept his pace unhurried, reveling in each easy glide, every silken inch.

Beneath him, she sighed and moaned, climbing closer and closer to release.

All too soon, Thorne felt himself approaching that dangerous edge. Slipping closer and closer to the unknown. If he fell over the brink, he wasn't sure what he'd do.

Panic built in his chest. He should withdraw. He should protect her.

She seemed to sense his struggle. One of her warm, slender legs wrapped over his.

"Don't leave me," she said. "I want all of you. Everything you have to give."

Her words spurred him faster. Soon his hips were

bucking with force, slapping against her thighs. The edge was near, and he raced toward it—for good or ill, determined not to hold anything back.

She cried out and clung to his neck, arching her back in the throes of bliss. He felt the sharp bite against his nape. Not her fingernails, no. His ring, on her finger. A razor edge of bliss.

He couldn't last long now. The climax built in his loins and the base of his spine. Pleasure surged through his veins as he pumped hard and fast. He was wild to get closer, deeper. So deep, where it would be safe.

He forced himself to keep his eyes open, focused on her face. She would be his anchor if he found himself flung somewhere else.

"God, Katie. Hold on to me. Tight."

She held him, and the climax seized him, too. And he did find himself flung somewhere else. But it wasn't a land of shadows and smoke and explosion. Instead, he found a landscape of luminous skin and perfect pink lips and eyes so wide and so deep, they were seas of love. Here, he was reasonably certain hearts had wings. He intended to make many return trips.

Above all, it was beautiful. It was so beautiful, he could have wept.

He wouldn't have wept alone. As he slowed to a stop, a few tears glistened on her cheeks. He didn't worry about them, just kissed them away.

"I love you, too," she said.

He lifted his head, surprised. "Did I say it?"

She smiled. "Only several times."

"Oh. Then good." He kissed her again. "I felt it enough for a thousand."

She stroked his hair, and he allowed himself a few

moments' rest, nestled close to her bosom. If he had to be a broken, fragmented man, liable to slip into strange territories from time to time and be unaware of his actions—he was glad to know he could do something good and loving on occasion.

"We should be getting back," he said, withdrawing from her embrace. "I should speak with Drewe."

"Kate?" The deep, masculine voice came from the corridor. "Kate, are you down here?"

Damn, damn, damn. Speak of the devil.

Thorne didn't panic. He rose and pulled Katie to her feet, moments before Drewe entered the room. As she stood, her carefully draped skirts fell naturally to the floor. No one would have known what had just gone on beneath them.

"We're in here, Drewe," Thorne called, trying to make his voice nonchalant.

"We?" Drewe asked, striding into the room.

Thorne tried to be calm as he buttoned his falls. He knew the shadows would hide him for a few moments, as Drewe's eyes adjusted to the candlelight.

Just one more closure . . .

Then the coat buttons. Drewe was halfway to them now.

One more button. There.

"Drewe." Thorne bowed. "I was looking for you."

The marquess eyed him warily. "Kate, what's going on?"

"Oh, nothing. Nothing."

Her protests were a little too strenuous for Thorne's liking, and Drewe was definitely suspicious. But he was reasonably certain they'd managed to cover any real evidence.

That was, until Drewe's gaze fell to the two discarded stockings on the floor.

Damn.

In the dark, his eyes flashed with unholy rage. "You rutting bastard," he seethed. "I'll kill you."

Chapter Twenty-three

"Evan, stop. Stop!" Kate grabbed her cousin by the sleeve, wrenching him away. "Don't do this. I'll explain. We're going to be married."

"Married?" Evan's face twisted. "To him?"

Thorne approached and placed one hand at the small of her back. "I meant to come speak with you, Drewe. I meant to ask for her hand properly, but—"

"But what? You decided to defile her in a darkened room first? You bastard."

Evan lunged at him again, and Kate jumped between the two men just in time.

"Wait," she called out. "We need to talk. All of us. But we'll never manage it if you're leaping at each other's throats."

She put one hand on either man's chest and pushed them toward opposite sides of the hall. "Just give me a few moments."

"Very well," Evan said. He added ominously, "A few moments."

More voices reached them from the shadowed corridor. "Kate? Evan? Is everything all right?"

Harry, Lark, and Aunt Marmoset stepped into the candlelit entryway of the long narrow hall.

"The dancing's been paused for supper. We were hoping to make the announcement soon," Harry said, eyeing the men's furious expressions and Kate's disheveled gown. "But it looks as though you're . . . busy. Corporal Thorne, what a surprise."

"We'll just pop back inside," Lark offered.

Aunt Marmoset smiled. "I hear there's a fresh bowl of punch."

"No, stay," Kate said. "Please, stay. All three of you. This concerns you, too." She laid a hand flat on her belly, just as she did when she needed support to sing loud and clear. "Corporal Thorne and I have reconciled. We're going to be married."

From his side of the hall, Evan fumed. "Kate, you can't. Do you have any idea who this man is? I had him investigated, you know. Back when we first arrived in Spindle Cove."

"You had him *investigated*?"

"Yes. I had your welfare in mind. And that of the family. I wanted to know just whom you were marrying. And it's a damned fortunate thing I made those inquiries, too. This man is a convicted felon, Kate. He spent years in prison."

"I know that. He's told me everything. He was convicted of poaching as a youth, but he was released to join the army."

"Where he committed even more villainous offenses."

"I know that, too. But then he mended his ways and served honorably under Lord Rycliff for years. Like I said, he's told me everything." She turned to Thorne. "I'm sorry to do so much speaking for you. Would you rather defend yourself?"

"Doesn't matter what I say," Thorne replied. "He'll see in me what he wants to see. My lord, I don't much care what you think of me, so long as Katie—"

"How dare you." A wash of red pushed from the line of Evan's crisp cravat all the way to his hairline. "How *dare* you speak of her in such a familiar fashion? She is Lady Katherine to you."

"He may speak to me however he wishes," Kate said, taken aback by the fury in Evan's voice. "We are in love. We're going to marry."

"Kate, you haven't even heard the worst of it yet. Do you know where this man came from? His mother was a harlot in some disgusting, low-class bawdy house in Sou—"

"In Southwark," Kate finished. "I know."

"He told you that?"

"No, I know because I remember it. Because I lived there, too."

The ladies gasped. Kate hated to shock them by bringing it up at this time and place, but could such an announcement ever come as anything *less* than shocking?

Evan said, "You lived together? The two of you, in a . . . ?"

"We were children, both of us. It seems that's where Elinor ended, after leaving Ambervale. She lived under a new name, Ellie Rose, and yes—I spent my first four years in a bawdy house. All my memories of it were hazy until just the last few days, but with Samuel's help I've pieced them together."

"He's lying," Evan said, eyeing Samuel with a dangerous glare. "He's convinced you of something that isn't true."

"I wish for my mother's sake that it weren't true. But I remember it, Evan. I can't imagine why she ended there.

Perhaps she was too afraid to seek help. Perhaps, as a farmer's daughter, she felt unequal to the task of living as a lady." On that score, Kate could sympathize.

She approached her cousin with caution. "Please don't worry about the family. We'll find some way. I'll . . . I'll simply sign everything over to you before the wedding. All the properties, all the money."

"Like the devil you will," Thorne said. "Your inheritance is your birthright, Katie. You grew up alone, with nothing. You deserve this now. That's why I came here tonight. I won't let you give it up. Not for me, and most definitely not for a puling reptile like him."

"And I won't let a convicted felon destroy what remains of my family's name," Evan interjected. "If you care for her at all, why would you connect her with that place again? Marry her, and the truth will come out. All England will know her as the marquess's daughter who was raised in a whorehouse."

"I don't care," Kate said. "I don't care about idle gossip, and neither does Samuel."

"But I care," Evan said. "I shall have no choice but to care. To have any hope of salvaging Lark's prospects, I would have to sever all acquaintance with you both. Publicly and completely. There would be no more outings or balls. No family holidays at Easter and Christmas." His voice lowered to a hoarse rasp. "Kate, we would be forced to cut you in the street. It would eviscerate me, no question. But I *would* do it, to protect my siblings."

Kate knew he would. He'd do anything for them. Her stomach knotted. "But you've already told me I can't simply disappear. Even if I don't marry Samuel, I'll be the subject of public scrutiny. I don't see how the revelation can be avoided."

"I do. You'll marry me, and we'll conceal all this ugliness from public view."

Samuel swore. "What the hell is this? She's not marrying you."

Evan ignored him and spoke directly to Kate. "If we marry, there will be no need for any court proceedings. Anything that's yours would legally become mine once we wed. No property needs to change hands. The Drewe title and Gramercy fortune will remain united. Then we can avoid all court inquiries and scandal."

"But Evan . . ." She tried to put the words kindly. "You and I don't love each other. Not that way."

"*Love.*" Evan snorted. "Love is a fierce and intoxicating thing, but I will tell you from bitter experience, it cannot balance the loss of fortune, reputation, and family. On this, Kate, I suspect your own parents would agree."

For the first time, her cousin's words gave Kate pause.

And Evan knew it.

"Simon and Elinor were in love," he said softly. "Passionate, desperate love. They scorned the rules of Society and disobeyed the wishes of their families to be together. Look how their story ended."

"It hasn't ended yet," Samuel said. "But I'll tell you how it will end. With their daughter being rightfully restored as Lady Katherine Gramercy, heiress to property and fortune."

Evan spoke only to her, levelly and forcefully. "Kate, think of the family."

Samuel tightened his arm about her middle. "If there's any tarnish on the Gramercy name, then be a gentleman, Drewe, and own it. You, or someone in your family, threw her mother to the streets. This convicted felon did what he could to save her from that. And I'll protect her to the grave now. If you ever—ever—try to shame her for what she could not help, with the aim of keeping your own life gilded and comfortable . . . ? You will answer to me, and there *will* be blood."

Evan lunged in anger.

"Stop this!" Kate cried. "Stop this, please."

She didn't know what to say or do. They were both misunderstanding each other's intentions so badly, and so willfully. Neither man was interested in hearing reason. They just wanted an excuse to hate each other, and she was it.

This was disaster in the making.

But there was one way she could end this entire argument. Much as it pained her to announce it to the group at large, she could see no alternative.

"Evan," she said, "I cannot marry you. Surely you must understand . . . Samuel and I have been intimate. I must marry him."

Evan was silent for a torturous eternity, simply breathing in and out. "No. You don't need to marry him."

"But didn't you hear me? I—"

"You need to marry *someone,* yes." He raised his head and turned a murderous look on Samuel. "That someone will be decided at dawn."

In unison, Harry, Lark, and Aunt Marmoset groaned.

"Oh, Evan."

"Not again."

"Six? Truly? *Six?* Five was impressive, but six is the setup for a bad joke."

Evan quelled the objections with a look. "By the rules of dueling, Thorne—I suspect you may not be so familiar with them, not being a gentleman—I issued the challenge, so the choice of weapons is yours."

Kate was in turmoil. Weren't pistols the traditional choice? But Samuel's right hand was still weakened from the adder venom. His aim with a pistol would be disastrous. He wouldn't have a chance in hell.

"She's made her choice," Samuel said. "There's not going to be any duel."

Oh, thank heaven. Thank God.

Evan strode about the hall, swinging his arms. "You're right, Thorne. A duel isn't necessary."

Truly? He would give up on the idea that easily? To Kate, this turn of events seemed too good to be true.

It was.

Evan stopped before one of the mounted suits of armor and drew the sword from the grasp of the phantom knight's gauntlet. "Why wait for the morning, when we can settle this tonight?"

Kate took back her prayers of thanksgiving and exchanged them for desperate pleas for deliverance.

Evan hefted the sword in his right hand, testing its balance. Though the weapon must have been centuries old, it was well cared for and polished to a mirror gleam.

He said, "Takes you back to the era of true chivalry, doesn't it, Thorne? The days when a man cared something for a lady's reputation."

Harry spoke up. "Evan, don't be ridiculous. Everyone here cares for Kate."

"I don't want anyone fighting over me," Kate said. "It's not worth it."

"Like hell it's not." Samuel turned to her. "Don't ever say you're not worth it, Katie. You're worth epic battles. Entire wars."

Her heart pinched. "Samuel . . ."

"Yes, Helen of Troy?" She thought she saw him wink

as he backed away, reaching for a sword to match Evan's.

After all this time . . . he *would* choose this moment to be charming.

"It's all right," Lark soothed, drawing her aside. "It's all a bit of show to preserve honor and save face. You know how gentlemen are."

It didn't matter how gentlemen were. Samuel wasn't a gentleman. He was not the sort of man to take up arms in a show of honor. He would *fight*.

Worse, any given blow might send him to that other place—that shadowy battlefield where he knew nothing but instinct and survival. Even if he wished to back down, he might be unable to do so in the heat of the struggle.

She saw no way this could end but badly—bloodily—for everyone concerned.

"Stop this," she cried. "Both of you, please. Evan, you don't understand. Samuel cares for me. He sacrificed everything to save me from that awful place."

"He stole your virtue. He's a blackguard."

Kate wanted to argue that she'd given herself willingly, and that the idea of a woman's virtue as a possession one man could steal from another was straight from the Dark Ages. But judging by the scene before her, accusations of medieval behavior would fall on deaf ears.

The men circled one another in the center of the hall, like two wild beasts bristling and snarling in warning. The bloodred carpet they trod upon did little to calm Kate's fears or ease the men's thirst for violence.

"You really want to do this, Thorne?" Evan asked.

"No. Because when I kill you, it will be sad for Katie and a mess for Sir Lewis's house staff."

"I spent four years fencing at Oxford."

"Child's play," Samuel scoffed. "I spent a decade fighting my way through enemy lines, using nothing but a bayonet."

I'm sure you did, Kate thought. But that was with a strong, healthy arm, not a grip weakened by snake venom.

"I won't surrender her," Samuel said. "You can't convince me you're the better man."

"Very well. Then I'll let my blade do the talking."

Kate cringed as Evan swung his sword, but Thorne parried the blow capably. They clashed several times in quick succession. The ringing clangs of metal against metal shivered through her bones.

Just as suddenly, they broke apart and retreated, each breathing hard. The ritual of mutual, animalistic circling began again.

"Don't do this, Samuel," she pleaded. "He's only desperate to save the family. It's his passion. He wants so much to take care of his siblings and for Lark to have—"

Samuel laughed bitterly. "There's nothing noble in this. Can't you see he's had this planned? He's been maneuvering you into marrying him all along. That's why he hasn't let you out of his sight since they arrived in Spindle Cove. He cares, all right. He cares about the money."

"And you don't?" Evan stopped circling and leveled his sword at Samuel. "Those American ambitions disappeared rather quickly once you learned of her inheritance. You want her money so badly, you're willing to drag her name through the gutter to get it."

"The gutter *you* left her in." Holding his blade pointed at Evan's chest, Thorne looked around the room, from one Gramercy to the next. "I will never believe that no one knew of her. That you could not have found her and saved her years of degradation and misery. You're either liars or fools."

"Samuel, look sharp!"

Evan took advantage of his opponent's distraction and made a slicing blow that caught Samuel's sword and sent it spiraling away, into the darkest corner of the room. But before Evan could even demand his surrender, Samuel shifted his weight back and made a full-force kick at Evan's wrist. Evan cried out in pain and dropped his sword. Rather than reach for it, Samuel kicked the weapon out of reach.

Both men were disarmed.

"Oh, thank heaven," Kate whispered. "Maybe now it will be over."

Harry shook her head. "You don't know my brother very well."

Evan turned to the next suit of armor in the row. This one held not a sword, but a shield and a long, slender javelin. He wrenched both shield and weapon from the pedestal. "Always fancied a go at this."

Across the hall, Thorne turned to the armored figure's counterpart and began to do the same.

Once they were identically armed, the men backed toward opposite ends of the hall, as if preparing for a joust.

"There's no doubt you're a lady now," Harriet said to Kate. "They've organized a full tournament for your affections."

"This is ridiculous!" Kate cried. "The midsummer fair was over weeks ago. What's next, squaring off with crossbows?"

"Don't give them any more ideas," Lark whispered.

"On three, Thorne," Evan called, raising his shield with his left hand and balancing the javelin with his right. He planted his boots firmly in the plush red carpet. "Three . . . two . . ."

"No!" Kate plucked her discarded stockings from the floor and dashed into the center of the hall, waving them like white, streaming banners of surrender. "Stop!"

The men stopped.

Everything stopped. Suddenly, the hall was completely, unearthly quiet. Because from the ballroom, they heard music. Not orchestral music. Just the gentle strains of the pianoforte and a familiar voice, lifted in song.

"Oh," Kate gasped, recognizing the tune. "It's Miss Elliott. At last, the brave dear. She's finally performing for her friends."

"Mozart," Evan said, recognizing the aria. "Excellent choice, Kate. It suits her voice very well. Do you attend the opera frequently, Thorne?"

"No," Samuel replied tightly.

Without taking his eyes from his opponent, Evan spoke to Kate. "Do you see? *I* will be good for you. I can give you not only the protection you need, but the companionship you deserve. We converse on politics and poetry, play brilliant duets." He waved his javelin at Thorne. "He might make your blood pound with illicit thrills, but he can't give you those things."

Kate slid her gaze to Samuel, worried. She knew Evan's words poked at his deepest feelings of unworthiness.

"What can you possibly offer her?" Evan demanded, as Miss Elliott's voice soared to operatic heights.

"You've no breeding. No education. Not even an honorable trade. You can't provide her with a home befitting a lady."

"I know." Samuel's expression hardened to that veneer of impenetrable stone.

"You're beneath her," Evan said, "in every possible way."

"I know that, too."

Don't agree with him, Kate shouted in her mind. *Don't ever believe it.*

Evan sneered. "Then how can you dare to ask for her hand?"

"Because I love her," Samuel replied in a low, quiet voice. "I have more love and devotion to give that woman than there is gold in England. And I have the manners not to prattle on while her pupil is singing." He made a menacing thrust with his javelin. "Shut it, or I'll skewer you."

After that, every soul in the room remained quiet and still until Miss Elliott sang her last, sweetly pure note. Kate's chest swelled with pride in her pupil and happiness for her friend.

Best of all, she had hope for the men's reconciliation.

"Thank you," she told the men, alternating her gaze from one end of the hall to the other. "I know you understand what that meant to me. How hard Miss Elliott worked."

She let her arms drop to her sides and retreated to the border of the hall, leaving them to regard one another. Surely now they must comprehend—no matter their differences as men, they both wanted what was best for her.

"Now," Kate asked, "can we put away Sir Lewis's artifacts and discuss this like rational people?"

Apparently not.

"One," Evan said.

The two men rushed at each other and collided in the center of the hall with an ugly crunch. The impact of javelins on shields sent them bouncing back, repulsed by the force of the impact. No one had been seriously hurt—which pleased Kate, but evidently frustrated the men. They threw their javelins aside.

Evan reached for a battle-axe next, but in pulling it down from its wall rack, he misjudged the weight. The horrific weapon crashed to the floor, narrowing missing his foot and sinking two inches into the parquet.

By now Lark, Harriet, and Aunt Marmoset had joined in the shouting. "Stop! Both of you, stop! This is absurd."

But apparently there were yet loftier heights of male absurdity, just begging to be explored. Both of them had moved to some place beyond logic or reason, where only male pride and bloodlust held sway.

Thorne plucked a quarterstaff from a rack. It was a long, wooden pole weighted at either end for the purpose of inflicting bone-crushing blows.

For his part, Evan now reached for a morning star—a heavy, spiked ball dangling at the end of a chain. He lifted the mace's handle with two hands and began to swing the menacing projectile in circles over his head. It made a fearful whistling noise as it picked up speed.

Everyone stared at it, rapt. The image was transfixing—this instrument of death swinging faster and faster through its drunken orbit.

Evan's face told her even *he* was wary of what he'd unleashed—and uncertain how to control or stop it. He shot Kate a bewildered look. His eyes seem to say, *Did I truly do this? Fight your betrothed with javelins and broadswords and then lift a bloody medieval mace over my head and start swinging it recklessly about in a room full of people?*

Yes, Evan. You truly did.

She was glad he'd finally come to his senses about this entire ridiculous battle.

But it was too late.

When he released that thing, it was going to fly fast and hard and wreak destruction in whatever direction it chose.

He said, in a very polite, calm, aristocratic voice, "I can't hold it much longer, I'm afraid."

"Katie," Samuel barked. "Get down."

All the ladies obeyed, diving into corners and taking cover under chairs. Kate ducked behind one of the discarded shields.

Thorne positioned himself as her human guard, lifting his quarterstaff in both hands and keeping his eye on the circling morning star. He looked like a cricketer, readying to bat—and in essence, he was. Brave, stupid man.

"Samuel, please! Just take cover!"

With a savage shout, Evan released his grip on the mace. Kate ducked instinctively, unable to watch any further.

She both heard and felt the horrific crash. The initial impact was sharp and jolting, then almost musical, with the plink and crack of shattered glass.

The ball must have found a window and taken its bloodthirsty spikes soaring out into the garden. She could not speak for the hedgehogs, but with luck, it would seem no people had been hurt.

Drawn by the sound of calamity, guests began pouring in from the ballroom. Several carried candles or lamps.

"What the devil's going on here?" Lord Rycliff demanded.

A good question. Sucking in what seemed to be her first proper breath in an hour, Kate emerged and assessed the scene.

Evan remained standing, staring at the broken window. On his brow, blood oozed from a small razor-thin cut. Otherwise, he appeared unharmed.

As for Samuel . . .

Oh no. Her worst fears were realized. He wasn't physically harmed, but mentally . . . His eyes were dilated. his nostrils flared. He wasn't there. Just the same as with the melon siege, with one important difference.

This time he was armed.

Chapter Twenty-four

As Kate watched in horror, Samuel tightened his grip on the quarterstaff. He held it in two hands, braced across his chest, parallel to the floor.

An inhuman growl originated somewhere low in his gut, building strength as it clawed its way up through his chest.

He was going to charge Evan. And dazed, unarmed, unwitting Evan wouldn't have a chance.

"Samuel, no!" Kate dashed to intercept him, gripping the quarterstaff with both hands.

She made eye contact, hoping he'd know her.

It's me. Come back.

Something flashed in his blue, unfocused gaze—but what it was, she couldn't tell.

The primal growl building deep in his chest now erupted from his throat. With a hoarse cry he lifted the quarterstaff, swinging both weapon and Kate with violent force, slamming her against the nearest wall.

Several ladies screamed.

Kate couldn't have screamed if she'd tried. The impact knocked all air from her lungs. For a moment she floated loose in her own body—robbed of sensation, of presence. She didn't feel any pain—not yet. But she was certain it must be coming. An impact that strong must have broken her somewhere. Her spine, perhaps. A few ribs at the very least.

Then a dizzying rush of air entered her lungs. Her vision sharpened. She could breathe again, freely. The pain still hadn't arrived.

After a moment's reflection she understood why. He'd slammed her not against the flat wall, but into a niche. As the quarterstaff was much wider than the recessed alcove, the beams on either side had taken the impact. She was unharmed.

Unharmed, but shaken to her marrow.

If he'd thrown her mere inches to either side, the full force of the quarterstaff would have crashed into her rib cage—wounding her, surely. Killing her, possibly. But even in his darkest, most unthinking moment, Thorne had protected her from himself.

He'd saved her. Now she had to return the favor.

She ignored the room packed with onlookers. She ignored the quarterstaff holding her pinned into the narrow niche. She kept her gaze locked with his. He was far away, and she had to bring him home.

"It's all right," she said, speaking in the lowest, most soothing tone she could manage. "Samuel, it's me. Katie. I'm unharmed, and so are you. You were having a disagreement with Lord Drewe here at Summerfield. But it's over now. It's all over. There's no danger any-more."

She caught a flicker of awareness in his eyes. He drew a sharp breath.

"Yes," she encouraged him. "Yes, that's it. Come back. Back to me. I love you."

If only she could touch him, it might make all the difference. But the quarterstaff kept them apart.

"Let her go." Evan appeared at Samuel's side, pressing a blade to his throat and undoing all Kate's efforts of the past minute.

"Evan, don't. Please. You'll make it worse."

"Get the hell away from her," he growled at Thorne.

"You don't understand, Evan. He didn't hurt me. He would never hurt me." She ignored her cousin then and focused on Thorne again, staring deeply into his eyes. "Samuel, you must come back to me. *Now*. I need you here."

That did it.

His breathing steadied and recognition smoothed the creases in his brow. His eyes focused—first on her face, then on the quarterstaff and their position against the wall.

"Oh, Jesus," he breathed. Anguish tweaked his voice. "Katie. What did I do to you?"

"Nothing," she assured him. "Nothing but remove me from the path of harm. I'm fine."

"Bollocks," said Evan. "You could have killed her."

"Don't believe him," Kate said. "I know the truth. You didn't hurt me at all. You'd never hurt me."

Bram appeared then, reaching for the quarterstaff. "Stand down, Thorne. The fight's over."

Samuel nodded, still clutching the weapon tight. "Yes. It's all over."

"Don't say that," Kate pleaded, pushing against the staff that kept her pinned. She needed to touch him, to hold him tight. If only she could get her arms around him, she could change his mind.

He seemed to know it, too.

"I can't risk it," he whispered, holding her off. "I can't.

I love you too much. I thought I could make myself into the man you need—a husband fit for a lady—but . . ." His face twisted as he swept a tormented gaze down and then up her body. "Look at this. I don't belong in this world anymore. If I ever did."

"Then we'll go find another world," she said. "Together. I'd give up everything for you."

He shook his head, still holding her off. "I can't let you do that. You say this life doesn't matter, but if I take you from it . . . you'll come to resent me, in time. I'll resent myself. Family means so much to you."

"You mean more."

"Drewe," he said, still staring into Kate's eyes, "how soon could you marry her?"

"Tomorrow," Evan answered.

"And you'll protect her? Against rumor, scandal. Against those who would treat her ill or use her for her fortune."

"With my life."

"Samuel, no." Kate fought back tears.

He nodded, still looking at her. "Then do it. I'll leave England as soon as I know it's done. As soon as I know she's safe."

"I won't marry him," Kate objected. "And Samuel, you won't let it happen. You say this now, but do you mean for me to believe you'll sit in the pews of St. Ursula's tomorrow morning and watch, while I walk down the aisle with another man?"

At that, he hesitated.

"You wouldn't let it happen. I know you wouldn't."

The argument seemed to make some inroads.

But unfortunately, they took him in the wrong direction.

"Bram," he called.

"Still here," Lord Rycliff answered.

"When you were shot in the knee, you made me swear, right there on the battlefield, that I wouldn't let them take your leg." Samuel spoke in a firm, controlled voice. "No matter what the surgeons said, no matter if you hovered at death's threshold. Even if you lost your mind with delirium. I swore I wouldn't let them amputate, and I didn't. I sat by your bedside with a pistol cocked, scaring off anyone with a saw. When they threatened me with court-martial, even when my own powers of reason argued against it . . . I stayed true to my word."

Bram nodded. "You did. I'm forever in your debt."

"You're going to repay me now."

"How?"

"Lock me in the village gaol. In irons, tonight. And no matter what happens—even if I rage or plead—give me your word right now that you won't release me until she's married. Swear it."

"Thorne, I can't—"

Samuel turned to him. "Don't question. Don't look at anyone else. This is you and me, and a debt you owe. Just do as I ask, and swear it."

Lord Rycliff relented. "Very well. You have my word. You can release her now."

"Get the irons first."

"For goodness' sake, Samuel!" Kate struggled again. "What are the chances that a pair of irons are just hanging about?"

She had forgotten to consider that in Sir Lewis Finch's house, the chances were apparently quite good. Someone produced a pair of iron cuffs, connected by a heavy chain.

Lord Rycliff opened one manacle and fitted it around Samuel's wrist.

Samuel stared deep into her eyes. "Thank you," he whispered. "For lighting up for me, just the once. That was worth everything."

Kate growled and kicked him in the shin—not that her bare foot could do much damage. "Don't pretend this is romantic, you stubborn, foolish man! If I didn't love you so much, I'd vow to hate you forever."

In response, he pressed an infuriating kiss to her brow.

Once the other cuff was fastened, he let go of the quarterstaff and released her.

Then he walked away in chains.

"I won't let it happen."

Lark stood in the center of the Queen's Ruby parlor, looking as firm-chinned and resolute as Kate had ever seen her.

"Kate," she said, "I love you dearly, but if you try to marry my brother today, I will stand up in the middle of St. Ursula's and object."

"Chicken," Harry soothed, "it's not yours to say. Evan and Kate are adults. Besides, the vicar will only be interested in your objection if it presents a legal impediment. There is none."

"There's an emotional impediment," Lark argued. "Kate can't marry Evan. She's in love with Corporal Thorne."

Kate squeezed her eyes shut. Of course she was in love with Thorne. If she weren't completely, eternally in love with him, she wouldn't feel so miserable sitting here this morning, discussing the possibility of marrying another man.

Her heart ached. Somewhere nearby, Samuel was in irons, locked up like an animal in a cage. He'd spent the entire night in gaol.

She knew how he'd suffered as a youth in prison. He should never have been subjected to confinement again, not even for one night. She was desperate to see him released, and he must have known she'd feel this way. He was holding himself ransom, and the price he demanded was her wedding to another.

The stubborn, impossible man. And to believe common wisdom, *women* were the sex prone to dramatics?

Lark continued, "What's more, Evan can't marry Kate. What about Claire?"

"Claire?" Harry echoed. "My dear pigeon, Claire is several years in the grave."

"But he loved her once. That's all I'm saying. He might fall in love again."

"Let's hope not," Harry muttered.

Lark confronted her sister. Anger burned red on her cheeks. "Really, Harriet. Our brother defended you when you broke three loveless engagements. He has supported you in your attachment to Ames. And this is how you repay him? By encouraging him to enter a marriage of convenience and hoping he never loves again?"

As she absorbed Lark's censure, Harry's eyebrows rose. "My my, starling. You are growing up so fast." She drummed her fingers on the arm of her chair, then stood. "Very well, I'll object, too."

"Your objections won't be necessary, I hope." Kate lifted Badger into her lap and drew him close. "I've no intention of marrying Evan, if it can possibly be helped. There must be some other way."

But even as she spoke the words, she doubted them. What other way could there be? All night long she'd been thinking on the dilemma. She'd exhausted all her powers of logic, imagination, and desperation, and still no solution had come to her.

"Harry and I tried appealing to Evan," Lark said. "If he withdrew his offer to Kate, Corporal Thorne would have to back down. But he won't budge, either."

"He feels too guilty," Harry said to Kate. "He's determined to give you the life you deserve, he says."

"But you all have given me so much already," she said. "You sought me out and welcomed me with open arms, even knowing it would change your lives in uncertain ways. Your kindness and faith in me has been remarkable, and I . . . I love you all for it."

"Oh, dear." Across the room, Aunt Marmoset pressed a hand to her chest. "Oh dear, oh dear."

"Aunt Marmoset, what is it? Not your heart?"

"No, no. My conscience." The old woman looked to Kate with red, teary eyes. "I must tell you the truth. It's my fault. It's all my fault that you were lost, dear. You mustn't feel beholden to us. I shouldn't blame you if you took all the family money and cast us out in the cold."

Kate shook her head, utterly confused. "I don't understand. Cast you out in the cold? I'd never do such a thing."

Lark patted her aunt's hand. "I'm sure it's not as bad as all that, Aunt Marmoset."

"But it is. It is." The old woman accepted a handkerchief from Harry. "After Simon died and your father inherited the title, I came to Rook's Fell. My sister needed me. You weren't even born yet, Lark. But Harry—surely you must remember that time. How difficult it was."

Harry nodded. "It was the year Father's illness began. There were so many doctors, coming and going. I remember Mother's face was always grim."

"Your lives had changed so much, so swiftly. A new

home, new titles, new responsibilities. I took over the running of the household. I oversaw the servants, attended to correspondence. I received any guests to the house . . ." She paused meaningfully. "So I was there the day Simon's lover came back, babe in arms. And I sent her away."

"*What?*"

At the words, Kate felt as though she'd been dunked underwater. The air felt slow and thick around her. Cold. Her vision went wavy and a dull pulse throbbed in her ears.

She couldn't breathe.

"You sent her away?" Lark's voice echoed from a great distance. "Aunt *Marmoset*. How could you do such a thing?"

Kate forced herself to surface, to listen.

"You've no idea," Aunt Marmoset said. She wrung Harry's handkerchief. "You've no idea how many charlatans crawl out of every ceiling crack after a marquess dies. Every day, I was chasing another away. Some came claiming his lordship owed back wages or gambling debts, others said that his lordship had promised them a living. More than one girl showed up with an infant in her arms. Liars, all. When Elinor arrived and claimed to have married him . . . I didn't believe her. A marquess, marry a tenant farmer's daughter? Preposterous. I never suspected, until the day we found the parish register, that the girl might have been telling the truth."

Kate's fingers went to the pendant dangling at her breastbone. She skimmed her fingertips over the polished teardrop of stone, begging the glossy smoothness to calm her emotions. "So that's why you had her pendant. You took it from her. You had it all along."

Aunt Marmoset nodded. "She offered it as some sort of proof. I didn't see what meaning it should have, just a chip of stone. I did save it, however, in case she came back. But she never did. She never went to the solicitors. She disappeared."

Lark paced the room, clearly struggling to contain her emotions. "Why didn't you tell us the truth weeks ago?"

"I was ashamed," the old woman said. "And what was done was done. I didn't see how it could do any good to relate the story now. We all agreed to make it right for Kate. We were going to welcome her to the family, give her all she was due. But then last night, when you told us about the bawdy house . . ." Aunt Marmoset's tears renewed. "Oh, it was my fault. I was so sharp with the girl. When she asked me where she should go or how she should live, I . . . I told her she wouldn't get a penny from us, and she should go live like the slattern she was."

"Oh, no." Kate covered her mouth with her hand. "You didn't."

Kate stared at Aunt Marmoset, uncertain what to say or do. In the past weeks, she'd come to think of this woman as . . . as the closest thing to a mother she would likely ever know. And now to learn she'd been turned away, even as an infant.

For a moment she was back in Miss Paringham's sitting room, swallowing dishwater tea and dodging blows from a cane. *No one wanted you then. Who on earth do you think will want you now?*

"I'm so sorry," Aunt Marmoset said. "I know you may never forgive me, and I'll understand if you don't. But I'm so fond of you, dear." She sniffed. "I truly am. I love you like one of my own. If I'd only known that my moment of peevishness would have such dire consequences . . ."

"You didn't know," Kate found herself saying. "You couldn't have known. I don't blame you."

"You don't?"

She shook her head honestly. "I don't."

Miss Paringham's scornful words that day hadn't altered the course of her life. She doubted a few moments' ugliness from Aunt Marmoset had been enough to determine her mother's entire future. For Elinor to grow so desperate, more than one door must have been closed in her face. Or perhaps she'd simply been unwilling to live by others' rules. Kate would never know.

Aunt Marmoset clasped Kate's hand. "Do you know how she responded that day, when I turned her away?"

Kate shook her head. "Tell me, please. I want to know everything."

"She lifted her chin, bade me a good day. And she walked away, smiling. She kept her dignity, even after I'd lost mine." The older woman's papery hand squeezed Kate's. "You have so much of your mother's fire."

Your mother's fire.

At last, Kate had a name for that small flame warming her heart. She did have something of her mother. She'd carried it inside her all along, and it was more precious than a memory of her face or a verse her mother might have sung. She had the courage to smile in the face of cruelty and indifference—to clutch her dignity tight when she had nothing else. That inner fire was how she'd survived.

She would find an answer to this situation, and it would not involve marrying anyone. Anyone other than Samuel, that was.

"Should we tell Evan this?" she asked. "Perhaps he'd feel less obligated to marry me if he knew that—"

"*Less* obligated?" Harry cried. "Surely you know him better than that, Kate. If Evan hears of this, he'll have us scraping your shoes in penance. He'll dress Lark in sackcloth and ashes for her debut. He will certainly not feel less obligated."

Kate chewed her lip, knowing Harry was right.

She did have one last source of hope, however. Susanna. Perhaps Susanna could make Lord Rycliff see sense and release Samuel from the gaol.

Just then, Susanna and Minerva entered through the parlor door. Badger scampered to the floor as Kate stood to welcome them.

Susanna wasted no time on pleasantries. "It's no good, I'm afraid."

"He won't be moved?" Kate asked, deflating back into her chair. "Oh no."

Susanna shook her head with so much agitation, her freckles blurred. "What good is a 'code of honor' if it flies in the face of all common sense? Bram insists that he's bound to do as Thorne asks, even if he personally disagrees. He won't hear any argument. It's all wrapped up in pride and brotherhood and his wounded leg. I tell you, whenever that dratted leg is concerned, Bram's impervious to reason. If the man ever had a sensible bone in his body, it must have been his right kneecap."

She sat down next to Kate. "I'm so sorry. I tried my best."

"I know you did."

Minerva added, "I considered asking Colin speak to him, as a last resort. But I worried it might work against us."

Kate tried to smile. "Thank you for the thought."

"Surely one of them can be worn down, over the course of days," Susanna said. "This can't last forever."

But even if it lasted days, it would be too much. No one could understand just what it meant for Samuel to be confined. Here was a man who'd etched the date of his release on his *own arm,* working carefully despite the teeth-gritting pain, because he knew he was in danger of losing all hope and forfeiting his last shred of humanity. Accepting chains must be torture for him.

"We'll find another way," Susanna said. She looked around the parlor at Lark, Harry, Aunt Marmoset, Minerva . . . finally coming back to Kate. "This is Spindle Cove. Here we have six intelligent, resourceful, strong-willed women in one room. We will not be thwarted by a few unreasonable men and their silly toy-soldier games."

"That's right," Minerva said. "Let's go through all the alternatives."

"I can't run away," Kate said, ticking them off on her fingers. "Marrying Evan is out of the question, as is marrying anyone else."

"I know!" Lark said. "Kate, you could take religious vows, so you're forbidden to marry anyone."

Aunt Marmoset coughed on her spice drop. "A Gramercy woman, sent to a nunnery? That would be unspeakably cruel—to the abbess, most of all."

Harry wagged a finger, eyes keen. "Wait a moment. Perhaps she could marry Evan just for a few minutes, and then apply for a dissolution or annulment."

"I can't do that," Kate said. "I did think of it, but the vicar told me annulments aren't easy to obtain. Plus, it would be dishonest. Evan's been so good to me—I couldn't lie to his face that way, reciting vows I've no intention to keep."

"Susanna had the right idea," Minerva declared. She adjusted her spectacles. "In this village, we beat the men at their own games. If they want to play soldiers, we'll assemble our own army of ladies. We'll have at them with bows, pistols, rifles—even a trebuchet, if Sir Lewis will lend it—and stage a jailbreak by force."

Aunt Marmoset perked up. "My dear, I like the way you think."

"No, no," Kate said. "That's certainly an . . . *exciting* . . . idea, Min. But we can't. There'd be too much chance of someone getting hurt, and the last thing Samuel needs is another siege."

His unpredictable reaction to blasts was at the very heart of the problem.

"Besides, even if we were to break him out of the gaol, that wouldn't change his mind. We'd just be back where we were last night."

Kate believed, with all her heart, that she and Samuel could build a happy life together. But when he'd made that bargain with Evan last night, he revealed his own doubts. He'd passed her into someone else's keeping, the same way he'd left her at Margate two decades ago. He doubted his own worth. And he didn't believe her when she said she'd give up everything for him. She had run out of ways to convince him with words.

And there was still the problem of public scandal. She couldn't adopt the family name, then turn around and drag it straight through the seediest lanes of Southwark. Even after Aunt Marmoset's confessions, she wouldn't wish that on any of the Gramercys—and she didn't want that cloud hanging over a marriage to Samuel.

In a nervous gesture, she twisted the ring on her

finger, turning the pale pink stone this way and that to catch golden flashes of sun. So beautiful. She couldn't imagine ever removing it. Samuel had chosen it especially for her.

The stone had inner fire. So did she.

"Well, we must do *something*," Minerva said. "Print pamphlets. Stage a hunger strike in the green. Go without our corsets until someone relents. This is Spindle Cove. Heaven forbid we let etiquette and convention carry the day. Just look at your dog. Even he agrees with me."

Kate looked down at Badger, who was happily gnawing his way through yet another copy of *Mrs. Worthington's Wisdom for Young Ladies*.

She bent and scratched him behind one funny, half-cocked ear and whispered, "This is all your fault, you know."

If not for Badger, she might never have pulled the truth from Samuel after the adder bite. She might never have come to know his softer side, and grown to love him for it. Melons would have far less meaning in her life.

In her mind, the wisp of an idea began to coalesce. Maybe . . . just maybe . . . Badger could be the key to this problem, too.

"I think I may know just what to do," she said, growing excited as she looked around the room at her family and friends. "But I'll need help getting dressed."

Chapter Twenty-five

So this was Spindle Cove's excuse for a gaol.

Thorne had always wondered about this tiny building settled on the village green, not far from St. Ursula's. At first he'd assumed it to be a well house for a spring that had long dried up. Then someone told him it used to be a baptistery for the original church.

At any rate, now it was the gaol.

The structure was small, round, and fashioned of windowless sandstone walls. It must have been built during the same era as the original Rycliff Castle—in other words, forever ago. The wood ceiling, of course, had long since rotted away. Instead, a lattice of iron bars overhead kept prisoners confined while admitting fresh air and golden shafts of sunlight. Here and there a bit of moss or fern sprouted from a crack in the wall.

As with all things in this village, it was a little too quaint and charming. But it would be effective enough. The only break in the stone walls was the single forged metal door. The handiwork of Aaron Dawes, no doubt, and Thorne knew him to be a capable smith.

A heavy set of iron cuffs encircled his wrists, linked by a chain. The shackles were genuine, taken from Sir Lewis's collection. The only keys to both cell door and irons were in Bram's possession, and he'd given his word.

Thorne was well and truly confined.

The night hadn't been easy. Sitting chained in the dark . . . the silence poked at the wild, feral creature in him. But the restraints were good, and the walls were solid. Even if he went a bit mad and his resolve crumbled, he wouldn't be muscling his way out of this cell.

Which was fortunate, because if he did muscle his way out of the cell, taking on the guards would be no difficulty.

"Tell me again how is it that *you* two," he asked, "are the village gaolers?"

Finn and Rufus Bright sat outside the cell's grated door with a pack of cards. They were twins, just nearing sixteen years old, and Thorne didn't like trusting them with a few hours' watch from the southeast turret of Rycliff Castle. He would have never set them to guard a dangerous criminal.

"Used to be our despicable sot of a father's duty," Rufus said. "He was the riding officer, before he switched sides of the law. Better money in smuggling, I suppose."

"Once he was gone," Finn said, "the task fell to Errol, as his eldest son."

"And Errol's gone to Dover this week." Rufus split and shuffled the deck of cards. "So lucky you, you get us."

Lucky them, the youth surely meant. As much hell as Thorne had given Spindle Cove's youngest militiamen over the past year, he could only imagine they were enjoying this.

He heard Bram's voice. "Finn, Rufus. I hope you're treating your prisoner well."

"Yes, Lord Rycliff."

"Thorne?" Bram peered through the door grate. "Not yet wasted to bones, I gather."

"Not even close."

"Don't think this isn't costing me. My wife is not pleased. And in case you're wondering, Miss Taylor— Lady Kate, I suppose I should call her now—is not pleased, either."

Thorne shrugged, indifferent.

Katie would be pleased, eventually. In time, she'd see that this was best. Drewe could keep her safe *and* make her happy. She might have put on a brave face for him last night, told him she'd leave behind everything to be with him—but he knew her too well. She'd longed for a family all her life, and he couldn't offer her anything to replace the Gramercys. And after last night, he knew he wasn't fit to be a lady's husband. He couldn't even keep her safe.

"So what's happening?" Thorne asked. "Have they seen the vicar for a license yet?"

"I'm not sure," Bram said. "But she's just come through the front door of the Queen's Ruby."

"How does she look?"

"Like she's about to be married."

A black, bottomless pit opened up in Thorne's chest. He contemplated jumping into it.

"She's walking toward the church," Bram said. "All the rooming house ladies are following her. The Gramercys, too."

"Tell me what she's wearing."

Bram cut him an annoyed look. "What do I look like to you? The Society columnist for the *Prattler*?"

"Just tell me."

"Ivory frock. Two flounces and a great deal of lace."

"Is she smiling?"

Stupid question. Her smile wouldn't give any clues to her inner emotions. His Katie would be bravely smiling, even if she were walking to a guillotine.

"Her hair," Thorne asked. "How is she wearing her hair?"

Bram growled. "Good God, man. I agreed to imprison you, not provide fashion reports."

"Just tell me."

"Her hair is up. You know how the ladies fix it— mass of curls on top, wound with ribbons. Someone's stuck little blossoms between the curls. Don't bother asking me what kind of flower. I don't know."

"Never mind," Thorne scraped out. "That's enough."

He could see her in his mind's eye. Floating in a lacy cloud, tiny stars of jasmine studded in her dark, shining hair. So feminine and beautiful. If she'd taken that much care with her appearance, she must be approaching her wedding with joy, not unwillingness or dread.

This was good, he told himself. The best possible outcome. He'd worried she might hold out longer, strictly for the sake of being stubborn. But she must have seen the wisdom of it, once she had a few hours to reflect.

"Susanna's with her," Bram said. "I'll go inquire about their plans."

Restless, Thorne paced the small round cell. He lifted and spread his arms, pulling against the irons. Every primal instinct in his body wanted to break free. He'd been prepared for this. This was why he'd exacted the promise from Bram—because when the time drew close, he knew only physical restraints could keep him from going after her.

Less than an hour now, surely, and it would be over. A matter of minutes, perhaps. When the church bells sounded, he'd know it was done.

Instead of church bells, however, he heard a scraping of metal in the lock. In response, his body screamed, *Make ready. Prepare to bolt.*

He turned his back on the door, clenching his hands in fists. "Devil take you, Bram. I told you not to open that door. You gave me your word."

"I'm not releasing you," Bram called. "I have a new prisoner, so you'll have to share the cell."

"A new prisoner?" Thorne glared hard at the wall as the door clanged shut. "I'm the first prisoner this gaol has seen in years. Now two in one morning? What's the offense?"

A soft, melodic voice answered him. "Possession of a nuisance animal. Destruction of property."

No.

His iron chains seemed to double in weight, and they pulled directly on his heart. He turned.

Of course it was Katie.

She was here, in gaol with him. And Bram had no future in Society columns, because his account of her appearance was a mere ghost of the reality. A man might as well witness a comet streaking across the sky and describe it as something resembling a glowworm.

Her frock was gauzy—sweet and revealing, all at once. Her hair was piled in dozens of intricate coils and twists, and her skin could have made angels weep. She was radiant.

A bit of fire flashed on her finger.

Sweet mercy. She was still wearing his ring.

Thorne pushed down the unwelcome surge of hope. His spirits shouldn't be buoyed by her presence. He shouldn't want her here at all. She didn't belong with him in a gaol of any sort—not even a relatively quaint and charming one.

"Well . . . ?" She twisted, trying to catch his approval. "I wanted to look my best for my wedding."

"You shouldn't be here," he said. "What the hell sort of game is Bram playing at?"

"It's not a game, unfortunately. I'm under arrest."

"For what?"

She pulled a thick black book from beneath her arm. "You were right. Letting Badger chew books was horrendous neglect on my part. Just look what the little beast has done."

Thorne couldn't risk drawing any closer to her, but he cocked his head and peered at the book. It was old, thick, bound with black leather . . . the gold leaf letters on the spine had been mostly destroyed, and most of the pages were shredded.

"Jesus," he breathed as realization dawned. "Tell me that's not what I think it is."

She nodded. "It's the St. Mary of the Martyrs parish register."

"Not the one that—"

"Contained my birth record. Yes. As well as the record of my parents' marriage."

Thorne couldn't believe this. "You allowed Badger to do that. On purpose."

"It doesn't really signify how and why it happened, does it? It's done." She squared her shoulders. "There's no paper record of Katherine Adele Gramercy. Not any longer."

The enormity of her words swamped his mind for a moment. He groped for some cord of reason or logic in the vast, nonsensical sea.

"It doesn't matter," he said. "Destroying that book doesn't change who you are. You're still Lady Katherine Gramercy."

"Oh, I know who I am. And the Gramercys know it, too. But this mishap"—she held up the mangled register—"makes my identity more difficult to prove. Evan says we'll need more witnesses before we even can approach the courts. It could take us years to have it all sorted out—until well after Lark's season, I expect, and after Evan has a chance to arrange the finances and prepare me to inherit."

"So you're saying . . ."

"I'm saying I'm free, for now, to do as I please." She approached him slowly. "I'm saying that someday I'll take the Gramercy name, legally and publicly. But in the meantime . . . I'm hoping to share yours." Her voice went husky with emotion. "I told you I'd give up everything, Samuel. I can't fathom any life without you in it."

Thorne stared at her a moment. Then he went to the door of the cell. "Bram!" He rattled the bars. "Bram, open this gate. Now."

Bram shook his head. "Not a chance. I gave my word."

"To hell with your word."

"Curse me all you like. Rattle your cage as you please. You asked for this. You told me to keep you in gaol until Miss Taylor is married."

"Well, she can't get married while she's locked in here."

"On the contrary," she said. "I believe I can."

He turned to find her gazing at him from beneath lowered lashes. A shy smile played about her lips.

"No. Don't think it. It's not going to happen."

"Why not?"

"For God's sake, I'm not going to marry you in a gaol."

"Would you rather we do it in the church?"

"No." He growled with frustration.

She tilted her head and regarded the sunlight streaming through the lattice of iron overhead. With her fingertips, she brushed a bit of ivy curling through the wall. "As prisons go, it's rather a romantic one. This is consecrated ground, so there's no difficulty on that score. We did have the banns read over the past few weeks. I'm all dressed for the occasion, and you're still wearing that devastating suit. There's no impediment whatsoever."

No, no, no. This was not going to happen.

"Lord Rycliff, would you kindly send for the vicar?" she asked.

"Don't," Thorne ordered. "Don't. I won't go through with it."

"I thought you might say that." Katie dropped onto the room's only bench—a simple wood plank. "Very well. I can wait."

"Don't sit on that," he exhorted. "Not in your wedding frock."

"Shall I stand and call for the vicar, then?" When he didn't answer, she stretched her legs out in front of her and crossed them at the ankles. "I'll just wait until you change your mind."

Thorne snorted. So that's how she meant to play this. A war of wills.

Well, she'd made the first fatal mistake in battle— underestimating her opponent.

He leaned against the wall—as far away from her as he could possibly put himself, in the small round cell.

"You can't wear me down," he told her. "You cannot outlast me."

"We'll just see, won't we?" She looked up at the shards of blue sky. "I'm not going anywhere."

Kate stayed true to her word. She didn't go anywhere.

Neither did he.

Of course, that didn't stop all Spindle Cove from coming to them. Over the course of the day it seemed every man, woman, and child in the village had a turn at peeking through the barred door and sharing words of encouragement or wisdom.

The vicar came to offer counsel. The Gramercys came to call. Evan gave them his blessing, in case Samuel was waiting on it. Samuel made it clear he wasn't. Aunt Marmoset passed Kate spice drops through the bars.

Mrs. Highwood dropped by to suggest, in rather obvious fashion, that if Lord Drewe were still interested in getting married today, her Diana would be available.

At suppertime the Fosburys brought over some food. Kate offered Thorne a morsel of cake with her fingertips, but he warned her off with a stern glare.

She popped it in her own mouth instead, making a show of licking her fingers clean.

Don't think you're hiding that flash in your eye.

He was so stubborn. After the fight last night, he'd thrown everything he had into building up one last fortified wall. But she would break it down. She'd be damned if she'd let him live in that cold, unfeeling prison he'd constructed. Not now, when she knew how much love and goodness he had to give.

And as Kate saw it, she was simply repaying a favor. All those years ago, he hadn't left her behind. His conscience hadn't let him leave the Hothouse without her. She would not leave this gaol without him.

By evening the whole village had gathered on the

green. Kate and Samuel's standoff had turned into an impromptu festival. Ale was flowing freely, thanks to the Bull and Blossom. The militiamen organized a betting pool, placing wagers on how long the couple's imprisonment would last.

As the sun was setting, Badger came by. After depositing the gift of a limp church mouse just outside the door, he settled down in the grass and propped his head on his paws. Waiting. For hours. Until moonlight poured through the gaps overhead, like streams of quicksilver.

"Think of the dog," she crooned. "Look at him. You know he won't leave. He's going to sit there all night long. Out, exposed in the elements. Poor little pup, shivering in the cold."

Thorne made a dismissive noise. "This is all his doing."

Well, if concern for the dog wouldn't move him . . .

"*I'm* cold." She trembled for effect. "Won't you come sit beside me, or are you just going to let me shiver, too?"

At last she'd found the argument to move him. With obvious reluctance, he came and sat beside her on the small, unyielding bench.

She caught his wrists by the iron manacles, still chained together, and ducked her head to slip into the circle of his arms. He didn't fight her as she leaned against his chest, snuggling into his warmth. Pressing her ear to his shirt front, she found his heartbeat, strong and steady.

"You should go," he murmured. "Go back to the Queen's Ruby and sleep in a warm bed."

"A warm bed sounds lovely indeed. But only if you're in it. I'll wait to go home with you."

His hands flattened against her back, pulling her

close. With his thumb, he stroked light caresses up and down her spine.

"I'm not leaving this place without you, Samuel. You didn't leave the Hothouse without me."

"That was decades ago. We were children. There's nothing you owe me now."

She laughed wryly. "Only my life, health, happiness, and all the love in my heart." She slid her arms around his waist and looked up at him. "This isn't about the past, Samuel. It's about our future. I can't imagine being happy without you."

"Katie, you must know . . . it's only because of you that I can imagine being happy at all."

She swallowed back a lump of emotion. "Then why are you resisting me now, after everything? Is it solely a matter of your bull-headed pride?"

A half smile tugged at his lips. "If my 'bull-headed pride' is inconvenient, you should know that any pride I have is entirely your fault."

He closed his eyes and pressed his brow to hers.

"It's all your fault." His voice was rough with emotion. "You listened when I needed it. Laughed when I needed that. You wouldn't go away, no matter how I scowled or raged. You loved me despite everything, and you made me look deep inside myself to find the strength to love you in return. I'm a different man because of you."

Her heart swelled with joy.

"But that's not enough. *I'm* not enough. What if I'd hurt you last night? What if it happens again?"

"You didn't hurt me," she insisted. "You've never hurt me. Even when you've . . . slipped away in the heat of the moment, you've always come back. You've always kept me safe."

"What if . . ." His voice trailed off. He cleared his throat and continued. "There'd be children. I worry about children."

She hugged him tight. "We needn't be in any rush to start a family. You've been one year back in England, after spending a decade on campaign. Give yourself some time to heal. You don't have to quarantine yourself to some uninhabited wilderness. The darkness *will* ebb eventually. When it does, I'll still be here."

"You shouldn't have to wait. You deserve someone who's not broken and brutish and . . ." He exhaled roughly and gripped her tight. "There are better men, Katie."

"Really? I've yet to meet one."

As she pressed her lips to his in a sweet, tender kiss, Kate could taste victory. The battle was nearly won.

She kissed the stubble-roughened edge of his jaw and made her voice a sultry whisper. "You know, we could be starting our honeymoon in less than an hour."

She twisted in his embrace just a little, letting her breasts rub against his chest. Teasing them both with the exquisite sensation. He moaned deep in his chest.

"Do you know what Aunt Marmoset told me once? She compared you to a spice drop. Overpowering and hard at first, but all sweetness at the center. I'll admit, I've been desperate to try an experiment." She gave him a teasing look. "How many times do you suppose I could lick you before you crack?"

His every muscle tightened.

Smiling, she tucked her face into the curve of his neck and ran her tongue seductively over his skin. "There's one."

"*Katie.*" The word was a low, throaty warning. It made her toes curl.

She nuzzled at the notch of his open shirt, pushing the fabric aside. The familiar musk of his skin stirred her in deep places.

With a teasing swirl of her tongue, she tasted the notch at the base of his throat. "Two . . ."

"Finn," he called in a booming voice, lifting his head. "Send for the vicar."

She pulled back, shocked. "*Two?* That's all, truly? Two? I'm not sure whether to feel proud or disappointed."

Finn's face appeared in the grate. "If it's all the same to you, Corporal, do you mind holding off another half hour? I've got midnight in the betting pool."

"Yes, I do mind. Fetch the vicar. Now."

Kate smiled. That was her future husband. When he finally made up his mind to do a thing, no one had better stand in his way. Thank God.

She smiled at Samuel in the dark. "I hope the blossoms in my hair aren't too wilted."

"They're perfect." His blue eyes roamed her face. "You're so beautiful, Katie. I haven't words."

She didn't need words. What woman could want flattery, when she could have such pure, raw adoration? The pride and love in his gaze were palpable.

She stroked his unshaven jaw. "You are unbearably handsome, as always. I couldn't have dreamed a more perfect wedding. All our family and friends are already gathered outside. With a few candles, this funny little building will make a romantic chapel. But do you think Lord Rycliff would remove the irons before we say our vows? I've heard men call matrimony 'getting shackled,' but this is a bit extreme."

"Extreme? This from the woman who tied me to a bed."

She laughed softly, ducking her head to rest against his chest.

His chin settled, square and heavy, on her crown. In the silence, she could feel him thinking, pondering. When he spoke again, his voice had that thoughtful tone—the one he could never seem to muster unless she'd turned her gaze away. She kept her face buried in his sleeve, unwilling to break the spell.

"Bram should leave the irons," he said, "until after. That's the oath he swore, and it seems fitting, somehow. For other men, marriage might be a trap or a prison. Not for me, Katie. Not for me." He pressed a kiss to the top of her head. "When I marry you, I'll walk free."

Epilogue

Several years later

"Hush! That's his horse in the drive."

Kate took a surreptitious peek from behind the blue velvet drapes. There he came, riding his gelding up the white gravel lane at a brisk canter.

He dismounted in one swift, agile motion and handed the reins to a waiting groom. Through the lingering twilight, she could make out the familiar, stern lines of his face. With every passing year, life etched those lines a little deeper, engraving his handsomeness as a permanent, eternal thing. And each time she glimpsed him after a separation, her heart still gave a girlish hop in her chest.

"He's arrived."

With one hand, she gathered her heavy silk skirts and hastened down the corridor in a smooth, practiced glide. It wasn't seemly for a lady to run, but a lady with three children had to learn to move fast.

But she wasn't the first to meet him at the door. Badger, even old as he was, raced her to the entrance hall, nails clicking over the travertine. He nosed around his master's boots, sniffing out the story of his journey.

As she watched the two old friends reunite, Kate smiled. "I see I'm not the first to welcome you home."

With a final rub to the dog's ear, Samuel straightened. "You're the loveliest."

He'd brought in with him a gust of cool, autumnal air. The woodsy-scented wind clung to his greatcoat. He shrugged out of the garment and removed his gloves.

Kate took both, and in exchange pressed a kiss to his chilled, weathered cheek.

"Where's Williams?" he asked, scanning the entry-way for the butler.

Kate bit her lip. "Oh, he's . . . elsewhere."

She turned away and took her time hanging the coat, afraid to look at him, worried he'd take the servants' absence as cause for suspicion. But his actions soon made it clear that he wasn't going to take the servants' absence as cause for suspicion. He meant to take it as an opportunity.

His hands framed her waist and he pulled her back-ward, drawing her tight against the firm expanse of his chest. With wind-chilled lips, he pressed kisses to her nape, sending ripples of cool and hot sensation down her spine.

Kate's eyelids fluttered with sensual abandon. She leaned against his chest and let her head roll to the side, offering more of herself to his kiss. Oh, how she'd missed him.

"How was Wimbley Park?" she murmured.

"A shambles." His teeth grazed her collarbone.

"The south fields again?"

He growled an affirmative answer as he suckled her earlobe. "Flooded ankle deep."

"Oh, dear," she sighed. "What about the drainage canals from last year? I thought—"

With a brisk push, he whirled her around to face him. The intensity in his eyes told her there'd be no more talk of drainage canals just now.

"*Katie.*"

He pulled her into a deep, stormy kiss. It told her everything another woman might wish to hear in words: *I want you. I need you. I love you. The whole time we were apart, I thought of no one but you.*

"Let's go upstairs." He fisted his hand in the back of her dress. "It's been an eternity."

She laughed against his lips. "It's been since Tuesday."

"Like I said. An eternity." He lifted her off her feet, as though he meant to simply toss her over his shoulder and haul her to the nearest mattress.

She put her hands to his chest, stopping him. "We can't. Not right now."

The gravity in her expression didn't escape his notice. As he set her back on her toes, his brow furrowed with protective concern. "What is it? What's wrong?"

"Nothing, just . . ." She swallowed hard. "Please don't be angry."

He took her by the shoulders. "Tell me. Now."

"Don't worry. No one's ill or bleeding." *Yet.* "And it's not really something I can explain. You'll have to see for yourself."

She took him by the hand and led him down the corridor. They walked slowly, quietly. He looked like a man marching toward his own funeral.

"I know how you hate these things," she said in an

advance apology. "But the boys have been asking ever since last summer, and then Bryony seized the idea and wouldn't let go." They came to a stop just outside the drawing room.

"It's too quiet," he suddenly noted. "Katie, I don't like this."

"I don't even know how it happened. It all spiraled out of control. But please know they had the best of intentions."

With a final, silent prayer for courage, Kate pushed open the double doors.

The drawing room erupted in color and noise.

"Surprise!" came the shout from several dozen of their closest family, servants, neighbors, and friends.

"It's a party," she said. "For you."

"Bloody hell."

She cringed, watching him as he surveyed the room, filled to bursting with people. She'd invited all the land-owners from neighboring estates, and as many old friends as she could lure to Ambervale. Lord Rycliff and Lord Payne had brought their families. Calista and Parker were there, and Harry and Ames. As always, Evan greeted Samuel with a warm handshake. They'd long been close friends.

"The children wanted to give you a birthday," she whispered, waving in Aunt Marmoset's direction. "Last summer they were asking why we never celebrate it, and I didn't know what to say. I just plucked a date from the air, because I thought they'd forget. But they didn't. They're stubborn, like their father."

"They're clever," he said. "And that's entirely your fault."

The children stood waiting in the center of the room. All three of them just bursting with self-satisfaction, knowing they'd managed to rattle their formidable papa.

Bryony Claire, almost eight years old now.

Brent Christopher, a few years behind.

The smallest, Benjamin Charles, tottered across the room and attached himself to his papa's boot.

They'd given all of them the initials B.C. With the first child, she'd talked Samuel into it. He'd suggested Simon or Elinor, for her parents, but she desperately wanted to give those letters inked beneath his heart a different meaning.

There was nothing of Bad Character in him now, if there ever had been. Only Doting Father, Fair-minded Employer, Loyal Friend . . . and Loving Husband. There wasn't a soul in this packed, unruly drawing room who didn't admire him.

But Kate didn't think anyone could love the man more than she.

She put a hand to her belly. If her suspicions of the past few queasy weeks proved true, they'd soon be racking their brains for another set of names. As virile as the man seemed to be, she only hoped they could stop short of using Bathsheba Cabbagewort.

When she caught his gaze, his eyebrow arched into a chastening bow. But she'd developed a talent for reading the subtle changes in his stony expression, and she could tell he wasn't angry.

He scooped little Benjamin off his feet and put him on his shoulders.

"Come see your cake!" Bryony tugged at her father's sleeve, pulling him toward a table laden with refreshments. In the center was a lumpy, slightly listing cake.

"Bryony iced it herself," Kate said.

Bryony went up on her toes with pride. "There's apricot preserves inside. We're going to sing for you later. Mama's taught us a new song." She twisted to and fro, swirling the skirts of her best gown. "Do you like your party, Papa?"

"No, I don't like it."

Kate sent him a pleading look. Samuel didn't care for fuss—much less cake—but she hoped he could bear it for the one evening.

With a big, weathered hand, he cupped his daughter's chin and tilted her hopeful face to his. "I love it. And I love you."

K.I.S.S. and Teal: Avon Books and the Ovarian Cancer National Alliance Urge Women to Know the Important Signs and Symptoms

September is National Ovarian Cancer Awareness month, and Avon Books is joining forces with the Ovarian Cancer National Alliance to urge women to start talking, and help us spread the **K.I.S.S. and Teal** message: **K**now the **I**mportant **S**igns and **S**ymptoms.

Ovarian cancer was long thought to be a silent killer, but now we know it isn't silent at all. The Ovarian Cancer National Alliance works to spread a life-affirming message that this disease doesn't have to be fatal if we all take the time to learn the symptoms.

The **K.I.S.S. and Teal** program urges women to help promote awareness among friends and family members. Avon authors are actively taking part in this mission, creating public service announcements and speaking with readers and media across the country to break the silence. Please log on to *www.kissandteal.com* to hear what they have to share, and to learn how you can further help the cause and donate.

You can lend your support to the Ovarian Cancer National Alliance by making a donation at:
www.ovariancancer.org/donate.
Your donation benefits all the women in our lives.

KT1 0912

Break the Silence:
The following authors are taking
part in the K.I.S.S. and Teal
campaign, in support of the

Ovarian Cancer National Alliance:

THE UGLY DUCHESS
Eloisa James

NIGHTWATCHER
Wendy Corsi Staub

THE LOOK OF LOVE
Mary Jane Clark

A LADY BY MIDNIGHT
Tessa Dare

THE WAY TO A DUKE'S HEART
Caroline Linden

CHOSEN
Sable Grace

SINS OF A VIRGIN
Anna Randol

For more information, log on to: **www.kissandteal.com**

AVON
An imprint of HarperCollins*Publishers*

www.ovariancancer.org
www.avonromance.com • *www.facebook.com/avonromance*

KT2 0912

This September,
the Ovarian
Cancer National
Alliance and Avon
Books urge you to
K.I.S.S. and Teal:

Know the **I**mportant **S**igns and **S**ymptoms

Ovarian cancer is the deadliest gynecologic cancer and a
leading cause of cancer deaths for women.

There is no early detection test, but women with the disease
have the following symptoms:

- **Bloating**
- **Pelvic and abdominal pain**
- **Difficulty eating or feeling full quickly**
- **Urinary symptoms (urgency or frequency)**

Learn the symptoms and tell other women about them!

Teal is the color of ovarian cancer awareness—help us
K.I.S.S. and Teal today!

Log on to **www.kissandteal.com** to learn more about the
symptoms and risk factors associated with ovarian cancer,
and donate to support women with the disease.

The Ovarian Cancer National Alliance is the foremost advocate
for women with ovarian cancer in the United States.

Learn more at www.ovariancancer.org

KT3 0912